Ben Jonson, Francis Cunningham, William Gifford

Works

With notes critical and explanatory and a biographical memoir. Vol. 5

Ben Jonson, Francis Cunningham, William Gifford

Works

With notes critical and explanatory and a biographical memoir. Vol. 5

ISBN/EAN: 9783337015848

Printed in Europe, USA, Canada, Australia, Japan

Cover: Foto ©Raphael Reischuk / pixelio.de

More available books at **www.hansebooks.com**

THE WORKS OF BEN JONSON.

The Muses' fairest light in no dark time ;
The wonder of a learned age ; the line
Which none can pass ; the most proportion'd wit,
To nature, the best judge of what was fit ;
The deepest, plainest, highest, clearest pen ;
The voice most echo'd by consenting men ;
THE SOUL WHICH ANSWER'D BEST TO ALL WELL SAID
BY OTHERS, AND WHICH MOST REQUITAL MADE.

CLEVELAND.

THE WORKS OF

WITH NOTES CRITICAL AND EXPLANATORY

AND A BIOGRAPHICAL MEMOIR

BY W. GIFFORD ESQ.

WITH INTRODUCTION AND APPENDICES BY

LIEUT.-COL. F. CUNNINGHAM

IN NINE VOLUMES

VOL. V

LONDON
BICKERS AND SON
HENRY SOTHERAN AND CO.
1875

CHISWICK PRESS :—PRINTED BY WHITTINGHAM AND WILKINS,
TOOKS COURT, CHANCERY LANE.

CONTENTS OF VOLUME V.

THE DEVIL IS AN ASS.

5 B

THE DEVIL IS AN ASS.] This Comedy was acted in 1616, by the King's Servants, at Blackfriars, but not put to the press till many years afterwards, when it appeared in the folio of 1631. The Editor of the *Biographia Dramatica*, who had but to open this volume to ascertain the true date, chooses rather to copy Langbaine, who is of no authority in this respect, and assign it to a later period. There is, indeed, another edition in folio, 1641, but it is of no authority, or even value, being full of errors.

In noticing the date of *Bartholomew Fair*, I had occasion to observe that Jonson appeared to concern himself little, if at all, with the printing of the plays in the present collection; and the *Devil is an Ass*, as well as the *Staple of News*, furnishes no slight proof of it. In the folio, 1616, which the author certainly revised, he is altogether sparing of his marginal directions, while the dramas just mentioned abound in them. They are, however, of the most trite and trifling nature; they tell nothing that is not told in action, and generally in the same words, and are, upon the whole, such a worthless incumbrance on the page, that the reader will thank me for discarding them altogether. They bear no trace of the poet's hand.

This comedy was revived immediately after the Restoration, and, as Downes informs us, "much to the satisfaction of the town." It originally appeared with this motto, from Horace:

Ficta voluptatis causâ, sint proxima veris.

THE PROLOGUE.

THE Devil is an Ass :[1] *that is, to-day,*
The name of what you are met for, a new
    play.
Yet, grandees, would you were not come to
grace
Our matter, with allowing us no place.
Though you presume Satan, a subtle thing,
And may have heard he's worn in a thumb-ring ;[2]

[1] *The Devil is an Ass.*] This is said by the prologue pointing
to the *title* of the play, which, as was then the custom, was painted
in large letters, and placed in some conspicuous part of the stage.
The remainder of the prologue alludes to a practice common at
that period to all the theatres, namely, that of crowding the stage
with stools for the accommodation of the spectators, who were thus
admitted into the court, "yea, even to the very throne of King
Cambyses."

[2] —— *worn in a thumb-ring.*] Nothing was more common, as
we learn from Lilly, than to carry about familiar spirits, shut up in
rings, watches, sword-hilts, and other articles of dress. Lest the
reader should be in pain for the close confinement of the demon in
the text, it may be proper to mention that the thumb-rings of Jonson's days were set with jewels of an extraordinary size. Frequent
mention of them occurs in our old dramatists : from which, however, we might be led to conclude, that they were more affected
by magistrates and grave citizens, than necromancers. The fashion
of wearing these weighty ornaments was prevalent in Addison's
time. "It is common (he says) for a stale virgin to set up a shop
in a place where she is not known, where the *large thumb-ring,*
supposed to be given her by her husband, quickly recommends

Do not on these presumptions force us act
In compass of a cheese-trencher.   This tract
Will ne'er admit our Vice, because of yours.
Anon, who worse than you, the fault endures
That yourselves make? when you will thrust and spurn,
And knock us on the elbows ; and bid, turn;
As if, when we had spoke, we must be gone,
Or, till we speak, must all run in, to one,
Like the young adders, at the old one's mouth !
Would we could stand due north, or had no south,
If that offend ; or were Muscovy glass,[3]
That you might look our scenes through as they pass.
We know not how to affect you.   If you'll come
To see new plays, pray you afford us room,
And shew this but the same face you have done
Your dear delight, The Devil of Edmonton.[4]
Or, if for want of room it must miscarry,

her to some wealthy neighbour, who takes a liking to the jolly widow, that would have overlooked the venerable spinster.   *Spec.* No. 614.

[3] *or were* Muscovy glass.]   "About the river Dwyna, towards the North Sea, there groweth a soft rocke, which they call Slude ; this they cut into pieces, and so tear it into thin flakes, which naturally it is apt for, and so use it for *glasse lanthorns,* and such like." Fletcher's *Russe Commonwealth.* 1591.   This is Jonson's Muscovy glass.

[4] *The Devil of Edmonton.*]   This pleasant old comedy had been several years on the stage when this was written, being incidentally noticed as a popular piece in 1604.   It is absurdly attributed to Shakspeare by Kirkman, and there wanted nothing perhaps but the knowledge of this *sneer* at it by Jonson (see vol. iv. p. 348), to induce the commentators to print it among his works.   One of them, indeed, observes that it is unworthy of our great poet; but it ill becomes any of those who burthened his reputation with such trash as *Pericles* and *Titus Andronicus*, to raise scruples about the present play.

Oldys ascribes the *Merry Devil of Edmonton* to Drayton ; but it bears no resemblance to any of his published works ; and if *Lingua* be the production of (Tony) Antony Brewer, he also must be relieved from the charge of writing it, notwithstanding the initials T. B. in the title-page.

'Twill be but justice that your censure tarry,
Till you give some: and when six times you have seen't,
If this play do not like,[5] the Devil is in't.

[5] *If this play do not* like, *&c.*] i. e. please. The quibble in the text had already furnished Decker with a title for his play of *Belphegor.*

DRAMATIS PERSONÆ.

SATAN, *the great devil.*
PUG, *the less devil.*
INIQUITY, *the Vice.*
FABIAN FITZDOTTREL, *a squire of Norfolk.*
MEERCRAFT, *the projector.*
EVERILL, *his champion.*
WITTIPOL, *a young gallant.*
EUSTACE MANLY, *his friend.*
ENGINE, *a broker.*
TRAINS, *the projector's man.*
THOMAS GILTHEAD, *a goldsmith.*
PLUTARCHUS, *his son.*
Sir PAUL EITHERSIDE, *a lawyer, and justice.*
AMBLER, *gentleman-usher to lady Tailbush.*
SLEDGE, *a smith, the constable.*
SHACKLES, *keeper of Newgate.*

Mrs. FRANCES FITZDOTTREL.
Lady EITHERSIDE.
Lady TAILBUSH, *the lady projectress.*
PITFALL, *her woman.*

Serjeants, Officers, Servants, Underkeepers, *&c.*

SCENE, London.

THE DEVIL IS AN ASS.

ACT I.

SCENE I.[6]

Enter SATAN *and* PUG.

Satan.

HOH, hoh, hoh, hoh, hoh, hoh, hoh,
    hoh![7]—
To earth! and why to earth, thou foolish
    spirit?
What wouldst thou do on earth?
  Pug. For that, great chief,
As time shall work. I do but ask my month

---

[6] This first scene must be laid " e'en where the reader pleases."
Satan and Pug, probably, make their entrance on the stage from a
trap-door, (some rude representation, perhaps, of Hell-mouth), and
the dialogue may be supposed to take place in their journey from
the infernal regions. For these, and a thousand other incongruities,
the absolute poverty and nakedness of the old stage furnished a
ready apology.

[7] *Hoh, hoh, &c.*] "The devil," Whalley says, in the old Mysteries and Moralities, "generally came roaring upon the stage with
a cry of Ho, ho, ho!" This, with a great deal more, which he has
taken from the commentators on Shakspeare, is all out of place
here. It is not the roar of terror; but the boisterous expression of
sarcastic merriment at the absurd petition of Pug, with which Satan
makes his first appearance.

Which every petty, puisne devil has;
Within that term, the court of hell will hear
Something may gain a longer grant, perhaps.
    Sat. For what? the laming a poor cow or two,
Entering a sow, to make her cast her farrow,
Or crossing of a market-woman's mare
'Twixt this and Tottenham? these were wont to be
Your main achievements, Pug : You have some plot
        now,
Upon a tunning of ale, to stale the yeast,
Or keep the churn so, that the butter come not,
Spite of the housewife's cord, or her hot spit :
Or some good ribibe,[8] about Kentish Town
Or Hogsden, you would hang now for a witch,
Because she will not let you play round Robin.
And you'll go sour the citizens' cream 'gainst Sunday,
That she may be accused for't, and condemn'd,
By a Middlesex jury,[9] to the satisfaction

---

[8] *Or some good* ribibe.]   Bawd, or mistress of a brothel.

> " This Sompnour, wayting evir on his pray,
>   Rode to summon an old wife, a *ribibe.*"
> *Frere's Tale.* WHAL.

Whalley, like Steevens, is too fond of licentious explanations.
Ribibe, together with its synonym *rebeck,* is merely a cant expression for an old woman. A ribibe, the reader knows, is a rude
kind of fiddle, and the allusion is probably to the inharmonious
nature of its sounds. The word is used in a similar sense by
Skelton :

> " There came an olde rybibe ;
>   She halted of a kybe," &c.

[9] *That she may be accused for't, and condemn'd*
    By a Middlesex jury, &c.]   A reproof no less severe than
merited. It appears from the records of those times, that many
unfortunate creatures were condemned and executed on charges of
the ridiculous nature here enumerated. In many instances, the
judge was well convinced of the innocence of the accused, and
laboured to save them ; but such were the gross and barbarous prejudices of the juries, that they would seldom listen to his recom-
mendations ; and he was deterred from shewing mercy, in the last
place, by the brutal ferociousness of the people, *whose teeth were*

Of their offended friends, the Londoners' wives,
Whose teeth were set on edge with't. Foolish fiend!
Stay in your place, know your own strength, and put
      not
Beyond the sphere of your activity :
You are too dull a devil to be trusted
Forth in those parts, Pug, upon any affair
That may concern our name on earth. It is not
Every one's work. The state of hell must care
Whom it employs, in point of reputation,
Here about London. You would make, I think,
An agent to be sent for Lancashire,[10]
Proper enough ; or some parts of Northumberland,
So you had good instructions, Pug.
    Pug. O chief,
You do not know, dear chief, what there is in me !
Prove me but for a fortnight, for a week,
And lend me but a Vice,[1] to carry with me,
To practise there with any play-fellow,
And you will see, there will come more upon't,

set on edge with't, and who clamoured tumultuously for the murder
of the accused.

   [10] *An agent to be sent for Lancashire.*] This was the very hot-bed
of witches. Not long before this play was written, fifteen of them
had been indicted at one time, of whom twelve were condemned.
Lancashire is still famous for its witches : they are said to frequent
balls and music meetings, and, being in possession of spells and
charms far more potent than those of their antiquated predecessors,
to do a great deal of mischief to such as venture within the sphere
of their influence.

   [1] *And lend me but a Vice.*] The buffoon of the old Mysteries
and Moralities. He appears to have been a perfect counterpart
of the Harlequin of the modern stage, and had a twofold office,—
to instigate the hero of the piece to wickedness, and, at the same
time, to protect him from the devil, whom he was permitted to
buffet and baffle with his wooden sword, till the process of the
story required that both the protector and the protected should
be carried off by the fiend ; or the latter driven roaring from the
stage by some miraculous interposition in favour of the repentant
offender.

Than you'll imagine, precious chief.
   Sat. What Vice?
What kind wouldst thou have it of?
   Pug. Why any : Fraud,
Or Covetousness, or lady Vanity,
Or old Iniquity.
   Sat. I'll call him hither.

Enter Iniquity.

   Iniq. What is he calls upon me, and would seem
        to lack a Vice?
Ere his words be half spoken, I am with him in a trice;
Here, there, and every where, as the cat is with the
        mice :
True *Vetus Iniquitas.* Lack'st thou cards, friend, or
        dice?
I will teach thee [to] cheat, child, to cog, lie and
        swagger,
And ever and anon to be drawing forth thy dagger :
To swear by Gogs-nowns, like a Lusty Juventus,[2]
In a cloak to thy heel, and a hat like a pent-house.
Thy breeches of three fingers, and thy doublet all belly,
With a wench that shall feed thee with cockstones
        and jelly.
   Pug. Is it not excellent, chief? how nimble he is![3]

---

[2] —— *like a* Lusty Juventus.] This is an allusion to the chief
personage in the Morality of that name, written so early as the
reign of Edward VI. by one Wever. The language which Iniquity
gives to Juventus, is taken from his licentious conversation, after
he had been perverted by *Hypocrisie*, the Vice of the piece. It has
a serious cast, and was professedly written to favour the Reformation.

   [3] —— *How nimble he is!*] A perfect idea of his activity may
be formed, as I have already observed, from the incessant skipping
of the modern Harlequin. In saying, however, that he would take
a leap from the *top of Paul's steeple*, Iniquity boasts of a feat which
he could not perform, inasmuch, as St. Paul's had no steeple. It

Iniq. Child of hell, this is nothing! I will fetch
          thee a leap
From the top of Paul's steeple to the standard in
          Cheap :
And lead thee a dance thro' the streets, without fail,
Like a needle of Spain,[4] with a thread at my tail.

was burnt, together with the tower, and a great part of the roof of
the church, in 1561, and though the latter was speedily repaired,
all attempts to rebuild the former came to nought. "Concerning
the *steeple* (Stow says) divers models were devised and made, but
little was done, through whose default God knoweth." 1598.   In
1632, Lupton writes, "The head of St. Paul's hath been twice
troubled with a burning fever, and so the city, to keep it from a
third danger, lets it stand without a head." *London Carbonadoed.*
In this state it was found by the great fire.   The Puritans took a
malignant pleasure in this mutilated state of the cathedral, for which
they are frequently reprimanded by the dramatic poets, who appear
to have been the most clear-sighted politicians of those troublous
times.   One example may suffice:

Mic. I am church-warden, and we are this year
         To build our *steeple* up ; now, to save charges,
         I'll get a high-crown'd hat with five low-bells
         To make a peal shall serve as well as Bow.
Col. 'Tis wisely cast,
         And like a careful steward of the church,
         Of which the steeple is no part, at least,
         No necessary.
Bird. Verily, 'tis true.
         They are but wicked synagogues where those instruments
         Of superstition and idolatry ring
         Warning to sin, and chime all in to the devil."
                              Muses Looking Glass.

  [4] *Like a needle of Spain.*]   Randolph, in his *Amyntas*, tells us that
" the spits of the fairies are made of *Spanish needles ;*" but, indeed,
the expression is too common for notice.   In the *Sun's Darling*, by
Ford, Folly says of one of the characters, "He is a French gentleman that trails a Spanish pike, a taylor."   Upon which the editor
observes, "I *cannot discover* the force of this allusion, except it be
to the thinness of the taylor's legs!"   The editor is not fortunate
in his guesses.   The allusion is to the taylor's needle, which, in
cant language, was commonly termed a *Spanish pike.*   In the satirical catalogue of books by Sir John Birkenhead is, "The Sting
of Conscience, a tract written with the sharp end of Arise Evans's

We will survey the suburbs, and make forth our sallies
Down Petticoat-lane and up the Smock-alleys,
To Shoreditch, Whitechapel, and so to St. Kathern's,
To drink with the Dutch there, and take forth their
        patterns :
From thence, we will put in at Custom-house key there,
And see how the factors and prentices play there
False with their masters, and geld many a full pack,
To spend it in pies, at the Dagger and the Woolsack.
    Pug. Brave, brave, Iniquity! will not this do, chief?
    Iniq. Nay, boy, I will bring thee to the bawds and
        the roysters,
At Billinsgate, feasting with claret-wine and oysters;
From thence shoot the Bridge, child, to the Cranes
        in the Vintry,
And see there the gimblets, how they make their
        entry !
Or if thou hadst rather to the Strand down to fall,
'Gainst the lawyers come dabbled from Westminster
        hall,
And mark how they cling, with their clients together,
Like ivy to oak, so velvet to leather :
Ha, boy, I wou'd shew thee—
    Pug. Rare, rare !
    Sat. Peace, dotard,
And thou, more ignorant thing, that so admir'st ;
Art thou the spirit thou seem'st ? so poor, to choose,
This for a Vice, to advance the cause of hell,
Now, as vice stands this present year ? Remember
What number it is, six hundred and sixteen.

Spanish pike.   Arise Evans was a tailor. Mr. Weber had not *discovered* that the best needles, as well as other sharp instruments,
were, in that age, and indeed long before and after it, imported
from Spain : if he had ever looked into Jonson, whom he is so forward to revile, he might have seen the "*force of the allusion,*" and,
probably, discovered, in addition to it, that the name of this great
poet might be cited for better purposes than the gratification of
wanton malice, or the sport of incorrigible folly.

Had it but been five hundred, though some sixty
Above ; that's fifty years agone, and six,
When every great man had his Vice stand by him,
In his long coat, shaking his wooden dagger,
I could consent, that then this your grave choice
Might have done that, with his lord chief, the which
Most of·his chamber can do now.   But, Pug,
As the times are, who is it will receive you ?
What company will you go to, or whom mix with ?
Where canst thou carry him, except to taverns,
To mount upon a joint-stool, with a Jew's trump,
To put down Cokely, and that must be to citizens ?
He ne'er will be admitted there, where Vennor comes.[5]
He may perchance, in tail of a sheriff's dinner,
Skip with a rhyme on the table, from New-nothing,
And take his Almain-leap into a custard,[6]
Shall make my lady mayoress and her sisters
Laugh all their hoods over their shoulders.   But
This is not that will do, they are other things
That are received now upon earth, for Vices ;

---

[5] *Cokely and Vennor.*]   Cokely is elsewhere mentioned by Jonson as master of a puppet-show; he seems also to have been famous for tricks of legerdemain.   Of Vennor, his superior in the art, I can give the reader no information.   In Taylor's *Cast over the Water*, he mentions

> " Poor old Vennor, that plain dealing man,
>   Who acted ' England's Joy ' at the Old Swan."

If the Vennor of the text be, as I suppose, the son of this person, he seems to have turn'd aside from the *plain dealing* of his father.

[6] *And take his* Almain-*leap into a custard.*]   In the earlier days, when the City kept a fool, it was customary for him, at public entertainments, to leap into a large bowl of custard set on purpose : there is an allusion to this piece of mirth in Shakspeare.   WHAL.

Whalley alludes to *All's well that end's well.*   " You have made a shift to run into it, boots and all, like him that leapt into the custard."   A. ii. S. 5.

Our old dramatists abound with pleasant allusions to the enormous size of these " quaking custards," which were served up at the

Stranger and newer : and changed every hour.
They ride them like their horses, off their legs,
And here they come to hell, whole legions of them,
Every week tired.　We still strive to breed,
And rear up new ones ; but they do not stand ;
When they come there, they turn them on our hands.
And it is fear'd they have a stud o' their own
Will put down ours : both our breed and trade
Will suddenly decay, if we prevent not.
Unless it be a vice of quality,
Or fashion now, they take none from us.　Carmen
Are got into the yellow starch, and chimney-sweepers
To their tobacco, and strong waters, Hum,
Meath and Obarni.[7]　We must therefore aim

city feasts, and with which such gross fooleries were played. Thus
Glapthorne :

> " I'll write the city annals
> In metre, which shall far surpass Sir Guy
> Of Warwick's history ; or John Stow's, upon
> The custard, with the four and twenty nooks
> At my lord mayor's feast."　　　　*Wit in a Const.*

Indeed, no common supply was required ; for, besides what the
Corporation (great devourers of custard) consumed on the spot, it
appears that it was thought no breach of city manners to send, or
take some of it home with them for the use of their ladies.　In
the excellent old play quoted above, Clara twits her uncle with this
practice :

> " Nor shall you, sir, as 'tis a frequent custom,
> 'Cause you're a worthy alderman of a ward,
> Feed me with custard, and perpetual white broth
> Sent from the lord mayor's feast, and kept ten days,
> Till a new dinner from the common hall
> Supply the large defect."

[7] ───────────────── *Carmen*
Are got into the yellow starch, *and chimney sweepers*
To their tobacco, and strong waters, Hum,
Meath *and* Obarni.]　The ridiculous fashion, affected both by
the great and small vulgar, of having their ruffs and linen stiffened
with a kind of *yellow starch* was an object of satire to the wits of
Jonson's age.　It was first brought into vogue by Mrs. Turner, one
of the persons employed by the countess of Essex in the poisoning

At extraordinary subtle ones now,
When we do send to keep us up in credit :
Not old Iniquities.   Get you e'en back, sir,
To making of your rope of sand again ;
You are not for the manner, nor the times.
They have their vices there, most like to virtues :
You cannot know them apart by any difference :
They wear the same clothes, eat the same meat,
Sleep in the self-same beds, ride in those coaches,
Or very like, four horses in a coach,
As the best men and women.   Tissue gowns,
Garters and roses, fourscore pound a pair,
Embroider'd stockings, cut-work smocks and shirts,
More certain marks of letchery now and pride,
Than e'er they were of true nobility !   [*Exit* INIQ.
But, Pug, since you do burn with such desire
To do the commonwealth of hell some service,
I am content, assuming of a body,
You go to earth, and visit men a day.
But you must take a body ready made, Pug ;
I can create you none : nor shall you form
Yourself an airy one, but become subject
To all impression of the flesh you take,

of sir Thomas Overbury : and as she was soon after executed for
her dealings in that affair, with a yellow starched ruff about her
neck, the mode became for a time disreputable.   WHAL.

Enough, and more than enough has been produced on this tritest
of all subjects, *yellow starch*.   On the strong waters mentioned in
the quotation, Whalley has nothing ; and I have very little to the
purpose.   Meath is familiar to every reader under the name of
metheglin.   *Hum*, I have always understood to be an infusion of
spirits in ale or beer.   It is mentioned by several of our old dramatists, and appears to have been considered as a kind of cordial.
Thus Fletcher : " Lord, what should I ail ! what a cold I have over
my stomach ; would I had some hum !"   *Wild Goose Chace.   Obarni*
is probably a preparation of usquebaugh ; but this is merely conjecture.   The word is an ἅπαξ λεγομενον, (as far as my knowledge
reaches,) and I have endeavoured in vain to ascertain the meaning
of it.

So far as human frailty.   So, this morning,
There is a handsome cut-purse hang'd at Tyburn,
Whose spirit departed, you may enter his body :
For clothes, employ your credit with the hangman,
Or let our tribe of brokers furnish you.
And look how far your subtilty can work
Thorough those organs, with that body, spy
Amongst mankind, (you cannot there want vices,
And therefore the less need to carry them with you,)
But as you make your soon at night's relation,
And we shall find it merits from the state,
You shall have both trust from us, and employment.
    Pug. Most gracious chief!
    Sat. Only thus more I bind you,
To serve the first man that you meet ; and him
I'll shew you now : observe him.   Yon is he,
        [*Shews him* FITZDOTTREL *coming out of his house*
                    at a distance.
You shall see first after your clothing.   Follow him :
But once engaged, there you must stay and fix ;
Not shift, until the midnight's cock do crow.
    Pug. Any conditions to be gone.
    Sat. Away then.   [*Exeunt severally.*

SCENE II.   *The Street before* FITZDOTTREL'S *House.*

Enter FITZDOTTREL.

Fitzdottrel.

Y, they do now name Bretnor, as before
    They talk'd of Gresham, and of doctor Fore-
            man,
Franklin, and Fiske, and Savory, he was in too ; [8]

---

  [8] *Ay, they do now name Bretnor, as before*
     They talk'd of Gresham, and of doctor Foreman,
       Franklin, and Fiske, and Savory, he was in too.]   These were
pretenders to soothsaying, in other words, receivers of stolen goods,

But there's not one of these that ever could
Yet shew a man the devil in true sort.
They have their crystals, I do know, and rings,
And virgin-parchment, and their dead men's sculls,
Their ravens' wings, their lights, and pentacles,
With characters ; I have seen all these.   But—
Would I might see the devil !   I would give
A hundred of these pictures to see him
Once out of picture.   May I prove a cuckold,
And that's the one main mortal thing I fear,
If I begin not now to think, the painters
Have only made him : 'slight, he would be seen
One time or other else ; he would not let
An ancient gentleman, of [as] good a house
As most are now in England, the Fitzdottrels,
Run wild, and call upon him thus in vain,
As I have done this twelvemonth.   If he be not
At all, why are there conjurers ? if they be not,[9]

pimps, and poisoners.   They were all, with the exception of Bretnor, who came later into notice, connected with the infamous countess of Essex and Mrs. Turner, in the murder of sir Thomas Overbury. Of Foreman the reader will find some account in a note to the *Silent Woman*, A. iv. S. 1.   Gresham succeeded him in the service of Mrs. Turner, and being, as Arthur Wilson says, "a *rotten* engine," was preserved, like his predecessor, from the gallows by an early death. Franklin was hanged at the same time with Mrs. Turner, "a swarthy, sallow, crook-backed fellow, (Wilson says,) as sordid in his death as pernicious in his life, and deserving not even so much as memory, p. 82.   He was the purveyor of the poison.   *Fiske* is often mentioned by Lilly ; and appears to have been just such another ignorant and impudent impostor as himself and Dr. Foreman.   "He was a licentiate in physick, exquisitely skilful in the art of directions upon nativities, and had a good genius in performing judgment thereupon —Oh learned esquire !" this pathetic apostrophe is to the dupe of these miscreants, the worthy Ashmole, "he died about the seventy-eighth year of his age, poor." *Lilly's History*, p. 44.   Fiske is introduced as *a cheating rogue*, in Fletcher's *Rollo Duke of Normandy.*

[9] ———— *if they be not, &c.*]   It is not a little amusing to find Fitzdottrel deep in the *Dialectics* of Chrysippus.   This is the very syllogism by which that acute philosopher triumphantly proved the reality of augury. *De Divinatione*, Lib. 1. § 71.

5   C

Why are there laws against them ? The best artists
Of Cambridge, Oxford, Middlesex and London,
Essex and Kent, I have had in pay to raise him,
These fifty weeks, and yet he appears not. 'Sdeath,
I shall suspect they can make circles only
Shortly, and know but his hard names. They do say,
He will meet a man, of himself, that has a mind to him.
If he would so, I have a mind and a half for him :
He should not be long absent.   Prithee come,
I long for thee :—an I were with child by him,
And my wife too, I could not more.   Come yet,
Good Beëlzebub.   Were he a kind devil,
And had humanity in him, he would come, but
To save one's longing.   I should use him well,
I swear, and with respect ; would he would try me !
Not as the conjurers do, when they have raised him,
Get him in bonds, and send him post on errands
A thousand miles ; it is preposterous, that ;
And, I believe, is the true cause he comes not :
And he has reason.   Who would be engaged,
That might live freely, as he may do ?   I swear,
They are wrong all.   The burnt child dreads the fire.
They do not know to entertain the devil :
I would so welcome him, observe his diet,
Get him his chamber hung with arras, two of 'em,
In my own house, lend him my wife's wrought pillows ;
And as I am an honest man, I think,
If he had a mind to her too, I should grant him,
To make our friendship perfect : so I would not
To every man.   If he but hear me now,
And should come to me in a brave young shape,
And take me at my word ?—

Enter PUG *handsomely shaped and apparelled.*
                            Ha ! who is this ?
    Pug. Sir, your good pardon, that I thus presume
Upon your privacy.   I am born a gentleman,
A younger brother, but in some disgrace

Now with my friends ; and want some little means
To keep me upright, while things be reconciled.[1]
Please you to let my service be of use to you, sir.

 Fitz. Service ! 'fore hell, my heart was at my mouth,
'Till I had view'd his shoes well : for those roses
Were big enough to hide a cloven foot.[2]— [*Aside.*
No, friend, my number's full. I have one servant,
Who is my all, indeed ; and from the broom
Unto the brush : for just so far I trust him.
He is my wardrobe-man, my cater, cook,
Butler, and steward : looks unto my horse ;
And helps to watch my wife. He has all the places
That I can think on, from the garret downward,
Even to the manger, and the curry-comb.

 Pug. Sir, I shall put your worship to no charge,
More than my meat, and that but very little ;
I'll serve you for your love.

 Fitz. Ha ! without wages ?
I'd hearken o' that ear, were I at leisure.
But now I am busy. Prithee, friend, forbear me—
An thou hadst been a devil, I should say
Somewhat more to thee : thou dost hinder now
My meditations.

 Pug. Sir, I am a devil.

 Fitz. How !

 Pug. A true devil, sir.

 Fitz. Nay, now you lie ;
Under your favour, friend, for I'll not quarrel.[3]

---

 [1] ———— while *things be reconciled,*] i. e. until.
 [2] —————— *for those* roses
  Were big enough to hide a cloven foot.] I have already noticed
the preposterous size of this fashionable article of dress ; a passage,
which was then overlooked, may serve to shew that the poet is
guilty of no exaggeration in the description of it. " He hath in the
shoe as much taffetie for the *tyings,* as would serve for an ancient :"
i. e. an ensign. Nashe's *Unfortunate Traveller,* 1598.
 [3] Under your favour, *friend, &c.*] This was one of the qualify-
ing expressions, by which, " according to the laws of the duello,"

I look'd on your feet afore, you cannot cozen me,
Your shoe's not cloven, sir, you are whole hoof'd.

   Pug. Sir, that's a popular error, deceives many :
But I am that I tell you.

   Fitz. What's your name ?

   Pug. My name is Devil, sir.

   Fitz. Say'st thou true ?

   Pug. Indeed, sir.

   Fitz. 'Slid, there's some omen in this ! What
      countryman ?

   Pug. Of Derbyshire, sir, about the Peak.

   Fitz. That hole
Belong'd to your ancestors ?

   Pug. Yes, Devil's arse, sir.

   Fitz. I'll entertain him for the name sake. Ha !
And turn away my t'other man, and save
Four pound a year by that ! there's luck and thrift too!
The very Devil may come hereafter as well. [*Aside.*
Friend, I receive you : but, withal, I acquaint you
Aforehand, if you offend me, I must beat you.
It is a kind of exercise I use ;
And cannot be without.

   Pug. Yes, if I do not
Offend, you can, sure.

   Fitz. Faith, Devil, very hardly :
I'll call you by your surname, 'cause I love it.

    Enter, behind, ENGINE, *with a cloke on his arm,*
         WITTIPOL, *and* MANLY.

   Eng. Yonder he walks, sir, I'll go lift him for you.

   Wit. To him, good Engine, raise him up by de-
      grees,

the lie might be given, without subjecting the speaker to the absolute necessity of receiving a challenge. To this Fitzdottrel alludes
in the next hemistich—*for I'll not quarrel.* The remainder of the
speech refers to the vulgar opinion respecting the devil, which is
also noticed by Shakspeare, "I look down towards his feet ;—but
that's a fable." *Othello.*

Gently, and hold him there too, you can do it.
Shew yourself now a mathematical broker.
   Eng. I'll warrant you, for half a piece.
   Wit. 'Tis done, sir.
   [ENGINE *goes to* FITZDOTTREL *and takes him aside.*
   Man. Is't possible there should be such a man !
   Wit. You shall be your own witness ; I'll not labour
To tempt you past your faith.
   Man. And is his wife
So very handsome, say you ?
   Wit. I have not seen her
Since I came home from travel ; and they say
She is not alter'd.   Then, before I went,
I saw her once ; but so, as she hath stuck
Still in my view, no object hath removed her.
   Man. 'Tis a fair guest, friend, beauty ; and once
      lodged
Deep in the eyes, she hardly leaves the inn.
How does he keep her ?
   Wit. Very brave ; however
Himself be sordid, he is sensual that way :
In every dressing he does study her.
   Man. And furnish forth himself so from the
      brokers ?
   Wit. Yes, that's a hired suit he now has on,
To see the DEVIL IS AN ASS, to day, in.
This Engine gets three or four pound a week by him—
He dares not miss a new play or a feast,
What rate soever clothes be at ; and thinks
Himself still new, in other men's old.
   Man. But stay,
Does he love meat so ?
   Wit. Faith, he does not hate it.
But that's not it : his belly and his palate
Would be compounded with for reason.   Marry,
A wit he has, of that strange credit with him,
'Gainst all mankind ; as it doth make him do

Just what it list : it ravishes him forth
Whither it please, to any assembly or place,
And would conclude him ruin'd, should he scape
One publick meeting, out of the belief
He has of his own great and catholic strengths,
In arguing and discourse.   It takes, I see :
He has got the cloke upon him.
 Fitz. [*after saying on the cloke.*] A fair garment,
By my faith, Engine !
 Eng. It was never made, sir,
For threescore pound, I assure you : 'twill yield thirty.
The plush, sir, cost three pound ten shillings a yard :
And then the lace and velvet !
 Fitz. I shall, Engine,
Be look'd at, prettily, in it : art thou sure
The play is play'd to-day ?
 Eng. O here's the bill, sir : [*He gives him the*
I had forgot to give it you.   *play-bill.*
 Fitz. Ha, the DEVIL !
I will not lose you, sirrah.   But, Engine, think you
The gallant is so furious in his folly,
So mad upon the matter, that he'll part
With's cloke upon these terms ?
 Eng. Trust not your Engine,
Break me to pieces else, as you would do
A rotten crane, or an old rusty jack,
That has not one true wheel in him.   Do but talk
  with him.
 Fitz. I shall do that, to satisfy you, Engine,
And myself too. [*comes forward.*]—With your leave,
  gentlemen.
Which of you is it,[4] is so mere idolater

---

 [4] *Which of you is it, &c.*] This adventure of the cloke, as
Langbaine observes, is from Boccacio, *Day* 3. *Nov.* 5.   It is there
told of Francisco Vergellesi, who parts with a horse on the conditions stipulated in the text.   Jonson has judiciously adapted his
bribe to the disposition of his characters ; but for a person who is

To my wife's beauty, and so very prodigal
Unto my patience, that, for the short parley
Of one swift hour's quarter, with my wife,
He will depart with (let me see) this cloke here,
The price of folly ?—Sir, are you the man ?
    Wit. I am that venturer, sir.
    Fitz. Good time ! your name
Is Wittipol ?
    Wit. The same, sir.
    Fitz. And 'tis told me
You have travell'd lately ?
    Wit. That I have, sir.
    Fitz. Truly,
Your travels may have alter'd your complexion ;
But sure your wit stood still.
    Wit. It may well be, sir ;
All heads have not like growth.
    Fitz. The good man's gravity,
That left you land, your father, never taught you
These pleasant matches.
    Wit. No, nor can his mirth,
With whom I make them, put me off.
    Fitz. You are
Resolved then ?
    Wit. Yes, sir.
    Fitz. Beauty is the saint,
You'll sacrifice your self into the shirt to ?
    Wit. So I may still clothe and keep warm your
       wisdom.
    Fitz. You lade me, sir ![5]
    Wit. I know what you will bear, sir.

now, perhaps, for the first time indebted to a preceding writer for
any part of his plot, the incident seems scarcely worth the borrowing.

   [5] *You* lade *me, sir !*]   This is equivalent to the modern phrase,
you do not spare me.   You lay what imputations you please upon
me.   The word occurs again in this sense, p. 33.

Fitz. Well, to the point. 'Tis only, sir, you say,
To speak unto my wife?
    Wit. Only to speak to her.
    Fitz. And in my presence?
    Wit. In your very presence.
    Fitz. And in my hearing?
    Wit. In your hearing; so
You interrupt us not.
    Fitz. For the short space
You do demand, the fourth part of an hour,
I think I shall, with some convenient study,
And this good help to boot, [*shrugs himself up in the
    cloke.*] bring myself to't.
    Wit. I ask no more.
    Fitz. Please you, walk toward my house,
Speak what you list; that time is yours; my right
I have departed with : but not beyond
A minute, or a second, look for.   Length,
And drawing out may advance much to these matches.
And I except all kissing : kisses are .
Silent petitions still with willing lovers.
    Wit. Lovers! how falls that o' your phantasy?
    Fitz. Sir,
I do know somewhat; I forbid all lip-work.
    Wit. I am not eager at forbidden dainties :
Who covets unfit things, denies himself.
    Fitz. You say well, sir; 'twas prettily said, that
        same :
He does indeed. I'll have no touches therefore,
Nor takings by the arms, nor tender circles
Cast 'bout the waste, but all be done at distance.
Love is brought up with those soft migniard handlings :
His pulse lies in his palm; and I defend
All melting joints and fingers, that's my bargain,
I do defend them any thing like action.[6]

[6] *I do* defend *them any thing like action.*] To *defend*, from the
Fr. *defendre*, is to forbid. This sense of the word is common in

But talk, sir, what you will.   Use all the tropes
And schemes, that prince Quintilian can afford you :
And much good do your rhetoric's heart.   You are
  welcome, sir.   [*Opens the door of his house.*
Engine, God be wi' you !
 Wit. Sir, I must condition
To have this gentleman by, a witness.
 Fitz. Well,
I am content, so he be silent.
 Man. Yes, sir.
 Fitz. Come, Devil, I'll make you room straight :
  but I'll shew you
First to your mistress, who's no common one,
You must conceive, that brings this gain to see her.
I hope thou'st brought me good luck.
 Pug. I shall do't, sir. [*They all enter the house.*

SCENE III. *A Room in* FITZDOTTREL'S *House.*

Enter WITTIPOL, MANLY, *and* ENGINE.

Wittipol.

NGINE, you hope of your half piece ? 'tis
  there, sir.
Be gone. [*Exit* ENGINE.]—Friend Manly,
  who's within here ? fixed !
     [*Knocks him on the breast.*
 Man. I am directly in a fit of wonder
What will be the issue of this conference.

our old writers.   Thus Chaucer, in *The Wife of Bath's Prologue,*
v. 59,
   " Where can you say in any manir age
    That ever God *defendid* marriage ?"
And Spenser,
   "That, O ye heavens, *defend !* and turn away."
     Faerie Queene, B. 5. C. 8. St. 10.

Wit. For that ne'er vex yourself till the event.
How like you him ?
  Man. I would fain see more of him.
  Wit. What think you of this ?
  Man. I am past degrees of thinking.
Old Afric, and the new America,
With all their fruit of monsters, cannot shew
So just a prodigy.
  Wit. Could you have believed,
Without your sight, a mind so sordid inward,
Should be so specious, and laid forth abroad,
To all the show that ever shop or ware was ?
  Man. I believe any thing now, though I confess
His vices are the most extremities
I ever knew in nature. But why loves he
The devil so ?
  Wit. O, sir ! for hidden treasure
He hopes to find ; and has proposed himself
So infinite a mass, as to recover,
He cares not what he parts with, of the present,
To his men of art, who are the race may coin him.
Promise gold mountains, and the covetous
Are still most prodigal.
  Man. But have you faith,
That he will hold his bargain ?
  Wit. O dear sir !
He will not off on't ; fear him not : I know him.
One baseness still accompanies another.
See ! he is here already, and his wife too.
  Man. A wondrous handsome creature, as I live !

Enter FITZDOTTREL, *with* Mrs. FRANCES *his wife.*

  Fitz. Come, wife, this is the gentleman ; nay,
    blush not.
  Mrs. Fitz. Why, what do you mean, sir, have you
    your reason ?
  Fitz. Wife,

I do not know that I have lent it forth
To any one ; at least, without a pawn, wife :
Or that I have eat or drunk the thing, of late,
That should corrupt it. Wherefore, gentle wife,
Obey, it is thy virtue ; hold no acts
Of disputation.
   Mrs. Fitz. Are you not enough
The talk of feasts and meetings, but you'll still
Make argument for fresh ?
   Fitz. Why, careful wedlock,
If I have a longing to have one tale more
Go of me, what is that to thee, dear heart ?
Why shouldst thou envy my delight, or cross it,
By being solicitous, when it not concerns thee ?
   Mrs. Fitz. Yes, I have share in this : the scorn
      will fall
As bitterly on me, where both are laugh'd at.
   Fitz. Laugh'd at, sweet bird ! is that the scruple ?
      come, come,
Thou art a niaise.[7] Which of your great houses,
(I will not mean at home here, but abroad,)
Your families in France, wife, send not forth
Something within the seven year, may be laugh'd at?
I do not say seven months, nor seven weeks,
Nor seven days, nor hours ; but seven year, wife :
I give them time. Once within seven year,
I think they may do something may be laugh'd at ;
In France, I keep me there still. Wherefore, wife,
Let them that list laugh still, rather than weep
For me. Here is a cloke cost fifty pound, wife,

---

   [7] *Thou art a* niaise.] A marginal note in the old copy says, "a
niaise is a young hawk taken crying out of the nest." This explanation could scarcely come from Jonson ; for it explains nothing.
A niaise (or rather *an eyas*, of which it is a corruption) is unquestionably a young hawk, but the niaise of the poet is the French
term for, " a simple, witless, inexperienced gull," &c. The word
is very common in our old writers.

Which I can sell for thirty, when I have seen
All London in't, and London has seen me.[8]
To-day I go to the Blackfriars play-house,
Sit in the view, salute all my acquaintance,
Rise up between the acts, let fall my cloke,
Publish a handsome man, and a rich suit,
As that's a special end why we go thither,
All that pretend to stand for't on the stage :
The ladies ask, who's that ? for they do come
To see us, love, as we do to see them.
Now I shall lose all this, for the false fear
Of being laugh'd at ! Yes, wusse. Let them laugh, wife.
Let me have such another cloke to-morrow,
And let them laugh again, wife, and again,
And then grow fat with laughing, and then fatter,
All my young gallants, let 'em bring their friends too;
Shall I forbid them ? No, let heaven forbid them :
Or wit, if it have any charge on 'em. Come, thy ear
      wife,
Is all I'll borrow of thee.—Set your watch, sir.—
Thou only art to hear, not speak a word, dove,
To aught he says : that I do give you in precept,
No less than counsel, on your wifehood, wife,
Not though he flatter you, or make court, or love,
As you must look for these, or say he rail ;
Whate'er his arts be, wife, I will have thee
Delude them with a trick, thy obstinate silence.
I know advantages ; and I love to hit
These pragmatic young men at their own weapons.
Is your watch ready ?   Here my sail bears for you :
Tack toward him, sweet pinnace. [*He disposes his
      wife to her place.*] Where's your watch ?

---

8   ———— *when I have seen
    All London in't and London has seen me.*]

Had Pope read this passage ?

    "Europe he saw, and Europe saw him too."

Wit. I'll set it, sir, with yours.

Mrs. Fitz. I must obey.   [*Aside.*

Man. Her modesty seems to suffer with her beauty,
And so, as if his folly were away,
It were worth pity.

Fitz. Now they are right; begin, sir.[9]
But first,.let me repeat the contract briefly.
I am, sir, to enjoy this cloke I stand in,
Freely, and as your gift; upon condition
You may as freely speak here to my spouse,
Your quarter of an hour, always keeping
The measured distance of your yard or more,
From my said spouse ; and in my sight and hearing.
This is your covenant ?

Wit. Yes, but you'll allow
For this time spent now ?

Fitz. Set them so much back.

Wit. I think I shall not need it.

Fitz. Well, begin, sir,
There is your bound, sir; not beyond that rush.

Wit. If you interrupt me, sir, I shall discloke you.—
The time I have purchased, lady, is but short ;
And therefore, if I employ it thriftily,
I hope I stand the nearer to my pardon.
I am not here to tell you, you are fair,
Or lovely, or how well you dress you, lady ;
I'll save myself that eloquence of your glass,
Which can speak these things better to you than I.
And 'tis a knowledge wherein fools may be
As wise as a court-parliament. Nor come I
With any prejudice or doubt, that you
Should, to the notice of your own worth, need
Least revelation. She's a simple woman,
Knows not her good, whoever knows her ill,

---

[9] *Now* they are *right,*] i. e. the watches. Whalley says that the
old copy has *Now* thou *art right,* meaning his wife ; but he is mistaken, it reads as in the text.

And at all caracts.[1] That you are the wife
To so much blasted flesh, as scarce hath soul,
Instead of salt, to keep it sweet ;[2] I think,
Will ask no witnesses to prove.   The cold
Sheets that you lie in, with the watching candle,
That sees, how dull to any thaw of beauty,
Pieces and quarters, half and whole nights sometimes,
The devil-given elfin squire, your husband,
Doth leave you, quitting here his proper circle.
For a much worse, in the walks of Lincoln's-inn,
Under the elms, t' expect the fiend in vain there,
Will confess for you.
   Fitz. I did look for this jeer.
   Wit. And what a daughter of darkness he does
      make you,
Lock'd up from all society, or object ;
Your eye not let to look upon a face,
Under a conjurer's, or some mould for one,
Hollow and lean like his, but by great means,
As I now make; your own too sensible sufferings,
Without the extraordinary aids
Of spells, or spirits, may assure you, lady.
For my part, I protest 'gainst all such practice,
I work by no false arts, medicines, or charms
To be said forward and backward.
   Fitz. No, I except—
   Wit. Sir, I shall ease you.
              [*He offers to discloke him.*
   Fitz. Mum.
   Wit. Nor have I ends, lady,
Upon you, more than this : to tell you how Love,

---

[1] *And at all* caracts,] i. e. to the nicest point, to the minutest circumstance. Caracts, as Whalley has somewhere before observed, are the weights by which gold and precious stones are weighed and valued.

[2] ——————— *As scarce hath soul,*
  Instead of salt to keep it sweet.]   See vol. iv. p. 447.

Beauty's good angel, he that waits upon her
At all occasions, and, no less than Fortune,
Helps the adventurous, in me makes that proffer,
Which never fair one was so fond to lose,
Who could but reach a hand forth to her freedom.
On the first sight I loved you, since which time,
Though I have travell'd, I have been in travail
More for this second blessing of your eyes,
Which now I've purchased, than for all aims else.
Think of it, lady, be your mind as active
As is your beauty : view your object well,
Examine both my fashion and my years ;
Things that are like, are soon familiar :
And nature joys still in equality.
Let not the sign of the husband fright you, lady ;
But ere your spring be gone, enjoy it.   Flowers,
Though fair, are oft but of one morning ; think,
All beauty doth not last until the autumn :
You grow old while I tell you this ;[3] and such
As cannot use the present, are not wise.
If Love and Fortune will take care of us,
Why should our will be wanting ?   This is all.
What do you answer, lady ?

   Fitz. Now the sport comes.
Let him still wait, wait, wait ; while the watch goes,
And the time runs, wife !

   Wit. How ! not any word ?
Nay, then I taste a trick in't.—Worthy lady,
I cannot be so false to my own thoughts
Of your presumed goodness, to conceive

---

  [3] *You grow old while I tell you this.*]
     Fugit hora : hoc quod loquor, inde est.   Pers. Sat. 5.
                             WHAL.
To be so near, and yet miss, is unlucky : is not the expression
rather from Horace ?
           ——————— *dum loquimur, fugerit invida*
  Ætas, carpe diem, &c.

This, as your rudeness, which I see's imposed.
Yet, since your cautelous jailor [4] here stands by you,
And you are denied the liberty of the house,
Let me take warrant, lady, from your silence,
Which ever is interpreted consent,
To make your answer for you ; which shall be
To as good purpose as I can imagine,
And what I think you'd speak.

Fitz. No, no, no, no.

Wit. I shall resume, sir.

Man. Sir, what do you mean ?

Wit. One interruption more, sir, and you go
Into your hose and doublet, nothing saves you :
And therefore hearken.   This is for your wife.

Man. You must play fair, sir.

Wit. Stand for me, good friend.—

[*Sets* MANLY *in his place, and speaks for the lady.*

---

[4] *Yet, since your* cautelous *jailor.*] Our old writers seem to have
included in this word not only the sense of wariness, but also of
something artful and insidious, ingrafted upon it.   In many instances, I will not say in all, it is clearly distinguished from cautious.
Thus Knolles, "The Turke began to shrinke from that he had before promised, by *cautelous* expositions of his meaning." *Hist. of
the Turks*, p. 904.

Now I am on this subject, I will take the opportunity " of pro-
testing against a singular practice " of the late editor of Beaumont
and Fletcher, very injurious to the reputation of those writers.
Whenever this gentleman is at a loss for the precise meaning of a
word, he sets down the first which occurs to him, and observes that
" its vague import is owing to the general laxity of language which
prevailed in those times."   It is not a little presumptuous in a
foreigner who, like Mr. Weber, grubs all his knowledge of English
out of glossaries and indexes, to call in question the proficiency of
such writers as Beaumont, Fletcher, and others, the politest scholars,
and best informed men of their time, in their own language.   The
fact is, (and I mention it for the sake of far other critics than Mr.
Weber,) that they were in possession of a more precise and co-
pious vocabulary than ourselves, and that they had a most profound
and critical knowledge of every part of it.   The difficulty which
Mr. Weber finds in ascertaining their meaning, originates in his
ignorance of the English tongue.

Troth, sir, 'tis more than true that you have utter'd
Of my unequal and so sordid match here,
With all the circumstances of my bondage.
I have a husband, and a two-legg'd one,
But such a moonling, as no wit of man,
Or roses can redeem from being an ass.[5]
He's grown too much the story of men's mouths,
To scape his lading : should I make't my study,
And lay all ways, yea, call mankind to help
To take his burden off; why, this one act
Of his, to let his wife out to be courted,
And at a price, proclaims his asinine nature
So loud, as I am weary of my title to him.
But, sir, you seem a gentleman of virtue,
No less than blood ; and one that every way
Looks as he were of too good quality,
To intrap a credulous woman, or betray her.
Since you have paid thus dear, sir, for a visit,
And made such venture on your wit and charge
Merely to see me, or at most, to speak to me,
I were too stupid, or, what's worse, ingrate
Not to return your venture. Think but how

[5] *But such a* moonling, *as no wit of man,*
Or roses *can redeem from being an* ass.] Here is an allusion to
the metamorphosis of Lucian into an *ass ;* who being brought into
the theatre to shew tricks, recovered his human shape, by eating
some *roses* which he found there. See the conclusion of the treatise, *Lucius, sive Asinus.* I am afraid that many of the audience,
in our author's days, were not apprised of these allusions. WHAL.
    It might be so : and yet I suspect that, generally speaking, the
audience then had more literature than the dramatic writers themselves now possess. The age was credulous, but not uninformed,
at least in classical matters. Other requisites than ignorance and
impudence were then required in dramatic writers; and, indeed,
with a solitary exception or two, all of them had received an university education.
    Moonling, which occurs in this line, is a pretty expression for
a fool or lunatic, which should not have been suffered to grow
obsolete.

5   D

I may with safety do it, I shall trust
My love and honour to you, and presume
You'll ever husband both, against this husband;
Who, if we chance to change his liberal ears
To other ensigns,[6] and with labour make
A new beast of him, as he shall deserve,
Cannot complain he is unkindly dealt with.
This day he is to go to a new play, sir,
From whence no fear, no, nor authority,
Scarcely the king's command, sir, will restrain him,
Now you have fitted him with a stage-garment,
For the mere name's sake, were there nothing else;
And many more such journeys he will make;
Which, if they now, or any time hereafter,
Offer us opportunity, you hear, sir,
Who'll be as glad and forward to embrace,
Meet, and enjoy it cheerfully, as you.

       [Shifts to his own place again.

I humbly thank you, lady——

 Fitz. Keep your ground, sir.
 Wit. Will you be lighten'd?
 Fitz. Mum.
 Wit. And but I am,

By the said contract, thus to take my leave of you
At this so envious distance, I had taught
Our lips ere this, to seal the happy mixture
Made of our souls: but we must both now yield
To the necessity.   Do not think yet, lady,
But I can kiss, and touch, and laugh, and whisper,
And do those crowning courtships too, for which
Day, and the public, have allow'd no name;
But now, my bargain binds me.   'Twere rude injury
To impórtune more, or urge a noble nature,
To what of its own bounty it is prone to:
Else I should speak——But, lady, I love so well,

<hr />

6 ———— *to change his liberal ears*
 To other ensigns,] i. e. to horns, the insignia of a cuckold.

As I will hope you'll do so too.—I have done, sir.
　Fitz. Well, then I have won ?
　Wit. Sir, and I may win too.
　Fitz. O yes ! no doubt on't.　I'll take careful order,
That she shall hang forth ensigns at the window,
To tell you when I am absent !　Or I'll keep
Three or four footmen, ready still of purpose,
To run and fetch you at her longings, sir !
I'll go bespeak me straight a gilt caroch,
For her and you to take the air in : yes,
Into Hyde-park, and thence into Blackfriars,
Visit the painters, where you may see pictures,
And note the properest limbs, and how to make them !
Or what do you say unto a middling gossip,[7]
To bring you ay together, at her lodging,
Under pretext of teaching of my wife
Some rare receipt of drawing almond-milk, ha ?
It shall be a part of my care.　Good sir, God be wi'
　　　you !
I have kept the contract, and the cloke's mine own.
　Wit. Why, much good do't you, sir : it may fall out,
That you have bought it dear, though I've not sold it.
　　　　　　　　　　　　　　　[Exit.

　Fitz. A pretty riddle ! fare you well, good sir.
Wife, your face this way ; look on me, and think
You had a wicked dream, wife, and forget it.
　Man. This is the strangest motion I e'er saw.
　　　　　　　　　　　　　　　[Exit.

　Fitz. Now, wife, sits this fair cloke the worse
　　　upon me
For my great sufferings, or your little patience, ha ?
They laugh, you think ?
　Mrs. Fitz. Why, sir, and you might see't.
What thought they have of you, may be soon collected
By the young gentleman's speech.

---

[7] *Or what do you say unto a* middling gossip?]　A go between,
an *internuntia*, as the Latin writers would have called her.　WHAL.

Fitz. Young gentleman !
Death, you are in love with him, are you ? could he
   not
Be named the gentleman, without the young ?
Up to your cabin again.
   Mrs. Fitz. My cage, you were best
To call it.
   Fitz. Yes, sing there.   You'd fain be making
Blanc-manger with him at your mother's ! I know
   you.
Go, get you up.—   [*Exit* Mrs. Fitz.

Enter Pug.

      How now ! what say you, Devil ?
   Pug. Here is one Engine, sir, desires to speak with
   you.
   Fitz. I thought he brought some news of a broker !
   well,
Let him come in, good Devil ; fetch him else.
                         [*Exit* Pug.

Re-enter Engine.

O, my fine Engine ! what's the affair, more cheats ?
   Eng. No, sir, the wit, the brain, the great projector,
I told you of, is newly come to town.
   Fitz. Where, Engine ?
   Eng. I have brought him (he's without)
Ere he pull'd off his boots, sir ; but so follow'd
For businesses !
   Fitz. But what is a projector ?
I would conceive.
   Eng. Why, one, sir, that projects
Ways to enrich men, or to make them great,
By suits, by marriages, by undertakings :
According as he sees they humour it.
   Fitz. Can he not conjure at all ?
   Eng. I think he can, sir,

To tell you true. But you do know, of late,
The state hath ta'en such note of 'em, and compell'd
  'em
To enter such great bonds, they dare not practise.
 Fitz. 'Tis true, and I lie fallow for't the while !
 Eng. O, sir, you'll grow the richer for the rest.
 Fitz. I hope I shall : but, Engine, you do talk
Somewhat too much o' my courses : my cloke-
  customer
Could tell me strange particulars.
 Eng. By my means ?
 Fitz. How should he have them else ?
 Eng. You do not know, sir,
What he has ; and by what arts : a money'd man, sir,
And is as great with your almanack-men as you are.
 Fitz. That gallant !
 Eng. You make the other wait too long here ;
And he is extreme punctual.
 Fitz. Is he a gallant ?
 Eng. Sir, you shall see : he's in his riding suit,
As he comes now from court : but hear him speak ;
Minister matter to him, and then tell me. [*Exeunt.*

ACT II.

SCENE I. *A Room in* FITZDOTTREL'S *House.*

Enter FITZDOTTREL, ENGINE, *and* MEERCRAFT, *followed by* TRAINS *with a bag, and three or four* Attendants.

Meercraft.

SIR, money is a whore, a bawd, a drudge;
    Fit to run out on errands : let her go.
    Via, pecunia ! when she's run and gone,
    And fled, and dead; then will I fetch her again
With *aqua vitæ*, out of an old hogshead !
While there are lees of wine, or dregs of beer,
I'll never want her ! Coin her out of cobwebs,
Dust, but I'll have her! raise wool upon egg shells,
Sir, and make grass grow out of marrow-bones,
To make her come.—Commend me to your mistress.
                     [To 1 Attendant.
Say, let the thousand pound but be had ready,
And it is done. [*Exit* 1 Atten.]—I would but see the creature
Of flesh and blood, the man, the prince indeed,
That could employ so many millions
As I would help him to.
    Fitz. How talks he ? millions !
    Meer. [*to* 2 Attendant.]—I'll give you an account
        of this to-morrow.   [*Exit* 2 Atten.
—Yes, I will take no less, and do it too;
If they were myriads : and without the Devil,

By direct means, it shall be good in law.

 Eng. Sir.

 Meer. [*to* 3 Atten.] Tell master Woodcock, I'll
  not fail to meet him

Upon the Exchange at night ; pray him to have
The writings there, and we'll dispatch it. [*Exit*
  3 Atten.]—Sir,
You are a gentleman of a good presence,
A handsome man ; I have consider'd you
As a fit stock to graft honours upon :
I have a project to make you a duke now.
That you must be one, within so many months
As I set down, out of true reasons of state,
You shall not avoid it.   But you must hearken, then.

 Eng. Hearken ! why, sir, do you doubt his ears ?
  Alas !
You do not know master Fitzdottrel.

 Fitz. He does not know me indeed ; I thank you,
  Engine,
For rectifying him.

 Meer. Good ! Why, Engine, then
I'll tell it you.   (I see you have credit here,
And, that you can keep counsel, I'll not question.)
He shall but be an undertaker with me,
In a most feasible business.   It shall cost him
Nothing.

 Eng. Good, sir.

 Meer. Except he please, but's countenance,
(That I will have) to appear in't, to great men,
For which I'll make him one.   He shall not draw
A string of's purse.   I'll drive his patent for him.
We'll take in citizens, commoners, and aldermen,
To bear the charge, and blow them off again,
Like so many dead flies, when it is carried.
The thing is for recovery of drown'd land,[8]

 [8] *The thing is for recovery of drown'd land.*] This was the age
of projects and monopolies ; and the prevailing humour is not un-

Whereof the crown's to have a moiety,
If it be owner; else the crown and owners
To share that moiety, and the recoverers
To enjoy the t'other moiety for their charge.
    Eng. Thoroughout England?

seasonably ridiculed by the poet. 'Tis probable, that a design of draining the fens was then talked of: and experience has since shewn, that the project was not wholly impracticable. WHAL.
    Thus Randolph:

> "I have a rare device to set Dutch windmills
> Upon Newmarket Heath and Salisbury Plain,
> *To drain the fens!" Muses' Looking-glass.*

But this was, as Whalley says, the age of projectors; and it is to the praise of the dramatic poets, that they spared no efforts to guard the public against them. Had not the scandalous rapacity of the courtiers found an interest in encouraging those daring depredators on the weak and wealthy, the united force of wit and satire must have driven them out of countenance. Our poet, who never loses sight of verisimilitude, is somewhat modest in his catalogue of *projects;* but his contemporaries wanton in their exposure of those pernicious follies. *The Court Beggar* of Brome is solely directed against them; and in that extraordinary drama, *The Antipodes,* they are attacked with no inconsiderable degree of humour. One example may be given: its pleasantry must apologize for its length.

>   " As for your *project*
> For putting down the infinite use of jacks,
> Whereby the education of young children
> In turning spits, is greatly hindered,
> It may be look'd into; and so may yours,
> Against the multiplicity of watches,
> Whereby much neighbourly familiarity,
> By asking " What d'ye guess it is o'clock?"
> Is lost, when every puny clerk can carry
> The time o' the day in's breeches. For the rest;
> This, for the increase of wool; that is to say,
> By flaying of live horses, and new-covering them
> With sheepskins, I do like exceedingly:
> And this, for keeping of tame owls in cities,
> To kill up rats and mice, whereby all cats
> May be destroyed, as an especial means
> To stop the growth of witchcraft." A. iv. S. 1.

Meer. Yes, which will arise
To eighteen millions, seven the first year :
I have computed all, and made my survey
Unto my acre : I'll begin at the pan,
Not at the skirts ; as some have done, and lost
All that they wrought,[9] their timber-work, their trench,
Their banks, all borne away, or else fill'd up,
By the next winter.   Tut, they never went
The way : I'll have it all.
    Eng. A gallant tract
Of land it is !
    Meer. 'Twill yield a pound an acre :
We must let cheap ever at first.   But, sir,
This looks too large for you, I see.   Come hither,
We'll have a less.   Here's a plain fellow, [*points to*
        TRAINS] you see him,
Has his black bag of papers there, in buckram,
Will not be sold for the earldom of Pancridge : draw,

----

9 ——————— *I'll begin at the* pan,
    Not at the skirts ; *as some have done, and lost*
    All that they wrought, &c.] *Pan* is not easily distinguished
from *skirt.* Both words seem to refer to the outer parts, or extremities. Perhaps Meercraft means—on a broader scale, on a more
extended front.   The remainder of the speech apparently alludes
to some well-known disaster of the time.   Many schemes were set
on foot about this period, not only for *draining the fens* of Lincolnshire, but for gaining land from the sea in various places ; of these
not a few failed ; but the attempts were not wholly lost to the community, since they taught later adventurers to avoid the errors of
the original projectors.
    The boldness of the plans for draining the fens, seems to have
startled the public more than all the others exhibited to their consideration : hence the perpetual allusions to it in our old dramatists.
One has just been mentioned ; another is now before me :
                "Our projector
    Will undertake the making of bay-salt,
    For a penny a bushel, to serve all the state ;
    Another *dreames* of building water-workes,
    Drying of fennes and marshes, like the Dutchmen."
                    Holland's Leaguer, A. i. S. 5.

Give me out one by chance. [TRAINS *gives him a*
    paper out of the bag.] "*Project four : Dogs'*
    skins."
Twelve thousand pound ! the very worst at first.
    Fitz. Pray you let's see it, sir.
    Meer. 'Tis a toy, a trifle !
    Fitz. Trifle ! twelve thousand pound for dogs'
    skins ?
    Meer. Yes,
But, by my way of dressing, you must know, sir,
And med'cining the leather to a height
Of improved ware, like your borachio
Of Spain,[1] sir, I can fetch nine thousand for't——
    Eng. Of the king's glover ?
    Meer. Yes ; how heard you that ?
    Eng. Sir, I do know you can.
    Meer. Within this hour ;
And reserve half my secret.   Pluck another ;
See if thou hast a happier hand ; [TRAINS *draws out*
    another.] I thought so.
The very next worse to it ! "*Bottle-ale.*"
Yet this is two and twenty thousand.   Prithee
Pull out another, two or three.
    Fitz. Good ; stay, friend—
By bottle-ale two and twenty thousand pound ?
    Meer. Yes, sir, it's cast to penny-halfpenny far-
    thing.
On the back-side, there you may see it, read,
I will not bate a Harrington of the sum.[2]

---

[1] ——————— *like your* borachio
    Of Spain.]   "Borachio (says Minshieu) is a bottle commonly
of a pigges skin, with the hair inward, dressed inwardly with
rozen, to keep wine or liquor sweet :"—Wines preserved in these
bottles contract a peculiar flavour, and are then said *to taste of the*
borachio.
    [2] *I will not bate a* Harrington *of the sum.*]   In 1613, a patent
was granted to John Stanhope, lord Harrington, Treasurer of the
Chambers, for the coinage of royal farthing tokens, of which he

I'll win it in my water, and my malt,
My furnaces, and hanging of my coppers,

seems to have availed himself with sufficient liberality. Some clamour was excited on the occasion; but it speedily subsided; for the Star Chamber kept a watchful eye on the first symptoms of discontent at these pernicious indulgences. "Now" (says the author of *the first fourteen years of king James*) "my lord Harrington obtained a patent of his majesty for the making of *brasse farthings*, a thing that brought with it some contempt, though lawful, for all things lawful are not expedient, who being enjoined to goe into the Low-countries with her Grace" (the princess Elizabeth, married to the Palsgrave) "by the way lost his life." From this nobleman they took the name of Harringtons in common conversation; thus sir Henry Wotton: "I have lost four or five friends, and not gotten the value of one Harrington." *Letters*, p. 558. Several of these little pieces were in the hands of Mr. Waldron, and Whalley caused one of them to be engraved; this I have copied, though it is too common, I suspect, to be an object either of interest or curiosity.

In that amusing collection of anecdotes, &c., the *Oxoniana*, there is a singular error respecting this word, which occurs in *Drunken Barnaby's Journal*:

> "*Veni Harrington, bonum omen!*
> *Vere amans illud nomen;*
> *Harringtoni dedi nummum,*
> *Et fortunæ penè summum,*
> *Indigenti postulanti*
> *Benedictionem danti.*"

> " Thence to Harrington, be it spoken,
> For name's sake, I gave a token
> To a beggar that did crave it
> And as cheerfully receive it.
> More he need not me impórtune,
> For, 'twas the utmost of my fortune."

From this passage, the surname of Harrington has been absurdly given to Barnaby—"though it must be observed," (the collector says) "that in the Latin there is little if any proof of Barnaby's

The tonning, and the subtlety of my yest;
And, then the earth of my bottles, which I dig,
Turn up, and steep, and work, and neal, myself,
To a degree of porcelane.   You will wonder
At my proportions, what I will put up
In seven years! for so long time I ask
For my invention.   I will save in cork,
In my mere stop'ling, above three thousand pound,
Within that term; by googing of them out
Just to the size of my bottles, and not slicing:
There's infinite loss in that.   [TRAINS *draws out
    another.*] What hast thou there?
O! "*Making wine of raisins:*" this is in hand now.
   Eng. Is not that strange, sir, to make wine of
        raisins?[3]
   Meer. Yes, and as true a wine as the wines of
        France,
Or Spain, or Italy: look of what grape
My raisin is, that wine I'll render perfect,
As of the Muscatel grape, I'll render Muscatel;
Of the Canary, his; the Claret, his;
So of all kinds: and bate you of the prices
Of wine throughout the kingdom half in half.
   Eng. But how, sir, if you raise the other commodity,
Raisins?
   Meer. Why, then I'll make it out of blackberries,

surname being Harrington, but only in the English translation."
vol. ii. p. 57.   In fact, there is no proof of it in either language.
Barnaby simply means to say, that when he reached *Harrington*,
he had in his pocket the *token* or farthing piece of that name,
which he looked on as a fortunate circumstance.   This *Harrington*
he bestowed in charity; and, as it was the whole of his stock, the
act may be placed as a small set-off against some of his drunken
frolics.
   [3] *Is not that strange, sir, to make wine of raisins?*]   Whatever
it might be in Fitzdottrel's days, it is sufficiently familiar in ours.
The late Mr. Beaufoy would have outgone Meercraft in his own
way; and his successors are thought to have improved even upon
his ingenuity.

And it shall do the same.   'Tis but more art,
And the charge less.   Take out another.
    Fitz. No, good sir,
Save you the trouble, I'll not look, nor hear
Of any but your first, there; the drown'd-land;
If't will do, as you say.
    Meer. Sir, there's not place
To give you demonstration of these things,
They are a little too subtle.   But I could shew you
Such a necessity in it, as you must be
But what you please; against the received heresy,
That England bears no dukes.[4] Keep you the land,
        sir,
The greatness of the estate shall throw't upon you.
If you like better turning it to money,
What may not you, sir, purchase with that wealth ?
Say you should part with two of your millions,
To be the thing you would, who would not do't ?
As I protest I will, out of my dividend,
Lay for some pretty principality
In Italy, from the church : now you, perhaps,
Fancy the smoke of England rather ? But——
Have you no private room, sir, to draw to,
To enlarge ourselves more upon ?
    Fitz. O yes.—Devil!

[4] ——————— *against the received heresy,*
    That England bears no dukes.] I know not when this *heresy*
crept in. There was apparently some unwillingness to create dukes,
as a title of honour, in the Norman race; probably because the
Conqueror, and his immediate successors, were dukes of Normandy,
and did not choose that a subject should enjoy similar dignities
with themselves.   The first of the English who bore the title was
Edward the black prince, (son of Edward III.) who was created
duke of Cornwall, by charter, as Collins says, in 1337. The dignity
being subsequently conferred on several of the blood-royal, and of
the nobility, who came to untimely ends, an idea seems to have been
entertained by the vulgar, that the title itself was ominous.   At the
accession of James I. to the crown of this country, there was, I
believe, no English peer of ducal dignity.

Meer. These, sir, are businesses ask to be carried
With caution, and in cloud.
    Fitz. I apprehend
They do, sir.—

Enter Pug.

                Devil, which way is your mistress ?
    Pug. Above, sir, in her chamber.
    Fitz. O that's well :
Then this way, good sir.
    Meer. I shall follow you.   Trains,
Give me the bag, and go you presently,
Commend my service to my lady. Tailbush.
Tell her I am come from court this morning ; say,
I have got our business mov'd, and well : entreat
       her,
That she give you the fourscore angels, and see them
Disposed of to my counsel, sir Paul Eitherside.
Some time, to-day, I'll wait upon her ladyship,
With the relation.   [*Exit* TRAINS.
    Eng. Sir, of what dispatch
He is ! do you mark ?   [*Aside to* FITZ.
    Meer. Engine, when did you see
My cousin Everill ? keeps he still your quarter
In the Bermudas ?
    Eng. Yes, sir, he was writing
This morning, very hard.
    Meer. Be not you known to him,
That I am come to town : I have effected
A business for him, but I would have it take him,
Before he thinks for't.
    Eng. Is it past ?
    Meer. Not yet.
'Tis well o' the way.
    Eng. O sir ! your worship takes
Infinite pains.
    Meer. I love friends to be active :

A sluggish nature puts off man, and kind.[5]
  Eng. And such a blessing follows it.
  Meer. I thank
My fate.—Pray you, let's be private, sir.
  Fitz. In, here.
  Meer. Where none may interrupt us.
                              [*Exeunt* MEER. *and* ENGINE.
  Fitz. You hear, Devil,
Lock the street-doors fast, and let no one in,
Except they be this gentleman's followers,
To trouble me.   Do you mark ?   You have heard
        and seen
Something to-day, and by it you may gather,
Your mistress is a fruit that's worth the stealing,
And therefore worth the watching. Be you sure, now,
You have all your eyes about you ; and let in
No lace-woman, nor bawd, that brings French masks,
And cut-works ; see you ? nor old croans with wafers,
To convey letters : nor no youths, disguised
Like country-wives, with cream and marrow-puddings.
Much knavery may be vented in a pudding,
Much bawdy intelligence : they are shrewd cyphers.
Nor turn the key to any neighbour's need ;
Be it but to kindle fire, or beg a little,
Put it out rather, all out, to an ash,
That they may see no smoke.   Or water, spill it ;
Knock on the empty tubs, that by the sound
They may be forbid entry.   Say, we are robb'd,
If any come to borrow a spoon or so :
I will not have Good Fortune, or God's Blessing
Let in, while I am busy.[6]
  Pug. I'll take care, sir ;

---

  [5] *A sluggish nature puts off* man *and* kind,] i. e. human nature.
See vol. iv. p. 212.
  [6] *I will not have Good Fortune, or God's Blessing*
    Let in, while I am busy.] "Once upon a time, there was an
old chuff; and when he brought home money he used to say,

They shall not trouble you if they would.
    Fitz. Well, do so.   [*Exit.*
    Pug. I have no singular service of this now,
Nor no superlative master! I shall wish
To be in hell again at leisure! bring
A Vice from thence! that had been such a subtlety,
As to bring broad-cloths hither, or transport
Fresh oranges into Spain.   I find it now;
My chief was in the right.   Can any fiend
Boast of a better Vice, than here by nature
And art they're owners of? Hell never own me,
But I am taken! the fine tract of it
Pulls me along! to hear men such professors
Grown in our subtlest sciences! My first act, now,
Shall be to make this master of mine, cuckold:
The primitive work of darkness I will practise.
I will deserve so well of my fair mistress
By my discoveries first, my counsels after,
And keeping counsel after that, as who
So ever is one, I will be another sure,
I'll have my share.   Most delicate damn'd flesh
She will be! O, that I could stay time, now!
Midnight will come too fast upon me, I fear,
To cut my pleasure——

'Wife, this must not be spent; it must be laid by for *good fortune.'*
As he did this often, a neighbour chanced to overhear him: so he
dressed himself like a way-faring man, and when the husband was
busy elsewhere, knocked at the door. 'Who are you?' said the
wife: 'I am Good Fortune, and I am come for the money which
your husband has laid by for me.'   So this simple woman gave it
to him, and, when her good man came home, told him very pleasantly that Good Fortune had called for the money which had been
so long kept for him."
    *Let us cast away nothing, for we know not what use we may have
for it.* This I had from my nurse some fifty years ago. She knew
no more of Jonson than I did; but her story gives an apt explanation of a passage which has puzzled far wiser heads than either of
ours, and might, perhaps, have been sought elsewhere, to very little
purpose.

Enter Mrs. FITZDOTTREL.

Mrs. Fitz. Look at the back-door,
One knocks, see who it is.
    Pug. Dainty she-Devil!   [*Aside and exit.*
    Mrs. Fitz. I cannot get this venture of the cloke
Out of my fancy, nor the gentleman's way
He took, which though 'twere strange, yet it was
      handsome,
And had a grace withal, beyond the newness.
Sure he will think me that dull stupid creature
He said, and may conclude it, if I find not
Some thought to thank the attempt. He did presume,
By all the carriage of it, on my brain,   ·
For answer; and will swear 'tis very barren,
If it can yield him no return.—

Re-enter PUG.

                  Who is it?
    Pug. Mistress, it is—but first, let me assure
The excellence of mistresses, I am,
Although my master's man, my mistress' slave,
The servant of her secrets, and sweet turns,
And know what fitly will conduce to either.
    Mrs. Fitz. What's this? I pray you come to your-
      self, and think
What your part is; to make an answer.   Tell,
Who is at the door?
    Pug. The gentleman, mistress,
Who was at the cloke-charge to speak with you
This morning; who expects only to take
Some small commandments from you, what you please,
Worthy your form, he says, and gentlest manners.
    Mrs. Fitz. O! you'll anon prove his hired man, I
      fear;
What has he given you for this message? sir,
Bid him put off his hopes of straw, and leave

  5   E

To spread his nets in view thus.   Though they take
Master Fitzdottrel, I am no such foul
Nor fair one, tell him, will be had with stalking; [7]
And wish him to forbear his acting to me,
At the gentleman's chamber-window in Lincoln's-inn
      there,
That opens to my gallery; else I swear
To acquaint my husband with his folly, and leave
      him
To the just rage of his offended jealousy.
Or if your master's sense be not so quick
To right me, tell him I shall find a friend
That will repair me.   Say, I will be quiet
In mine own house.   Pray you, in those words give
      it him.

   Pug. This is some fool turn'd!   [*Exit.*
   Mrs. Fitz. If he be the master,
Now, of that state and wit which I allow him,
Sure, he will understand me : I durst not
Be more direct; for this officious fellow,
My husband's new groom, is a spy upon me,
I find already.   Yet, if he but tell him
This in my words, he cannot but conceive
Himself both apprehended and requited.

---

[7] ——————— *Though they take*
Master Fitzdottrel, I am no such foul
Nor fair *one, tell him, will be had with* stalking.] This punning
allusion of *foul* to *fowl*, is introduced for the sake of playing upon
the word dottrel, (the name of her husband,) a silly bird usually taken
by *stalking*, in the plain sense of the word.   " The dotterel (Fuller
tells us) is avis γιλοποιος, a mirth-making bird, so ridiculously
mimical, that he is easily caught, or rather catcheth himself by his
over-active imitation.   As the fowler stretcheth forth his arms and
legs, stalking towards the bird, so the bird extendeth his legs and
wings, approaching the fowler till he is surprised in the net."   To
this simplicity of the dottrel, there are allusions in every part of this
play.   Fuller adds a very comfortable consideration.   " It is observed, that the foolisher the woodcock, dotterel, codshead, &c., the
finer the flesh thereof."   See his *Lincolneshire.*

I would not have him think he met a statue,
Or spoke to one, not there, though I were silent.

Re-enter PUG.

How no ? have you told him ?
   Pug. Yes.
   Mrs. Fitz. And what says he ?
   Pug. Says he !
That which myself would say to you, if I durst.
That you are proud, sweet mistress ; and withal,
A little ignorant, to entertain
The good that's proffer'd ; and, by your beauty's leave,
Not all so wise as some true politic wife
Would be ; who having match'd with such a nupson
(I speak it with my master's peace)[8] whose face
Hath left to accuse him, now, for it doth confess him,
What you can make him ; will yet (out of scruple,
And a spiced conscience) defraud the poor gentleman,
At least delay him in the thing he longs for,
And makes it his whole study, how to compass
Only a title.   Could but he write cuckold,
He had his ends : for, look you——
   Mrs. Fitz. This can be
None but my husband's wit.   [*Aside.*
   Pug. My precious mistress—
   Mrs. Fitz. It creaks his engine : the groom never
      durst
Be else so saucy.   [*Aside.*
   Pug. If it were not clearly
His worshipful ambition, and the top of it,
The very forked top too, why should he

---

[8] *I speak it with my master's peace,*] i. e. respectfully, reverently :
a bad translation of *cum pace domini. Nupson*, which occurs in
the preceding line, is used by our old writers for a gull, an easy
dupe.   As they sometimes write it *nup*, it may be corrupted from
the Greek νηπ. Both nup and nupson are found in the old comedy
of *Lingua.*   See vol. i. p. 111.

Keep you thus mured up in a back room, mistress,
Allow you ne'er a casement to the street,
Fear of engendering by the eyes, with gallants ?
Forbid you paper, pen and ink, like a rat's-bane ;
Search your half pint of muscatel, lest a letter
Be sunk in the pot ; and hold your new-laid egg
Against the fire, lest any charm be writ there ?
Will you make benefit of truth, dear mistress,
If I do tell it you ?   I do't not often :
I am set over you, employ'd indeed
To watch your steps, your looks, your very breathings,
And to report them to him.   Now, if you
Will be a true, right, delicate, sweet mistress,
Why, we will make a Cokes of this Wise Master,
We will, my mistress, an absolute fine Cokes,
And mock, to air, all the deep diligences
Of such a solemn and effectual ass,
An ass to so good purpose as we'll use him.
I will contrive it so, that you shall go
To plays, to masques, to meetings, and to feasts :
For, why is all this rigging and fine tackle, mistress,
If your neat handsome vessels, of good sail,
Put not forth ever and anon with your nets
Abroad into the world ?   It is your fishing.
There, you shall choose your friends, your servants,
        lady,
Your squires of honour ; I'll convey your letters,
Fetch answers, do you all the offices
That can belong to your blood and beauty.   And,
For the variety, at my times, although
I am not in due symmetry, the man
Of that proportion ; or in rule
Of physic, of the just complexion ;
Or of that truth of Picardil, in clothes,[9]

  [9] *Or of that truth of* Picardil *in clothes.*] This alludes to the fashion
then in vogue : *Picardils* were the stiff upright collars that were
fastened on to the coat ; and Pug means by the expression, that

To boast a sovereignty o'er ladies ; yet
I know to do my turns, sweet mistress. Come, kiss—
   Mrs. Fitz. How now !
   Pug. Dear delicate mistress, I am your slave,
Your little worm, that loves you ; your fine monkey,
Your dog, your Jack, your Pug, that longs to be
Styled, o' your pleasures.
   Mrs. Fitz. [*aloud.*] Hear you all this ?[1] Sir, pray you
Come from your standing, do, a little, spare
Yourself, sir, from your watch, t'applaud your squire,
That so well follows your instructions !

Enter FITZDOTTREL.

   Fitz. How now, sweet heart ! what is the matter ?
   Mrs. Fitz. Good !
You are a stranger to the plot ! you set not
Your saucy Devil here, to tempt your wife,
With all the insolent uncivil language,
Or action, he could vent !
   Fitz. Did you so, Devil ?
   Mrs. Fitz. Not you !
You were not planted in your hole to hear him,

---

his clothes, perhaps, were not made enough in the reigning mode,
to captivate a lady's fancy. WHAL.
   Whalley did not perceive that Pug (unless the author has forgotten himself) is affecting modesty, since he had not only assumed
a handsome body, but also a fashionable dress, "made new" for a
particular occasion. See A. v. S. 1. With respect to the *piccadil*,
or, as Jonson writes it, Picardil, (as if he supposed the fashion of
wearing it to be derived from Picardy,) the term is simply a dimin-
utive of picca (Span. and Ital.) a spear-head, and was given to this
article of foppery, from a fancied resemblance of its stiffened plaits
to the bristled points of those weapons. Blount thinks, and apparently with justice, that Piccadilly took its name from the sale
of the " small stiff collars, so called," which was first set on foot in
a house near the western extremity of the present street, by one
Higgins, a tailor.
   [1] *Hear you all this, &c.*] This is addressed to her husband,
whom, as the margin of the old copy says, she supposes to be on
the watch.

Upon the stairs, or here behind the hangings!
I do not know your qualities! he durst do it,
And you not give directions!
 Fitz. You shall see, wife,
Whether he durst or no, and what it was,
I did direct.   [*Exit.*
 Pug. Sweet mistress, are you mad?

   Re-enter FITZDOTTREL *with a cudgel.*

 Fitz. You most mere rogue! you open manifest
  villain!
You fiend apparent, you! you declared hell-hound!
 Pug. Good sir.
 Fitz. Good knave, good rascal, and good traitor.
Now, I do find you parcel Devil indeed.
Upon the point of trust! in your first charge,
The very day of your probation,
To tempt your mistress! [*Beats* PUG.] You do see,
  good wedlock,
How I directed him?
 Mrs. Fitz. Why where, sir, were you?
 Fitz. Nay, there is one blow more for exercise:
        [*Strikes him again.*
I told you, I should do it.
 Pug. Would you had done, sir.
 Fitz. O wife, the rarest man!—(yet there's another
To put you in mind o' the last)—[*Beats him again.*]
  such a brave man, wife!
Within, he has his projects, and does vent them
The gallantest!—Were you tentiginous, ha?
Would you be acting of the incubus?
Did her silk's rustling move you?
 Pug. Gentle sir!
 Fitz. Out of my sight. If thy name were not
  Devil,
Thou should'st not stay a minute with me. In,
Go, yet stay, yet go too. I am resolv'd

What I will do, and you shall know't aforehand,
Soon as the gentleman is gone, do you hear?
I'll help your lisping. [*Exit* PUG.]—Wife, such a man,
    wife!
He has such plots! he will make me a duke!
No less, by heaven! six mares to your coach, wife!
That's your proportion! and your coachman bald,[2]
Because he shall be bare enough. Do not you laugh,
We are looking for a place, and all, in the map,
What to be of. Have faith, be not an infidel.
You know I am not easy to be gull'd.
I swear, when I have my millions, else, I'll make
Another, dutchess; if you have not faith.
    Mrs. Fitz. You'll have too much, I fear, in these
        false spirits.
    Fitz. Spirits! O, no such thing, wife; wit, mere wit.
This man defies the Devil and all his works,
He does't by engine, and devices, he!
He has his winged ploughs, that go with sails,
Will plough you forty acres at once! and mills
Will spout you water ten miles off! All Crowland
Is ours, wife; and the fens, from us, in Norfolk,
To the utmost bounds in Lincolnshire! we have
    view'd it,
And measur'd it within all, by the scale:
The richest tract of land, love, in the kingdom!
There will be made seventeen or eighteen millions,
Or more, as 't may be handled! wherefore think,
Sweet-heart, if thou hast a fancy to one place
More than another, to be dutchess of,
Now name it; I will have't, whate'er it cost,
(If 'twill be had for money) either here,

---

[2] ——————— *and your coachman bald*
    Because he shall be bare *enough.*] It appears from innumerable passages in our old plays, that it was then considered as a particular mark of state and grandeur for the coachman to be uncovered.

Or in France, or Italy.

Mrs. Fitz. You have strange phantasies !

Enter MEERCRAFT *and* ENGINE.

Meer. Where are you, sir ?

Fitz. I see thou hast no talent
This way, wife. Up to thy gallery, do, chuck,
Leave us to talk of it who understand it.

                            [*Exit* Mrs. FITZ.

Meer. I think we have found a place to fit you
    now, sir.

Gloucester.

Fitz. O no, I'll none.

Meer. Why, sir ?

Fitz. 'Tis fatal.[3]

Meer. That you say right in. Spenser, I think the
    younger,
Had his last honour thence. But he was but earl.

Fitz. I know not that, sir. But Thomas of Wood-
    stock,
I'm sure was duke, and he was made away
At Calice, as duke Humphrey was at Bury :
And Richard the Third, you know what end he
    came to.

Meer. By my faith you are cunning in the chronicle,
    sir.

Fitz. No, I confess I have it from the play books,[4]

---

[3] *'Tis fatal.*] See p. 45.

[4] *No; I confess I have it from the* play-books,
    And think they are more authentic.] This harmless passage
has drawn a world of obloquy on the poet from the commentators
on Shakspeare. Malone and Steevens, in particular, are never
weary of recurring to it with spiteful triumph. " In the *Devil's an
Ass* (says the former), *all* Shakspeare's historical plays are ridiculed." And in a dissertation to prove that *Henry VI.* was *not*
written by Shakspeare, he observes—" the *malignant* Ben, in his
Devil's an Ass, sneers at our author's pieces, which were probably
then the *only historical dramas on the stage.*" And this is advanced

And think they are more authentic.

Eng. That is sure, sir.

Meer. [*whispers him.*] What say you to this then?

Fitz. No, a noble house

Pretends to that. I will do no man wrong.

Meer. Then take one proposition more, and hear it
As past exception.

Fitz. What is that?

in the very face of his own arguments, to prove that there were
scores, perhaps hundreds, of others on it at the time !—In the very
same page in which this wanton burst of impotent malice appears,
he contends, that "it is clear Shakspeare was not the first who
dramatized our old *chronicles;* and that the principal events of the
English history were *familiar to the ears of his audience,* before he
commenced a writer for the stage." Why then was Jonson accused of aiming at Shakspeare for plays which he did *not* write?
"Some (Mr. Malone remarks in another place) have supposed that
Shakspeare was the first dramatic poet who introduced dramas,
formed on the *Chronicles,* but this is an undoubted error. Every
one of the subjects on which he constructed his historical plays,
appears to have been brought upon the scene before his time."
And yet Jonson could mean no one but Shakspeare ! though, in
fact, he merely puts into the mouth of his conceited simpleton, a
trite observation which had probably been made by a hundred
others. Mr. Malone is such a blind Bayard in his hostility to our
poet, that it is seldom necessary to do more than to quote him
against himself, to refute his charges. After proving from Gosson
that the *Chronicles* had been ransacked for plays before 1580, while
Shakspeare perhaps was "killing calves," as Aubrey says, "in a
high style," he adds : Lodge urges in defence of plays, that "they
dilucidate and well explain many darke obscure *histories,* imprint-
ing them in men's minds in such indelible characters that they can
hardly be obliterated." And Heywood in his *Apology for Actors,*
1612, (four years prior to the date of the present drama,) says,
"Plays have taught the unlearned the knowledge of many famous
histories, instructed such as cannot read in the discovery of our
English Chronicles : and what man have you now of that weake
capacity that being possest of their true use, cannot discourse of
any notable thing recorded even from *William the Conqueror,* until
this day?" Yet Jonson with all this, and ten times more, before
him, could not forsooth lightly touch on the same subject without
being taxed from volume to volume, with *malignantly sneering* at
Shakspeare !

Meer. To be
Duke of those lands you shall recover : take
Your title thence, sir, DUKE OF THE DROWN'D LANDS,
Or, DROWN'D LAND.
　Fitz. Ha ! that last has a good sound :
I like it well.　The duke of Drown'd-land ?
　Eng. Yes;
It goes like Groen-land, sir, if you mark it.
　Meer. Ay ;
And drawing thus your honour from the work,
You make the reputation of that greater,
And stay it the longer in your name.
　Fitz. 'Tis true.
DROWN'D LANDS will live in drown'd-land !
　Meer. Yes, when you [5]
Have no foot left; as that must be, sir, one day.
And though it tarry in your heirs some forty,
Fifty descents, the longer liver at last, yet,
Must thrust them out on't, if no quirk in law,
Or odd vice of their own not do it first.
We see those changes daily : the fair lands
That were the client's, are the lawyer's now ;

[5] *Yes, when you*
　Have no foot left, as that must be, sir, one day, &c.]
The venturing upon so sad a truth in the midst of a project of
deceit, is artful in the highest degree, and tends to throw an air of
sincerity over the whole.

The speech itself is adapted with the most imposing gravity from
Horace :

> *Nam propriæ telluris herum natura, neque illum*
> *Nec me, nec quenquam statuit ; nos expulit ille,*
> *Illum aut nequities, aut vafri inscitia juris,*
> *Postremo expellat certe vivacior hæres.*

What follows is admirably turned by Pope :

> "Shades that to Bacon might retreat afford,
> 　Become the portion of a booby lord ;
> 　And Helmsley, once proud Buckingham's delight,
> 　Slides to a scrivener, or city knight."

And those rich manors there of goodman Taylor's,
Had once more wood upon them, than the yard
By which they were measured out for the last pur-
    chase.
Nature hath these vicissitudes.   She makes
No man a state of perpetuity, sir.
    Fitz. You are in the right.   Let's in then, and
    conclude.—

Re-enter PUG.

In my sight again ! I'll talk with you anon.
                [*Exeunt* FITZ. MEER. *and* ENGINE.
    Pug. Sure he will geld me if I stay, or worse,
Pluck out my tongue, one of the two.   This fool,
There is no trusting of him ; and to quit him,
Were a contempt against my chief past pardon.
It was a shrewd disheartening this, at first !
Who would have thought a woman so well harness'd,
Or rather well caparison'd, indeed,
That wears such petticoats, and lace to her smocks,
Broad seaming laces (as I see them hang there)
And garters which are lost, if she can shew them,[6]
Could have done this ? Hell ! why is she so brave ?
It cannot be to please duke Dottrel, sure,
Nor the dull pictures in her gallery,
Nor her own dear reflection in her glass ;
Yet that may be : I have known many of them
Begin their pleasure, but none end it there :
(That I consider, as I go along with it)
They may, for want of better company,

---

   [6] *And garters which are lost if she can shew them.*]   So the old
copies read : but the sense seems to require the addition of *not*,
which might be dropt at the press.   "Garters of fourscore pound
a pair," are mentioned by Satan in the first scene, and we may be
pretty confident that some mode of displaying them was in use.
Pug could see the lace of his lady's smock, and it is probable that
the embroidered extremities of her garters were permitted to *hang*,
as he says, quite as low as that.

Or that they think the better, spend an hour,
Two, three, or four, discoursing with their shadow;
But sure they have a farther speculation.
No woman drest with so much care and study,
Doth dress herself in vain.   I'll vex this problem
A little more, before I leave it sure.   [*Exit.*

SCENE II.   MANLY'S *Chambers in Lincoln's Inn,*
opposite FITZDOTTREL'S *House.*

Enter WITTIPOL *and* MANLY.

Wittipol.

THIS was a fortune happy above thought,
      That this should prove thy chamber; which
            I fear'd
Would be my greatest trouble! this must be
The very window, and that the room.
   Man. It is.
I now remember, I have often seen there
A woman, but I never mark'd her much.
   Wit. Where was your soul, friend?
   Man. Faith, but now and then
Awake unto those objects.
   Wit. You pretend so.
Let me not live, if I am not in love
More with her wit, for this direction now,
Than with her form, though I have praised that
            prettily,
Since I saw her and you to-day.   Read those:
                        [*Gives him the copy of a song.*
They'll go unto the air you love so well.
Try them unto the note, may be the music
Will call her sooner; light, she's here! sing quickly.

Mrs. Fitzdottrel *appears at a window of her house*
fronting that of Manly's *Chambers.*[7]

Mrs. Fitz. Either he understood him not ; or else,
The fellow was not faithful in delivery
Of what I bade.   And, I am justly pay'd,
That might have made my profit of his service,
But by mistaking, have drawn on his envy,[8]
And done the worse defeat upon myself.

> [Manly *sings.*

How ! music ? then he may be there : and is sure.

Enter Pug *behind.*

Pug. O ! is it so ? is there the interview !
Have I drawn to you, at last, my cunning lady ?
The Devil is an ass ! fool'd off, and beaten !
Nay, made an instrument, and could not scent it !
Well, since you have shewn the malice of a woman,
No less than her true wit and learning, mistress,
I'll try, if little Pug have the malignity
To recompense it, and so save his danger.
'Tis not the pain, but the discredit of it,
The Devil should not keep a body entire.

> [*Aside and exit.*

Wit. Away, fall back, she comes.
Man. I leave you, sir,
The master of my chamber : I have business. [*Exit.*
Wit. Mistress !

---

[7] This scene, the margin of the old copy tells us, is "acted at two windows as out of two contiguous buildings." Whoever has noticed the narrow streets or rather lanes of our ancestors, and observed how story projected beyond story, till the windows of the upper rooms almost touched on different sides, will easily conceive the feasibility of every thing which takes place between Wittipol and his mistress, though they make their appearance in different houses.

[8] *But by mistaking, have drawn on his* envy,] i. e. ill-will, displeasure. As this sense of the word is altogether obsolete. it seems just necessary to notice it.

Mrs. Fitz. [*advances to the window.*] You make me
    paint, sir.[9]
    Wit. They are fair colours,
Lady, and natural ! I did receive
Some commands from you, lately, gentle lady,
But so perplex'd, and wrapt in the delivery,
As I may fear to have misinterpreted :
But must make suit still, to be near your grace.
    Mrs. Fitz. Who is there with you, sir ?
    Wit. None but myself.
It falls out, lady, to be a dear friend's lodging ;
Wherein there's some conspiracy of fortune
With your poor servant's blest affections.
    Mrs. Fitz. Who was it sung ?
    Wit. He, lady, but he's gone,
Upon my entreaty of him, seeing you
Approach the window.   Neither need you doubt him,
If he were here ; he is too much a gentleman.
    Mrs. Fitz. Sir, if you judge me by this simple action,
And by the outward habit, and complexion
Of easiness it hath, to your design ;
You may with justice say, I am a woman ;
And a strange woman.   But when you shall please
To bring but that concurrence of my fortune
To memory, which to-day yourself did urge ;
It may beget some favour like excuse,
Though none like reason.
    Wit. No, my tuneful mistress ?
Then surely love hath none, nor beauty any ;

---

[9] *You make me* paint,] i. e. blush.   This word is prettily applied
by Emily in the *Two Noble Kinsmen.*

> " Of all flowers
>   Methinks the rose is best :
>   It is the very emblem of a maid ;
>   For when the west wind courts her gently,
>   How modestly she blows and *paints* the sun
>   With her chaste blushes ! "

Nor nature, violenced in both these :
With all whose gentle tongues you speak, at once.
I thought I had enough remov'd already
That scruple from your breast, and left you all reason ;
When through my morning's perspective I shew'd you
A man so above excuse, as he's the cause,
Why any thing is to be done upon him ;
And nothing call'd an injury, misplaced.
I rather now had hope, to shew you how love
By his accesses grows more natural :
And what was done this morning with such force,
Was but devised to serve the present, then.
That since Love hath the honour to approach
These sister-swelling breasts ;[1] and touch this soft
And rosy hand ; he hath the skill to draw
Their nectar forth, with kissing ; and could make
More wanton salts from this brave promontory,[2]
Down to this valley, than the nimble roe ;
Could play the hopping sparrow 'bout these nets ;
And sporting squirrel in these crisped groves ;

[1] *These* sister-swelling breasts.]   This is an elegant and poetical rendering of the *sororiantes mammæ* of the Latins, which Festus thus explains : " *Sororiare puellarum mammæ dicuntur, cum primum tumescunt.*"   *Here* (the margin says) *he grows more familiar in his courtship.*   And again, *Wittipol plays with her paps, kisses her hands, &c.*   This is, indeed, *growing familiar !* but; strange as it may appear, liberties very similar to these were, in the poet's time, permitted by ladies, who would have started at being told that they had foregone all pretensions to delicacy.

I am half inclined to think that, when Hotspur tells his lady it is no time

"To *toy with mammets*, or to tilt with lips,"

he alludes to some such play with the paps, as Wittipol is engaged in. *Mammet* undoubtedly signifies a girl ; but the Italians use both this word (mammette) and mammille for a bosom, and our old dramatists adopt terms of this kind from them without scruple. Italian was, in those days, the favourite language.

[2] ———————— *And could make*

More wanton salts,] i. e. leapings, or boundings, from the Latin *saltus*. WHAL.

Bury himself in every silk-worm's kell,
Is here unravell'd ; run into the snare,
Which every hair is, cast into a curl,
To catch a Cupid flying ! bathe himself
In milk and roses here, and dry him there ;
Warm his cold hands, to play with this smooth, round,
And well-torn'd chin,[3] as with the billiard ball ;
Roll on these lips, the banks of love, and there
At once both plant and gather kisses.   Lady,
Shall I, with what I have made to-day here, call
All sense to wonder, and all faith to sign
The mysteries revealed in your form ?
And will Love pardon me the blasphemy
I utter'd, when I said, a glass could speak
This beauty, or that fools had power to judge it ?

> *Do but look on her eyes, they do light*
>   *All that love's world compriseth !*
> *Do but look on her hair, it is bright*
>   *As love's star when it riseth !*
> *Do but mark, her forehead's smoother*
>   *Than words that soothe her !*
> *And from her arched brows, such a grace*
>   *Sheds itself through the face ;*
> *As alone, there triumphs to the life,*
>   *All the gain, all the good, of the elements strife !*
> *Have you seen but a bright lily grow,*
>   *Before rude hands have touch'd it ?*
> *Have you mark'd but the fall of the snow,*
>   *Before the soil hath smutch'd it ?*
> *Have you felt the wool of the beaver ?*
>   *Or swan's down ever ?*
> *Or have smelt o' the bud of the brier ?*
>   *Or the nard in the fire ?*
> *Or have tasted the bag of the bee ?*
>   *O, so white ! O, so soft ! O, so sweet is she !*

---

[3] *Well*-torn'd,] i. e. rounded and polished as by the wheel.

FITZDOTTREL *appears at his* Wife's *back.*

Fitz. Is she so, sir? and I will keep her so,
If I know how, or can : that wit of man
Will do't, I'll go no farther.   At this window
She shall no more be buzz'd at. Take your leave on't,
If you be sweet meats, wedlock, or sweet flesh,
All's one : I do not love this hum about you.
A fly-blown wife is not so proper; in !—
For you, you, sir, look to hear from me.
 Wit. So I do, sir.
 Fitz. No, but in other terms. There's no man offers
This to my wife, but pays for't.
 Wit. That have I, sir.
 Fitz. Nay then, I tell you, you are——
 Wit. What am I, sir?
 Fitz. Why, that I'll think on, when I have cut your
  throat.
 Wit. Go, you are an ass.
 Fitz. I am resolv'd on't, sir.[4]
 Wit. I think you are.
 Fitz. To call you to a reckoning.
 Wit. Away, you broker's block, you property !
 Fitz. 'Slight, if you strike me, I will strike your
  mistress. [*Strikes* Mrs. FITZ. *and leads her out.*
 Wit. O ! I could shoot mine eyes at him for that
  now,
Or leave my teeth in him, were they cuckold's bane,
Enough to kill him.   What prodigious,
Blind, and most wicked change of fortune's this ?
I have no air of patience : all my veins
Swell, and my sinews start at th' iniquity of it.
I shall break, break.   [*Exit.*

---

[4] *I am* resolv'd *on't, sir.*] Fitzdottrel and Wittipol are at cross
purposes. The former uses *resolv'd* in the sense of determined;
and the latter affects to take it in that of convinced, which was,
then, no uncommon acceptation of the word.

SCENE III. *Another Room in* FITZDOTTREL'S *House.*

Enter PUG.

Pug.

THIS for the malice of it,
      And my revenge may pass ! but now my con-
      science
Tells me, I have profited ·the cause of hell
But little, in the breaking off their loves.
Which, if some other act of mine repair not,
I shall hear ill of in my account !

Enter FITZDOTTREL *and his* Wife.

Fitz. O, bird,
Could you do this ? 'gainst me ! and at this time now !
When I was so employ'd, wholly for you,
Drown'd in my care (more than the land, I swear,
I have hope to win) to make you peerless, studying
For footmen for you, fine-paced huishers, pages,
To serve you on the knee ; with what knight's wife
To bear your train, and sit with your four women
In council, and receive intelligences
From foreign parts, to dress you at all pieces !
You've almost turn'd my good affection to you ;⁵
Sour'd my sweet thoughts, all my pure purposes :
I could now find in my very heart to make
Another, lady dutchess ; and depose you.
Well, go your ways in. [*Exit* Mrs. FITZ.]—Devil,
      you have redeem'd all ;
I do forgive you : and I'll do you good. [*Exit* PUG.

⁵ *You're almost* turn'd *my good affection to you.*] Not diverted or
changed its course ; but, as appears from what follows, soured it.
The word is used in a similar sense by Shakspeare :

      " Has friendship such a faint and *milky* heart,
         It *turns* in less than two nights !"   *Timon,* A. iii. S. 2.

Enter MEERCRAFT *and* ENGINE.

Meer. Why have you these excursions? where
  have you been, sir?

Fitz. Where I have been vex'd a little with a toy.

Meer. O sir, no toys must trouble your grave head,
Now it is growing to be great.   You must
Be above all those things.

Fitz. Nay, nay, so I will.

Meer. Now you are toward the lord, you must put off
The man, sir.

Eng. He says true.

Meer. You must do nothing
As you have done it heretofore; not know,
Or salute any man.

Eng. That was your bedfellow
The other month.

Meer. The other month! the week.
Thou dost not know the privileges, Engine,
Follow that title; nor how swift: to-day,
When he has put on his lord's face once, then—

Fitz. Sir, for these things I shall do well enough
There is no fear of me: but then my wife is
Such an untoward thing, she'll never learn
How to comport with it: I am out of all
Conceit, on her behalf.

Meer. Best have her taught, sir.

Fitz. Where? are there any schools for ladies? is
  there
An academy for women? I do know
For men there was; I learn'd in it myself,
To make my legs, and do my postures.

Eng. [*whispers* MEERCRAFT.] Sir,
Do you remember the conceit you had——
Of the Spanish gown at home?

Meer. Ha! I do thank thee
With all my heart, dear Engine.——Sir, there is

A certain lady, here about the town,
An English widow, who hath lately travell'd,
But she is call'd the Spaniard, 'cause she came
Latest from thence, and keeps the Spanish habit.
Such a rare woman! all our women here,
That are of spirit and fashion, flock unto her,
As to their president, their law, their canon ;
More than they ever did to oracle Foreman.
Such rare receipts she has, sir, for the face,
Such oils, such tinctures, such pomatums,
Such perfumes, med'cines, quintessences, *et cætera ;*
And such a mistress of behaviour,
She knows from the duke's daughter to the doxy,
What is their due just, and no more!
　　Fitz. O sir!
You please me in this, more than mine own greatness.
Where is she ? Let us have her.
　　Meer. By your patience,
We must use means, cast how to be acquainted—
　　Fitz. Good, sir, about it.
　　Meer. We must think how, first.
　　Fitz. O!
I do not love to tarry for a thing,
When I have a mind to it. You do not know me,
If you do offer it.
　　Meer. Your wife must send
Some pretty token to her, with a compliment,
And pray to be received in her good graces.
All the great ladies do it.
　　Fitz. She shall, she shall.
What were it best to be ?
　　Meer. Some little toy,
I would not have it any great matter, sir :
A diamond ring of forty or fifty pound
Would do it handsomely, and be a gift
Fit for your wife to send, and her to take.
　　Fitz. I'll go and tell my wife on't straight. [*Exit.*

Mcer. Why, this
Is well! the clothes we have now, but where's this lady?
If we could get a witty boy now, Engine,
That were an excellent crack,[6] I could instruct him
To the true height : for any thing takes this Dottrel.
    Eng. Why, sir, your best will be one of the players !
    Mcer. No, there's no trusting them : they'll talk
        of it,
And tell their poets.
    Eng. What if they do ! the jest
Will brook the stage.   But there be some of them
Are very honest lads : there's Dickey Robinson [7]
A very pretty fellow, and comes often
To a gentleman's chamber, a friend of mine. We had
The merriest supper of it there, one night,
The gentleman's landlady invited him
To a gossip's feast: now he, sir, brought Dick
        Robinson,
Drest like a lawyer's wife, amongst them all :

---

[6] *That were an excellent* crack.]   A clever lively lad.   See vol.
ii. p. 211.
    [7] *There's* Dickey Robinson.]   He was a comedian, and famous
for acting women's parts.   The vogue he was in appears from these
verses of Cowley, addressed to sir Kenelm Digby, and prefixed to
Love's Riddle:
        "Nor has't a part for *Robinson,* whom they
        At school account essential to a play."
He was a performer in our author's *Catiline.*   WHAL.
    Robinson (who undoubtedly played the part of Wittipol in
this piece) followed the fortunes of his sovereign, and obtained
a commission in the royal army.   He was murdered at the siege of
Basinge-house by Harrison, who shot him through the head after
he had laid down his arms, exclaiming in the blasphemous cant of
those ferocious times, " cursed be he that doeth the work of the
Lord negligently !"
    It is worth observing, that Jonson, who is never mentioned at
present, but as the "libeller of the players," has written more in
praise of them than all the other poets of his time put together.
Such is the discrimination, and such the justice of our critical
luminaries !

I lent him clothes—But to see him behave it,
And lay the law, and carve and drink unto them,
And then talk bawdy, and send frolics ![8] O,
It would have burst your buttons, or not left you
A seam.

    Meer. They say he's an ingenious youth.

    Eng. O sir ! and dresses himself the best, beyond
Forty of your very ladies ! did you never see him ?

    Meer. No, I do seldom see those toys. But think
        you
That we may have him ?

    Eng. Sir, the young gentleman
I tell you of can command him : shall I attempt it ?

    Meer. Yes, do it.

Re-enter FITZDOTTREL.

    Fitz. 'Slight, I cannot get my wife
To part with a ring on any terms, and yet
The sullen monkey has two.

    Meer. It were 'gainst reason
That you should urge it : sir, send to a goldsmith,
Let not her lose by it.

    Fitz. How does she lose by it ?
Is it not for her ?

    Meer. Make it your own bounty,
It will have the better success ; what is a matter
Of fifty pound to you, sir ?

    Fitz. I have but a hundred

---

[8] ———————— *and send* frolics !] *Frolics* are couplet, commonly of an amatory or satirical nature, written on small slips of
paper, and wrapt round a sweetmeat. A dish of them is usually
placed on the table after supper, and the guests amuse themselves
with sending them to one another, as circumstances seem to render
them appropriate : this is occasionally productive of much mirth. I
do not believe that the game is to be found in England ; though
the drawing on Twelfth Night may be thought to bear some kind of
coarse resemblance to it.   On the continent I have frequently been
present at it.

Pieces to shew here ; that I would not break—
 Meer. You shall have credit, sir. I'll send a ticket
Unto my goldsmith.—

Enter TRAINS.

       Here my man comes too,
To carry it fitly.—How now, Trains ! what birds ?
 Trains. Your cousin Everill met me, and has beat
  me,
Because I would not tell him where you were :
I think he has dogg'd me to the house too.
 Meer. Well——
You shall go out at the back-door then, Trains.
You must get Gilthead hither by some means.
 Trains. It is impossible !
 Fitz. Tell him we have venison,
I'll give him a piece, and send his wife a pheasant.
          [*Exit.*

 Trains. A forest moves not, 'till that forty pound
You had of him last be paid. He keeps more stir
For that same petty sum, than for your bond
Of six, and statute of eight hundred.
 Meer. Tell him
We'll hedge in that. Cry up Fitzdottrel to him,
Double his price : make him a man of metal.
 Trains. That will not need, his bond is current
  enough.   [*Exeunt.*

ACT III.

Scene I. *A Room in* Fitzdottrel's *House.*

Enter Thomas Gilthead *and* Plutarchus.

Gilthead.

ALL this is to make you a gentleman!
 I'll have you learn, son. Wherefore have
   I placed you
 With sir Paul Eitherside, but to have so
 much law
To keep your own? Besides, he is a justice,
Here in the town; and dwelling, son, with him,
You shall learn that in a year, shall be worth twenty
Of having staid you at Oxford or at Cambridge,
Or sending you to the inns of court, or France.
I'm call'd for now in haste by master Meercraft,
To trust master Fitzdottrel, a good man,[9]
I have enquired him, eighteen hundred a year,
(His name is current) for a diamond ring
Of forty, shall not be worth thirty; that's gain'd;
And this is to make you a gentleman!
 Plu. O, but good father, you trust too much.
 Gilt. Boy, boy,
We live by finding fools out to be trusted.
Our shop-books are our pastures, our corn-grounds,
We lay 'em open, for them to come into;

---

 [9] ———— *a good man.*] "My meaning in saying he is a *good man*, is, to have you understand me, that he is sufficient." *Merch. of Venice.*

And when we have them there, we drive them up
Into one of our two pounds, the compters, straight,
And this is to make you a gentleman !
We citizens never trust, but we do cozen :
For if our debtors pay, we cozen them ;
And if they do not, then we cozen ourselves.
But that's a hazard every one must run,
That hopes to make his son a gentleman !

Plu. I do not wish to be one, truly, father.
In a descent or two, we come to be,
Just in their state, fit to be cozen'd, like them :
And I had rather have tarried in your trade.
For, since the gentry scorn the city so much,
Methinks we should in time, holding together,
And matching in our own tribes, as they say,
Have got an act of common-council for it,
That we might cozen them out of *rerum natura*.

Gilt. Ay, if we had an act first to forbid
The marrying of our wealthy heirs unto them,
And daughters with such lavish portions :
That confounds all.

Plu. And makes a mongrel breed, father.
And when they have your money, then they laugh
          at you,
Or kick you down the stairs.   I cannot abide them :
I would fain have them cozen'd, but not trusted.

Enter MEERCRAFT.

Meer. O, is he come !   I knew he would not fail
          me.—
Welcome, good Gilthead, I must have you do
A noble gentleman a courtesy here,
In a mere toy, some pretty ring or jewel,
Of fifty or threescore pound.—Make it a hundred,
And hedge in the last forty that I owe you,
And your own price for the ring.   [*Aside to* GILT-
          HEAD.]   He's a good man, sir,

And you may hap see him a great one! he
Is likely to bestow hundreds and thousands
With you, if you can humour him.   A great prince
He will be shortly.   What do you say?
   Gilt. In truth, sir,
I cannot : 't has been a long vacation with us.
   Meer. Of what, I pray thee, of wit or honesty ?
Those are your citizens' long vacations.
   Plu. Good father, do not trust them.
   Meer. Nay, Tom Gilthead,
He will not buy a courtesy and beg it ;
He'll rather pay than pray.   If you do for him,
You must do cheerfully : his credit, sir,
Is not yet prostitute.   Who's this, thy son ?
A pretty youth ! what is his name ?
   Plu. Plutarchus, sir.
   Meer. Plutarchus ! how came that about ?
   Gilt. That year, sir,
That I begot him, I bought Plutarch's lives,
And fell so in love with the book, as I call'd my son
By his name, in hope he should be like him,
And write the lives of our great men.—
   Meer. In the city !
And do you breed him there ?
   Gilt. His mind, sir, lies
Much to that way.
   Meer. Why, then he's in the right way.
   Gilt. But now, I had rather get him a good wife,
And plant him in the country, there to use
The blessing I shall leave him.
   Meer. Out upon't !
And lose the laudable means thou hast at home here,
To advance and make him a young alderman ?
Buy him a captain's place, for shame ; and let him
Into the world early, and with his plume
And scarfs march through Cheapside, or along Corn-
      hill,

And by the virtue of those, draw down a wife
There from a window, worth ten thousand pound!
Get him the posture-book and's leaden men
To set upon a table, 'gainst his mistress
Chance to come by, that he may draw her in,
And shew her Finsbury battles.
  Gilt. I have placed him
With justice Eitherside, to get so much law——
  Meer. As thou hast conscience. Come, come, thou
   dost wrong
Pretty Plutarchus, who had not his name
For nothing, but was born *to train the youth
Of London in the military truth*——[1]
That way his genius lies.—

Enter EVERILL.

        My cousin Everill!
  Ever. O, are you here, sir! pray you let us
   whisper.   [*Takes* MEER. *aside.*
  Plu. Father, dear father, trust him if you love me.
  Gilt. Why, I do mean it, boy, but what I do
Must not come easily from me : we must deal
With courtiers, boy, as courtiers deal with us.
If I have a business there with any of them,
Why, I must wait, I am sure on't, son ; and though
My lord dispatch me, yet his worshipful man
Will keep me for his sport a month or two,
To shew me with my fellow-citizens :
I must make his train long, and full, one quarter,
And help the spectacle of his greatness. There,
Nothing is done at once but injuries, boy,

---

[1] ——————— *to train the youth
Of London in the military truth*—] This is probably a quotation from one of those posture-books, which were frequent in Jonson's age, and contained coarse representations of the manual
exercises, evolutions, &c., practised in the Artillery Yard. Jonson
amuses himself again with this couplet in his *Underwoods.*

And they come headlong : all their good turns move
    not,
Or very slowly.
    Plu. Yet, sweet father, trust him.
    Gilt. Well, I will think.   [*They walk aside.*
    Ever. Come, you must do't, sir.
I am undone else, and your lady Tailbush
Has sent for me to dinner, and my clothes
Are all at pawn.   I had sent out this morning,
Before I heard you were come to town, some twenty
Of my epistles, and no one return——
    Meer. Why, I have told you of this.   This comes
       of wearing
Scarlet, gold-lace, and cut-works ! your fine gartering,
With your blown roses, cousin ! and your eating
Pheasant, and godwit, here in London, haunting
The Globes and Mermaids,[2] wedging in with lords
Still at the table, and affecting letchery
In velvet ! where, could you have contented yourself
With cheese, salt butter, and a pickled herring,
In the Low Countries ; there worn cloth and fustian,
Been satisfied with a leap o' your host's daughter,
In garrison, a wench of a storer, or
Your sutler's wife in the leaguer, of two blanks ![3]
You never then had run upon this flat,

    [2] *The* Globes *and* Mermaids.] Playhouses and taverns. The
Globe was on the Bank-side, the Mermaid (tavern) in Cornhill.
    [3] ——— *a wench of a* storer ; *or*
Your sutler's wife in the leaguer, *of two* blanks !] Whalley says,
in the margin of his copy, he "suspects a line to be dropt here, as
he cannot make out the poet's meaning." The poet's meaning is
clear enough, and to a scholar, like Whalley, ought to have presented no difficulty. Jonson had Horace in his thoughts, and has,
not without some ingenuity, parodied several loose passages of one
of his satires. Either by accident or design, Whalley reads *storer*
for *stoter*, and I have retained his variation. *Leaguer*, as every one
knows, is camp ; *blanks* are silver coins worth about as much as the
livre. They were struck in France by Henry V. and never had
much currency in this country.

To write your letters missive, and send out
Your privy seals, that thus have frighted off
All your acquaintance, that they shun you at distance,
Worse than you do the bailiffs.
    Ever. Pox upon you!
I come not to you for counsel, I lack money.
    Meer. You do not think what you owe me already.
    Ever. I!
They owe you that mean to pay you: I'll be sworn
I never meant it. Come, you will project,
I shall undo your practice, for this month, else:
You know me.
    Meer. Ay, you are a right sweet nature!
    Ever. Well, that's all one!
    Meer. You'll leave this empire one day;
You will not ever have this tribute paid
Your scepter of the sword!
    Ever. Tie up your wit,
Do, and provoke me not——
    Meer. Will you, sir, help
To what I shall provoke another for you?
    Ever. I cannot tell; try me: I think I am not
So utterly, of an ore un-to-be-melted,
But I can do myself good, on occasions.

Enter FITZDOTTREL.

    Meer. Strike in, then, for your part. [*They go up
        to* FITZ.]—Master Fitzdottrel,
If I transgress in point of manners, afford me
Your best construction; I must beg my freedom
From your affairs, this day.
    Fitz. How, sir!
    Meer. It is
In succour of this gentleman's occasions,
My kinsman—
    Fitz. You'll not do me that affront, sir?
    Meer. I am sorry you should so interpret it.

But, sir, it stands upon his being invested
In a new office, he has stood for, long :
Master of the Dependences ! a place
Of my projection too, sir, and hath met
Much opposition ; but the state, now, sees
That great necessity of it, as after all
Their writing, and their speaking against duels,
They have erected it.   His book is drawn——
For, since there will be differences daily
'Twixt gentlemen, and that the roaring manner
Is grown offensive ; that those few, we call
The civil men of the sword, abhor the vapours ;
They shall refer now, hither, for their process ;
And such as trespass 'gainst the rule of court
Are to be fined.
      Fitz. In troth, a pretty place !
      Meer. A kind of arbitrary court 'twill be, sir.
      Fitz. I shall have matter for it, I believe,
Ere it be long ; I had a distaste.[4]
      Meer. But now, sir,
My learned counsel, they must have a feeling,
They'll part, sir, with no books, without the hand-gout
Be oil'd : and I must furnish.   If't be money,
To me straight ; I am mine, mint, and exchequer,
To supply all.   What is't, a hundred pound ?
      Ever. No, the harpy now stands on a hundred
            pieces.[5]
      Meer. Why, he must have them, if he will.   To-
            morrow, sir,
Will equally serve your occasions—
And therefore, let me obtain, that you will yield

------

      [4] *I had a* distaste,] i. e. an insult offered me : he alludes to his
quarrel with Wittipol.
      [5] *What is't, a hundred* pound ?
      No, the harpy now stands on a hundred pieces.] It may be
necessary to observe, once for all, that the *piece* (the double sovereign) went for two and twenty shillings : a hundred pieces, therefore, were equivalent to a hundred and ten pounds.

To timing a poor gentleman's distresses,
In terms of hazard.
    Fitz. By no means.
    Meer. I must
Get him this money, and will——
    Fitz. Sir, I protest,
I had rather stand engaged for it myself;
Than you should leave me.
    Meer. O good sir! do you think
So coarsely of our manners, that we would,
For any need of ours, be prest to take it;
Though you be pleased to offer it?
    Fitz. Why, by heaven,
I mean it.
    Meer. I can never believe less.
But we, sir, must preserve our dignity,
As you do publish yours: by your fair leave, sir.
                            [*Offers to be gone.*

    Fitz. As I am a gentleman, if you do offer
To leave me now, or if you do refuse me,
I will not think you love me.
    Meer. Sir, I honour you,
And with just reason, for these noble notes
Of the nobility you pretend to: but, sir,
I would know why? a motive (he a stranger)
You should do this?
    Ever. [*Aside to* MEER.] You'll mar all with your
    fineness.[6]

[6] *You'll mar all with your* fineness.] Mr. Sympson imagines it
should be *finesse;* but that word, I believe, came into use since
our author's days. *Fineness* is the same with *shyness*, or *coyness;*
and that sense is not incongruous to the rest of the passage.
                                       WHAL.

    Neither Whalley nor Sympson seems to have entered into the
poet's meaning. The words are evidently directed, in a side speech,
to Meercraft, by his confederate, who is apprehensive that he will
refine too much; in other words, carry his pretended refusal too far.
Fineness, of which both the commentators have mistaken the sense,
is an overstrained and factitious scrupulousness.

Fitz. Why that's all one, if 'twere, sir, but my
    fancy.—
But I have a business, that perhaps I would have
Brought to his office.
    Meer. O sir! I have done then ;
If he can be made profitable to you.
    Fitz. Yes, and it shall be one of my ambitions
To have it the first business : may I not ?
    Ever. So you do mean to make 't a perfect business.
    Fitz. Nay, I'll do that, assure you ; shew me once.
    Meer. Sir, it concerns, the first be a perfect business,
For his own honour.
    Ever. Ay, and the reputation
Too, of my place.
    Fitz. Why, why do I take this course, else ?
I am not altogether an ass, good gentlemen.
Wherefore should I consult you, do you think ?
To make a song on 't ? How's your manner ? tell us.
    Meer. Do, satisfy him ; give him the whole course.
    Ever. First, by request, or otherwise, you offer
Your business to the court ; wherein you crave
The judgment of the master and the assistants.
    Fitz. Well, that is done now ; what do you upon it ?
    Ever. We straight, sir, have recourse to the spring-
    head :
Visit the ground, and so disclose the nature ;
If it will carry, or no.   If we do find,
By our proportions, it is like to prove
A sullen and black business ; that it be
Incorrigible, and out of treaty ; then
We file it, a dependence !
    Fitz. So, 'tis filed :
What follows ? I do love the order of these things.
    Ever. We then advise the party, if he be
A man of means and havings, that forthwith
He settle his estate ; if not, at least
That he pretend it : for, by that, the world

Takes notice, that it now is a dependence :
And this we call, sir, publication.

    Fitz. Very sufficient : after publication, now ?

    Ever. Then we grant out our process, which is
        diverse ;

Either by chartel, sir, or ore-tenus,
Wherein the challenger and challengee,
Or, with your Spaniard, your provocador
And provocado, have their several courses—

    Fitz. I have enough on't : for an hundred pieces !

Yes, for two hundred, under-write me, do.
Your man will take my bond ?

    Meer. That he will, sure :

But these same citizens, they are such sharks !
There's an old debt of forty, I gave my word
                     [*Aside to* FITZ.

For one is run away to the Bermudas,[7]
And he will hook in that, or he'll not do.

    Fitz. Why, let him. That and the ring, and a
        hundred pieces,

Will all but make two hundred.

    Meer. No, no more, sir.

What ready arithmetic you have !—Do you hear ?
                   [*Aside to* GILTHEAD.

A pretty morning's work for you, this ! do it,
You shall have twenty pound on't.

    Gilt. Twenty pieces ?

    Plu. Good father, do't.

    Meer. You will hook still ? well,

Shew us your ring. You could not have done this now,
With gentleness, at first, we might have thank'd you ?
But groan, and have your courtesies come from you
Like a hard stool, and stink ! A man may draw
Your teeth out easier than your money.   Come,

---

   [7] *For one is run away to the* Bermudas.]   Not to the islands, but
to the alleys of this name ; the receptacles of thieves, fraudulent
debtors, &c., already mentioned.   See vol. iv. p. 407.

  5   G

Were little Gilthead here, no better a nature,
I should ne'er love him, that could pull his lips off,
    now.   [*Pulls him by the lips.*
Was not thy mother a gentlewoman?
    Plu. Yes, sir.
    Meer. And went to the court at Christmas, and St.
        George-tide,
And lent the lords' men chains?
    Plu. Of gold and pearl, sir.
    Meer. I knew thou must take after somebody,
Thou could'st not be else.   This was no shop-look!
I'll have thee captain Gilthead, and march up,
And take in Pimlico, and kill the bush
At every tavern.   Thou shalt have a wife,
If smocks will mount, boy.   [*Turns to* GILTHEAD.
           How now! you have there now
Some Bristol stone, or Cornish counterfeit
You'd put upon us!
    Gilt. No, sir, I assure you:
Look on his lustre, he will speak himself!
I'll give you leave to put him in the mill:
He is no great large stone, but a true paragon,
He has all his corners, view him well.
    Meer. He's yellow.
    Gilt. Upon my faith, sir, of the right black water,
And very deep! he's set without a foil, too.
Here's one of the yellow-water, I'll sell cheap.
    Meer. And what do you value this at, thirty pound?
    Gilt. No, sir, he cost me forty ere he was set.
    Meer. Turnings, you mean? I know your equi-
        vokes:
You are grown the better fathers of 'em o' late.[8]

---

[8] —————— *I know your* equivokes:
    You're grown the better fathers of 'em o' late.] Satirically
reflecting on the Jesuits, the great patrons of *equivocation.* WHAL.
    Or rather on the Puritans, I think; who were sufficiently ob-
noxious to this charge.   The Jesuits would be out of place here.

Well, where it must go 'twill be judged, and therefore
Look you't be right.   You shall have fifty pound for't,
Not a denier more.—[*To* Fitz.] And because you would
Have things dispatch'd, sir, I'll go presently,
Inquire out this lady.   If you think good, sir,
Having an hundred pieces ready, you may
Part with those now, to serve my kinsman's turns,
That he may wait upon you anon the freer;
And take them, when you have seal'd, again, of Gilt-
     head.
    Fitz. I care not if I do.
    Meer. And dispatch all
Together.
    Fitz. There, they are just a hundred pieces;
I have told them over twice a day these two months.
                     [*Turns them out on the table.*
    Meer. Well, go and seal then, sir; make your return
As speedy as you can.
    [*Exeunt* Fitzdottrel, Gilthead, *and* Plutarchus.
    Ever. Come, give me.   [*They fall to sharing.*
    Meer. Soft, sir.
    Ever. Marry, and fair too then; I'll no delaying, sir.
    Meer. But you will hear?
    Ever. Yes, when I have my dividend.
    Meer. There's forty pieces for you.
    Ever. What is this for?
    Meer. Your half: you know, that Gilthead must
     have twenty.
    Ever. And what's your ring there? Shall I have
     none o' that?
    Meer. O, that is to be given to a lady.
    Ever. Is it so?
    Meer. By that good light, it is.
    Ever. Come, give me
Ten pieces more, then.
    Meer. Why?

Ever. For Gilthead, sir !
Do you think I'll allow him any such share ?
   Meer. You must.
   Ever. Must I! do you your musts, sir, I'll do mine :
You will not part with the whole, sir, will you? Go to,
Give me ten pieces !
   Meer. By what law do you this ?
   Ever. Even lion-law, sir, I must roar else.
   Meer. Good !
   Ever. You have heard how the ass made his divi-
      sions wisely ?
   Meer. And I am he !—I thank you.
   Ever. Much good do you, sir.
   Meer. I shall be rid of this tyranny one day.
   Ever. Not
While you do eat, and lie about the town here,
And cozen in your bullions ;[1] and I stand,
Your name of credit, and compound your business,
Adjourn your beatings every term, and make
New parties for your projects. I have now
A pretty task of it, to hold you in
With your lady Tailbush : but the toy will be
How we shall both come off!
   Meer. Leave you your doubting,
And do your portion, what's assign'd you : I
Never fail'd yet.
   Ever. With reference to your aids !—
You'll still be unthankful. Where shall I meet you,
      anon ?

---

[1] *And cozen in your* bullions.] I have little to add to what has
been already advanced on this word in the last edition of Massinger.
See vol. iii. p. 390. It appears to be some article (trunk-hose, or
doublet) of spurious finery, furnished with globular gilt buttons, and
adopted by gamblers and others, as a mark of wealth, to entrap
the unwary. The word occurs in Brome. "I'll impeach you for
foul incontinence, and shaking your old *bullion trunks* on my truckle-
bed." *The Sparagus Garden.* Here the person spoken of is a wealthy
usurer.

You have some feat to do alone, now, I see ;
You wish me gone ; well, I will find you out,
And bring you after to the audit.   [*Exit.*
   Meer. 'Slight,
There's Engine's share, too, I had forgot ! this reign
Is too-too-unsupportable ; I must
Quit myself of this vassalage.—

   Enter ENGINE, *followed by* WITTIPOL.
             Engine ! welcome.
How goes the cry ?
   Eng. Excellent well.
   Meer. Will it do ?
Where's Robinson ?
   Eng. Here is the gentleman, sir,
Will undertake it himself.   I have acquainted him.
   Meer. Why did you so ?
   Eng. Why, Robinson would have told him,
You know : and he's a pleasant wit, will hurt
Nothing you purpose.   Then he's of opinion,
That Robinson might want audacity,
She being such a gallant.   Now, he has been
In Spain, and knows the fashions there ; and can
Discourse ; and being but mirth, he says, leave much
To his care.
   Meer. But he is too tall !
   Eng. For that,
He has the bravest device (you'll love him for't)
To say, he wears cioppinos ; and they do so
In Spain : and Robinson's as tall as he.
   Meer. Is he so ?
   Eng. Every jot.
   Meer. Nay, I had rather
To trust a gentleman with it, of the two.
   Eng. Pray you go to him then, sir, and salute him.
   Meer. Sir, my friend Engine has acquainted you
With a strange business here.

Wit. A merry one, sir.
The duke of Drown'd-land and his dutchess?
    Meer. Yes, sir.
Now that the conjurors have laid him by,
I have made bold to borrow him a while.
    Wit. With purpose, yet, to put him out, I hope,
To his best use.
    Meer. Yes, sir.
    Wit. For that small part
That I am trusted with, put off your care :
I would not lose to do it, for the mirth
Will follow of it ; and well, I have a fancy.
    Meer. Sir, that will make it well.
    Wit. You will report it so.
Where must I have my dressing?
    Eng. At my house, sir.
    Meer. You shall have caution, sir, for what he yields,
To sixpence.
    Wit. You shall pardon me : I will share, sir,
In your sports only, nothing in your purchase.[2]
But you must furnish me with compliments,
To the manner of Spain ; my coach, my guarda-
        duennas.
    Meer. Engine's your provedoré.   But, sir, I must,
Now I have entered trust with you thus far,
Secure still in your quality, acquaint you
With somewhat beyond this.   The place design'd
To be the scene for this our merry matter,
Because it must have countenance of women,
To draw discourse, and offer it, is here by,
At the lady Tailbush's.
    Wit. I know her, sir,
And her gentleman-usher.

---

[2] —— *nothing in your* purchase,] i.e. in the unlawful profits you
expect to make of Fitzdottrel. *Compliments* in the next line is used
in the old and proper sense of the word ; for whatever was necessary to the completion of the business in hand.

Meer. Master Ambler?

Wit. Yes, sir.

Meer. Sir, it shall be no shame to me, to confess,
To you, that we poor gentlemen that want acres,
Must for our needs turn fools up, and plough ladies
Sometimes, to try what glebe they are : and this
Is no unfruitful piece.   She and I now
Are on a project for the fact, and venting
Of a new kind of fucus, paint for ladies,
To serve the kingdom : wherein she herself
Hath travailed, specially, by way of service
Unto her sex, and hopes to get the monopoly
As the reward of her invention.

Wit. What is her end in this ?

Meer. Merely ambition,
Sir, to grow great, and court it with the secret,
Though she pretend some other.   For she's dealing
Already upon caution for the shares ;
And master Ambler he is named examiner
For the ingredients, and the register
Of what is vented, and shall keep the office.
Now, if she break with you of this, (as I
Must make the leading thread to your acquaintance,
That, how experience gotten in your being
Abroad, will help our business,) think of some
Pretty additions, but to keep her floating ;
It may be she will offer you a part :
Any strange names of——

Wit. Sir, I have my instructions.
Is it not high time to be making ready ?

Meer. Yes, sir.

Eng. The fool's in sight, Dottrel.

Meer. Away then. [*Exeunt* ENGINE *and* WITTIPOL.

Re-enter FITZDOTTREL.

Meer. Return'd so soon !

Fitz. Yes, here's the ring : I have seal'd.

But there's not so much gold in all the Row,[3] he
    says—
Till it come from the mint : 'tis ta'en up for the games-
    ters.
    Meer. There's a shop-shift ! plague on 'em !
    Fitz. He does swear it.
    Meer. He'll swear and forswear too, it is his trade ;
You should not have left him.
    Fitz. 'Slid, I can go back,
And beat him yet.
    Meer. No, now let him alone.
    Fitz. I was so earnest after the main business,
To have this ring gone.
    Meer. True, and it is time.
I have learn'd, sir, since you went, her ladyship eats
With the lady Tailbush, here hard by.
    Fitz. In the lane here ?
    Meer. Yes ; if you had a servant now of presence,
Well clothed, and of an airy, voluble tongue,
Neither too big nor little for his mouth,
That could deliver your wife's compliment,
To send along withal.
    Fitz. I have one, sir,
A very handsome gentleman-like fellow,
That I do mean to make my dutchess' usher——
I entertain'd him but this morning too :
I'll call him to you.   The worst of him is his name.
    Meer. She'll take no note of that, but of his message.
    Fitz. Devil !—

            Enter PUG.

How like you him, sir ?—Pace, go a little,
Let's see you move.

---

[3] —————— *in all the* Row.] " That part of Cheapside between
the end of Broad-street and the Cross, is called Goldsmith's *Row*,
from its being inhabited by Goldsmiths." *Stow's Survey*, p. 391.
Edit. 1633.

Meer. He'll serve, sir; give it him,
And let him go along with me, I'll help
To present him and it.
    Fitz. Look you do, sirrah,
Discharge this well, as you expect your place.
Do you hear? go on, come off with all your honours.
I would fain see him do it.
    Meer. Trust him with it.
    Fitz. Remember kissing of your hand, and answering
With the French time, and flexure of your body.
I could now so instruct him——and for his words——
    Meer. I'll put them in his mouth.
    Fitz. O, but I have them
Of the very academies.
    Meer. Sir, you'll have use for them
Anon yourself, I warrant you, after dinner,
When you are call'd.
    Fitz. 'Slight, that will be just play-time.
It cannot be, I must not lose the play!
    Meer. Sir, but you must, if she appoint to sit,
And she is president.
    Fitz. 'Slid, it is the DEVIL.
    Meer. An 'twere his dam too, you must now apply
Yourself, sir, to this wholly, or lose all.
    Fitz. If I could but see a piece——
    Meer. Sir, never think on't.
    Fitz. Come but to one act, and I did not care—
But to be seen to rise and go away,
To vex the players, and to punish their poet;
Keep him in awe——
    Meer. But say that he be one
Will not be aw'd, but laugh at you; how then?
    Fitz. Then he shall pay for's dinner himself.
    Meer. Perhaps,
He would do that twice, rather than thank you.[1]

---

[1] *Perhaps,*
    He would do that twice, rather than thank you.]   This ill-timed

Come get the Devil out of your head, my lord,
(I'll call you so in private still,) and take
Your lordship in your mind.   You were, sweet lord,
In talk to bring a business to the office.
 Fitz. Yes.
 Meer. Why should not you, sir, carry it on yourself,
Before the office be up, and shew the world
You had no need of any man's direction,
In point, sir, of sufficiency?   I speak
Against a kinsman, but as one that tenders
Your grace's good.
 Fitz. I thank you ; to proceed——
 Meer. To publication : have your deed drawn pre-
  sently,
And leave a blank to put in your feoffees,
One, two, or more, as you see cause.
 Fitz. I thank you ;
Heartily, I do thank you : not a word more,
I pray you, as you love me.   Let me alone.
That I could not think of this as well as he !
O, I could beat my infinite blockhead. [*Exeunt.*

SCENE II. *The Lane near the Lady* TAILBUSH'S
     House.

Enter MEERCRAFT *followed by* PUG.

Meercraft.

OME, we must this way.
 Pug. How far is't ?
 Meer. Hard by here,
Over the way. [*They cross over.*] Now, to achieve
  this ring

compliment to himself, Jonson might have spared, with some advantage to his judgment, at least, if not his modesty.

From this same fellow, that is, to assure it,
Before he give it.　Though my Spanish lady
Be a young gentleman of means, and scorn
To share, as he doth say, I do not know
How such a toy may tempt his ladyship;
And therefore I think best it be assured.　　*[Aside.*
　Pug. Sir, be the ladies brave we go unto?
　Meer. O, yes.
　Pug. And shall I see them, and speak to them?
　Meer. What else?

Enter TRAINS.

Have you your false beard about you, Trains?
　Trains. Yes.
　Meer. And is this one of your double clokes?[5]
　Trains. The best of them.
　Meer. Be ready then.　　　　　　　　*[Exeunt.*

SCENE III. *A Hall in Lady* TAILBUSH'S *House.*

Enter MEERCRAFT *and* PUG, *met by* PITFALL.

Meercraft.

WEET Pitfall!
　　Come, I must buss——　　*[Offers to kiss her.*
　　　Pit. Away.
　Meer. I'll set thee up again.
Never fear that : canst thou get ne'er a bird?
No thrushes hungry! stay till cold weather come,
I'll help thee to an ousel or a fieldfare.
Who's within, with madam?

---

[5] *Your* double clokes,] i. e. a cloke adapted for disguises,
which might be worn on either side.　It was of different colours,
and fashions.　This turned cloke with a false beard (of which the
cut and colour varied) and a black or yellow peruke, furnished a
ready and effectual mode of concealment, which is now lost to the
stage.

Pit. I'll tell you straight.   [*Exit hastily.*
Meer. Please you stay here a while, sir, I'll go in.
                                   [*Exit.*

Pug. I do so long to have a little venery
While I am in this body! I would taste
Of every sin a little, if it might be,
After the manner of man.—Sweet-heart!

Re-enter PITFALL.

Pit. What would you, sir?   [PUG *runs to her.*
Pug. Nothing but fall in to you; be your black-
      bird,
My pretty Pit, as the gentleman said, your throstle,
Lie tame, and taken with you; here is gold,
To buy you so much new stuffs from the shop,
As I may take the old up——

Enter TRAINS, *in his false beard and cloke.*

Trains. You must send, sir,
The gentleman the ring.
Pug. There 'tis. [*Exit* TRAINS.]—Nay look,
Will you be foolish, Pit?
Pit. This is strange rudeness.
Pug. Dear Pit.
Pit. I'll call, I swear.

Enter MEERCRAFT.

Meer. Where are you, sir?
Is your ring ready? Go with me.
Pug. I sent it you.
Meer. Me! when? by whom?
Pug. A fellow here, e'en now,
Came for it in your name.
Meer. I sent none, sure.
My meaning ever was, you should deliver it
Yourself; so was your master's charge, you know.

Re-enter TRAINS *dressed as at first.*

What fellow was it, do you know him?
  Pug. Here,
But now, he had it.
  Meer. Saw you any, Trains?
  Trains. Not I.
  Pug. The gentlewoman saw him.
  Meer. Enquire.
  Pug. I was so earnest upon her, I mark'd not.
My devilish chief has put me here in flesh,
To shame me! this dull body I am in,
I perceive nothing with, I offer at nothing
That will succeed!   [*Aside.*
  Trains. Sir, she saw none, she says.
  Pug. Satan himself has ta'en a shape to abuse me;
It could not be else!   [*Aside.*
  Meer. This is above strange.
That you should be so rechless! What will you do, sir,
How will you answer this, when you are question'd?
- *Pug.* Run from my flesh, if I could; put off man-
      kind.
This is such a scorn, and will be a new exercise
For my arch-duke! Woe to the several cudgels
Must suffer on this back![6] [*Aside.*]—Can you no
      succours, sir?
  Meer. Alas! the use of it is so present.[7]
  Pug. I ask,
Sir, credit for another but till to-morrow.
  Meer. There is not so much time, sir; but, however,
The lady is a noble lady, and will,
To save a gentleman from check, be entreated

---

  [6] ————————— *Woe to the several cudgels*
    Must suffer on this back!] This is from Jonson's favourite
poet, and is given with kindred spirit and humour.
  [7] *Alas! the use of it is so* present.] i. e. so immediate, so important to our ends. A latinism sufficiently harsh.

To say, she has received it.
   Pug. Do you think so ?
Will she be won ?
   Meer. No doubt, to such an office,
It will be a lady's bravery and her pride.
   Pug. And not be known on't after, unto him ?
   Meer. That were a treachery : Upon my word,
Be confident.   Return unto your master,
My lady president sits this afternoon,
Has ta'en the ring, commends her services
Unto your lady dutchess.   You may say
She is a civil lady, and does give her
All her respects already : bad you tell her,
She lives but to receive her wish'd commandments,
And have the honour here to kiss her hands,
For which she'll stay this hour yet.   Hasten you
Your prince, away.
   Pug. And, sir, you will take care
The excuse be perfect ?
   Meer. You confess your fears
Too much.
   Pug. The shame is more.
   Meer. I'll quit you of either.[8]   [*Exeunt.*

[8] Pug. *The shame is more, I'll quit you of either.*] The latter
part of this line, though all the editions concur in giving it to Pug,
evidently belongs to Meercraft, and is an answer to Pug's appre-
hensions of being discovered. WHAL.

ACT IV.

SCENE I. *A Room in Lady* TAILBUSH'S *House.*

Enter Lady TAILBUSH *and* MEERCRAFT.

Lady Tailbush.

POX upon referring to commissioners !
I had rather hear that it were past the seals:
You courtiers move so snail-like in your
       business.
Would I had not begun with you !
   Meer. We must move,
Madam, in order, by degrees ; not jump.
   Lady T. Why, there was sir John Moneyman
      could jump
A business quickly.
   Meer. True, he had great friends ;
But, because some, sweet madam, can leap ditches,
We must not all shun to go over bridges.
The harder parts, I make account, are done,
Now 'tis referr'd : you are infinitely bound
Unto the ladies, they have so cried it up !
   Lady T. Do they like it then ?
   Meer. They have sent the Spanish lady
To gratulate with you.
   Lady T. I must send them thanks,
And some remembrances.
   Meer. That you must, and visit them.
Where's Ambler ?
   Lady T. Lost, to-day, we cannot hear of him.
   Meer. Not, madam !
   Lady T. No, in good faith : they say he lay not

At home to-night.   And here has fallen a business
Between your cousin and master Manly, has
Unquieted us all.
 Meer. So I hear, madam.
Pray you, how was it?
 Lady T. Troth, it but appears
Ill on your kinsman's part.   You may have heard,
That Manly is a suitor to me, I doubt not.
 Meer. I guess'd it, madam.
 Lady T. And it seems, he trusted
Your cousin to let fall some fair reports
Of him unto me.
 Meer. Which he did!
 Lady T. So far
From it, as he came in, and took him railing
Against him.
 Meer. How! And what said Manly to him?
 Lady T. Enough, I do assure you; and with that
  scorn
Of him and the injury, as I do wonder
How Everill bore it; but that guilt undoes
Many men's valours.

Enter MANLY.

 Meer. Here comes Manly.
 Man. Madam, I'll take my leave——
 Lady T. You shall not go, i' faith.
I'll have you stay and see this Spanish miracle,
Of our English lady.
 Man. Let me pray your ladyship,
Lay your commands on me some other time.
 Lady T. Now, I protest; and I will have all pieced,
And friends again.
 Man. It will be but ill-solder'd!
 Lady T. You are too much affected with it.
 Man. I cannot,
Madam, but think on't for the injustice.

Lady T. Sir,
His kinsman here is sorry.
  Meer. Not I, madam,
I am no kin to him, we but call cousins :
And if he were, sir, I have no relation
Unto his crimes.
  Man. You are not urged with them.
I can accuse, sir, none but mine own judgment ;
For though it were his crime so to betray me,
I am sure, 'twas more mine own, at all to trust him :
But he therein did use but his old manners,
And savour strongly what he was before.
  Lady T. Come, he will change.
  Man. Faith, I must never think it ;
Nor were it reason in me to expect,
That, for my sake, he should put off a nature
He suck'd in with his milk.   It may be, madam,
Deceiving trust is all he has to trust to :
If so, I shall be loth, that any hope
Of mine should bate him of his means.
  Lady T. You are sharp, sir :
This act may make him honest.
  Man. If he were
To be made honest by an act of parliament,
I should not alter in my faith of him.

Enter Lady EITHERSIDE.

  Lady T. Eitherside !
Welcome, dear Eitherside ! how hast thou done, good
        wench ?
Thou hast been a stranger : I have not seen thee this
        week.
  Lady E. Ever your servant, madam.
  Lady T. Where hast thou been ?
I did so long to see thee.
  Lady E. Visiting, and so tired !
I protest, madam, 'tis a monstrous trouble.

  5   H

Lady T. And so it is. I swear I must to-morrow
Begin my visits, would they were over, at court :
It tortures me to think on them.
    Lady E. I do hear
You have cause, madam, your suit goes on.
    Lady T. Who told thee ?
    Lady E. One that can tell ; master Eitherside.
    Lady T. O, thy husband.
Yes faith, there's life in't now ; it is referr'd.
If we once see it under the seals, wench, then,
Have with them for the great caroch, six horses,
And the two coachmen, with my Ambler bare,
And my three women ; we will live, i'faith,
The examples of the town, and govern it :
I'll lead the fashion still.
    Lady E. You do that now,
Sweet madam.
    Lady T. O but then, I'll every day
Bring up some new device. Thou and I, Eitherside,
Will first be in it, I will give it thee ;
And they shall follow us. Thou shalt, I swear,
Wear every month a new gown out of it.
    Lady E. Thank you, good madam.
    Lady T. Pray thee call me Tailbush,
As I thee Eitherside ; I love not this madam.
    Lady E. Then I protest to you, Tailbush, I am glad
Your business so succeeds.
    Lady T. Thank thee, good Eitherside.
    Lady E. But master Eitherside tells me, that he
        likes
Your other business better.
    Lady T. Which ?
    Lady E. Of the tooth-picks.
    Lady T. I never heard of it.
    Lady E. Ask master Meercraft.
    Meer. Madam ! [*Aside to* MANLY.]—He is one, in
        a word, I'll trust his malice

With any man's credit, I would have abused.

   Man. Sir, if you think you do please me in this,
You are deceived.

   Meer. No, but because my lady
Named him my kinsman, I would satisfy you
What I think of him ; and pray you upon it
To judge me.

   Man. So I do ; that ill men's friendship
Is as unfaithful as themselves.

   Lady T. Do you hear ?
Have you a business about tooth-picks ?

   Meer. Yes, madam ;
Did I ne'er tell it you ? I meant to have offer'd it
Your ladyship, on the perfecting the patent.

   Lady T. How is it ?

   Meer. For serving the whole state with tooth-picks ;
Somewhat an intricate business to discourse : but
I show how much the subject is abused,
First, in that one commodity ; then what diseases
And putrefactions in the gums are bred,
By those are made of adulterate and false wood ;
My plot for reformation of these, follows :
To have all tooth-picks brought unto an office,
There seal'd ; and such as counterfeit them, mulcted.
And last, for venting them, to have a book
Printed, to teach their use, which every child
Shall have throughout the kingdom, that can read,
And learn to pick his teeth by : which beginning
Early to practise, with some other rules,
Of never sleeping with the mouth open, chewing
Some grains of mastick, will preserve the breath
Pure and so free from taint——

       Enter TRAINS, *and whispers him.*

             Ha ! what is't, say'st thou ?

   Lady T. Good faith, it sounds a very pretty business !

Lady E. So master Eitherside says, madam.

Meer. The lady is come.

Lady T. Is she! good, wait upon her in.   [*Exit*
         MEERCRAFT.]—My Ambler

Was never so ill absent.   Eitherside,
How do I look to-day, am I not drest
Spruntly ?[9]   [*Looks in her glass.*

Lady E. Yes verily, madam.

Lady T. Pox o' madam!
Will you not leave that ?

Lady E. Yes, good Tailbush.

Lady T. So!
Sounds not that better ? What vile fucus is this
Thou hast got on ?

Lady E. 'Tis pearl.

Lady T. Pearl ! oyster-shells ;
As I breathe, Eitherside, I know't.   Here comes,
They say, a wonder, sirrah, has been in Spain,
Will teach us all! she's sent to me from court,
To gratulate with me : prithee let's observe her,
What faults she has, that we may laugh at them,
When she is gone.

Lady E. That we will heartily, Tailbush.

Re-enter MEERCRAFT, *introducing* WITTIPOL *dressed
              as a Spanish lady.*

Lady T. O me, the very infanta of the giants!

Meer. Here is a noble lady, madam, come

---

[9] ———— *am I not drest*
   Spruntly ?] i. e. sprucely. I know not the etymon of this word ;
but it is extended through several languages. Sprunt, sprack,
spree or spry, and spruce, have all the same derivation, and bear
the same import : applied to the mind, they mean acute, active,
clever; to the body, neat, smart, elegant. Dr. Johnson, who merely
copies Ainsworth, says " *sprunt*, any thing that is short, and that
will not easily bend."   In some of our northern provinces a stout
lad, is, indeed, called a good *sprunt* lad; but this scarcely seems to
support Ainsworth's explanation.

From your great friends at court, to see your lady-
    ship,
And have the honour of your acquaintance.
    Lady T. Sir,
She does us honour.
    Wit. Pray you, say to her ladyship,
It is the manner of Spain to embrace only,
Never to kiss. She will excuse the custom.
    Lady T. Your use of it is law. Please you, sweet
    madam,
To take a seat.
    Wit. Yes, madam. I have had
The favour, through a world of fair report,
To know your virtues, madam ; and in that
Name, have desired the happiness of presenting
My service to your ladyship.
    Lady T. Your love, madam ;
I must not own it else.
    Wit. Both are due, madam,
To your great undertakings.
    Lady T. Great ! In troth, madam,
They are my friends, that think them any thing :
If I can do my sex, by 'em, any service,
I have my ends, madam.
    Wit. And they are noble ones,
That make a multitude beholden, madam ;
The commonwealth of ladies must acknowledge from
    you.
    Lady E. Except some envious, madam.
    Wit. You are right in that, madam,
Of which race, I encounter'd some but lately,
Who, it seems, have studied reasons to discredit
Your business.
    Lady T. How, sweet madam !
    Wit. Nay, the parties
Will not be worth your pause——most ruinous things,
    madam,

That have put off all hope of being recover'd
To a degree of handsomeness.
    Lady T. But their reasons, madam,
I would fain hear.
    Wit. Some, madam, I remember.
They say that painting quite destroys the face——
    Lady E. O, that's an old one, madam.
    Wit. There are new ones too.
Corrupts the breath ; hath left so little sweetness
In kissing, as 'tis now used but for fashion ;
And shortly will be taken for a punishment.
Decays the fore-teeth that should guard the tongue ;
And suffers that run riot everlasting !
And, which is worse, some ladies when they meet,
Cannot be merry and laugh, but they do spit
In one another's faces.
    Man. I should know
This voice and face too.   [*Aside.*
    Wit. Then, they say, 'tis dangerous
To all the fall'n, yet well disposed mad-ams,
That are industrious, and desire to earn
Their living with their sweat : for any distemper
Of heat and motion may displace the colours ;
And if the paint once run about their faces,
Twenty to one they will appear so ill-favour'd,
Their servants run away too, and leave the pleasure
Imperfect, and the reckoning also unpaid.
    Lady E. Pox ! these are poets' reasons.
    Lady T. Some old lady,
That keeps a poet, has devised these scandals.
    Lady E. Faith, we must have the poets banish'd,
        madam,
As master Eitherside says.
    Meer. Master Fitzdottrel,
And his wife!
    Wit. Where ?

Enter Mr. *and* Mrs. FITZDOTTREL, *followed by* PUG.

    Meer. [*To* WIT.] Madam, the duke of Drown'd-
        land,[1]
That will be shortly.

    Wit. Is this my lord ?

    Meer. The same.

    Fitz. Your servant, madam!

    Wit. [*Takes* MANLY *aside.*] How now, friend!
        offended,
That I have found your haunt here ?

    Man. No, but wondering
At your strange-fashion'd venture hither.

    Wit. It is
To shew you what they are you so pursue.

    Man. I think 'twill prove a med'cine against
        marriage ;
To know their manners.

    Wit. Stay, and profit then.

    Meer. The lady, madam, whose prince has brought
        her here
To be instructed.   [*Presents* Mrs. FITZDOTTREL.

    Wit. Please you sit with us, lady.

    Meer. That's lady-president.

    Fitz. A goodly woman !
I cannot see the ring, though.

    Meer. Sir, she has it.

    Lady T. But, madam, these are very feeble reasons.

    Wit. So I urg'd, madam, that the new complexion
Now to come forth, in name of your ladyship's fucus,
Has no ingredient——

    Lady T. But I durst eat, I assure you.

---

[1] Meer. *Master Fitzdottrel, &c.*] The old copy reads,
        Meer. Master Fitzdottrel
      And his wife : where ? madam, &c.
which I have attempted to regulate, as the reader now has it.
There is no end to the mistakes of the speakers in this ill-printed
play.

Wit. So do they in Spain.

Lady T. Sweet madam, be so liberal,
To give us some of your Spanish fucuses.

Wit. They are infinite, madam.

Lady T. So I hear.

Wit. They have
Water of gourds, of radish, the white beans,
Flowers of glass, of thistles, rose-marine,
Raw honey, mustard seed, and bread dough-baked,
The crums of bread, goats-milk, and whites of eggs,
Camphire, and lily-roots, the fat of swans,
Marrow of veal, white pigeons, and pine-kernels,
The seeds of nettles, purseline, and hares-gall;
Limons, thin skinn'd——

Lady E. How her ladyship has studied
All excellent things!

Wit. But ordinary, madam:
No, the true rarities are the alvagada
And argentata of queen Isabella.

Lady T. Ay, what are their ingredients, gentle
madam?

Wit. Your allum scagliola, or pol di pedra;
And zuccarino; turpentine of Abezzo,
Wash'd in nine waters: soda di levante,
Or your fern ashes; benjamin di gotta:
Grasso di serpe; porceletto marino;
Oils of lentisco; zucche mugia; make
The admirable varnish for the face,
Gives the right lustre; but two drops rubb'd on
With a piece of scarlet, makes a lady of sixty
Look as sixteen. But above all, the water
Of the white hen, of the lady Estifania's.

Lady T. O, ay, that same, good madam, I have
heard of:
How is it done?

Wit. Madam, you take your hen,
Plume it, and skin it, cleanse it o' the inwards;

Then chop it, bones and all ; add to four ounces
Of carravicins, pipitas, soap of Cyprus,
Make the decoction, strain it ; then distil it,
And keep it in your gallipot well gliddered : [2]
Three drops preserves from wrinkles, warts, spots,
            moles,
Blemish, or sun burnings ; and keeps the skin
In decimo sexto, ever bright and smooth,
As any looking-glass ; and indeed is call'd
The Virgins-Milk for the face, oglio reale ;
A ceruse, neither cold nor heat will hurt ;
And mix'd with oil of myrrh, and the red gilliflower,
Call'd cataputia, and flowers of rovistico,
Makes the best muta or dye of the whole world.
      Lady T. Dear madam, will you let us be familiar ?
      Wit. Your ladyship's servant.
      Meer. How do you like her ?
      Fitz. Admirable !
But yet I cannot see the ring.
      Pug. Sir !
      Meer. I must
Deliver it, or mar all : this fool's so jealous ! [*Aside.*
Madam—[*whispers Wit.*] Sir, wear this ring, and
            pray you take knowledge,
'Twas sent you by his wife ; and give her thanks.
Do not you dwindle, sir, bear up.   [*Aside to* PUG.
      Pug. I thank you, sir.
      Lady T. But for the manner of Spain.   Sweet
            madam, let us

---

[2] ———— *your gallipot well* gliddered,] i. e. glazed over with
some tenacious lacker.   I could easily have furnished the reader
with the literal meaning of the foregoing terms ; but as this could
convey no very precise idea of their real import in these days, it
seemed more eligible to be silent altogether.   With respect to the
poet, he wantons here, as in alchemy, and indeed in every other
art and science, in a profusion of minute knowledge, which the
ordinary bounds of human life will rarely permit the most industrious student to acquire.

Be bold, now we are in : are all the ladies
There in the fashion ?
    Wit. None but grandees, madam,
Of the clasp'd train, which may be worn at length too,
Or thus, upon my arm.
    Lady T. And do they wear
Cioppinos all ?
    Wit. If they be drest in punto, madam.
    Lady T. Gilt as those are, madam ?
    Wit. Of goldsmith's work, madam,
And set with diamonds ; and their Spanish pumps,
Of perfumed leather.
    Lady T. I should think it hard
To go in them, madam.
    Wit. At the first it is, madam.
    Lady T. Do you never fall in them ?
    Wit. Never.
    Lady E. I swear I should,
Six times an hour.
    Lady T. But you have men at hand still,
To help you, if you fall ?
    Wit. Only one, madam,
The guarda-duennas, such a little old man
As this.   [*Points to* TRAINS.
    Lady E. Alas, he can do nothing, this !
    Wit. I'll tell you, madam, I saw in the court of
        Spain once,
A lady fall in the king's sight, along ;
And there she lay, flat spread, as an umbrella,
Her hoop here crack'd ; no man durst reach a hand
To help her, till the guarda-duennas came,
Who is the person only allow'd to touch
A lady there, and he but by this finger.
    Lady E. Have they no servants, madam, there,
        nor friends ?
    Wit. An escudero, or so, madam, that waits
Upon them in another coach, at distance ;

And when they walk or dance, holds by a hand-
    kerchief,
Never presumes to touch them.
    Lady E. This is scurvy,
And a forced gravity !   I do not like it :
I like our own much better.
    Lady T. 'Tis more French,
And courtly, ours.
    Lady E. And tastes more liberty.
We may have our dozen of visitors at once
Make love to us.
    Lady T. And before our husbands.
    Lady E. Husband !
As I am honest, Tailbush, I do think,
If no body should love me but my poor husband,
I should e'en hang myself.
    Lady T. Fortune forbid, wench,
So fair a neck should have so foul a necklace !
    Lady E. 'Tis true, as I am handsome.
    Wit. I received, lady,
A token from you, which I would not be
Rude to refuse, being your first remembrance.
    Fitz. O, I am satisfied now !   [*Aside to* MEER.
    Meer. Do you see it, sir ?
    Wit. But since you come to know me nearer, lady,
I'll beg the honour you will wear it for me,
It must be so. [*Gives the ring to* Mrs. FITZDOTTREL.
    Mrs. Fitz. Sure I have heard this tongue. [*Aside.*
    Meer. What do you mean, sir ?   [*Aside to* WIT.
    Wit. Would you have me mercenary ?
We'll recompense it anon in somewhat else.
                [*Exeunt* MEER. *and* TRAINS.
    Fitz. I do not love to be gull'd, though in a toy,
Wife, do you hear ? [*Takes* Mrs. FITZ. *aside.*] you
    are come into the school, wife,
Where you may learn, I do perceive it, any thing.
How to be fine, or fair, or great, or proud,

Or what you will, indeed, wife ; here 'tis taught :
And I am glad on't, that you may not say,
Another day, when honours come upon you,
You wanted means.   I have done my parts ; been,
To-day, at fifty pound charge ; first, for a ring,
To get you enter'd ; then left my new play,
To wait upon you here, to see't confirmed,
That I may say, both to mine eyes and ears,
Senses, you are my witness, she hath enjoy'd
All helps that could be had for love, or money——
    Mrs. Fitz. To make a fool of her.
    Fitz. Wife, that's your malice,
The wickedness of your nature, to interpret
Your husband's kindness thus : but I'll not leave
Still to do good, for your depraved affections ;
Intend it ; bend this stubborn will ; be great.
    Lady T. Good madam, whom do they use in
       messages ?
    Wit. They commonly use their slaves, madam.
    Lady T. And does your ladyship
Think that so good, madam ?
    Wit. No indeed, madam ; I
Therein prefer the fashion of England far,
Of your young delicate page, or discreet usher.
    Fitz. And I go with your ladyship in opinion,
Directly for your gentleman usher :
There's not a finer officer goes on ground.
    Wit. If he be made and broken to his place once.
    Fitz. Nay, so I presuppose him.
    Wit. And they are fitter
Managers too, sir ; but I would have them call'd
Our escuderos.
    Fitz. Good.
    Wit. Say I should send
To your ladyship, who, I presume, has gather'd
All the dear secrets, to know how to make
Pastillos of the dutchess of Braganza,

Coquettas, almoiavanas, mantecadas,
Alcorcas, mustaccioli ; or say it were
The peladore of Isabella, or balls
Against the itch, or aqua nanfa, or oil
Of jessamine for gloves, of the marquesse Muja ;
Or for the head and hair ; why, these are offices——
   Fitz. Fit for a gentleman, not a slave.
   Wit. They only
Might ask for your piveti, Spanish coal,
To burn, and sweeten a room : but the arcana
Of ladies' cabinets——
   Fitz. Should be elsewhere trusted
You are much about the truth.—Sweet honour'd ladies,
Let me fall in with you : I have my female wit,
As well as my male ; and I do know what suits
A lady of spirit, or a woman of fashion.
   Wit. And you would have your wife such ?
   Fitz. Yes, madam, airy,
Light ; not to plain dishonesty, I mean :
But somewhat o' this side.
   Wit. I take you, sir :—
He has reason, ladies. I'll not give this rush
For any lady that cannot be honest
Within a thread.
   Lady T. Yes, madam, and yet venture
As far for the other, in her fame——
   Wit. As can be :
Coach it to Pimlico, dance the saraband,
Hear and talk bawdy, laugh as loud as a larum,
Squeak, spring, do any thing.
   Lady E. In young company, madam.
   Lady T. Or afore gallants. If they be brave, or
      lords,
A woman is engaged.
   Fitz. I say so, ladies.
It is civility to deny us nothing.
   Pug. You talk of a university ! why, hell is

A grammar-school to this !   [*Aside.*
   Lady E. But then
She must not lose a look on stuffs or cloth, madam.
   Lady T. Nor no coarse fellow.
   Wit. She must be guided, madam,
By the clothes he wears, and company he is in,
Whom to salute, how far——
   Fitz. I have told her this ;
And how that bawdry too, upon the point,
Is in itself as civil a discourse——
   Wit. As any other affair of flesh whatever.
   Fitz. But she will ne'er be capable, she is not
So much as coming, madam ; I know not how,
She loses all her opportunities,
With hoping to be forced.   I have entertain'd
A gentleman, a younger brother, here,
Whom I would fain breed up her escudero,
Against some expectations that I have,
And she'll not countenance him.
   Wit. What's his name ?
   Fitz. Devil of Derbyshire.
   Lady E. Bless us from him !
   Lady T. Devil !
Call him De-vile, sweet madam.
   Mrs. Fitz. What you please, ladies.
   Lady T. De-vile's a prettier name.
   Lady E. And sounds, methinks,
As it came in with the conqueror——
   Man. Over smocks !
What things they are ! that nature should be at leisure
Ever to make them !   My wooing is at an end.
        [*Aside, and exit with indignation.*
   Wit. What can he do ?
   Lady E. Let's hear him.
   Lady T. Can he manage ?
   Fitz. Please you to try him, ladies.—Stand forth,
     Devil.

Pug. Was all this but the preface to my torment ?
                                              [*Aside.*
Fitz. Come, let their ladyships see your honours.
Lady E. O,
He makes a wicked leg.[3]
Lady T. As ever I saw.
Wit. Fit for a devil.
Lady T. Good madam, call him De-vile.
Wit. De-vile, what property is there most required,
In your conceit now, in the escudero ?
Fitz. Why do you not speak ?
Pug. A settled discreet pace, madam.
Wit. I think, a barren head, sir, mountain-like,
To be exposed to the cruelty of weathers——
Fitz. Ay, for his valley is beneath the waist, madam,
And to be fruitful there, it is sufficient.
Dulness upon you ! could not you hit this ?
                                              [*Strikes him.*

Pug. Good sir.
Wit. He then had had no barren head :
You daw him too much in troth, sir.[4]
Fitz. I must walk
With the French stick, like an old verger, for you.
Pug. O chief, call me to hell again, and free me !
                                              [*Aside.*

Fitz. Do you murmur now ?
Pug. Not I, sir.
Wit. What do you take,
Master De-vile, the height of your employment,
In the true perfect escudero ?
Fitz. When !
What do you answer ?
Pug. To be able, madam,
First to enquire, then report the working

---

[3] *He makes a* wicked leg,] i. e. an awkward or clownish scrape
with the leg, the constant accompaniment of a bow in those days.
   [4] *You* daw *him*,] i. e. daunt or put him out of countenance.

Of any lady's physick, in sweet phrase.

    Wit. Yes, that's an act of elegance and importance:
But what above?

    Fitz. O, that I had a goad for him.

    Pug. To find out a good corn-cutter.

    Lady T. Out on him!

    Lady E. Most barbarous!

    Fitz. Why did you do this now?
Of purpose to discredit me, you damn'd devil!

    Pug. Sure, if I be not yet, I shall be.—All
My days in hell were holidays, to this!   [*Aside.*

    Lady T. 'Tis labour lost, madam.

    Lady E. He is a dull fellow,
Of no capacity.

    Lady T. Of no discourse.
O, if my Ambler had been here!

    Lady E. Ay, madam,
You talk of a man; where is there such another?

    Wit. Master De-vile, put case one of my ladies
       here
Had a fine brach, and would employ you forth
To treat 'bout a convenient match for her;
What would you observe?

    Pug. The colour and the size, madam.

    Wit. And nothing else?

    Fitz. The moon, you calf, the moon!

    Wit. Ay, and the sign.

    Lady T. Yes, and receipts for proneness.

    Wit. Then when the puppies came, what would
       you do?

    Pug. Get their nativities cast.

    Wit. This is well.   What more?

    Pug. Consult the almanac-man which would be
       least,
Which cleanliest.

    Wit. And which silent'st? This is well, madam.
And while she were with puppy?

Pug. Walk her out,
And air her every morning.
   Wit. Very good!
And be industrious to kill her fleas?
   Pug. Yes.
   Wit. He will make a pretty proficient.
   Pug. Who,
Coming from hell, could look for such a catechising?
The Devil is an Ass, I do acknowledge it.   [*Aside.*
   Fitz. The top of woman! all her sex in abstract!
I love her, to each syllable falls from her.
                    [*Aside, and looking at* WITTIPOL.
   Lady T. Good madam, give me leave to go aside
      with him,
And try him a little.
   Wit. Do, and I'll withdraw, madam,
With this fair lady, read to her the while.
   Lady T. Come, sir.
   Pug. Dear chief, relieve me, or I perish!   [*Aside.*
   Wit. Lady, we'll follow.—You are not jealous, sir?
   Fitz. O, madam, you shall see.—Stay, wife;—
      behold,
I give her up here absolutely to you;
She is your own, do with her what you will:
Melt, cast, and form her as you shall think good;
Set any stamp on: I'll receive her from you
As a new thing, by your own standard.   [*Exit.*
   Wit. Well, sir!
      [*Exeunt* WITTIPOL *with* Mrs. FITZ., *and* TAILBUSH
         and EITHERSIDE *with* PUG.

SCENE II.   *Another Room in the same.*

Enter MEERCRAFT *and* FITZDOTTREL.

Meercraft.

BUT what have you done in your dependence
         since ?
      Fitz. O, it goes on ; I met your cousin, the
   master——
Meer. You did not acquaint him, sir ?
Fitz. Faith but I did, sir,
And, upon better thought, not without reason.
He being chief officer might have taken it ill else,
As a contempt against his place, and that
In time, sir, have drawn on another dependence :
No, I did find him in good terms, and ready
To do me any service.
Meer. So he said to you!
But, sir, you do not know him.
Fitz. Why, I presumed,
Because this bus'ness of my wife's required me,
I could not have done better : and he told
Me, that he would go presently to your counsel,
A knight here in the lane——
Meer. Yes, justice Eitherside.
Fitz. And get the feoffment drawn, with a letter of
      attorney,
For livery and seisin.
Meer. That I know's the course.
But, sir, you mean not to make him feoffee ?
Fitz. Nay, that I'll pause on.

Enter PITFALL.

Meer. How now, little Pitfall !
Pit. Your cousin, master Everill, would come in—

But he would know if master Manly were here.
    Meer. No, tell him; if he were, I have made his
        peace.—   *[Exit* PITFALL.
He's one, sir, has no state, and a man knows not
How such a trust may tempt him.
    Fitz. I conceive you.

           Enter EVERILL *and* PLUTARCHUS.

    Ever. Sir, this same deed is done here.
    Meer. Pretty Plutarchus!
Art thou come with it? and has sir Paul view'd it?
    Plu. His hand is to the draught.
    Meer. Will you step in, sir,
And read it?
    Fitz. Yes.
    Ever. I pray you, a word with you. *[Aside to* FITZ.
Sir Paul Eitherside will'd me give you caution
Whom you did make feoffee; for 'tis the trust
Of your whole state; and though my cousin here
Be a worthy gentleman, yet his valour has
At the tall board been question'd; and we hold
Any man so impeach'd of doubtful honesty.
I will not justify this, but give it you
To make your profit of it; if you utter it,
I can forswear it.
    Fitz. I believe you, and thank you, sir.   *[Exeunt.*

      SCENE III.   *Another Room in the same.*

    Enter WITTIPOL *and* Mrs. FITZDOTTREL.

            Wittipol.

E not afraid, sweet lady; you are trusted
    To love, not violence, here: I am no ravisher,
    But one whom you by your fair trust again
May of a servant make a most true friend.

MANLY *enters behind.*

Mrs. Fitz. And such a one I need, but not this way.
Sir, I confess me to you, the mere manner
Of your attempting me this morning, took me ;
And I did hold my invention, and my manners,
Were both engaged to give it a requital,
But not unto your ends : my hope was then,
Though interrupted ere it could be utter'd,
That whom I found the master of such language,
That brain and spirit for such an enterprize,
Could not, but if those succours were demanded
To a right use, employ them virtuously,
And make that profit of his noble parts
Which they would yield. Sir, you have now the ground
To exercise them in : I am a woman
That cannot speak more wretchedness of myself,
Than you can read ; match'd to a mass of folly,
That every day makes haste to his own ruin ;
The wealthy portion that I brought him, spent,
And, through my friends' neglect, no jointure made
        me.
My fortunes standing in this precipice,
'Tis counsel that I want, and honest aids ;
And in this name I need you for a friend ;
Never in any other ; for his ill
Must not make me, sir, worse.
    Manly. [*comes forward.*] O, friend, forsake not
The brave occasion virtue offers you
To keep you innocent : I have fear'd for both,
And watch'd you, to prevent the ill I fear'd.
But since the weaker side hath so assured me,
Let not the stronger fall by his own vice,
Or be the less a friend, 'cause virtue needs him.
    Wit. Virtue shall never ask my succours twice ;
Most friend, most man, your counsels are commands.—
Lady, I can love goodness in you, more

Than I did beauty; and do here intitle
Your virtue to the power upon a life
You shall engage in any fruitful service,
Even to forfeit.

Enter MEERCRAFT.

Meer. Madam!——Do you hear, sir ?
                                        [*Aside to* WITTIPOL.
We have another leg strain'd for this Dottrel.[5]
He has a quarrel to carry, and has caused
A deed of feoffment of his whole estate
To be drawn yonder : he has't within; and you
Only he means to make feoffee.   He is fallen
So desperately enamour'd on you, and talks
Most like a madman : you did never hear
A phrenetic so in love with his own favour !
Now you do know, 'tis of no validity
In your name, as you stand : therefore advise him
To put in me !——

Enter FITZDOTTREL, EVERILL, *and* PLUTARCHUS.

                          He's come here.   You shall share, sir.
Fitz. Madam, I have a suit to you ; and aforehand
I do bespeak you ; you must not deny me,
I will be granted.
    Wit. Sir, I must know it, though.
    Fitz. No, lady, you must not know it : yet you
                        must too,
For the trust of it, and the fame indeed,
Which else were lost me.   I would use your name,

---

[5] *We have another leg strain'd for this Dottrel.*]   See p. 50.
Beaumont and Fletcher frequently allude to this mode of catching
dottrels:
            " All other loves are mere catching of dottrels,
                Stretching of legs out only."   *Bonduca.*
    Again :
            "See ! they stretch out their legs like dottrels," &c.
                                        Sea Voyage.

But in a feoffment, make my whole estate
Over unto you : a trifle, a thing of nothing,
Some eighteen hundred.
    Wit. Alas! I understand not
Those things, sir ; I am a woman, and most loth
To embark myself——
    Fitz. You will not slight me, madam ?
    Wit. Nor you'll not quarrel me ?
    Fitz. No, sweet madam.   I have
Already a dependence;⁶ for which cause
I do this : let me put you in, dear madam,
I may be fairly kill'd.
    Wit. You have your friends, sir,
About you here for choice.
    Ever. She tells you right, sir.
    Fitz. Death, if she do, what do I care for that ?
Say, I would have her tell me wrong !
    Wit. Why, sir,
If for the trust you'll let me have the honour
To name you one.
    Fitz. Nay, you do me the honour, madam.
Who is't ?
    Wit. This gentleman.   [*Pointing to* MANLY.
    Fitz. O no, sweet madam,
He's friend to him with whom I have the dependence.
    Wit. Who might he be ?
    Fitz. One Wittipol ; do you know him ?
    Wit. Alas, sir, he ! a toy : this gentleman
A friend to him ! no more than I am, sir.
    Fitz. But will your ladyship undertake that, madam ?
    Wit. Yes, and what else, for him, you will engage me.
    Fitz. What is his name ?

---

⁶ —————— *I have*
    Already a dependence,] i. e. a dispute to be settled according
to the laws of the duello ; which was to determine under what head
of quarrelling it came, and whether it admitted of "your peace-
maker, *if*," or was to be referred to "mortal arbitriment."

Wit. His name is Eustace Manly.

Fitz. Whence does he write himself?

Wit. Of Middlesex, esquire.

Fitz. Say nothing, madam.—Clerk, come hither;
                              [*To* PLUTARCHUS.
Write Eustace Manly, squire of Middlesex.

Meer. What have you done, sir? [*Aside to* WIT.

Wit. Named a gentleman,
That I'll be answerable for to you, sir:
Had I named you, it might have been suspected;
This way 'tis safe.

Fitz. Come, gentlemen, your hands
For witness.

Man. What is this?

Ever. You have made election
Of a most worthy gentleman!

Man. Would one of worth
Had spoke it! but now whence it comes, it is
Rather a shame unto me, than a praise.

Ever. Sir, I will give you any satisfaction.

Man. Be silent then: Falsehood commends not
    truth.

Plu. You do deliver this sir, as your deed,
To the use of master Manly?

Fitz. Yes: and sir——   [*To* MANLY.
When did you see young Wittipol? I am ready
For process now: sir, this is publication.
He shall hear from me; he would needs be courting
My wife, sir.

Man. Yes; so witnesseth his cloke there.

Fitz. Nay, good sir—Madam, you did undertake—

Wit. What?

Fitz. That he was not Wittipol's friend.

Wit. I hear,
Sir, no confession of it.

Fitz. O, she knows not;
Now I remember.—Madam, this young Wittipol

Would have debauch'd my wife, and made me cuckold
Thorough a casement; he did fly her home
To mine own window; but, I think, I sous'd him,[7]
And ravish'd her away out of his pounces.
I have sworn to have him by the ears; I fear
The toy will not do me right.
 Wit. No! that were pity:
What right do you ask, sir? here he is will do't you.
          [*Discovers himself.*

 Fitz. Ha! Wittipol!
 Wit. Ay, sir; no more lady now,
Nor Spaniard.
 Man. No indeed, 'tis Wittipol.
 Fitz. Am I the thing I fear'd?
 Wit. A cuckold! No, sir;
But you were late in possibility,
I'll tell you so much.
 Man. But your wife's too virtuous.
 Wit. We'll see her, sir, at home, and leave you
  here,
To be made duke of Shoreditch with a project.
 Fitz. Thieves! ravishers!
 Wit. Cry but another note, sir,
I'll mar the tune of your pipe.
 Fitz. Give me my deed then.
 Wit. Neither: that shall be kept for your wife's
  good,
Who will know better how to use it.
 Fitz. Ha!
To feast you with my land?
 Wit. Sir, be you quiet,
Or I shall gag you ere I go; consult
Your master of dependences, how to make this

---

[7] *But I* sous'd *him.*] All the copies of the folio which I have
examined, read *sou't*, of which I can make nothing but sought or
sous'd; and I prefer the latter. Whalley reads *fought;* but he
evidently had not consulted the old copy.

A second business, you have time, sir.

> [*Baffles him,*[8] *and exit with* MANLY.

Fitz. Oh!
What will the ghost of my wise grandfather,
My learned father, with my worshipful mother,
Think of me now, that left me in this world
In state to be their heir? that am become
A cuckold, and an ass, and my wife's ward;
Likely to lose my land, have my throat cut;
All by her practice!

Meer. Sir, we are all abused.

Fitz. And be so still! who hinders you, I pray you?
Let me alone, I would enjoy myself,
And be the duke of Drown'd-land you have made me.

Meer. Sir, we must play an after-game of this.

Fitz. But I am not in case to be a gamester,
I tell you once again——

Meer. You must be ruled,
And take some counsel.

Fitz. Sir, I do hate counsel,
As I do hate my wife, my wicked wife!

Meer. But we may think how to recover all,
If you will act.

Fitz. I will not think, nor act,
Nor yet recover; do not talk to me:
I'll run out of my wits, rather than hear;
I will be what I am, Fabian Fitzdottrel,
Though all the world say nay to't.   [*Exit.*

Meer. Let us follow him.   [*Exeunt.*

Baffles *him,*] i. e. passes him with some act of contempt.

ACT V.

SCENE I. *A Room in* TAILBUSH'S *House.*

Enter AMBLER *and* PITFALL.

Ambler.

BUT has my lady miss'd me?
    Pit. Beyond telling.
Here has been that infinity of strangers!
And then she would have had you, to have
    sampled you
With one within, that they are now a teaching,
And does pretend to your rank.
    Amb. Good fellow Pitfall,
Tell master Meercraft I entreat a word with him.
                      [*Exit* PITFALL.
This most unlucky accident will go near
To be the loss of my place, I am in doubt.

Enter MEERCRAFT.

    Meer. With me!—What say you, master Ambler?
    Amb. Sir,
I would beseech your worship, stand between
Me and my lady's displeasure, for my absence.
    Meer. O, is that all! I warrant you.
    Amb. I would tell you, sir,
But how it happen'd.
    Meer. Brief, good master Ambler,
Put yourself to your rack; for I have task
Of more importance.
    Amb. Sir, you'll laugh at me:
But (so is truth) a very friend of mine,

Finding by conference with me, that I lived
Too chaste for my complexion, and indeed
Too honest for my place, sir, did advise me,
If I did love myself,—as that I do,
I must confess—
    Meer. Spare your parenthesis.
    Amb. To give my body a little evacuation——
    Meer. Well, and you went to a whore?
    Amb. No, sir, I durst not
(For fear it might arrive at somebody's ear
It should not) trust myself to a common house;
                [Tells this with extraordinary speed.
But got the gentlewoman to go with me,
And carry her bedding to a conduit-head,
Hard by the place toward Tyburn, which they call
My Lord Mayor's banqueting-house.[9]   Now, sir, this
     morning
Was execution; and I never dreamt on't,
Till I heard the noise of the people, and the horses;
And neither I, nor the poor gentlewoman,
Durst stir, till all was done and past : so that,
In the interim, we fell asleep again.   *[He flags.*
    Meer. Nay, if you fall from your gallop, I am
     gone, sir.
    Amb. But when I waked, to put on my clothes, a
     suit
I made new for the action, it was gone,
And all my money, with my purse, my seals,

---

[9] ————————— *to a conduit-head,*
Hard by the place toward Tyburn, which they call
My Lord Mayor's banqueting-house.] *Tyburn* was anciently a
village, taking its name from the rivulet *Tyburn;* and at the north-
east corner of the bridge over it, was the Lord Mayor's banqueting-
house, near which were nine conduits, erected about 1238 for sup-
plying the city with water.   Here it was usual for the Lord Mayor
and Aldermen to repair, accompanied with their ladies, to view the
conduits, after which was an entertainment at the banqueting-house.
It was taken down in the year 1737.   WHAL.

My hard-wax, and my table-books, my studies,
And a fine new device I had to carry
My pen and ink, my civet, and my tooth-picks,
All under one.　But that which grieved me, was
The gentlewoman's shoes, (with a pair of roses,
And garters, I had given her for the business,)
So as that made us stay till it was dark :
For I was fain to lend her mine, and walk
In a rug, by her, barefoot, to St. Giles's.
　　Meer. A kind of Irish penance ![10]　Is this all, sir ?
　　Amb. To satisfy my lady.
　　Meer. I will promise you, sir.
　　Amb. I have told the true disaster.
　　Meer. I cannot stay with you,
Sir, to condole ; but gratulate your return.　[*Exit.*
　　Amb. An honest gentleman ; but he's never at
　　　　leisure
To be himself, he has such tides of business.　[*Exit.*

SCENE II.　*Another Room in the Same.*

Enter PUG.

Pug.

CALL me home again, dear chief, and put me
To yoking foxes, milking of he-goats,
Pounding of water in a mortar, laving
The sea dry with a nut-shell, gathering all
The leaves are fallen this autumn, drawing farts
Out of dead bodies, making ropes of sand,
Catching the winds together in a net,

[10] *A kind of* Irish penance !]　There is the same allusion to the
rug gowns of the wild Irish, in the *Night Walker* of Fletcher :

　　" We have divided the sexton's household stuff
　　　Among us ; one has the *rug,* and he's turn'd *Irish.*"

Mustering of ants, and numbering atoms ; all
That hell and you thought exquisite torments, rather
Than stay me here a thought more : I would sooner
Keep fleas within a circle,[1] and be accomptant
A thousand year, which of them, and how far,
Out-leap'd the other, than endure a minute
Such as I have within.   There is no hell
To a lady of fashion ; all your tortures there
Are pastimes to it ! 'Twould be a refreshing
For me, to be in the fire again, from hence——

Enter AMBLER, *and surveys him.*

Amb. This is my suit, and those the shoes and
    roses !   [*Aside.*
Pug. They have such impertinent vexations,
A general council of devils could not hit——
Ha! [*sees* AMBLER.] this is he I took asleep with his
    wench,
And borrow'd his clothes.   What might I do to balk
    him ?   [*Aside.*
Amb. Do you hear, sir ?
Pug. Answer him, but not to the purpose. [*Aside.*
Amb. What is your name, I pray you, sir ?
Pug. Is't so late, sir ?
Amb. I ask not of the time, but of your name, sir.
Pug. I thank you, sir : yes, it does hold, sir, certain.
Amb. Hold, sir ! what holds ? I must both hold,
    and talk to you
About these clothes.

---

[1] ————————— *I would sooner*
Keep fleas within a circle, &c.] This is taken from an employment of the same kind, which Aristophanes has given to Socrates:

Ανηρετ' αρτι Χαιρεφωντα Σωκρατης
Ψυλλαν ὑποσους αλλοιτο τους αυτης ποζας ; &c.

                      Nubes, A. i. S. 2.   WHAL.

  This, I believe, Whalley took from Upton : the resemblance between the two passages is somewhat like that between Fluellin's
two rivers—"there is" fleas "in both."

Pug. A very pretty lace ;
But the tailor cozen'd me.
　Amb. No, I am cozen'd
By you ; robb'd.
　Pug. Why, when you please, sir ; I am,
For three-penny gleek, your man.
　Amb. Pox o' your gleek,
And three-pence ! give me an answer.
　Pug. Sir,
My master is the best at it.
　Amb. Your master !
Who is your master ?
　Pug. Let it be Friday-night.
　Amb. What should be then ?
　Pug. Your best song's *Tom o' Bethlem.*
　Amb. I think you are he.—Does he mock me,
　　trow, from purpose,
Or do not I speak to him what I mean ?—
Good sir, your name.
　Pug. Only a couple of cocks, sir ;
If we can get a widgeon, 'tis in season.
　Amb. He hopes to make one of these sceptics of me,
(I think I name them right,) and does not fly me ;
I wonder at that : 'tis a strange confidence !
I'll prove another way, to draw his answer.
　　　　　　　　　　　[Exeunt severally.

SCENE III. *A Room in* FITZDOTTREL'S *House.*

Enter MEERCRAFT, FITZDOTTREL, *and* EVERILL.

Meercraft.

T is the easiest thing, sir, to be done,
　　As plain as fizzling : roll but with your eyes,
　　And foam at the mouth. A little castle-soap
Will do't, to rub your lips ; and then a nut-shell,

With tow, and touch-wood in it, to spit fire.
Did you ne'er read, sir, little Darrel's tricks
With the boy of Burton,[2] and the seven in Lancashire,
Somers at Nottingham? all these do teach it.
And we'll give out, sir, that your wife has bewitch'd you.
    Ever. And practised with those two, as sorcerers.
    Meer. And gave you potions, by which means you
        were
Not *compos mentis*, when you made your feoffment.
There's no recovery of your state but this;
This, sir, will sting.

---

[2] *Did you ne'er read, sir, little* Darrel's tricks
With the boy of Burton, &c.] Impostures of this kind, the inventions of the jesuits, were frequent in the age of Jonson. Dr. Harsnet, who died archbishop of York, was fortunate in the discovery of the tricks made use of by these artists; and published them to the world. There is a pamphlet of his entituled, *A discovery of the fraudulent practices of John Darrel, minister,* in answer to a *True narration of the strange and grievous vexation by the devil of seven persons in Lancashire, and William Somers of Nottingham.* As the book is not easily to be met with, I am unable to give the reader the particulars of the cheat. WHAL.

Dr. Harsnet's *Discovery,* which is a book of considerable size, was published in 1599. Darrel, who was a puritan preacher at Mansfield, replied to it in the following year, in a treatise full of "sound and fury," and has contrived to render it somewhat doubtful, whether he was a dupe or an impostor. In any case, there was assuredly more efficient agency than his at hand; there were *spirits at work* of whom he knew little or nothing. The *Boy of Burton* was one Thomas Darling, for the bewitching of whom, a poor old woman of the name of Alice Goodridge was condemned to the gallows, which she only escaped by dying in prison. Darrel dispossessed this booby of a spirit which Alice had sent to torment him: the credit which he got by this notable achievement, he lost by *Somers of Nottingham;* and in consequence of the discovery of the imposture, which yet he always affected to maintain, he was degraded from the ministry, and committed to prison. This took place in 1598. The *seven in Lancashire* belonged to the family of a Mr. Starkey, a mischievous crack-brained idiot, who accused one Edmund Hartley of bewitching them, and had credit enough with a judge and jury, as weak and credulous as himself, to get the poor man condemned and executed, at Lancaster, in 1597.

Ever. And move in a court of equity.

Meer. For it is more than manifest, that this was
A plot of your wife's, to get your land.

Fitz. I think it.

Ever. Sir, it appears.

Meer. Nay, and my cousin has known
These gallants in these shapes——

Ever. To have done strange things, sir,
One as the lady, the other as the squire.

Meer. How a man's honesty may be fool'd ! I
    thought him
A very lady.

Fitz. So did I ; renounce me else.

Meer. But this way, sir, you'll be revenged at
    height.

Ever. Upon them all.

Meer. Yes, faith, and since your wife
Has run the way of woman thus, e'en give her——

Fitz. Lost, by this hand, to me ; dead to all joys
Of her dear Dottrel ; I shall never pity her,
That could [not] pity herself.

Meer. Princely resolv'd, sir,
And like yourself still, *in potentiâ.*

Enter GILTHEAD, PLUTARCHUS, SLEDGE, *and* Serjeants.

Meer. Gilthead ! what news ?

Fitz. O, sir, my hundred pieces !
Let me have them yet.

Gilt. Yes, sir.—Officers,
Arrest him.

Fitz. Me !

1 *Serj.* I arrest you.

Sledge. Keep the peace,
I charge you, gentlemen.

Fitz. Arrest me ! why ?

Gilt. For better security, sir. My son Plutarchus
Assures me, you are not worth a groat.

Plu. Pardon me, father,
I said his worship had no foot of land left :
And that I'll justify, for I writ the deed.
    Fitz. Have you these tricks in the city ?
    Gilt. Yes, and more :
Arrest this gallant too, here, at my suit.
                            [*Points to* MEERCRAFT.
    Sledge. Ay, and at mine: he owes me for his
        lodging
Two year and a quarter.
    Meer. Why, master Gilthead,—landlord,
Thou art not mad, though thou art constable,
Puft up with the pride of the place. Do you hear, sirs,
Have I deserv'd this from you two, for all
My pains at court, to get you each a patent ?
    Gilt. For what ?
    Meer. Upon my project of the forks.
    Sledge. Forks ! what be they ?
    Meer. The laudable use of forks,
Brought into custom here, as they are in Italy,[3]
To the sparing of napkins : that, that should have made
Your bellows go at the forge, as his at the furnace.
I have procured it, have the signet for it,
Dealt with the linen-drapers on my private,
Because I fear'd they were the likeliest ever
To stir against, to cross it : for 'twill be

---

[3] —— *the laudable use of* forks,
Brought into custom here, as they are in Italy.] The practice of
eating with forks, which had its rise in Italy, came about this time
into England : and some kind of affectation in the use of them,
probably gave the poet an occasion to ridicule the invention itself.
The German divine, indeed, who preached against the custom,
thought it an insult on providence not to touch one's meat with
one's fingers. Tom Coriat tells us that this custom was not used
in any other country that he saw in his travels, nor by any other
nation of Christendom, but only Italy. After having described the
manner of holding the knife and fork at large, " Hereupon," says
he, " I myself thought good to imitate the Italian fashion, by this
forked cutting of meate, not only while I was in Italy, but also in

A mighty saver of linen through the kingdom,
As that is one o' my grounds, and to spare washing.
Now, on you two had I laid all the profits :
Gilthead to have the making of all those
Of gold and silver, for the better personages ;
And you, of those of steel for the common sort :
And both by patent. I had brought you your seals in,
But now you have prevented me, and I thank you.
   Sledge. Sir, I will bail you, at mine own apperil.[4]

Germany, and oftentimes in England since I came home." *Cru-*
dities, p. 90.
   The use of forks is bantered likewise by Beaumont and Fletcher,
as the mark of both a traveller and courtier :

> " It doth express th' enamoured courtier,
>   As full as your *fork-carving* traveller."
>   *Queen of Corinth*, A. iv. S. 1.

And so in *Monsieur Thomas*, A. i. S. 2.

>   " he eats with *picks !*
>   Utterly spoil'd."

A project of tooth-picks has been just mentioned, which was another object of satire to our author's contemporaries. So Fletcher,

> " You that enhance the daily price of *tooth-picks*."

And Shakspeare could not omit it in his description of the finical
traveller, in *King John*. WHAL.
   [4] *Sir, I will bail you, at mine own* apperil.] *Sledge is brought about*
(the margin says) by this hopeful project. But I have yet an observation to make on this line. In *Timon of Athens*, at the state
banquet, A. i. S. 2, Apemantus says,

> " Let me stay at thine *apperil*, Timon,
>   I come to observe," &c.

Here Mr. Steevens and Mr. Malone, who profess such entire vene-
ration for the purity of Shakspeare's text, interpose their judgment,
and corrupt it to

> " Let me stay at thine *own peril*, Timon ;"

and the latter adds, " I have not been able to find such a word as
apperil in any dictionary, nor is it reconcilable to etymology ! I
have therefore adopted the *emendation* made by Mr. Steevens."
   " *Apperil*," subjoins Mr. Ritson, " may be right, though *no other*
instance of it has been, or *possibly can be produced !* "
   If these notes serve for no better purpose, they will at least suffice

Meer. Nay, choose.

Plu. Do you so too, good father.

Gilt. I like the fashion of the project well,
The forks! it may be a lucky one! and is
Not intricate, as one would say, but fit for
Plain heads, as ours, to deal in.—Do you hear, .
Officers, we discharge you.   [*Exeunt* Serjeants.

Meer. Why, this shews
A little good-nature in you, I confess;
But do not tempt your friends thus.—Little Gilthead,
Advise your sire, great Gilthead, from these courses :
And, here, to trouble a great man in reversion,
For a matter of fifty, in a false alarm !
Away, it shews not well.   Let him get the pieces
And bring them : you'll hear more else.

Plu. Father.   [*Exeunt* GILT. *and* PLU.

Enter AMBLER, *dragging in* PUG.

Amb. O, master Sledge, are you here ?   I have
        been to seek you.
You are the constable, they say.   Here's one

to prove how diligently Jonson has been studied by those eternal
calumniators of his talents and reputation.   The word occurs again
in the *Magnetic Lady.*

Now I am on the subject, I will trouble the reader with another
example of this rash mode of assertion, without a competent degree
of information.   In *Henry IV.* 1st Part, the king says,

" As far as *to* the sepulchre of Christ,
    Forthwith a power of English shall we *levy.*"

" To levy a power as far as to the sepulchre of Christ," subjoins
Mr. Steevens, " is an expression *quite* unexampled, if not corrupt;"
—and he accordingly proposes to read *lead* for *levy !* But there is
no occasion.   The expression is neither *unexampled* nor *corrupt;*
but good authorized English.   One instance of it is before me.
"Scipio, before he *levied* his force *to* the walles of Carthage, gave
his soldiers the print of the citie in a cake to be devoured." Gosson's *School of Abuse,* 1587, E. 4.   Mr. Douce will see from this,
that he also is mistaken.

That I do charge with felony, for the suit
He wears, sir.
   Meer. Who ? master Fitzdottrel's man !
Ware what you do, master Ambler.

Enter FITZDOTTREL.

   Amb. Sir, these clothes
I'll swear are mine ; and the shoes the gentlewoman's
I told you of : and have him afore a justice
I will.
   Pug. My master, sir, will pass his word for me.
   Amb. O, can you speak to purpose now ?
   Fitz. Not I,
If you be such a one, sir, I will leave you [5]
To your godfathers in law : let twelve men work.
   Pug. Do you hear, sir, pray, in private.
[*Takes him aside.*

   Fitz. Well, what say you ?
Brief, for I have no time to lose.
   Pug. Truth is, sir,
I am the very Devil, and had leave
To take this body I am in to serve you ;
Which was a cut-purse's, and hang'd this morning :
And it is likewise true, I stole this suit
To clothe me with ; but, sir, let me not go
To prison for it.   I have hitherto
Lost time, done nothing ; shown, indeed, no part
Of my devil's nature : now, I will so help
Your malice, 'gainst these parties ; so advance
The business that you have in hand, of witchcraft,
And your possession, as myself were in you ;

-----

[5] ——————— *I will leave you*
   To your godfathers in law, &c.] This seems to have been a
standing joke for a jury.   It is used by Shakspeare and by writers
prior to him.   Thus Bulleyn, speaking of a knavish ostler, says, " I
did see him ones aske blessying to xii godfathers at ones." *Dialogue*, 1564.

Teach you such tricks to make your belly swell,
And your eyes turn, to foam, to stare, to gnash
Your teeth together, and to beat yourself,
Laugh loud, and feign six voices——

    Fitz. Out, you rogue !
You most infernal counterfeit wretch, avant !
Do you think to gull me with your Æsop's fables ?
Here, take him to you, I have no part in him.

    Pug. Sir——

    Fitz. Away ! I do disclaim, I will not hear you.
                     [*Exit* SLEDGE *with* PUG.

    Meer. What said he to you, sir ?

    Fitz. Like a lying rascal,
Told me he was the Devil.

    Meer. How ! a good jest.

    Fitz. And that he would teach me such fine
        devil's tricks
For our new resolution.

    Ever. O, pox on him !
'Twas excellent wisely done, sir, not to trust him.

    Meer. Why, if he were the Devil, we shall not
        need him,
If you'll be ruled.   Go throw yourself on a bed,
        sir,
And feign you ill.   We'll not be seen with you
Till after, that you have a fit ; and all
Confirm'd within.   Keep you with the two ladies,
                    [*To* EVERILL.
And persuade them.   I will to justice Eitherside,
And possess him with all.   Trains shall seek out
        Engine,
And they two fill the town with't ; every cable
Is to be veer'd.   We must employ out all
Our emissaries now.   Sir, I will send you
Bladders and bellows.   Sir, be confident,
'Tis no hard thing t'outdo the Devil in ;
A boy of thirteen year old made him an ass,

But t'other day.[6]
    Fitz. Well, I'll begin to practise,
And scape the imputation of being cuckold,
By mine own act.
    Meer. You are right.   [*Exit* FITZ.
    Ever. Come, you have put
Yourself to a simple coil here, and your friends,
By dealing with new agents, in new plots.
    Meer. No more of that, sweet cousin.
    Ever. What had you
To do with this same Wittipol, for a lady?
    Meer. Question not that; 'tis done.
    Ever. You had some strain
Bove *e-la*?

[6] *'Tis no hard thing t'outdo the Devil in;*
    A boy of thirteen year old made him an ass,
      But t'other day.] This is evidently an allusion to the boy of Bilson in Staffordshire, who was practised on by some jesuits, and counterfeited possession by the devil. The cheat was discovered by Dr. Morton, at that time bishop of the diocese. The story, with all the particulars, may be met with in Wilson's history of James the First. The same imposture seems to be referred to by the poet, in the third scene of this act:

      "Did you ne'er read, sir, little Darrel's tricks
      With the boy of Burton?"———

But either Jonson's memory deceived him, or the passage is corrupted; unless Bilson be in the neighbourhood or parish of Burton: for I know of no other imposture so remarkable about that time. WHAL.

Bilson and Burton are both in Staffordshire:—but the *deception* rests with the commentator, not the poet. Jonson could not allude to the "boy of Bilson," as the juggling of this young impostor did not take place till 1620, four years after the appearance of this play; and twenty-five, at least, after the adventure of the "boy of Burton," with whom Whalley most strangely confounds him. The person to whom the text alludes, is Thomas Harrison, a youth of *twelve years old*, better known as the *boy of Norwich*. He was subject to fits, and those about him had the art to make him pass for a demoniac. His possession, which created no small trouble to the clergy, and "made asses" of more than Jonson speaks of, was at the height in 1605.

Meer. I had indeed.

Ever. And now you crack for't.

Meer. Do not upbraid me.

Ever. Come, you must be told on't;
You are so covetous still to embrace
More than you can, that you lose all.

Meer. 'Tis right :
What would you more than guilty ?   Now, your
         succours.   [*Exeunt.*

SCENE IV. *A Cell in Newgate.*

Enter SHACKLES, *with* PUG *in chains.*

Shackles.

ERE you are lodged, sir; you must send your
         garnish,
      If you'll be private.

Pug. There it is, sir : leave me. [*Exit* SHACKLES.
To Newgate brought ! how is the name of devil
Discredited in me ! what a lost fiend
Shall I be on return ! my chief will roar
In triumph, now, that I have been on earth
A day, and done no noted thing, but brought
That body back here, was hang'd out this morning.
Well ! would it once were midnight, that I knew
My utmost.   I think Time be drunk and sleeps,
He is so still, and moves not ! I do glory
Now in my torment.   Neither can I expect it,
I have it with my fact.   .

Enter INIQUITY.

Iniq. Child of hell, be thou merry :
Put a look on as round, boy, and red as a cherry.
Cast care at thy posterns, and firk in thy fetters :

They are ornaments, baby, have graced thy betters :
Look upon me, and hearken.   Our chief doth salute
   thee,
And lest the cold iron should chance to confute thee,[7]
He hath sent thee grant-parole by me, to stay longer
A month here on earth, against cold, child, or hunger.
 Pug. How! longer here a month?
 Iniq. Yes, boy, till the session,
That so thou mayst have a triumphal egression.
 Pug. In a cart, to be hang'd!
 Iniq. No, child, in a car,
The chariot of triumph, which most of them are.
And in the mean time, to be greasy, and bouzy,
And nasty, and filthy, and ragged, and lousy,
With damn me! renounce me! and all the fine
   phrases,
That bring unto Tyburn the plentiful gazes.
 Pug. He is a devil, and may be our chief,
The great superior devil, for his malice !
Arch-devil ! I acknowledge him.   He knew
What I would suffer, when he tied me up thus
In a rogue's body; and he has, I thank him,
His tyrannous pleasure on me, to confine me
To the unlucky carcase of a cut-purse,
Wherein I could do nothing.

Enter SATAN.

 Sat. Impudent fiend,
Stop thy lewd mouth.[8]   Dost thou not shame and
   tremble

---

 [7] —— *Our chief doth salute thee,*
  And lest the cold iron *should chance to* confute *thee.*] This is a
pure Latinism. *Confutare* is properly to pour cold water into a
pot, to prevent it from boiling over; and hence metaphorically, the
signification of *confuting*, reproving, or controlling. So Tully uses
the expression, *confutare audaciam.* WHAL.
 [8] *Stop thy* lewd *mouth,*] i. e. thy licentious and ignorant censure.
I should scarcely have thought this worthy of a note, had not the

To lay thine own dull, damn'd defects upon
An innocent case there ? Why, thou heavy slave !
The spirit that did possess that flesh before,
Put more true life in a finger and a thumb,
Than thou in the whole mass : yet thou rebell'st
And murmur'st ! What one proffer hast thou made,
Wicked enough, this day, that might be call'd
Worthy thine own, much less the name that sent thee ?
First, thou didst help thyself into a beating,
Promptly, and with't endangered'st too thy tongue :
A devil, and could not keep a body entire
One day ! that, for our credit : and to vindicate it,
Hinder'dst, for aught thou know'st, a deed of dark-
      ness :
Which was an act of that egregious folly,
As no one, toward the devil, could have thought on.

last editor of Beaumont and Fletcher, with his usual ill fortune,
stumbled upon this word and misinterpreted it. " Lewd (he says)
is continually used for *idle* by old authors. So in Ben Jonson's
Volpone :

     ———— " ' they are most *lewd* impostors,
     Made all of terms and shreds.' "   Vol. xiv. p. 58.

   This interpretation proves one of two things, either that Mr.
Weber never read the passage in Jonson, or that he does not understand it : perhaps it proves both. Sir Politick and Peregrine
are talking of Mountebanks. The former observes :

   " They are the only *knowing* men of Europe,
    Great general scholars, excellent physicians,
    Most admired statesmen," &c.

To this the latter replies :

   " And I have heard they are most *lewd* impostors,
    Made all of terms and shreds."

What, in the name of consistency, has *idle* to do here ? Can any
thing be clearer than that *lewd* is used in its genuine and ancient
sense, of *ignorant* and *illiterate ?* It is quite enough for Mr. Weber
to *explain* Fletcher and Ford : the author of *Volpone* is almost as
much above his comprehension as he has proved to be above his
malice ; and prudence, no less than justice, should have checked
his meddling.

This for your acting.—But, for suffering !—why
Thou hast been cheated on, with a false beard,
And a turn'd cloke : faith, would your predecessor
The cut-purse, think you, have been so ?   Out upon
        thee !
The hurt thou hast done, to let men know their
        strength,
And that they are able to outdo a devil
Put in a body, will for ever be
A scar upon our name !   Whom hast thou dealt with,
Woman or man, this day, but have outgone thee
Some way, and most have proved the better fiends ?
Yet you would be employ'd !   yes ; hell shall make you
Provincial of the cheaters, or bawd-ledger,
For this side of the town !   no doubt, you'll render
A rare account of things !   Bane of your itch,
And scratching for employment !   I'll have brimstone
To allay it sure, and fire to singe your nails off.—
But that I would not such a damn'd dishonour
Stick on our state, as that the devil were hang'd,
And could not save a body, that he took
From Tyburn, but it must come thither again ;
You should e'en ride.   But up, away with him—
               [INIQUITY *takes him on his back*.
  Iniq. Mount, dearling of darkness, my shoulders
      are broad :
He that carries the fiend, is sure of his load.
The devil was wont to carry away the Evil,
But now the Evil outcarries the devil.   [*Exeunt*.
               [*A loud explosion, smoke, &c.*

Enter SHACKLES, *and the* Under-keepers, *affrighted*.
  Shack. O me !
  1 *Keep.* What's this ?
  2 *Keep.* A piece of Justice-hall[9]

  [9] *Justice-hall.*]   The name of the Sessions-house in the Old
Bailey.

Is broken down.

3 *Keep.* Fough! what a steam of brimstone
Is here!

4 *Keep.* The prisoner's dead, came in but now.

Shack. Ha! where?

4 *Keep.* Look here.

1 *Keep.* 'Slid, I should know his countenance:
It is Gill Cutpurse, was hang'd out this morning.

Shack. 'Tis he!

2 *Keep.* The devil sure has a hand in this!

3 *Keep.* What shall we do?

Shack. Carry the news of it
Unto the sheriffs.

1 *Keep.* And to the justices.

4 *Keep.* This is strange.

3 *Keep.* And savours of the devil strongly.

2 *Keep.* I have the sulphur of hell-coal in my nose.

1 *Keep.* Fough!

Shack. Carry him in.

1 *Keep.* Away.

2 *Keep.* How rank it is!   [*Exeunt with the body.*

SCENE V.   *A Room in* FITZDOTTREL'S *House.*

FITZDOTTREL *discovered in bed;* Lady EITHERSIDE,
TAILBUSH, AMBLER, TRAINS, *and* PITFALL, *standing
by him.*

Enter Sir PAUL EITHERSIDE, MEERCRAFT, *and*
EVERILL.

Sir P. Eitherside.

THIS was the notablest conspiracy
That e'er I heard of.

Meer. Sir, they had given him potions,
That did enamour him on the counterfeit lady—

Ever. Just to the time o' delivery of the deed.
Meer. And then the witchcraft 'gan to appear, for
     straight
He fell into his fit.
     Ever. Of rage at first, sir,
Which since has so increased.
     Lady T. Good sir Paul, see him,
And punish the impostors.
     Sir P. Eith. Therefore I come, madam.
     Lady E. Let master Eitherside alone, madam.
     Sir P. Eith. Do you hear?
Call in the constable, I will have him by;
He's the king's officer: and some citizens
Of credit; I'll discharge my conscience clearly.
     Meer. Yes, sir, and send for his wife.
     Ever. And the two sorcerers,
By any means.   [*Exit* AMBLER.
     Lady T. I thought one a true lady,
I should be sworn: so did you, Eitherside.
     Lady E. Yes, by that light, would I might ne'er
          stir else, Tailbush.
     Lady T. And the other, a civil gentleman.
     Ever. But, madam,
You know what I told your ladyship.
     Lady T. I now see it.
I was providing of a banquet for them,
After I had done instructing of the fellow,
De-vile, the gentleman's man.
     Meer. Who is found a thief, madam,
And to have robb'd your usher, master Ambler,
This morning.
     Lady T. How!
     Meer. I'll tell you more anon.
     Fitz. *Give me some garlic, garlic, garlic, garlic!*
                              [*He begins his fit.*
     Meer. Hark, the poor gentleman, how he is tor-
          mented!

Fitz. My wife is a whore, I'll kiss her no more : and
    why ?
May'st not thou be a cuckold as well as I ?
Ha, ha, ha, ha, ha, ha, ha !
    Sir P. Eith. That is the devil speaks and laughs
        in him.
    Meer. Do you think so, sir ?
    Sir P. Eith. I discharge my conscience.
    Fitz. And is not the devil good company ? yes, wis.
    Ever. How he changes, sir, his voice !
    Fitz. And a cuckold is,
Wherever he put his head, with a wannion,
If his horns be forth, the devil's companion.
Look, look, look, else !
    Meer. How he foams !
    Ever. And swells !
    Lady T. O me, what's that there rises in his belly ?
    Lady E. A strange thing : hold it down.
    Tra. Pit. We cannot, madam.
    Sir P. Eith. 'Tis too apparent this !
    Fitz. Wittipol, Wittipol !

Enter WITTIPOL, MANLY, *and* Mrs. FITZDOTTREL.

    Wit. How now ! what play have we here ?
    Man. What fine new matters ?
    Wit. The cockscomb and the coverlet.
    Meer. O strange impudence,
That these should come to face their sin !
    Ever. And outface
Justice ! they are the parties, sir.
    Sir P. Eith. Say nothing.
    Meer. Did you mark, sir, upon their coming in,
How he call'd Wittipol ?
    Ever. And never saw them.
    Sir P. Eith. I warrant you did I : let them play
        awhile.
    Fitz. Buz, buz, buz, buz !

Lady T. 'Las, poor gentleman,
How he is tortured!
Mrs. Fitz. [*goes to him.*] Fie, master Fitzdottrel!
What do you mean to counterfeit thus?
Fitz. O, O!
She comes with a needle, and thrusts it in,
She pulls out that, and she puts in a pin,
And now, and now, I do not know how, nor where,
But she pricks me here, and she pricks me there: Oh, oh!
Sir P. Eith. Woman, forbear.
Wit. What, sir?
Sir P. Eith. A practice foul
For one so fair.
Wit. Hath this, then, credit with you?
Man. Do you believe in't?
Sir P. Eith. Gentlemen, I'll discharge
My conscience : 'tis a clear conspiracy,
A dark and devilish practice! I detest it.
Wit. The justice sure will prove the merrier man.
Man. This is most strange, sir.
Sir P. Eith. Come not to confront
Authority with impudence ; I tell you,
I do detest it.—

Re-enter AMBLER, *with* SLEDGE *and* GILTHEAD.

Here comes the king's constable,
And with him a right worshipful commoner,
My good friend, master Gilthead.   I am glad
I can, before such witnesses, profess
My conscience, and my detestation of it.
Horrible! most unnatural! abominable!
Ever. You do not tumble enough.
Meer. Wallow, gnash.   [*They whisper him.*
Lady T. O, how he is vexed!
Sir P. Eith. 'Tis too manifest.
Ever. Give him more soap to foam with.   [*To*
   MEER.] Now lie still.
Meer. And act a little.

Lady T. What does he now, sir ?

Sir P. Eith. Shew
The taking of tobacco, with which the devil
Is so delighted.

Fitz. *Hum !*

Sir P. Eith. And calls for hum.
You takers of strong waters and tobacco,
Mark this.

Fitz. *Yellow, yellow, yellow, yellow !*

Sir P. Eith. That's starch ! the devil's idol of that
        colour.
He ratifies it with clapping of his hands ;
The proofs are pregnant.[1]

---

[1] *That's starch ! the devil's idol of that colour.*
    He ratifies it with clapping of his hands ;
    The proofs are pregnant.] *The Justice* (as the margin tells us)
interprets all. The whole of this ridiculous scene is a close copy of
the tricks which were actually played by the impostors who pretended to be bewitched, and in consequence of which, many unfortunate creatures, guilty of age and poverty, were barbarously
sacrificed. There were, at that time, on the bench of justices
many sir Paul Eithersides, hard, unfeeling, superstitious wiseacres ;
but the person who sat for the sir Paul of the text, was John Darrel, whose explication of the dumb shew of the pretended demoniacs, is literally taken from Harsnett's *Discourse.* Fitzdottrel is
Somers ; and the resemblance is no less perfect in this than in the
former case. The *mouse*, the *soap*, the *bellows*, the *contortions*, the
crambo-rhymes, the *jargon in different languages*, &c., were all real
circumstances, and are mentioned in various parts of the bishop's
book. "Somers acted (says Dr. Hutchinson) all the sins of Nottingham by signs, and Darrel explained them to the people, as
Somers acted them." *Impostures detected*, p. 248. A ballad was
made upon the subject ; part of it ran thus :

> " But when that master Darrel came,
>   The Devil was vexed with the same ;
>   His limbs he *rack'd*, he *rent*, he *tore*,
>   Far worser than he did before ;
>   He play'd the *antick* there in scorns
>   And flouted men, in *making horns :*
>   And after that, he did bewray
>   How men at *cards and dice do play ;*
>   And by the *clapping of his hands*,
>   He shew'd the *starching* of our bands," &c.

Gilt. How the devil can act!

Sir P. Eith. He is the master of players, master
    Gilthead,
And poets too : you heard him talk in rhyme,
I had forgot to observe it to you, erewhile !

Lady T. See, he spits fire !

Sir P. Eith. O no, he plays at figgum ;
The devil is the author of wicked figgum.[2]

Man. Why speak you not unto him ?

Wit. If I had
All innocence of man to be endanger'd,
And he could save or ruin it, I'd not breathe
A syllable in request, to such a fool
He makes himself.

   Fitz. O they whisper, whisper, whisper,
We shall have more of devils a score,
To come to dinner, in me the sinner.

   Lady E. Alas, poor gentleman !

Sir P. Eith. Put them asunder ;
Keep them one from the other.

   Man. Are you phrenetic, sir ?
Or what grave dotage moves you to take part
With so much villainy ? we are not afraid
Either of law or trial ; let us be
Examined what our ends were, what the means
To work by, and possibility of those means :
Do not conclude against us ere you hear us.

   Sir P. Eith. I will not hear you, yet I will conclude

---

  [2] *See, he spits fire !*
   O no, he plays at figgum.] "Sir Paul (the margin says) interprets *figgum* to be a juggler's game !" this however affords little
information as to its nature. In some of our old dictionaries, *fid*
is explained to caulk with oakum : figgum, or fig'em, may therefore be a vulgar derivative from this term, and signify the lighted
flax or tow with which jugglers stuff their mouths when they pre-
pare to amuse the rustics by breathing out smoke and flames :

      ———— "a nut-shell
With tow, and touch-wood in it, to spit fire." p. 126.

Out of the circumstances.

Man. Will you so, sir ?

Sir P. Eith. Yes, they are palpable.

Man. Not as your folly.

Sir P. Eith. I will discharge my conscience, and
    do all

To the meridian of justice.

Gilt. You do well, sir.

Fitz. *Provide me to eat, three or four dishes o' good
    meat,*

I'll feast them and their trains, a justice head and brains
Shall be the first.—

Sir P. Eith. The devil loves not justice,

There you may see.

Fitz. *A spare rib of my wife,*

And a whore's purtenance; a Gilthead whole.

Sir P. Eith. Be not you troubled, sir, the devil
    speaks it.

Fitz. *Yes, wis, knight, shite, Poul, joul, owl, foul,
    troul, boul!*

Sir P. Eith. Crambo! another of the devil's games.

Meer. Speak, sir, some Greek, if you can. [*Aside
    to* FITZ.] Is not the justice

A solemn gamester ?

Ever. Peace.

Fitz. Οἰ μοὶ, κακοδαίμων,

Καὶ τρισκακοδαίμων, καὶ τετράκις, καὶ πεντάκις,

Καὶ δωδεκάκις καὶ μυριάκις.[3]

Sir P. Eith. He curses

In Greek, I think.

Ever. Your Spanish, that I taught you.

                    [*Aside to* FITZ.

Fitz. *Quebrémos el ojo de burlas.*

Ever. How !—your rest——

   [3] *Fitz.* Οἰ μοὶ, κακοδαίμων,

      Καὶ τρισκακοδαίμων, &c.] This is from the *Plutus* of
Aristophanes, Act iv. S. 3. WHAL.

5   L

Let's break his neck in jest, the devil says.

    Fitz. *Di gratia, signòr mio, se havete denari fata-*
      méne parte.

    Meer. What! would the devil borrow money?

    Fitz. *Ouy, ouy, monsieur, un pauvre diable, diablctin.*

    Sir P. Eith. It is the devil, by his several lan-
      guages.

    Enter SHACKLES, *with the things found on the*
      body of the Cut-purse.

    Shack. Where's sir Paul Eitherside?

    Sir P. Eith. Here; what's the matter?

    Shack. O, such an accident fallen out at Newgate,
      sir:

A great piece of the prison is rent down!
The devil has been there, sir, in the body
Of the young cut-purse, was hang'd out this morning,
But in new clothes, sir; every one of us know him.
These things were found in his pocket.

    Amb. Those are mine, sir.

    Shack. I think he was committed on your charge,
      sir,

For a new felony.

    Amb. Yes.

    Shack. He's gone, sir, now,

And left us the dead body; but withal, sir,
Such an infernal stink and steam behind,
You cannot see St. Pulchre's steeple yet:
They smell't as far as Ware, as the wind lies,
By this time, sure.

    Fitz. [*starts up.*] Is this upon your credit, friend?

    Shack. Sir, you may see, and satisfy yourself.

    Fitz. Nay then, 'tis time to leave off counterfeit-
      ing.——

Sir, I am not bewitch'd, nor have a devil,
No more than you; I do defy him, I,
And did abuse you: these two gentlemen

Put me upon it.   (I have faith against him.)
They taught me all my tricks.   I will tell truth,
And shame the fiend.   See here, sir, are my bellows,
And my false belly, and my mouse, and all
That should have come forth.
 Man. Sir, are you not ashamed
Now of your solemn, serious vanity?
 Sir P. Eith. I will make honourable amends to
  truth.
 Fitz. And so will I.   But these are cozeners still,
And have my land, as plotters, with my wife;
Who, though she be not a witch, is worse, a whore.
 Man. Sir, you belie her: she is chaste and virtuous,
And we are honest.   I do know no glory
A man should hope, by venting his own follies;
But you'll still be an ass in spite of providence.
Please you go in, sir, and hear truths, then judge 'em,
And make amends for your late rashness: when
You shall but hear the pains, and care was taken
To save this fool from ruin, his Grace of Drown'd-
  land——
 Fitz. My land is drown'd indeed——
 Sir P. Eith. Peace.
 Man. And how much
His modest and too worthy wife hath suffer'd
By misconstruction from him, you will blush,
First, for your own belief, more for his actions.
His land is his; and never by my friend,
Or by myself, meant to another use,
But for her succours, who hath equal right.
If any other had worse counsels in it,
(I know I speak to those can apprehend me)
Let them repent them, and be not detected.——
It is not manly to take joy or pride
In human errors: we do all ill things;
They do them worst that love them, and dwell there,
Till the plague comes.   The few that have the seeds

Of goodness left, will sooner make their way
To a true life, by shame, than punishment.
               [*He comes forward for the Epilogue.*

Thus the projector here is overthrown;
But I have now a project of mine own,
If it may pass, that no man would invite
The poet from us, to sup forth to-night,
If the play please.   If it displeasant be,
We do presume that no man will, nor we.   [*Exeunt.*

So much has incidentally appeared in the notes, on the two great
objects of this drama, the powerful ridicule of monopolists and projectors, and the exposure of pretended demoniacs and witch-finders,
(the crying evils of the time,) that little or nothing remains to be
added on either, in this place.   Another opportunity will be afforded
of recurring to the subject of witchcraft, and the subsequent play
brings forward another set of projectors.

There is much good writing in this comedy.   All the speeches
of Satan are replete with the most biting satire, delivered with an
appropriate degree of spirit.   Fitzdottrel is one of those characters
which Jonson delighted to draw, and in which he stood unrivalled,
a *gull*, i.e. a confident coxcomb, selfish, cunning, and conceited.
Mrs. Fitzdottrel possesses somewhat more interest than the gene-
rality of our author's females, and is, indeed, a well-sustained character.   In action, the principal amusement of the scene (exclusive
of the admirable burlesque of witchery in the conclusion) was probably derived from the mortification of poor Pug, whose stupid
stare of amazement at finding himself made an *ass* of on every possible occasion, must, if pourtrayed as some then on the stage were
well able to pourtray it, have been exquisitely comic.

This play is strictly moral in its conception and conduct.   Knavery
and folly are shamed and corrected, virtue is strengthened and re-
warded, and the ends of dramatic justice are sufficiently answered
by the simple exposure of those whose errors are merely subservient to the minor interests of the piece.

THE STAPLE OF NEWS.

THE STAPLE OF NEWS.] This Comedy was first acted by "his Majesty's Servants" in 1625, and entered soon after in the Stationers' Books, though no earlier copy of it is known than that of the old folio, which bears date in 1631. Nine years had elapsed since our author's last appearance on the stage ; in the interval he appears to have spent a great part of his time not unpleasantly. He was engaged in writing masques for the court and divers of the nobility, at whose houses probably he occasionally resided ; and he visited Scotland. During this period too, some of the works which perished in the conflagration of his library, must have been composed, as is proved from the *Execration on Vulcan*. Want, perhaps, originating in illness, drove him again to the stage, for an unfavourable change in his circumstances seems to have taken place about this period.

With respect to the printing of this play, I think of it as I did of the preceding one, and as I continue to do of all the rest which appear in the folio of 1631,[1] or, as it should rather be called, of 1641, that Jonson gave himself no concern about the matter.

The motto to the old edition is from Horace ; it is sufficiently trite, and had been more than once applied by the poet to his preceding labours :

> *Aut prodesse volunt, aut delectare poetæ :*
> *Aut simul et jucunda, et idonea dicere vitæ.*

---

[1] The only play which, according to my opinion, Jonson gave to the press after the folio of 1616, was the *New Inn*, which he printed in small 8vo. this year (1631), and for the publication of which, he had probably his private reasons. He was now on a sick bed, feeble and paralytic ; and though poverty might impel him to write, it might not drive him to print, which, at that time, was neither a very profitable nor a sure resource.

THE INDUCTION.

The Stage.

Enter PROLOGUE.

Prologue.

*F*OR *your own sakes, not his²——*

Enter Gossip MIRTH, Gossip TATTLE, Gossip EXPECTATION, *and* Gossip CENSURE, *four* Gentlewomen, *lady-like attired.*

Mirth. *Come, gossip, be not ashamed. The play is* THE STAPLE OF NEWS, *and you are the mistress and lady of Tattle,—let's have your opinion of it.—Do you hear, gentleman? what are you, gentleman-usher to the play? Pray you help us to some stools here.*

Pro. *Where? on the stage, ladies!*

Mirth. *Yes, on the stage; we are persons of quality, I assure you, and women of fashion, and come to see and to be seen. My gossip Tattle here, and gossip Expectation, and my gossip Censure, and I am Mirth, the daughter of Christmas, and spirit of Shrovetide. They say, It's merry when gossips meet; I hope your play will be a merry one.*

Pro. *Or you will make it such, ladies. Bring a form here.* [A bench is brought in.] *But what will the noblemen think, or the grave wits here, to see you seated on the bench thus?*

---

² The folio reads *ours*, but erroneously. See p. 157.

Mirth. Why, what should they think, but that they had mothers as we had; and those mothers had gossips (if their children were christened) as we are; and such as had a longing to see plays, and sit upon them, as we do, and arraign both them and their poets?

Pro. O, is that your purpose! Why, mistress Mirth and madam Tattle, enjoy your delights freely.

Tat. Look your News be new and fresh, master Prologue, and untainted; I shall find them else, if they be stale or fly-blown, quickly.

Pro. We ask no favour from you; only we would entreat of madam Expectation——

Expect. What, master Prologue?

Pro. That your ladyship would expect no more than you understand.

Expect. Sir, I can expect enough.

Pro. I fear, too much, lady; and teach others to do the like.

Expect. I can do that too, if I have cause.

Pro. Cry you mercy, you never did wrong, but with just cause.[3] *What's this, lady?*

[3] *You never did wrong, but with just cause.*] This is meant as a satire on a line in Shakspeare's *Julius Cæsar*, though it nowhere occurs as it is here represented. WHAL.

The commentators are right at last. Here is evidently an allusion to Shakspeare, and, for once, "old Ben speaks out."

The attacks on Jonson for this quotation, which are multiplied beyond credibility, are founded on two charges, first, that he has falsified the passage, and secondly that he was actuated by malignity in adverting to it at all. I cannot believe that the passage is "quoted (as Steevens says) unfaithfully." It is sufficient to look at it in the printed copy, to be convinced that it never came, in this form, from the pen of Shakspeare. One of the conspirators, Metellus Cimber by name, kneels at the feet of Cæsar, with this short address,

> "Metellus Cimber throws before thy seat,
>   An humble heart."—

And what is Cæsar's reply?

> "Know Cæsar *doth not wrong*, nor without cause
>   Will he be satisfied."

Mirth. *Curiosity, my lady Censure.*

Pro. *O, Curiosity! you come to see who wears the new suit to-day; whose clothes are best penn'd, what-*

How satisfied, and of what? Here is no congruity, and the poetry is as mean as the sense. In Jonson it stands thus:

> "*Met.* Cæsar, *thou dost me wrong.*
> *Cæs.* Cæsar *did never wrong,* but with just cause."

Here is, at least, a reference to something. The fact seems to be that this verse, which closely borders upon absurdity without being absolutely absurd, escaped the poet in the heat of composition, and being unluckily one of those quaint slips which are readily remembered, became a jocular and familiar phrase for reproving, as here, the perverse and unreasonable expectations of the male or female gossips of the day.

To suppose, with Steevens and Malone, that Jonson derived all his knowledge of Shakspeare from his printed works, is not a little ridiculous: those gentlemen choose to forget that he passed his life among play-houses and players, and that he must have frequently seen *Julius Cæsar* on the stage. There he undoubtedly heard the expression which he has quoted. He tells us himself that, till he was past the age of forty, he could repeat every thing that he had written. His memory therefore was most retentive, and as his veracity was never called in question, but by the duumvirate just mentioned, I cannot but believe that he has faithfully given the words as they were uttered. When the *Staple of News* was written, cannot be told, but it was acted in 1625, nine years after Shakspeare's death; it seems, however, not to have been published till 1641, when the author himself had long been dead; though the title page bears date 1631. *Julius Cæsar* was printed in 1623; but it does not necessarily follow from this, that Jonson consulted the players' copy. He had no occasion to look into it for what he already knew; and if he had opened it at all, the probability is, that he would have paid no attention to their botchery (for theirs I am persuaded it was) when the genuine words were already so familiar to him. He wrote and spoke at a time when he might easily have been put to shame, if his quotation had been unfaithful.

I am sorry to be compelled to repeat so often, that whenever Jonson is concerned, Mr. Malone is the weakest of all reasoners, the blindest of all accusers. Similar to the case before us, is the attack made on the poet in a previous passage. " I *remember* (says Ben) the players *have often mentioned* it as an honour to Shakspeare, that in writing (whatsoever he penned) he never blotted out a line." Here Mr. Malone bristles up, and gives him *the lie valiant.*

ever the part be; which actor has the best leg and foot; what king plays without cuffs, and his queen without gloves; who rides post in stockings, and dances in boots.

Cen. *Yes, and which amorous prince makes love in drink, or does over-act prodigiously in beaten satin, and, having got the trick on't, will be monstrous still, in despite of counsel.*[4]

Book-holder. [within.] *Mend your lights, gentlemen.—Master Prologue, begin.*

"This is NOT true," he exclaims, "*they* only say, *in their preface to his plays*, that his mind and hand went together, and what he thought, he uttered with that easiness, that a blot in his papers has *scarce* been received from him." This is playing at cross purposes with a witness! Jonson, who remembered every thing, and who lived in habits of daily intercourse with all the players, the contemporaries of Shakspeare, gives us the results of his *frequent conversations* with them; Mr. Malone, who forgets himself from page to page, comes two centuries afterwards, and charges him with a deliberate falsehood *because*—Heminge and Condell, two of them, *print*, in a preface which was not extant, perhaps, when Jonson wrote the passage just quoted, that they had *scarce received a blot* in Shakspeare's papers!

To have done with this long note.—After relieving Jonson from the heaviest part of the charge—that of sophisticating a line "for the gratification of his malignity," I have no desire to push the matter further, or seek, in any way, to exonerate him from the crime of having produced it at all. *Valeat quod valeat.* Whether it be a *satire*, as Whalley, a *sneer*, as Malone, a *scoff*, as Steevens, a piece of wanton *malice*, as Tyrwhitt calls it, or all of them together, as others say, the reader may determine at his pleasure. I would only remind him that this is THE FIRST PLACE in Jonson's works, in which I have found any expression that could be construed (whether fairly or not) into an attack on Shakspeare, and that a small portion of the tenderness which is felt for this great poet, would not be altogether cast away on Marlow, Lilly, Kidd, and others of some note in their day, whom he incessantly ridicules without stint and without mercy, though he had obligations to some of them, and had received provocation from none.

[4] *And having got the trick on't, will be monstrous still, in despite of counsel.*] There can be no doubt but this is particular satire, though it is not easy to say at whom it points. WHAL.

Enter the Tire-men *to mend the lights.*

Tat. *Ah me!*

Expect. *Who's that?*

Pro. *Nay, start not, ladies; these carry no fireworks to fright you, but a torch in their hands, to give light to the business. The truth is, there are a set of gamesters within, in travail of a thing called a play, and would fain be deliver'd of it: and they have entreated me to be their man-midwife, the prologue; for they are like to have a hard labour on't.*

Tat. *Then the poet has abused himself, like an ass as he is.*

Mirth. *No, his actors will abuse him enough, or I am deceived. Yonder he is within (I was in the tiring-house awhile to see the actors drest) rolling himself up and down like a tun in the midst of them, and purges, never did vessel of wort or wine work so! his sweating put me in mind of a good Shroving-dish, (and I believe would be taken up for a service of state somewhere, an't were known) a stewed poet! he doth sit like an unbraced drum, with one of his heads beaten out; for that you must note, a poet hath two heads, as a drum has; one for making, the other repeating! and his repeating head is all to pieces; they may gather it up in the tiring-house; for he hath torn the book in a poetical fury, and put himself to silence in dead sack, which, were there no other vexation, were sufficient to make him the most miserable emblem of patience.*

Cen. *The Prologue, peace.*

PROLOGUE.

(For the Stage.)

OR your own sakes, not his, he bad me say,
Would you were come to hear, not see a play.
Though we his actors, must provide for those
Who are our guests here, in the way of shows,
The maker hath not so ; he'd have you wise,
Much rather by your ears, than by your eyes ;
And prays you'll not prejudge his play for ill,
Because you mark it not, and sit not still ;
But have a longing to salute, or talk
With such a female, and from her to walk
With your discourse, to what is done, and where,
How, and by whom, in all the town, but here.
Alas ! what is it to his scene, to know
How many coaches in Hyde-park did show
Last spring, what fare to-day at Medley's was,
If Dunstan or the Phœnix best wine has ? [5]

[5] ———— *what fare at Medley's was,*
If Dunstan or the Phœnix best wine has ?] *Medley's* was an
ordinary or eating-house. *Dunstan* was better known in the poet's
time by the name of the Devil Tavern.* Here was the famous
club, at which Jonson presided as perpetual chairman; and at
which Shakspeare, Beaumont, Fletcher, Selden, Martin, a man of

---

* Mr. Waldron informs me that this tavern was shut up, and the
sign (the Devil peeping over the shoulder of St. Dunstan) taken
down about the year 1788. See the *Leges Conviviales.*

They are things—but yet the stage might stand as well,
If it did neither hear these things, nor tell.
Great noble wits, be good unto yourselves,
And make a difference 'twixt poetic elves,
And poets : all that dabble in the ink,
And defile quills, are not those few can think,
Conceive, express, and steer the souls of men,
As with a rudder, round thus, with their pen.
He must be one that can instruct your youth,
And keep your acme[6] in the state of truth,
Must enterprise this work ; mark but his ways.
What flight he makes, how new : and then he says,
If that not like you, that he sends to-night,
'Tis you have left to judge, not he to write.

PROLOGUE.

(For the Court.)

A WORK not smelling of the lamp, to-night,
But fitted for your Majesty's disport,
And writ to the meridian of your court,
We bring ; and hope it may produce delight :
The rather being offered as a rite,
To scholars, that can judge, and fair report
The sense they hear, above the vulgar sort
Of nut-crackers, that only come for sight.

infinite humour, Morley, afterwards Bishop of Winchester, Hodgson, and others, rarely equalled in aftertimes, occasionally assisted. The *Phœnix* was situated somewhere near the playhouse of that name, in Drury-lane.

[6] *And keep your* acme,] i. e. I presume, your mature age ; but the expression is a strange one. The conclusion of this prologue cannot be praised for its modesty ; but the audiences heard a language not much unlike it from others. Ben alludes to his long absence from the Stage, (nine years,) during which he fears not to affirm that, whatever change (for the worse) may have taken place

Wherein although our title, sir, be News,
We yet adventure here to tell you none,
But shew you common follies, and so known,
That though they are not truths, the innocent Muse,
Hath made so like, as phant'sy could them state,
Or poetry, without scandal, imitate.[1]

in them, he has suffered no deterioration. He is not much out in the present case; but the *wolves were imperceptibly advancing upon Mœris.*

[1] This address to the Court is not without merit. It is terse and neat, and will probably remind the reader of the style and construction of some of Milton's sonnets.

DRAMATIS PERSONÆ.

PENNYBOY, *the son, the heir and suitor.*
PENNYBOY, *the father, the Canter.*
PENNYBOY, *Richer, the uncle, the usurer.*
CYMBAL, *master of the* STAPLE, *and prime jeerer.*
FITTON, *emissary Court, and jeerer.*
ALMANAC, *doctor in physic, and jeerer.*
SHUNFIELD, *sea-captain, and jeerer.*
MADRIGAL, *poetaster and jeerer.*
PICKLOCK, *man o' law, and emissary Westminster.*
PIEDMANTLE, *pursuivant at arms, and heraldet.*
REGISTER, *of the staple, or office.*
NATHANIEL, *first clerk of the office.*
THOMAS, *Barber, second clerk of the office.*
BROKER, *secretary, and gentleman-usher to* PECUNIA.
LICKFINGER, *master-cook, and parcel-poet.*
FASHIONER, *the tailor of the times.*
LEATHERLEG, *shoemaker.*
Linener.
Haberdasher.
Spurrier.
Customers, *male and female.*
Porter.
BLOCK *and* LOLLARD, *two dogs.*
BUZ, AMBLER, *grooms; Fiddlers, Singing-boy, Attendants, &c.*

INTERMEAN *or* CHORUS. Gossips MIRTH, TATTLE, EXPECTATION, *and* CENSURE.

PECUNIA, *infanta of the mines.*
MORTGAGE, *her nurse.*
STATUTE, *first woman.*
BAND, *second woman.*
WAX, (ROSE,) *chambermaid.*

SCENE, London.

THE STAPLE OF NEWS.

ACT I.

SCENE I. *The Lodgings of* PENNYBOY, *jun.*

Enter PENNYBOY, *jun. and* LEATHERLEG *with a new pair of boots.*

P. *jun.* [LEATH. *pulls on his boots.*]

GRAMERCY, Leatherleg: get me the
        spurrier,
And thou hast fitted me.
    Leath. I'll do it presently.   [*Exit.*
    P. *jun.* [*walks up and down in his
        gown, waist-coat, and trowses,*[1]
expecting his tailor.]
Look to me, wit, and look to my wit, land,
That is, look on me, and with all thine eyes,
Male, female, yea, hermaphroditic eyes,
And those bring all your helps and perspicils,[2]

[1] *In his* trowses.] *Trowses* are the close drawers over which the
hose or slops (the loose breeches) were drawn. I know not why
Whalley constantly alters the word to *trowsers.*

[2] *Perspicils.*] Optic glasses. We find the word in *Albumazar,*
A. i. S. 3.

      "Sir, 'tis a *perspicil,* the best under heaven."   WHAL.

This certainly (like many other quotations which might be pointed
out) does not prove what it was brought to prove ; but the word is
nevertheless rightly explained.

5   M

To see me at best advantage, and augment
My form as I come forth ; for I do feel
I will be one worth looking after shortly ;
Now, by and by, that's shortly,—[*draws forth his
            watch, and sets it on the table.*]   It strikes !
      one, two,
Three, four, five, six.   Enough, enough, dear watch,
Thy pulse hath beat enough.   Now sleep and rest ;
Would thou couldst make the time to do so too :
I'll wind thee up no more.   The hour is come
So long expected ! there, there, drop my wardship,
                              [*Throws off his gown.*
My pupillage and vassalage together.——
And, Liberty, come throw thyself about me,
In a rich suit, cloke, hat, and band, for now
I'll sue out no man's livery, but mine own ;
I stand on my own feet, so much a year,
Right round and sound, the lord of mine own ground.
And (to rhyme to it) threescore thousand pound !
Not come ? not yet ?—[*Goes to the door and looks.*]
      Tailor, thou art a vermin,
Worse than the same thou prosecut'st and prick'st
In subtle seam—Go to, I say no more——
Thus to retard my longings, on the day
I do write man, to beat thee !   One and twenty
Since the clock struck, complete ! and thou wilt feel it,
Thou foolish animal !——I could pity him,
An I were not heartily angry with him now,
For this one piece of folly he bears about him,
To dare to tempt the fury of an heir
T' above two thousand a year, yet hope his custom !
Well, master Fashioner, there's some must break—
A head, for this your breaking.—

            Enter FASHIONER.
                              Are you come, sir ?
Fash. God give your worship joy !

P. jun. What! of your staying,
And leaving me to stalk here in my trowses,
Like a tame her'nsew for you?
    Fash. I but waited
Below, till the clock struck.
    P. jun. Why, if you had come
Before a quarter, would it so have hurt you,
In reputation, to have waited here?
    Fash. No, but your worship might have pleaded
        nonage,
If you had got them on, ere I could make
Just affidavit of the time.
    P. jun. That jest
Has gain'd thy pardon, thou hadst lived condemn'd
To thine own hell else, never to have wrought
Stitch more for me, or any Pennyboy,
I could have hinder'd thee : but now thou art mine.
For one and twenty years, or for three lives,
Choose which thou wilt, I'll make thee a copyholder,
And thy first bill unquestion'd.   Help me on.
    Fash. Presently, sir: [*says his suit.*[3]] I am bound
        unto your worship.
    P. jun. Thou shalt be, when I have seal'd thee a
        lease of my custom.
    Fash. Your worship's barber is without.
    P. jun. Who? Tom?—
Come in, Tom.

            Enter THOMAS, Barber.

            Set thy things upon the board,
And spread thy cloths, lay all forth in *procinctu*,
And tell's what news?
    Tho. O sir, a STAPLE OF NEWS!
Or the New Staple, which you please.

---

[3] —*says his suit.*] Tries it on. Thus Evadne in the *Rebellion.*
" I wonder why the tailor makes gowns so imperfect, that they need
so many *says ?*"

P. jun. What's that ?

Fash. An office, sir, a brave young office set up :
I had forgot to tell your worship.

P. jun. For what ?

Tho. To enter all the News, sir, of the time.

Fash. And vent it as occasion serves : a place
Of huge commèrce it will be !

P. jun. Pray thee, peace ;
I cannot abide a talking tailor : let Tom,
(He is a barber) by his place relate it.
What is't, an office, Tom ?

Tho. Newly erected
Here in the house, almost on the same floor,
Where all the news of all sorts shall be brought,
And there be examined, and then register'd,
And so be issued under the seal of the office,
As Staple News ; no other news be current.

P. jun. 'Fore me, thou speak'st of a brave business, Tom.

Fash. Nay, if you knew the brain that hatch'd it,
sir——

P. jun. I know thee well enough : give him a loaf,
Tom ;[4]
Quiet his mouth, that oven will be venting else.
Proceed——

Tho. He tells you true, sir ; master Cymbal
Is master of the office, he projected it,
He lies here, in the house ; and the great rooms
He has taken for the office, and set up
His desks and classes, tables and his shelves.

Fash. He is my customer, and a wit, sir, too.
But he has brave wits under him——

Tho. Yes, four emissaries.

——

4 —— *give him a* loaf, *Tom.*] Again ! Our old writers are
never weary of this jest. In the *Rebellion*, by Rawlins, allusions to
this artophagous propensity of the tailors occur in almost every
page.

P. jun. Emissaries ? stay, there's a fine new word,
    Tom;
Pray God it signify anything! what are emissaries ?
    Tho. Men employ'd outward, that are sent abroad
To fetch in the commodity.
    Fash. From all regions
Where the best news are made.
    Tho. Or vented forth.
    Fash. By way of exchange, or trade.
    P. jun. Nay, thou wilt speak——
    Fash. My share, sir, there's enough for both.
    P. jun. Go on then,
Speak all thou canst : methinks the ordinaries
Should help them much.
    Fash. Sir, they have ordinaries,
And extraordinaries, as many changes,
And variations, as there are points in the compass.
    Tho. But the four cardinal quarters.
    P. jun. Ay those, Tom——
    Tho. The Court, sir, Paul's, Exchange, and West-
        minster-hall.
    P. jun. Who is the chief ? which hath precedency ?
    Tho. The governor of the Staple, master Cymbal,
He is the chief; and after him the emissaries :
First emissary Court, one master Fitton,
He is a jeerer too.
    P. jun. What's that ?
    Fash. A wit.
    Tho. Or half a wit, some of them are half-wits,
Two to a wit, there are a set of them.
Then master Ambler, emissary Paul's,
A fine-paced gentleman, as you shall see walk
The middle aisle : and then my froy Hans Buz,
A Dutchman ; he is emissary Exchange.
    Fash. I had thought master Burst, the merchant
        had had it.
    Tho. No,

He has a rupture, he has sprung a leak.
Emissary Westminster's undisposed of yet;
Then the examiner, register, and two clerks,
They manage all at home, and sort, and file,
And seal the news, and issue them.
  P. jun. Tom, dear Tom,
What may my means do for thee? ask and have it,
I'd fain be doing some good: it is my birthday.
And I would do it betimes, I feel a grudging
Of bounty, and I would not long lie fallow.
I pray thee think and speak, or wish for something.
  Tho. I would I had but one of the clerks' places
In this News-office.
  P. jun. Thou shalt have it, Tom,
If silver or gold will fetch it; what's the rate?
At what is it set in the market?
  Tho. Fifty pound, sir.
  P. jun. An 'twere a hundred, Tom, thou shalt not
      want it.
  Fash. O noble master! [*Leaps and embraces him.*
  P. jun. How now, Æsop's ass!
Because I play with Tom, must I needs run
Into your rude embraces? stand you still, sir;
Clowns' fawnings are a horse's salutations.——
How dost thou like my suit, Tom?
  Tho. Master Fashioner
Has hit your measures, sir, he has moulded you,
And made you, as they say.
  Fash. No, no, not I,
I am an *ass*, old *Æsop's ass*.
  P. jun. Nay, Fashioner,
I can do thee a good turn too; be not musty,
Though thou hast moulded me, as little Tom says:
—I think thou hast put me in mouldy pockets
                    [*Draws out his pockets.*
  Fash. As good,
Right Spanish perfume, the lady Estifania's;—

They cost twelve pound a pair.
 P. jun. Thy bill will say so.
I pray thee tell me, Fashioner, what authors
Thou read'st to help thy invention : Italian prints ?
Or arras hangings ? they are tailors' libraries.
 Fash. I scorn such helps.
 P. jun. O ! though thou art a silkworm,
And deal'st in satins and velvets, and rich plushes,
Thou canst not spin all forms out of thyself ;
They are quite other things : I think this suit
Has made me wittier than I was.
 Fash. Believe it, sir,
That clothes do much upon the wit, as weather
Does on the brain ; and thence [sir] comes your pro-
   verb,
The tailor makes the man : I speak by experience
Of my own customers.   I have had gallants,
Both court and country, would have fool'd you up
In a new suit, with the best wits in being,[5]
And kept their speed as long as their clothes lasted
Handsome and neat ; but then as they grew out
At the elbows again, or had a stain or spot,
They have sunk most wretchedly.
 P. jun. What thou report'st,
Is but the common calamity, and seen daily ;
And therefore you've another answering proverb,
A broken sleeve keeps the arm back.

---

[5] —— *would have* fool'd *you up*
 In a new suit, with the best wits in being.] Whalley would read,
follow'd you up : but he overlooks the contrast between *fool* and
wit ; and quite mistakes the meaning of the expression which he
quotes.   He might have learned from Shakspeare that, to play the
fool well, *does ask a kind of wit.*—But Jonson satirically alludes to
the hardihood with which a *well-dressed* coxcomb will venture to
say and do the most extravagant things, on the credit of his clothes.
For the rest, to *fool up* is a very common expression in our old
writers, and means,—to practise, or humour, any act of folly, to a
ridiculous excess.

Fash. 'Tis true, sir.
And thence we say, that such a one plays at *peep-arm*.
     P. jun. Do you so? it is wittily said.   I wonder,
          gentlemen
And men of means will not maintain themselves
Fresher in wit, I mean in clothes, to the highest :
For he that's out of clothes is out of fashion,
And out of fashion is out of countenance,
And out of countenance is out of wit.
Is not rogue haberdasher come ?

     Enter Haberdasher, Linener, *and* Hatter *and*
          Shoemaker.

     Hab. Yes, here, sir.
I have been without this half hour.
     P. jun. Give me my hat.
Put on my girdle, rascal : fits my ruff well ?
     Lin. In print.
     P. jun. Slave !
     Lin. See yourself.
     P. jun. Is this same hat
Of the block-passant ? Do not answer me,
I cannot stay for an answer.   I do feel
The powers of one and twenty, like a tide,
Flow in upon me, and perceive an heir
Can conjure up all spirits in all circles.
Rogue ! rascal ! slave ! give tradesmen their true
          names,
And they appear to him presently.
     Lin. For profit.
     P. jun. Come, cast my cloke about me, I'll go see
This office, Tom, and be trimm'd afterwards.
I'll put thee in possession, my prime work !

     Enter Spurrier.

Ods so, my spurrier ! put them on, boy, quickly ;
I had like to have lost my spurs with too much speed.

Enter PENNYBOY Canter, *in a patched and ragged eloke, singing.*

P. Can. *Good morning to my joy! my jolly Penny-*
    boy!
The lord, and the prince of plenty!
I come to see what riches, thou bearest in thy breeches,
    The first of thy one and twenty.
What, do thy pockets jingle? or shall we need to mingle
    Our strength both of foot and of horses!
These fellows look so eager, as if they would beleaguer
    An heir in the midst of his forces!
I hope they be no serjeants, that hang upon thy
        margents—
    This rogue has the joul of a jailor!
P. jun. [*answers in tune.*] *O founder, no such matter,*
    my spurrier, and my hatter,
My linen-man, and my tailor.
Thou should'st have been brought in too, shoemaker,
If the time had been longer, and Tom Barber.
How dost thou like my company, old Canter?
Do I not muster a brave troop,[6] all bill-men?
Present your arms before my founder here,
This is my Founder, this same learned Canter!
He brought me the first news of my father's death,
I thank him, and ever since I call him founder.
Worship him, boys; I'll read only the sums,
And pass them straight.
    Sho. Now ale——
    Rest. And strong ale bless him.
    P. jun. Ods so, some ale and sugar for my founder!

---

[6] —— *all* bill-men?
    Present your arms, &c.] The old quibble between a trades-
man's bill, and the weapon of war so called. The word rarely
suggests itself to any of our ancient dramatists without furnishing
matter for an equivoke. Instances of it are familiar to every
reader. *Time,* which occurs in the line above, is synonymous with
tune.

Good bills, sufficient bills, these bills may pass.
                              [*Puts them in his pockets.*
   P. Can. I do not like these paper-squibs, good
     master.
They may undo your store, I mean, of credit,
And fire your arsenal, if case you do not
In time make good those outer-works, your pockets,
And take a garrison in of some two hundred,
To beat those pioneers off, that carry a mine
Would blow you up, at last. Secure your casamates.
Here, master Picklock, sir, your man of law,
And learn'd attorney, has sent you a bag of munition.
   P. jun. [*takes the bag.*] What is't ?
   P. Can. Three hundred pieces.
   P. jun. I'll dispatch them.
   P. Can. Do ; I would have your strengths lined,
     and perfumed
With gold, as well as amber.
   P. jun. God-a-mercy,
Come, *ad solvendum,* boys! there, there, and there,
I look on nothing but *totalis.*   [*Pays all their bills.*
   P. Can. See !
The difference 'twixt the covetous and the prodigal !
The covetous man never has money, and
The prodigal will have none shortly !   [*Aside.*
   P. jun. Ha,
What says my founder ? [*they make legs to him.*] I
     thank you, I thank you, sirs.
   All. God bless your worship, and your worship's
     Canter !
    [*Exe.* Shoemaker, Linener, Haber. *and* Hatter.
   P. Can. I say 'tis nobly done, to cherish shop-
     keepers,
And pay their bills, without examining thus.
   P. jun. Alas! they have had a pitiful hard time
     on't,
A long vacation from their cozening.

Poor rascals ! I do it out of charity :
I would advance their trade again, and have them
Haste to be rich, swear and forswear wealthily.
What do you stay for, sirrah ?   [*To the* Spurrier.
 Spur. To my box, sir.
 P. jun. Your box ! why, there's an angel ; if my
  spurs
Be not right Rippon [1]——
 Spur. Give me never a penny
If I strike not thorough your bounty with the rowels.
           [*Exit.*

 P. jun. Dost thou want any money, founder ?
 P. Can. Who, sir, I ?
Did I not tell you I was bred in the mines,
Under sir Bevis Bullion.
 P. jun. That is true,
I quite forgot, you mine-men want no money,
Your streets are pav'd with't : there the molten silver
Runs out like cream on cakes of gold.
 P. Can. And rubies
Do grow like strawberries.
 P. jun. 'Twere brave being there !——
Come, Tom, we'll go to the office now.
 P. Can. What office ?
 P. jun. News-office, the New Staple ; thou shalt
  go too ;
'Tis here in the house, on the same floor, Tom says :
Come, founder, let us trade in ale and nutmegs.
           [*Exeunt.*

---

[1] —— *right Rippon.*] Rippon (a town in Yorkshire) was
famous for the spurs made there. They are mentioned by several
of our old writers, and among the rest by Sir W. Davenant. "Whip
me with wire, headed with rowels of sharp *Rippon spurs.*" *The Wits.*

SCENE II.   *Another part of the same.   An outer
Room of the Office.*

Enter REGISTER *and* NATHANIEL.

Register.

W HAT, are those desks fit now ? Set forth the
        table,
    The carpet[8] and the chair ; where are the news
That were examined last ? have you filed them up ?
    Nath. Not yet, I had no time.
    Reg. Are those news registered
That emissary Buz sent in last night,
Of Spinola and his eggs ?
    Nath. Yes, sir, and filed.
    Reg. What are you now upon ?
    Nath. That our new emissary
Westminster gave us, of the golden heir.
    Reg. Dispatch ; that's news indeed, and of impor-
        tance.—

Enter a Countrywoman.

What would you have, good woman ?
    Wom. I would have, sir,
A groatsworth of any news, I care not what,
To carry down this Saturday to our vicar.
    Reg. O ! you are a butter-woman ; ask Nathaniel,
The clerk there.
    Nath. Sir, I tell her she must stay

[8] ———— *set forth the table,
The* carpet, *&c.*] The embroidered rug with which tables were
then covered. " In the fray one of their spurs engaged into a
carpet upon which stood a very fair looking-glass, and two noble
pieces of porcelain, drew all *to the ground,* broke the glass," &c.
Character of England, Harleian Miscel. vol. x. p. 189.

Till emissary Exchange, or Paul's send in,
And then I'll fit her.

Reg. Do, good woman, have patience;
It is not now, as when the captain lived.[9]

[9] Reg. *O! you are a* butter-woman; *ask Nathaniel,*
The clerk there.
   Nath. *Sir, I tell her she must stay——*
   Reg. *Do, good woman, have patience;*
It is not now, as when the captain *lived.*] Fletcher's *Fair Maid of
the Inn,* which appeared a few months after the *Staple of News,* has
a close imitation of this and similar passages.

For. It shall be the ghost of some lying stationer, a spirit shall
look as if *butter* would not melt in his mouth; a new Mercurius-
Gallo-Belgicus.

Cox. O, there was a *captain* was rare at it.

For. Never think of him: though that captain writ a full hand-
gallop, and wasted more harmless paper than ever did laxative
physic, yet will I make you to out-scribble him.   Act iv. S. 2.

Not one of the poet's editors appears to have suspected the allusion here, or to have understood the passage.   Both Jonson and
Fletcher had in view *Nathaniel Butter,* who, if we may trust the
present account of him, was bred a *stationer,* failed in his profession, and betook himself to the compilation of *news* from all quarters.   It appears, from Mr. Chalmers's inquiries, that he began his
labours as early (at least) as 1611, and if he was not the most successful, he was undoubtedly the most indefatigable of all the news-
writers of his age.   I have seen pamphlets (for such were most of
his publications, whether occasional or weekly) by him, of the date
of 1634, when he had swelled the firm to Butter and Co., and he
probably continued to publish much longer.   His foreign *news,*
which is extremely jejune, is merely a bald translation from some
of the continental Mercuries; when he ventures to add a remark
of his own, it is somewhat in the style of old Tiresias, or Jeffrey
Neve——What I say *will either fall out or not*——so that he was
not likely to conciliate much of Jonson's respect.

   The verse which mentions the *captain* is a parody of one in poor
old *Jeronimo* :

   " It is not now as when Andrea lived."

   The captain, of whom I have nothing certain to say, appears to
have rivalled Butter in the dissemination of news.   In that age the
middle aisle of St. Paul's swarmed with disbanded or broken ancients, lieutenants, &c., who, on the strength of having served a few
months in the Low Countries, assumed, like *Cavaliero Shift,* an
acquaintance with all the great officers in the field, and amused

Nath. You'll blast the reputation of the office
Now in the bud, if you dispatch these groats
So soon : let them attend, in name of policy.

the idle citizens with pretended intelligence from the armies. One
of these (the *captain* of Jonson and Fletcher) seems to have turned
his inventive faculties to account, and printed his imaginary corre-
spondence, instead of detailing it *vivâ voce.* This is all that I can
say,* but Mr. Weber goes farther. Fletcher, he subjoins, informs
us that the *captain* was the principal writer in the Mercurius-Gallo-
Belgicus! which was one of the first *newspapers* that appeared in
England. This gentleman's ignorance is pitiable ; but his careless-
ness deserves the severest reproof. Gallo-Belgicus was not a newspaper, nor was it printed in England. If he had turned for information to the history of newspapers given in the *Life of Ruddiman,*
instead of the Index to Reed's *Old Plays,* (his constant resource,)
he would have seen the very passage on which he so confidently
relies, proved to be groundless in every part. With respect to the
quotation from Fletcher, it is sufficient to observe that Mr. Weber
does not understand a word of it.

But we have not yet done.

> " *For.* You know the juggling captain.
> *Clown.* Ay ; there's a sure card.
> *For.* Only the foreman of their jury's dead,
> But he died like a Roman.
> *Clown.* Else, 'tis thought
> He had made work for the hangman."

"This *juggling* captain (the editor says) was perhaps the principal writer in the Mercurius-Gallo-Belgicus, mentioned above."

---

* In the *Great Assizes,* (a singular poem, which seems to have
escaped Mr. Chalmers,) mention is made of a *captain Rashingham,*
a great compiler of news, whose occupation was invaded by a
swarm of " paper-wasters," &c.

> " Who weekly uttered such a mass of lies,
> Under the specious name of *novelties,*"

that the poor captain found his trade over-run, and was obliged to
betake himself to " plucking tame pigeons " (tricking) for a liveli-
hood.

This was written nearly twenty years after the *Staple of News ;*
bully Rashingham, therefore, may be too late for the captain of
the text : the note, however, will serve to prove that men of this
description were commonly engaged in these pursuits. See also
the first scene of Shirley's *Love Tricks.*

Enter CYMBAL *and* FITTON, *introducing*
PENNYBOY, *jun.*

P. jun. In troth they are dainty rooms ; what place
is this ?

Cym. This is the outer room, where my clerks sit,
And keep their sides, the register in the midst ;
The examiner, he sits private there, within ;
And here I have my several rolls and files
Of news by the alphabet, and all put up
Under their heads.

P. jun. But those too subdivided ?

Cym. Into authentical, and apocryphal——

Fit. Or news of doubtful credit, as barbers' news—

Cym. And tailors' news, porters', and watermen's
news.

Fit. Whereto, beside the Coranti, and Gazetti—

Cym. I have the news of the season——

Fit. As vacation news,
Term-news, and christmas-news.

Cym. And news of the faction.

Fit. As the reformed-news ; Protestant-news ;—

Cym. And pontificial-news ; of all which several,

What, again ! " The *foreman of the jury* probably alludes to the
celebrated Banks, whose horse, &c.—this Banks and his horse
went abroad, and according to a vulgar report were both burned
at Rome by order of the Pope, to which the words *died like a Roman*, seem to allude." This stupidity is intolerable. Does Mr.
Weber suppose that the Romans were burned to death ! Can any
thing be plainer than that the *juggling captain* was one of a gang of
cheats, that the *foreman of the jury*, i. e. the most daring of them,
being suspected or seized, died like a Roman, that is, by his own
hand, and thus probably escaped the gallows ! Pity for our great
dramatists is swallowed up in indignation at the conduct of the
publishers of their works ; who wantonly sacrifice the reputation
and glory of the country, and ask not how well, but how cheaply a
jobber by the piece will illustrate manners to which he is a stranger,
in a language which he does not understand.

The day-books, characters, precedents are kept,
Together with the names of special friends——
    Fit. And men of correspondence in the country—
    Cym. Yes, of all ranks, and all religions.——
    Fit. Factors and agents——
    Cym. Liegers, that lie out
Through all the shires of the kingdom.
    P. jun. This is fine,
And bears a brave relation! But what says
Mercurius Britannicus[1] to this?
    Cym. O sir, he gains by't half in half.
    Fit. Nay more,
I'll stand to't.   For where he was wont to get
In hungry captains, obscure statesmen——
    Cym. Fellows
To drink with him in a dark room in a tavern,
And eat a sausage——
    Fit. We have seen it.
    Cym. As fain to keep so many politic pens
Going, to feed the press——
    Fit. And dish out news,
Were't true or false——
    Cym. Now all that charge is saved.
The public chronicler——
    Fit. How do you call him there?
    Cym. And gentle reader——
    Fit. He that has the maidenhead
Of all the books.

---

[1] —————— *But what says*
    Mercurius Britannicus.]   A news-journal then published with
that title.   WHAL.
    Whalley speaks entirely at random on this subject.   Mercurius
Britannicus was the assumed name of the composer of the " journal,"
or rather pamphlet, which was called the *Weekly News*.   Who this
person was, I cannot inform the reader.   He was evidently en-
couraged by the success of Butter.   There were two writers who
subsequently joined him, Watts and Bourne ;—one of these might
have been his competitor : but this is merely guess-work.

Cym. Yes, dedicated to him——

Fit. Or rather prostituted——

P. jun. You are right, sir.

Cym. No more shall be abused; nor country parsons
Of the inquisition, nor busy justices
Trouble the peace, and both torment themselves,
And their poor ignorant neighbours, with enquiries
After the many and most innocent monsters,
That never came in the counties they were charged
    with.

P. jun. Why, methinks, sir, if the honest common
    people
Will be abused, why should not they have their
    pleasure,
In the believing lies are made for them ;
As you in the office, making them yourselves ?

Fit. O sir ! it is the printing we oppose.

Cym. We not forbid that any news be made,
But that it be printed ; for when news is printed,
It leaves, sir, to be news ; while 'tis but written——

Fit. Tho' it be ne'er so false, it runs news still.

P. jun. See divers men's opinions ! unto some
The very printing of 'em makes them news ;
That have not the heart to believe anything,
But what they see in print.

Fit. Ay, that's an error
Has abused many ; but we shall reform it,
As many things beside, (we have a hope,)
Are crept among the popular abuses.

Cym. Nor shall the stationer cheat upon the time,
By buttering o'er again——[2]

---

[2] *Nor shall the* stationer *cheat upon the time,*
   By buttering *o'er again.*] Here is another allusion to Nathaniel,
nor is this the last. I shall not repeat my notice of it, though the
reader will do well to bear it in mind. Jonson had borrowed
several passages from himself in this place. See the masques of
News from the New World, and *Neptune's Triumph.*

5   N

Fit. Once in seven years,
As the age doats——
   Cym. And grows forgetful of them,
His antiquated pamphlets with new dates :
But all shall come from the mint.
   Fit. Fresh and new stamp'd.
   Cym. With the office seal, staple-commodity.
   Fit. And if a man will assure his news, he may ;
Two-pence a sheet he shall be warranted,
And have a policy for it.
   P. jun. Sir I admire
The method of your place ; all things within't
Are so digested, fitted, and composed,
As it shews Wit had married Order.
   Fit. Sir.
   Cym. The best we could to invite the times.
   Fit. It has
Cost sweat and freezing.
   Cym. And some broken sleeps,
Before it came to this.
   P. jun. I easily think it.
   Fit. But now it has the shape——
   Cym. And is come forth——
   P. jun. A most polite neat thing, with all the limbs,
As sense can taste !
   Cym. It is, sir, though I say it,
As well begotten a business, and as fairly
Help'd to the world.
   P. jun. You must be a midwife, sir,
Or else the son of a midwife (pray you pardon me)
Have help'd it forth so happily !—What news have
      you ?
News of this morning ? I would fain hear some
Fresh from the forge ; as new as day, as they say.
   Cym. And such we have, sir.
   Reg. Shew him the last roll,
Of emissary Westminster's, *The heir.*

Enter BARBER.

P. jun. Come nearer, Tom!

Nath. *There is a brave young heir*
Is come of age this morning, master Pennyboy.

P. jun. That's I? [*Aside.*

Nath. *His father died on this day seven-night.*

P. jun. True! [*Aside.*

Nath. *At six o' the clock in the morning, just a week*
Ere he was one and twenty.

P. jun. I am here, Tom!—
Proceed, I pray thee.

Nath. *An old canting beggar*
Brought him first news, whom he has entertain'd
To follow him since.

P. jun. Why, you shall see him;—Founder!
Come in—

Enter PENNYBOY, Canter.

No follower, but companion:
I pray thee put him in, friend; [*to* NATH.] there's an
　　　angel——
Thou dost not know, he is a wise old fellow,
Though he seem patch'd thus, and made up of pieces.
　　　　　　　　　　　　　　　　[*Exit* NATH.
Founder, we are in here, in, i' the News-office!
In this day's roll already!—I do muse
How you came by us, sirs.

Cym. One master Picklock,
A lawyer that hath purchased here a place
This morning of an emissary under me——

Fit. Emissary Westminster.

Cym. Gave it into the office.

Fit. For his essay, his piece.

P. jun. My man of law!
He's my attorney, and solicitor too!
A fine pragmatic! what is his place worth?

Cym. A *nemo-scit*, sir.

Fit. 'Tis as news come in.

Cym. And as they are issued. I have the just moiety
For my part : then the other moiety
Is parted into seven : the four emissaries,
Whereof my cousin Fitton here's for Court,
Ambler for Paul's, and Buz for the Exchange,
Picklock for Westminster, with the examiner,
And register, they have full parts : and then one part
Is under-parted to a couple of clerks.
And there's the just division of the profits.

P. jun. Have you those clerks, sir ?

Cym. There is one desk empty,
But it has many suitors.

P. jun. Sir, may I
Present one more, and carry it, if his parts
Or gifts, which you will call them——

Cym. Be sufficient, sir.

P. jun. What are your present clerk's habilities ?
How is he qualified ?

Cym. A decay'd stationer
He was, but knows news well, can sort and rank them.

Fit. And for a need can make them.

Cym. True Paul's, bred
In the church-yard.

P. jun. And this at the west-door
On the other side ; he is my barber, Tom,
A pretty scholar, and a master of arts,
Was made, or went out master of arts in a throng,[3]
At the university ; as before, one Christmas,
He got into a masque at court, by his wit,
And the good means of his cittern,[4] holding up thus

---

[3] *Went out master of arts in a* throng, *&c.*] i. e. when honorary
degrees were conferred, in compliment to some person of high rank,
foreign prince, &c., who visited the University.

[4] *And the good means of his* cittern.] " For you know (says Tom
Brown) that a *cittern is as natural to a barber*, as milk to a calf, or
dancing-bears to a bag-piper." Vol. iii. p. 74.

For one of the music : he's a nimble fellow,
And alike skill'd in every liberal science,
As having certain snaps of all ; a neat
Quick vein in forging news too : I do love him,
And promised him a good turn, and I would do it.
What is your price ? the value ?

    Cym. Fifty pounds, sir.

    P. jun. Get in, Tom, take possession, I instal thee.
Here, tell your money. Give thee joy, good Tom !
And let me hear from thee every minute of news,
While the New Staple stands, or the office lasts,
Which I do wish may ne'er be less, for thy sake.

Re-enter NATHANIEL.

    Nath. The emissaries, sir, would speak with you
And master Fitton ; they have brought in news,
Three bale together.

    Cym. Sir, you are welcome here.

    Fit. So is your creature.

    Cym. Business calls us off, sir,
That may concern the office.

    P. jun. Keep me fair, sir,
Still in your staple ; I am here your friend,
On the same floor.

    Fit. We shall be your servants.

             [*Exeunt all but* P. jun. *and* P. Cant.

    P. jun. How dost thou like it, founder ?

    P. Can. All is well,
But that your man of law, methinks, appears not
In his due time. O ! here comes master's worship.

Enter PICKLOCK.

    Pick. How does the heir, bright master Pennyboy ?
Is he awake yet in his one and twenty ?——
Why, this is better far, than to wear cypress,
Dull smutting gloves, or melancholy blacks,
And have a pair of twelve-penny broad ribands,

Laid out like labels.
    P. jun. I should have made shift
To have laugh'd as heartily in my mourner's hood,
As in this suit, if it had pleased my father
To have been buried with the trumpeters.
    Pick. The heralds of arms, you mean.
    P. jun. I mean,
All noise that is superfluous !
    Pick. All that idle pomp,
And vanity of a tombstone, your wise father
Did by his will prevent.   Your worship had——
    P. jun. A loving and obedient father of him,
I know it [I]; a right kind-natured man,
To die so opportunely.
    Pick. And to settle
All things so well! compounded for your wardship
The week afore, and left your state entire,
Without any charge upon't.
    P. jun. I must needs say,
I lost an officer of him, a good bailiff,
And I shall want him : but all peace be with him !
I will not wish him alive again, not I,
For all my fortune.   Give your worship joy
Of your new place, your emissaryship
In the News-office !
    Pick. Know you why I bought it, sir ?
    P. jun. Not I.
    Pick. To work for you, and carry a mine
Against the master of it, master Cymbal,
Who hath a plot, upon a gentlewoman
Was once design'd for you, sir.
    P. jun. Me ?
    Pick. Your father,
Old master Pennyboy, of happy memory,
And wisdom too, as any in the county,
Careful to find out a fit match for you,
In his own life-time, (but he was prevented,)

Left it in writing in a schedule here,
To be annexed to his will, that you,
His only son, upon his charge and blessing,
Should take due notice of a gentlewoman
Sojourning with your uncle, Richer Pennyboy.
    P. jun. A Cornish gentlewoman ; I do know her,
Mistress Pecunia Do-all.
    Pick. A great lady,
Indeed, she is, and not of mortal race,
Infanta of the mines ; her grace's grandfather
Was duke, and cousin to the king of Ophyr,
The Subterranean.   Let that pass.   Her name is,
Or rather her three names are (for such she is)
Aurelia Clara Pecunia, a great princess,
Of mighty power, though she live in private,
With a contracted family !   Her secretary——
    P. Can. Who is her gentleman-usher too.
    Pick. One Broker ;
And then two gentlewomen, mistress Statute
And mistress Band, with Wax the chambermaid,
And mother Mortgage the old nurse, two grooms,
Pawn and his fellow : you have not many to bribe, sir.
The work is feasible, and the approaches easy,
By your own kindred.   Now, sir, Cymbal thinks,
The master here, and governor of the Staple,
By his fine arts, and pomp of his great place,
To draw her !   He concludes, she is a woman,
And that so soon as she hears of the new office,
She'll come to visit it, as they all have longings,
After new sights and motions !   But your bounty,
Person, and bravery, must achieve her.
    P. Can. She is
The talk o' the time ! the adventure of the age !
    Pick. You cannot put yourself upon an action
Of more importance.
    P. Can. All the world are suitors to her.
    Pick. All sorts of men, and all professions.

P. Can. You shall have stall-fed doctors, cramm'd
　　divines,
Make love to her, and with those studied
And perfumed flatteries, as no room can stink
More elegant, than where they are.
　　Pick. Well chanted,
Old Canter ! thou sing'st true.
　　P. Can. And, by your leave,
Good master's worship, some of your velvet coat
Make corpulent curt'sies to her, till they crack for't.
　　Pick. There's doctor Almanac woos her, one of the
　　jeerers,
A fine physician.
　　P. Can. Your sea-captain, Shunfield,
Gives out, he'll go upon the cannon for her.
　　Pick. Though his loud mouthing get him little
　　credit.
　　P. Can. Young master Piedmantle, the fine herald,
Professes to derive her through all ages,
From all the kings and queens that ever were.
　　Pick. And master Madrigal, the crowned poet
Of these our times, doth offer at her praises
As fair as any, when it shall please Apollo
That wit and rhyme may meet both in one subject.
　　P. Can. And you to bear her from all these, it will
　　be——
　　Pick. A work of fame.
　　P. Can. Of honour.
　　Pick. Celebration.
　　P. Can. Worthy your name.
　　Pick. The Pennyboys to live in't.
　　P. Can. It is an action you were built for, sir.
　　Pick. And none but you can do it.
　　P. jun. I'll undertake it.
　　P. Can. And carry it.
　　P. jun. Fear me not ; for since I came
Of mature age, I have had a certain itch

In my right eye, this corner here, do you see?
To do some work, and worthy of a chronicle.

        [*Exeunt.*

    Mirth. *How now, gossip! how does the play please
you?*

    Cen. *Very scurvily, methinks, and sufficiently
naught.*

    Expect. *As a body would wish: here's nothing but
a young prodigal come of age, who makes much of the
barber, buys him a place in a new office, in the air, I
know not where; and his man of law to follow him,
with a beggar to boot, and they two help him to a wife.*

    Mirth. *Ay, she is a proper piece! that such creatures
can broke for.*

    Tat. *I cannot abide that nasty fellow, the beggar; if
he had been a court-beggar in good clothes, a beggar in
velvet, as they say, I could have endured him.*

    Mirth. *Or a begging scholar in black, or one of these
beggarly poets, gossip, that could hang upon a young
heir like a horseleech.*

    Expect. *Or a threadbare doctor of physic, a poor
quacksalver.*

    Cen. *Or a sea-captain half starved.*

    Mirth. *Ay, these were tolerable beggars, beggars of
fashion! you shall see some such anon.*

    Tat. *I would fain see the fool, gossip; the fool is the
finest man in the company, they say, and has all the
wit: he is the very justice o' peace of the play, and can
commit whom he will, and what he will, error, absurdity, as the toy takes him, and no man say black is
his eye, but laugh at him.*

    Mirth. *But they have no fool in this play, I am
afraid, gossip.*

    Tat. *It is a wise play, then!*

    Expect. *They are all fools, the rather, in that.*

    Cen. *Like enough.*

Tat. *My husband, Timothy Tattle, God rest his
poor soul! was wont to say,[5] there was no play without
a fool and a devil in't; he was for the devil still, God
bless him! The devil for his money, would he say, I
would fain see the devil. And why would you so fain
see the devil? would I say. Because he has horns,
wife, and may be a cuckold as well as a devil, he would
answer. You are e'en such another! husband, quoth I.
Was the devil ever married? Where do you read, the
devil was ever so honourable to commit matrimony?
The play will tell us that, says he, we'll go see it to-
morrow, the* Devil is an Ass. *He is an errant learned*

---

[5] ———— *there was no play without a* fool *and a devil in't, &c.*]
" It was wont," says good master John Geb, (Coll. Ex.) " when an
Enterlude was to be acted in a countrey town, the first question
that an hob-nailed spectator made before he would pay his penny
to goe in, was, *Whether there bee a devile and a foole in the play?*
And if the foole get upon the divell's backe, and beate him with his
coxcombe till he rore, the play is complete." *The foot out of the
Snare,* p. 68.

This alludes to the old Moralities : the fool or clown of the new
comedy, however, succeeded to all the celebrity of his predecessor,
and was inquired after with equal impatience. Goffe, a great admirer of Jonson, has a pleasant passage in his *Careless Shepherdess,*
which enters completely into mistress Tattle's idea of the subject.

> " Why, I would have the fool in every act,
> Be it comedy or Tragedy. I have laughed
> Until I cry'd again, to see what faces
> The rogue will make. O, it does me good
> To see him hold out's chin, hang down his hands,
> And twirle his bawble : there is never a part
> About him but breaks jests.
> I had rather hear him leap, or laugh, or cry,
> Than hear the gravest speech in all the play.
> I never saw *Reade* peeping thro' the curtain,
> But ravishing joy enter'd into my heart."

Emanuel Reade, the person here mentioned, was one of the original
actors in Beaumont and Fletcher's plays : these, however, could
have afforded him no scope for the fine acting which gave such delight to the good landlord in Goffe's *Prelude;* and which probably
took place in some of Shakspeare's pieces.

*man that made it, and can write, they say, and I am
foully deceived but he can read too.*

Mirth. *I remember it, gossip, I went with you; by
the same token Mistress Trouble-truth dissuaded us,
and told us he was a profane poet, and all his plays
had devils in them; that he kept school upon the stage,
could conjure there, above the school of Westminster,
and doctor Lamb[6] too : not a play he made but had a
devil in it ; and that he would learn us all to make our
husbands cuckolds at plays : by another token, that a
young married wife in the company said, she could find
in her heart to steal thither, and see a little of the
vanity through her mask, and come practise at home.*

Tat. *O, it was mistress——*

Mirth. *Nay, gossip, I name nobody : It may be
'twas myself.*

Expect. *But was the devil a proper man, gossip?*

Mirth. *As fine a gentleman of his inches as ever I
saw trusted to the stage, or any where else ; and loved
the commonwealth as well as ever a patriot of them all :
he would carry away the Vice on his back, quick to hell,
in every play where he came, and reform abuses.*

Expect. *There was the Devil of Edmonton, no such
man, I warrant you.*

---

[6] Dr. Lamb.] He passed for a conjurer with the vulgar, but was
an ignorant and impudent impostor.   He was indicted at Worces-
ter, 5 *Jac.* I. for diabolical witchcrafts and inchantments, and at the
assizes of the same county, in the following year, for his invocation
and entertainment of evil spirits ; but for both these, judgment was
suspended.   Convicted of a rape, 21 *Jac.* I. upon the body of a
girl of eleven years old in Southwark, but had interest enough to
get the king's pardon.   He was pelted by the mob, from the Fortune play-house to the Old Jewry, on the 13th of June, 1628, and
died the next morning in the Poultry-compter ; one of his eyes
being beaten out, and his skull fractured.   The rabble were possessed that the doctor dealt with the devil, and assisted the duke
of Buckingham in misleading the king ; at which instant the parliament were making a remonstrance.   WHAL.

Cen. *The conjurer cozened him with a candle's end;*[7]
he was an ass.

Mirth. *But there was one Smug, a smith, would have
made a horse laugh, and broke his halter, as they say.*[8]

Tat. *O, but the poor man had got a shrewd mis-
chance one day.*

Expect. *How, gossip?*

Tat. *He had drest a rogue jade in the morning, that
had the staggers, and had got such a spice of them himself by noon, as they would not away all the play-time,
do what he could for his heart.*

Mirth. *'Twas his part, gossip; he was to be drunk
by his part.*

Tat. *Say you so? I understood not so much.*

Expect. *Would we had such another part, and such
a man in this play! I fear 'twill be an excellent dull
thing.*

Cen. *Expect, intend it.*

[7] *The conjurer cozen'd him with a* candle's end.] This alludes
to a story told of Peter Fabel.—When the time for which he had
sold his soul was expired, and the devil came to fetch him, he
begged permission to live till the taper, then nearly finished, was
burnt out: this indulgence being granted to his earnest entreaties,
he seized the *candle end*, and before the devil was aware, plunged
it into a vessel of holy water! Here it was secure from the devil's
clutches, who vanished in great dudgeon, without his errand. In
the *Devil of Edmonton*, however, as we now have it, Peter Fabel
escapes by a different contrivance.

[8] *There was one* Smug, *a smith, would have made a horse laugh,
&c.*] Smug is a character in this old play. He is, as Mirth says,
a *smith*, and a deer-stealer: but it is not easy to guess what particular amusement his part afforded, unless, as the sequel seems to
insinuate, the performer was actually intoxicated at the time of
representation. Blague, the host, seems to be meant for the principal buffoon of the piece.

ACT II.

SCENE I. *A Room in* PENNYBOY senior's *House.*

Enter PENNYBOY sen., PECUNIA, MORTGAGE, STATUTE,
BAND *and* BROKER.

Pennyboy senior.

YOUR grace is sad, methinks, and melan-
choly,
    You do not look upon me with that face
    As you were wont, my goddess, bright
    Pecunia!
Altho' your grace be fallen off two in the hundred,[9]
In vulgar estimation; yet am I
Your grace's servant still: and teach this body
To bend, and these my aged knees to buckle,
In adoration, and just worship of you.
Indeed, I do confess, I have no shape
To make a minion of, but I am your martyr,
Your grace's martyr. I can hear the rogues,
As I do walk the streets, whisper and point,
"There goes old Pennyboy, the slave of money,
Rich Pennyboy, lady Pecunia's drudge,
A sordid rascal, one that never made

---

[9] *Although your grace be* fallen off two in the hundred, &c.] The
rate of interest was fixed, by a law passed in the thirty-seventh year
of Henry VIII. and confirmed in the thirteenth of Elizabeth, to *ten*
per cent. per annum ; but by the statute of the twenty-first of James
(the year before this play appeared,) it was reduced to *eight*. This
was a grievous affliction to the Pennyboys (misers) of the time, and
to this the text here and elsewhere alludes.

Good meal in his sleep, but sells the acates are sent
        him,[1]
Fish, fowl, and venison, and preserves himself,
Like an old hoary rat, with mouldy pie-crust!"
This I do hear, rejoicing I can suffer
This, and much more for your good grace's sake.
    Pec. Why do you so, my guardian? I not bid you:
Cannot my grace be gotten, and held too,
Without your self-tormentings and your watches,
Your macerating of your body thus,
With cares and scantings of your diet and rest?
    P. sen. O no, your services, my princely lady,
Cannot with too much zeal of rites be done,
They are so sacred.
    Pec. But my reputation
May suffer, and the worship of my family,
When by so servile means they both are sought.
    P. sen. You are a noble, young, free, gracious lady,
And would be every body's in your bounty,
But you must not be so.   They are a few
That know your merit, lady, and can value it.
Yourself scarce understands your proper powers,
They are all-mighty, and that we, your servants,
That have the honour here to stand so near you,
Know and can use too.   All this nether world [2]

---

1 ———— *sells the* acates *are sent him,*
   Fish, fowl, and venison, and preserves himself
   With mouldy pie-crust!] Pope has very happily transferred this
(for he did not find it in Horace) to the character of Avidienus,
whom, like Pennyboy, he makes to

        " Sell his *presented partridges and fruits,*
          And humbly live on rabbits and on roots."

2 ———— *All this nether world*
   Is yours, you command it, &c.]

                ——— *Omnis enim res,*
        Virtus, fama, decus, divina humanaque pulchris
        Divitiis parent.   Hor. L. ii. Sat. 3.

Is yours, you command it, and do sway it ;
The honour of it, and the honesty,
The reputation, ay, and the religion,
(I was about to say, and had not err'd,)
Is queen Pecunia's : for that style is yours,
If mortals knew your grace, or their own good.
   Mor. Please your grace to retire.
   Band. I fear your grace
Hath ta'en too much of the sharp air.
   Pec. O, no !
I could endure to take a great deal more,
(And with my constitution,) were it left
Under my choice : what think you of it, Statute ?
   Sta. A little now and then does well, and keeps
Your grace in your complexion.
   Band. And true temper.
   Mor. But too much, madam, may increase cold
       rheums,
Nourish catarrhs, green sicknesses, and agues,
And put you in consumption.
   P. sen. Best to take
Advice of your grave women, noble madam,
They know the state of your body, and have studied
Your grace's health.
   Band. And honour.   Here'll be visitants,

And again :

         ——*fidemque et amicos,*
    Et genus, et formam, Regina Pecunia *donat.* Lib. i. Ep. 6.

But Jonson has an eye constantly on Aristophanes, and has introduced various allusions to the highly humorous scene in which Chremylus and his servant let Plutus into the secret of his own importance.

   Χρ.   —— ὥστε του Διος
     Την δυναμιν, ην λυπῃ τι, καταλυσεις μονος.
   Πλ. Τι λεγεις ; εἰ εμε θυουσιν αυτῳ ;
   Χρ. Φημ' εγω.
     Και νη Δι', ει τι γ' εστι λαμπρον και καλον,
     Ἡ χαριεν ανθρωποισι, δια σε γιγνεται.
     Ἀπαντα τῳ πλουτειν γαρ εσθ' υπηκοα. κ. τ. α. 145.

Or suitors by and by; and 'tis not fit
They find you here.
    Sta. 'Twill make your grace too cheap
To give them audience presently.
    Mor. Leave your secretary
To answer them.
    Pec. Wait you here, Broker.
    Bro. I shall, madam,   [*Exeunt all but* BROKER.
And do your grace's trusts with diligence.

Enter PIEDMANTLE.

    Pie. What luck is this? I am come an inch too late!
Do you hear, sir? is your worship of the family
Unto the lady Pecunia?
    Bro. I serve her grace, sir,
Aurelia Clara Pecunia, the Infanta.
    Pie. Has she all those titles, and her grace besides?
I must correct that ignorance and oversight,
Before I do present. Sir, I have drawn
A pedigree for her grace, though yet a novice
In that so noble study.
    Bro. A herald at arms?
    Pie. No, sir, a pursuivant, my name is Piedmantle.
    Bro. Good master Piedmantle.
    Pie. I have deduced her——
    Bro. From all the Spanish mines in the West-
        Indies,
I hope; for she comes that way by her mother,
But by her grandmother she is duchess of mines.
    Pie. From man's creation I have brought her.
    Bro. No farther!
Before, sir, long before, you have done nothing else;
Your mines were before Adam, search your office,
Roll five and twenty, you will find it so.
I see you are but a novice, master Piedmantle,
If you had not told me so.
    Pie. Sir, an apprentice

In armory.   I have read the Elements,
And Accidence, and all the leading books ;[3]
And I have now upon me a great ambition
How to be brought to her grace, to kiss her hands.
    Bro. Why, if you have acquaintance with mistress
        Statute,
Or mistress Band, my lady's gentlewomen,
They can induce you.   One is a judge's daughter,
But somewhat stately ; the other, mistress Band,
Her father's but a scrivener, but she can
Almost as much with my lady as the other,
Especially if Rose Wax the chambermaid
Be willing.   Do you not know her sir, neither ?
    Pie. No, in troth, sir.
    Bro. She's a good pliant wench,
And easy to be wrought, sir ; but the nurse,
Old mother Mortgage, if you have a tenement,
Or such a morsel, though she have no teeth,
She loves a sweet-meat, any thing that melts
In her warm gums, she could command it for you
On such a trifle, a toy.   Sir, you may see
How for your love, and this so pure complexion,
(A perfect sanguine) I have ventur'd thus,
The straining of a ward, opening a door
Into the secrets of our family.
    Pie. I pray you let me know, sir, unto whom
I am so much beholden ; but your name.
    Bro. My name is Broker ; I am secretary
And usher to her grace.
    Pie. Good master Broker !
    Bro. Good master Piedmantle !
    Pie. Why, you could do me,
If you would, now, this favour of yourself.

[3] ———— *I have read the* Elements,
    And Accidence, *and all the leading books.*] The *Elements of Armory,* by Edm. Bolton, printed in 1610.   And the *Accedence of Armorye,* by Leigh, printed in 1562.   WHAL.

5   O

Bro. Truly I think I could; but if I would,
I hardly should, without, or mistress Band,
Or mistress Statute, please to appear in it;
Or the good nurse I told you of, mistress Mortgage.
We know our places here, we mingle not
One in another's sphere, but all move orderly
In our own orbs; yet we are all concentrics.
    Pie. Well, sir, I'll wait a better season.
    Bro. Do,   [*Makes a mouth at him.*
And study the right means; get mistress Band
To urge on your behalf, or little Wax.
    Pie. I have a hope, sir, that I may, by chance,
Light on her grace, as she is taking the air.
    Bro. That air of hope has blasted many an aiery
Of castrils like yourself, good master Piedmantle.
                                [*Exit* PIEDMANTLE.
    P. sen. [*springs forward.*] Well said, master
        secretary, I stood behind
And heard thee all. I honour thy dispatches.
If they be rude, untrained in our method,
And have not studied the rule, dismiss them quickly.
Where's Lickfinger, my cook, that unctuous rascal?
He'll never keep his hour, that vessel of kitchen-stuff!

Enter LICKFINGER.

    Bro. Here he is come, sir.
    P. sen. Pox upon him, kidney,
Always too late!
    Lick. To wish them you, I confess,
That have them already.
    P. sen. What?
    Lick. The pox!
    P. sen. The piles,
The plague, and all diseases light on him
Knows not to keep his word! I'd keep my word,
        sure;
I hate that man that will not keep his word.

When did I break my word ?
   Lick. Or I, till now ?
And 'tis but half an hour.
   P. sen. Half a year,
To me, that stand upon a minute of time :
I am a just man, I love still to be just.
   Lick. Why, you think I can run like light-foot
      Ralph,
Or keep a wheel-barrow with a sail in town here,
To whirl me to you.   I have lost two stone
Of suet in the service, posting hither :
You might have followed me like a watering-pot,
And seen the knots I made along the street ;
My face dropt like the skimmer in a fritter-pan,
And my whole body is yet, to say the truth,
A roasted pound of butter, with grated bread in't !
   P. sen. Believe you he that list ; you staid of
      purpose
To have my venison stink, and my fowl mortified,
That you might have them——
   Lick. A shilling or two cheaper !
That is your jealousy.
   P. sen. Perhaps it is.
Will you go in, and view, and value all ?
Yonder is venison sent me, fowl, and fish,
In such abundance, I am sick to see it ;
I wonder what they mean ! I have told them of it !
To burden a weak stomach, and provoke
A dying appetite ! thrust a sin upon me
I ne'er was guilty of ! nothing but gluttony,
Gross gluttony, that will undo this land !
   Lick. And bating two in the hundred.
   P. sen. Ay, that same's
A crying sin, a fearful damn'd device,
Eats up the poor, devours them——
   Lick. Sir, take heed
What you give out.

P. sen. Against your grave great Solons,
Numæ Pompilii, they that made that law,
To take away the poor's inheritance!
It was their portion, I will stand to it;
And they have robb'd them of it, plainly robb'd
    them.
I still am a just man, I tell the truth.
When moneys went at ten in the hundred, I,
And such as I, the servants of Pecunia,
Could spare the poor two out of ten, and did it :
How say you, Broker?
    Lick. Ask your echo!
    Bro. You did it.
    P. sen. I am for justice; when did I leave justice?
We knew 'twas theirs, they had right and title to't :
Now——
    Lick. You can spare them nothing.
    P. sen. Very little.
    Lick. As good as nothing.
    P. sen. They have bound our hands
With their wise solemn act, shorten'd our arms.
    Lick. Beware those worshipful ears, sir, be not
        shorten'd,
And you play Crop in the Fleet, if you use this license.
    P. sen. What license, knave, informer?
    Lick. I am Lickfinger,
Your cook.
    P. sen. A saucy Jack you are, that's once.
What said I, Broker?
    Bro. Nothing that I heard, sir.
    Lick. I know his gift, he can be deaf when he list.
    P. sen. Have you provided me my bushel of eggs
I did bespeak? I do not care how stale
Or stinking that they be; let 'em be rotten :
For ammunition here to pelt the boys
That break my windows.
    Lick. Yes, sir, I have spared them

Out of the custard-politic for you, the mayor's.[4]

P. sen. 'Tis well; go in, take hence all that excess,
Make what you can of it, your best: and when
I have friends that I invite at home, provide me
Such, such, and such a dish, as I bespeak;
One at a time, no superfluity.
Or if you have it not, return me money:
You know my ways.[5]

Lick. They are a little crooked.

P. sen. How, knave?

Lick. Because you do indent.

P. sen. 'Tis true, sir,
I do indent you shall return me money.

Lick. Rather than meat, I know it; you are just still.

P. sen. I love it still; and therefore if you spend
The red-deer pies in your house, or sell them forth, sir,
Cast so, that I may have their coffins all
Return'd here,[6] and piled up: I would be thought

---

[4] *The* custard-politic,] i. e. the huge custard prepared for the Lord Mayor's feast. See p. 13.

[5] *You know my ways.*
Lick. *They are a little crooked—*
Because you do indent.] A pun upon the old meaning of the law word *indentare,* (————) to make an impression on the wax of the seal with the teeth, which, before writing was common, Cowel tells us, was the mode of testifying the execution of covenants, deeds, &c.

[6] *Cast so, that I may have their* coffins *all*
Return'd here,] i. e. the raised crust, or cavities of the pies. The word is familiar, in this sense, to all our old writers. One instance of it is given in vol. ii. p. 3,

"Cold as the turkies *coffin'd* up in *crust,*"

which will be thought sufficient, perhaps, to exemplify so common an expression.

It may be added, however, that this word, *coffin,* was in ill repute under Elizabeth. The good queen, as the call for one to inclose *the dearest morsel of the earth* became more pressing, grew more solicitous to exclude all thoughts of it. "She would chide her lords if they mentioned the *coffin of a pie* before her, and would make them say *crust,* for she loved not words of sad omen."

To keep some kind of house.

    Lick. By the mouldy signs !

    P. sen. And then remember meat for my two dogs :

Fat flaps of mutton, kidneys, rumps of veal,

Good plenteous scraps ; my maid shall eat the relics.

    Lick. When you and your dogs have dined ! a
        sweet reversion.

    P. sen. Who's here ? my courtier, and my little
        doctor ?

My muster-master ? And what plover's that

They have brought to pull ?

    Bro. I know not, some green plover.

I'll find him out.

       Enter FITTON, ALMANAC, SHUNFIELD, *and*
            MADRIGAL.

    P. sen. Do, for I know the rest :

They are the jeerers, mocking, flouting Jacks.

    Fit. How now, old Moneybawd ! We are come—

    P. sen. To jeer me,

As you were wont ; I know you.

    Alm. No, to give thee

Some good security, and see Pecunia.

    P. sen. What is't ?

    Fit. Ourselves.

    Alm. We'll be one bound for another.

    Fit. This noble doctor here.

    Alm. This worthy courtier.

    Fit. This man of war, he was our muster-master.

    Alm. But a sea-captain now, brave captain Shun-
        field.   [P. sen. *holds up his nose.*

    Shun. You snuff the air now, has the scent dis-
        pleased you ?

    Fit. Thou need'st not fear him, man, his credit is
        sound.

    Alm. And season'd too, since he took salt at sea.

    P. sen. I do not love pickled security ;

Would I had one good fresh man in for all :
For truth is, you three stink.
 Shun. You are a rogue.
 P. sen. I think I am ; but I will lend no money
On that security, captain.
 Alm. Here's a gentleman,
A fresh-man in the world, one master Madrigal.
  Fit. Of an untainted credit ; what say you to
   him ?   [*Exit* MADRIGAL *with* BROKER.
  Shun. He's gone, methinks ; where is he ?—
   Madrigal !
  P. sen. He has an odd singing name : is he an
   heir ?
  Fit. An heir to a fair fortune.
  Alm. And full hopes :
A dainty scholar, and a pretty poet !
  P. sen. You have said enough. I have no money,
   gentlemen,
An he go to't in rhyme once, not a penny.
        [*He snuffs again.*
  Shun. Why, he's of years, though he have little
   beard.
  P. sen. His beard has time to grow : I have no
   money.
Let him still dabble in poetry. No Pecunia
Is to be seen.
  Alm. Come, thou lov'st to be costive
Still in thy courtesy ; but I have a pill,
A golden pill, to purge away this melancholy.
  Shun. 'Tis nothing but his keeping of the house
   here,
With his two drowsy dogs.
  Fit. A drench of sack
At a good tavern, and a fine fresh pullet,
Would cure him.
  Lick. Nothing but a young heir in white-broth ;
I know his diet better than the doctor.

Shun. What, Lickfinger, mine old host of Ram-alley![7]
You have some market here.

Alm. Some dosser of fish
Or fowl, to fetch off.

Fit. An odd bargain of venison
To drive.

P. sen. Will you go in, knave?

Lick. I must needs,
You see who drives me, gentlemen.

[P. sen. *thrusts him in.*

Alm. Not the Devil.

Fit. He may in time, he is his agent now.

P. sen. You are all cogging Jacks, a covey of wits,
The jeerers, that still call together at meals,
Or rather an aiery; for you are birds of prey,
And fly at all; nothing's too big or high for you;
And are so truly fear'd, but not beloved
One of another, as no one dares break
Company from the rest, lest they should fall
Upon him absent.

Alm. O, the only oracle
That ever peep'd or spake out of a doublet![8]

Shun. How the rogue stinks! worse than a fish-
      monger's sleeves.[9]

---

[7] ——— *mine old host of Ram-alley.*] This alley, which leads
from Fleet-street into the Temple, was in Jonson's time principally
inhabited by cooks, and victuallers. Thus, in the old drama of
that name,

"What, though *Ram-alley* stinks with *cooks* and ale," &c.

[8] Alm. *O! the only* oracle
That ever peep'd or spake out of a doublet!] The allusion is to the heathen priests, who were Ἐγγαστριμυθοι, or had the
art of keeping their voice within, as if the demon spoke in their
belly. There is an allusion to this in the prophet *Isaiah;* "And
when they shall say unto you, seek unto them who have familiar
spirits, and unto wizards that *peep*, and that mutter." viii. 19.
WHAL.

Instead of *peep*, Lowth has *speak inwardly*.

[9] ——— *worse than a fishmonger's sleeves.*] This reproach is

Fit. Or currier's hands.

Shun. And such a parboil'd visage !

Fit. His face looks like a dyer's apron, just.

Alm. A sodden head, and his whole brain a pos-
    set-curd.

P. sen. Ay, now you jeer, jeer on ; I have no
    money.

Alm. I wonder what religion he is of.

Fit. No certain species sure : a kind of mule,
That's half an ethnic, half a Christian !

P. sen. I have no money, gentlemen.

Shun. This stock,
He has no sense of any virtue, honour,
Gentry, or merit.

P. sen. You say very right,
My meritorious captain, as I take it,
Merit will keep no house, nor pay no house-rent.
Will mistress Merit go to market, think you,
Set on the pot, or feed the family ?
Will gentry clear with the butcher, or the baker,
Fetch in a pheasant, or a brace of partridges,
From good-wife poulter, for my lady's supper ?

Fit. See this pure rogue !

P. sen. This rogue has money though ;
My worshipful brave courtier has no money ;
No, nor my valiant captain.

Shun. Hang you, rascal.

P. sen. Nor you, my learned doctor.   I loved you
While you did hold your practice, and kill tripe wives,
And kept you to your urinal ; but since your thumbs
Have greased the Ephemerides, casting figures,
And turning over for your candle-rents,
And your twelve houses in the zodiac,
With your almutens, alma-cantaras,

of no modern date.   The reader remembers the spiteful reflection
on Horace, whose father is supposed by some to have been a dealer
in fish ; *Quoties ego vidi patrem tuum brachio se emungentem ?*

Troth you shall cant alone for Pennyboy.

Shun. I told you what we should find him, a mere
  bawd.

Fit. A rogue, a cheater.

P. sen. What you please, gentlemen :
I am of that humble nature and condition,
Never to mind your worships, or take notice
Of what you throw away thus.   I keep house here,
Like a lame cobler, never out of doors,
With my two dogs, my friends ; and, as you say,
Drive a quick pretty trade, still.   I get money :
And as for titles, be they rogue or rascal,
Or what your worships fancy, let them pass,
As transitory things ; they are mine to-day,
And yours to-morrow.

Alm. Hang thee, dog !

Shun. Thou cur !

P. sen. You see how I do blush, and am ashamed
Of these large attributes ! yet you have no money.

Alm. Well, wolf, hyena, you old pocky rascal,
You will have the hernia fall down again
Into your scrotum, and I shall be sent for :
I will remember then, that, and your fistula
In ano, I cured you of.

P. sen. Thank your dog-leech craft !
They were wholesome piles afore you meddled with
  them.

Alm. What an ungrateful wretch is this !

Shun. He minds
A courtesy no more than London bridge
What arch was mended last.[10]

Fit. He never thinks,

[10] *He minds*
   A courtesy no more than London bridge
   What arch was mended last.] Two hundred years have nearly
elapsed since this was written, and the observation still holds. This
pernicious structure has wasted more money in perpetual repairs
than would have sufficed to build a dozen safe and commodious

More than a log, of any grace at court
A man may do him ; or that such a lord
Reach'd him his hand.

P. sen. O yes ! if grace would strike
The brewer's tally, or my good lord's hand
Would quit the scores : but, sir, they will not do it.
Here is a piece, my good lord Piece doth all ;
Goes to the butcher's, fetches in a mutton ;
Then to the baker's, brings in bread, makes fires,
Gets wine, and does more real courtesies
Than all my lords I know : my sweet lord Piece !
                              [*Holds up a piece of gold.*
You are my lord, the rest are cogging Jacks,
Under the rose.

Shun. Rogue, I could beat you now.

P. sen. True, captain, if you durst beat any other,
I should believe you ; but indeed you are hungry ;
You are not angry, captain, if I know you
Aright, good captain. No Pecunia
Is to be seen, though mistress Band would speak,
Or little blushet Wax be ne'er so easy ;
I'll stop mine ears with her, against the Syrens,
Court, and philosophy. God be wi' you, gentlemen !
Provide you better names, Pecunia is for you. [*Exit.*

Fit. What a damn'd harpy it is ! Where's Mad-
        rigal ?
Is he sneak'd hence ?

Shun. Here he comes with Broker,
Pecunia's secretary.

Re-enter MADRIGAL *and* BROKER.

Alm. He may do some good

bridges, and cost the lives, perhaps, of as many thousand people.
This may seem little to those whom it concerns—but there is blood
on the city ; and a heavy account is before them. Had an alderman
or a turtle been lost there, the nuisance would have been long since
removed.

With him perhaps.—Where have you been, Mad-
    rigal?

Mad. Above, with my lady's women, reading
    verses.

Fit. That was a favour.—Good morrow, master
    Secretary!

Shun. Good morrow, master Usher!

Alm. Sir, by both
Your worshipful titles, and your name, mas Broker,
Good morrow!

Mad. I did ask him if he were
Amphibion Broker.

Shun. Why?

Mad. A creature of two natures,
Because he has two offices.

Bro. You may jeer,
You have the wits, young gentlemen : but your hope
Of Helicon will never carry it here,
With our fat family ; we have the dullest,
Most unbored ears for verse amongst our females !
I grieved you read so long, sir ; old nurse Mortgage
She snored in the chair, and Statute,if you mark'd her,
Fell fast asleep, and mistress Band she nodded,
But not with any consent to what you read.
They must have somewhat else to chink than rhymes.
If you could make an epitaph on your land,
(Imagine it on departure,) such a poem
Would wake them, and bring Wax to her true
    temper.

Mad. I'faith, sir, and I'll try.

Bro. It is but earth,
Fit to make bricks and tiles of.

Shun. Pox upon't,
'Tis but for pots, or pipkins at the best.
If it would keep us in good tobacco-pipes——

Bro. It were worth keeping.

Fit. Or in porcelain dishes,

There were some hope.
 Alm. But this is a hungry soil,
And must be help'd.
 Fit. Who would hold any land,
To have the trouble to marl it ?
 Shun. Not a gentleman.
 Bro. Let clowns and hinds affect it, that love
   ploughs,
And carts and harrows, and are busy still
In vexing the dull element.
 Alm. Our sweet songster
Shall rarify 't into air.
 Fit. And you, mas Broker,
Shall have a feeling.
 Bro. So it supple, sir,
The nerves.
 Mad. O, it shall be palpable,
Make thee run thorough a hoop, or a thumb-ring
The nose of a tobacco-pipe, and draw
Thy ductile bones out like a knitting-needle,
To serve my subtile turns.
 Bro. I shall obey, sir,
And run a thread, like an hour-glass.

   Re-enter PENNYBOY sen.

 P. sen. Where is Broker ?
Are not these flies gone yet ? Pray quit my house,
I'll smoke you out else.
 Fit. O the prodigal !
Will you be at so much charge with us, and loss ?
 Mad. I've heard you have offer'd, sir, to lock up
   smoke,[1]

---

[1] *Mad. I've heard you have offer'd, sir, to lock up smoke.*] This,
with what follows, is improved with true comic humour from the
subsequent passage in the *Aulular.* of Plautus :

  Quin Divûm atque hominum clamat continuo fidem,
  De suo tigillo fumus si qua exit foras.
  Quin, quum it dormitum, follem obstringit ob gulam. WHAL.

The *Aulularia* was a great favourite with Jonson, who has more

And calk your windows, spar up all your doors,[2]
Thinking to keep it a close prisoner with you,
And wept when it went out, sir, at your chimney.

Fit. And yet his eyes were drier than a pumice.

Shun. A wretched rascal, that will bind about
The nose of his bellows, lest the wind get out
When he's abroad.

Alm. Sweeps down no cobwebs here,
But sells them for cut fingers ; and the spiders,
As creatures rear'd of dust, and cost him nothing,
To fat old ladies' monkeys.

Fit. He has offer'd
To gather up spilt water, and preserve
Each hair falls from him, to stop balls withal.

Shun. A slave, and an idolater to Pecunia !

P. sen. You all have happy memories, gentlemen,
In rocking my poor cradle.   I remember too,
When you had lands and credit, worship, friends,
Ay, and could give security : now you have none,
Or will have none right shortly.   This can time,
And the vicissitude of things ! I have
All these, and money too, and do possess them,
And am right heartily glad of all our memories,
And both the changes.

Fit. Let us leave the viper.

[*Exeunt all but* P. sen. *and* BROKER.

P. sen. He's glad he is rid of his torture, and so
     soon.—

Broker, come hither ; up, and tell your lady,

---

obligations to it than Whalley was probably aware of. Fitton's *jeers*
are from the same source as Madrigal's :

> *Pumex non æque est aridus, atque hic est senex,*
> *Aquam hercle plorat, quom lavat, profundere:*
> *Quin ipsi pridem tonsor ungues demserat,*
> *Collegit, &c.*   A ii. S. 4.

[2] ———— spar *up all your doors,*] i. e. bar or bolt them.   The
word is still in use.

She must be ready presently, and Statute,
Band, Mortgage, Wax : my prodigal young kinsman
Will straight be here to see her ; top of our house,
The flourishing and flaunting Pennyboy !
We were but three of us in all the world,
My brother Francis, whom they call'd Frank Penny-
  boy,
Father to this ; he's dead : this Pennyboy
Is now the heir ! I, Richer Pennyboy,
Not Richard, but old Harry Pennyboy,
And, to make rhyme, close, wary Pennyboy,
I shall have all at last, my hopes do tell me.
Go, see all ready ; and where my dogs have faulted,
Remove it with a broom, and sweeten all
With a slice of juniper, not too much, but sparing,
We may be faulty ourselves else, and turn prodigal,
In entertaining of the prodigal.   [*Exit* BROKER.
Here he is, and with him—what ? a clapper-dudgeon ![3]

---

[3] *What ? a* clapper-dudgeon !] A clapper-dudgeon, the *Canting
Dictionary* informs us, is "a thorough-bred beggar, a beggar born
of a beggar."

In the *Captain*, by Beaumont and Fletcher, Jacomo says,

   ————— "though I am plain and *dudgeon*,
  I would not be an ass ; and to sell parcels,
  I can as soon be hang'd."

Dudgeon, as the last commentator assures us, "occurs here *in a
very unusual manner*," vol. ix. 162. If this jargon means, *in a very
unusual sense*, Mr. Weber is mistaken. The word occurs in a very
common sense. "It probably means," he adds, "a *fighting* man."
It means no such thing. Applied to persons, it means, as in the
text, *coarse, rude, blunt, inelegant*. But this is not all ; "a *dudgeon*
(he says) was a particular kind of dagger, as the commentators on
Shakspeare have proved by many quotations, though they have
overlooked Cotgrave's *simple* interpretation of *dague à roëlles*, 'a
Scottish dagger, or *dudgeon-haft* dagger !' "

It is somewhat remarkable that Mr. Weber should charge the
commentators with having *overlooked* this *simple* interpretation, as
he is pleased to call it, when he had himself but just before copied
it verbatim from one of them. Of the meaning of *dague à roëlles*, he
has not, I will venture to affirm, the slightest idea :—It may not be

That's a good sign, to have the beggar follow him
So near, at his first entry into fortune.

Enter PENNYBOY jun. PENNYBOY Canter, *and*
PICKLOCK.[4]

P. jun. How now, old uncle ?   I am come to see
        thee,

amiss therefore to add a few words in explanation of an expression
thus idly transferred from volume to volume.

   Whoever has looked into our old plays, must have noticed the
laudable pains taken by their editors, to account for the facility with
which the heroines of them produce daggers upon all occasions. In
the case of Juliet, (for example,) Mr. Steevens supposes—that she
was furnished with one, *as a bride;* while Mr. Malone, who finds
her in possession of it before the bridal robes were on, conjectures
that she *secretly* procured it " immediately after her father had
threatened to force her to marry Paris." It so happens (no uncommon case) that both these gentlemen are wrong.   Daggers, or,
as they were more commonly called, knives, were worn at all times,
by every woman in England—whether they were so in Italy, Shakspeare, I believe, never enquired, and I cannot tell. In the haft
of this universal appendage (for men also wore them) there was
of course much variety.   The homeliest was that *à roelles*, a plain
piece of wood with an orbicular rim of iron for a guard : the next,
in degree, was the *dudgeon*, in which the wood was googed out in
crooked channels, like what is now, and perhaps was then, called
snail-creeping.   It is needless to speak of steel, silver, amber, and
gold hafted daggers ; but the reader who knows how ambitious our
ancestors were of finery, will easily conceive by what process dudgeon (wooden) came to be used as a term of contempt, and from a
simple characteristic of poverty to be frequently employed in de-
noting the meaner passions.

   To return to Jonson.   *A clapper-dudgeon* literally signifies one
who claps his *wooden* dish at the door, for broken meat, &c., as was
once the practice.

   I should blush at the length of this note, were it not that I have
grown old in the love of the great masters of the English tongue,
and think no pains ill bestowed in seeking to rescue them from the
united attacks of ignorance and temerity.

  [4] After this, there occurs a marginal note, taken, with the rest of
this play, from the book-holder's copy.   *Broker, Pecunia, Statute,
Band, Wax, and Mortgage, hid in the study :* which is evidently the
prompter's call on the actors required for the ensuing scene.

And the brave lady here, the daughter of Ophir,
They say thou keep'st.
    P. sen. Sweet nephew, if she were
The daughter of the Sun, she's at your service,
And so am I, and the whole family,
Worshipful nephew.
    P. jun. Say'st thou so, dear uncle !
Welcome my friends then : here is domine Picklock,
My man of law, solicits all my causes,
Follows my business, makes and compounds my
        quarrels
Between my tenants and me ; sows all my strifes,
And reaps them too ; troubles the country for me,
And vexes any neighbour that I please.
    P. sen. But with commission ?
    P. jun. Under my hand and seal.
    P. sen. A worshipful place !
    Pick. I thank his worship for it.
    P. sen. But what is this old gentleman ?
    P. Can. A rogue,
A very canter, I, sir, one that maunds
Upon the pad :[5] we should be brothers though ;
For you are near as wretched as myself,
You dare not use your money, and I have none.
    P. sen. Not use my money, cogging Jack ! who
        uses it
At better rates, lets it for more in the hundred
Than I do, sirrah ?
    P. jun. Be not angry, uncle.

---

[5] *A* rogue,
   A very canter, *I, sir, one that* maunds
   Upon the pad.] *Rogue* is used here in its more ancient sense
of confirmed or sturdy vagrant. *Canter* has precisely the same
meaning.—" *Cant*, or *canting*," says a sensible old writer, " is a
term by which we do usually express the gibberish of beggars and
vagabonds." To *maund on the pad* is to beg on the highway—
somewhat, I believe, after the impressive manner of Gil Blas' dis-
abled soldier.

5   P

P. sen. What ! to disgrace me, with my queen, as if
I did not know her value.

P. Can. Sir, I meant,
You durst not to enjoy it.

P. sen. Hold your peace,
You are a Jack.

P. jun. Uncle, he shall be a John,
An you go to that ; as good a man as you are :
And I can make him so, a better man ;
Perhaps I will too.   Come, let us go.   [*Going.*

P. sen. Nay, kinsman,
My worshipful kinsman, and the top of our house,
Do not your penitent uncle that affront,
For a rash word, to leave his joyful threshold,
Before you see the lady that you long for,
The Venus of the time and state, Pecunia !
I do perceive your bounty loves the man,
For some concealed virtue that he hides
Under those rags.

P. Can. I owe my happiness to him,
The waiting on his worship, since I brought him
The happy news welcome to all young heirs.

P. jun. Thou didst indeed, for which I thank thee
          yet.
Your fortunate princess, uncle, is long a coming.

P. Can. She is not rigg'd, sir ; setting forth some
          lady
Will cost as much as furnishing a fleet.—
Here she is come at last, and like a galley
Gilt in the prow.

>   *Enter* PECUNIA *in state, attended by* BROKER,
>   STATUTE, BAND, WAX, *and* MORTGAGE.

P. jun. Is this Pecunia ?

P. sen. Vouchsafe my toward kinsman, gracious
          madam,
The favour of your hand.

Pec. Nay, of my lips, sir,   [*Kisses him.*
To him.

P. jun. She kisses like a mortal creature. [*Aside.*
Almighty madam, I have long'd to see you.

Pec. And I have my desire, sir, to behold
That youth and shape, which in my dreams and wakes
I have so oft contemplated, and felt
Warm in my veins, and native as my blood.
When I was told of your arrival here,
I felt my heart beat, as it would leap out
In speech ; and all my face it was a flame :
But how it came to pass, I do not know.

P. jun. O, beauty loves to be more proud than
          nature,
That made you blush.   I cannot satisfy
My curious eyes, by which alone I am happy,
In my beholding you.   [*Kisses her.*

P. Can. They pass the compliment
Prettily well.

Pick. Ay, he does kiss her, I like him.

P. jun. My passion was clear contrary, and doubtful,
I shook for fear, and yet I danced for joy,
I had such motions as the sun-beams make
Against a wall,[6] or playing on a water,
Or trembling vapour of a boiling pot——

P. sen. That's not so good ; it should have been a
          crucible

[6] *I had such motions as the sun-beams make*
    Against a wall, &c.]

          —————— *magno curarum fluctuat æstu,*
    Sicut aquæ tremulum labris ubi lumen aënis,
    Sole repercussum, aut radiantis imagine lunæ,
    Omnia pervolitat latè loca, jamque sub auras
    Erigitur, summique ferit laquearia tecti.
                              Æneid, lib. viii. v. 25.

In the speech of Pecunia, just above, there is an allusion to a very
beautiful passage in Apol. Rhodius, descriptive of the rising passion
of Medea.

With molten metal, she had understood it.

P. jun. I cannot talk, but I can love you, madam :
Are these your gentlewomen ? I love them too.

[*Kisses them.*

And which is mistress Statute ? mistress Band ?
They all kiss close, the last stuck to my lips.

Bro. It was my lady's chambermaid, soft Wax.

P. jun. Soft lips she has, I am sure on't. Mother
    Mortgage
I'll owe a kiss, till she be younger. Statute,
Sweet mistress Band, and honey little Wax,
We must be better acquainted.   [*Kisses them again.*

Sta. We are but servants, sir.

Band. But whom her grace is so content to grace,
We shall observe.

Wax. And with all fit respect.

Mor. In our poor places.

Wax. Being her grace's shadows.

P. jun. A fine, well-spoken family !—What's thy
    name ?

Bro. Broker.

P. jun. Methinks my uncle should not need thee,[7]
Who is a crafty knave enough, believe it.

[*Aside to* BROKER.

Art thou her grace's steward ?

Bro. No, her usher, sir.

P. jun. What, of the hall ? thou hast a sweeping
    face,
Thy beard is like a broom.

Bro. No barren chin, sir ;
I am no eunuch, though a gentleman-usher.

P. jun. Thou shalt go with us.—Uncle, I must have
My princess forth to-day.

P. sen. Whither you please, sir ;
You shall command her.

    [7] *Methinks my uncle, &c.*] This is not the first allusion which
we have had to the old proverb, *A crafty knave needs no broker.*

Pec. I will do all grace
To my new servant.

P. sen. Thanks unto your bounty ;
He is my nephew, and my chief, the point,
Tip, top, and tuft of all our family !—
But, sir, condition'd always you return
Statute and Band home, with my sweet soft Wax,
And my good nurse here, Mortgage.

P. jun. O, what else ?

P. sen. By Broker.

P. jun. Do not fear.

P. sen. She shall go with you,
Whither you please, sir, any where.

P. Can. I see
A money-bawd is lightly a flesh-bawd too.

Pick. Are you advised ?[8] Now, on my faith, this
          Canter
Would make a good grave burgess in some barn.

P. jun. Come, thou shalt go with us, uncle.

P. sen. By no means, sir.

P. jun. We'll have both sack and fidlers.

P. sen. I'll not draw
That charge upon your worship.

P. Can. He speaks modestly,
And like an uncle.

P. sen. But mas Broker here,
He shall attend you, nephew ; her grace's usher.
And what you fancy to bestow on him,
Be not too lavish, use a temperate bounty,
I'll take it to myself.

P. jun. I will be princely,
While I possess my princess, my Pecunia.

P. sen. Where is't you eat ?

P. jun. Hard by, at Picklock's lodging,

---

[8] *Are you* advised,] i. e. have you found out that ! Has it struck
you ! It is a proverbial phrase, and used as a gentle note of
admiration.

Old Lickfinger's the cook, here in Ram-alley.

    P. sen. He has good cheer; perhaps I'll come and
        see you.

    P. Can. O fie! an alley, and a cook's shop, gross!
'Twill savour, sir, most rankly of them both:
Let your meat rather follow you to a tavern.

                               [To P. jun.

    Pick. A tavern's as unfit too for a princess.

    P. Can. No, I have known a princess, and a great
        one,
Come forth of a tavern.

    Pick. Not go in, sir, though.

    P. Can. She must go in, if she came forth: the
        blessed
Pokahontas, as the historian calls her,[9]

---

[9] —————————————— *the* blessed

    Pokahontas, as the historian calls her, &c.] This historian was
John Smith, a famous traveller, and by far the most enterprizing of
the first Virginia settlers. He seems to have been the prototype
of John Bunkle, and in the dedication of his curious *History of
Virginia* to the Duchess of Richmond, thus enumerates his *bonnes
fortunes:* "Yet my comfort is, that heretofore honourable and
virtuous ladies, and comparable but among themselves, have offered
me rescue and protection in my greatest dangers. Even in forraine
parts, I have felt relief from that sex. The beauteous Lady Tra-
bigzonda, when I was a slave to the Turks, did all she could to
secure me. When I overcame the Bashaw of Nalbritz in Tartaria,
the charitable Lady Callamata supplyed my necessities. In the
utmost of my extremities, that *blessed Pokahontas, the great king's
daughter of Virginia,* oft saved my life," &c.

    With respect to this *blessed* lady, captain Smith does her no more
than justice. While little more than a child, she contrived to acquaint Smith and his men with a plot which Powhatan, her father,
had treacherously laid to cut them all off; and thus preserved the
infant colony. She continued her kindness to the new settlers,
and in 1612, married a Mr. Rolfe. By this gentleman she was instructed in the principles of the Christian religion, and baptized,
by the name of Rebecca. She came to England in 1616, with a
letter from captain Smith, strongly recommending her to the queen
(Anne) for her services to the colony: in consequence of which she
was very graciously received. Pokahontas died the following year,

And great king's daughter of Virginia,
Hath been in womb of tavern ;—and besides,
Your nasty uncle will spoil all your mirth,
And be as noisome.—
   Pick. That is true.
   P. Can. No, 'faith,
Dine in Apollo with Pecunia,
At brave duke Wadloe's,[10] have your friends about
     you,
And make a day on't.
   P. jun. Content, i'faith ;
Our meat shall be brought thither : Simon the king
Will bid us welcome.
   Pick. Patron, I have a suit.
   P. jun. What's that ?
   Pick. That you will carry the Infanta
To see the Staple ; her grace will be a grace

on board the ship George at Gravesend, as she was on her return
to Virginia, leaving an infant son.   In her last moments she was
deeply impressed with religious sentiments, and her death might
have been made, if not more profitable to herself, more exemplary
to the world, if she had not fallen into the hands of fanatics, who
disgraced her end by a mixture of familiarity and profaneness similar to that which shocks the well disposed mind in the death-bed
scenes of those ignorant enthusiasts, whose ravings are periodically
recorded in a pernicious publication called the *Methodists' Magazine*.
To sum up all, Pokahontas had many claims on the gratitude of
this country, nor would she be mentioned as she is, by Jonson, had
he not been disgusted by the accounts of her " godly end," (some
of which I have seen,) equally repugnant to true taste and genuine
piety.
   Smith himself died in 1631, (the year in which this play was
printed) and was buried, as Stow tells us, in St. Sepulchre's church :
where a long epitaph once told in wretched doggrel, how "in
honour of his God and Christendom, he did divide from pagans
three, their heads and lives," &c.
   [10] P. Can. *No, 'faith,*
     Dine in Apollo *with Pecunia,*
     At brave duke Wadloe's.] *Apollo* is the room so called, where
Jonson and his friends held their club, at the Devil Tavern in Fleet-
street, then kept by *Simon Wadloe*. WHAL.

To all the members of it.

P. jun. I will do it,
And have her arms set up there, with her titles,[1]
Aurelia Clara Pecunia, the Infanta,
And in Apollo! Come, sweet princess, go.

P. sen. Broker, be careful of your charge.

Bro. I warrant you.   [*Exeunt.*

Cen.. *Why, this is duller and duller! intolerable,
scurvy, neither devil nor fool in this play! pray God
some on us be not a witch, gossip, to forespeak the matter
thus.*[2]

Mirth. *I fear we are all such, an we were old
enough: but we are not all old enough to make one
witch. How like you the Vice in the play?*

Expect. *Which is he?*

Mirth. *Three or four: Old Covetousness, the sordid
Pennyboy, the Money-bawd, who is a flesh-bawd too,
they say.*

Tat. *But here is never a fiend to carry him away.
Besides, he has never a wooden dagger! I would not
give a rush for a Vice, that has not a wooden dagger
to snap at every body he meets.*

Mirth. *That was the old way, gossip, when Iniquity
came in like Hokos Pokos, in a jugler's jerkin, with
false skirts, like the knave of clubs; but now they are
attired like men and women of the time, the vices male
and female. Prodigality, like a young heir, and his*

---

[1] *And have her arms set up there, with her titles.*] It was the custom for foreign princes and noblemen of high rank or office, to *set
up* their arms and titles in the places through which they passed,
or the inns in which they lodged. Thus our author, in his *Discoveries;* "The German lord, when he went out of Newgate into
the cart, took order to have his *arms set up* in his last harborough."
Nor is the custom unknown in this country. The arms and titles
of the Lords Lieutenants of Ireland are usually set up in the inns
in which they occasionally rest on their journey to the coast.

[2] —— *to* forespeak *the matter thus,*] i. e. to foretell, and thus incur
the suspicion of dealing with a familiar. See vol. ii. p. 258.

mistress Money, (whose favours he scatters like coun-
ters,) pranked up like a prime lady, the Infanta of the
mines.

Cen. *Ay, therein they abuse an honourable princess,*
it is thought.

Mirth. *By whom is it so thought? or where lies the*
abuse?

Cen. *Plain in the styling her Infanta, and giving*
her three names.[3]

Mirth. *Take heed it lie not in the vice of your inter-*
pretation; what have Aurelia, Clara, Pecunia, to do
with any person? do they any more but express the pro-
perty of Money, which is the daughter of Earth, and
drawn out of the mines? Is there nothing to be call'd
Infanta, but what is subject to exception? why not the
infanta of the beggars, or infanta of the gypsies, as well
as king of beggars, and king of gypsies?

Cen. *Well, an there were no wiser than I, I would*
sew him in a sack, and send him by sea to his princess.

Mirth. *Faith, an he heard you, Censure, he would*
go near to stick the ass's ears to your high dressing, and
perhaps to all ours for hearkening to you.

Tat. *By'r lady, but he should not to mine; I would*
hearken, and hearken, and censure, if I saw cause, for
the other princess' sake Pokahontas, surnamed the
Blessed, whom he has abused indeed, and I do censure
him, and will censure him :—To say she came forth of
a tavern, was said like a paltry poet.[4]

---

[3] *In the styling her Infanta, and giving her three names.*] I cannot give the reader the *three names* of the Infanta Maria of Spain;
but this is plainly an allusion to them. Charles returned from his
ill-fated visit to the princess, in October 1623, and the match was
finally broken off a few months before the appearance of this play;
Gossip Censure therefore might have spared her zeal on the young
lady's account, who was not much in favour at this time.

[4] *To say she came forth of a tavern was said like a paltry poet.*]
This is said, however, by the writers of her life. The blessed
Pokahontas was *in womb of tavern*, both at Deptford and Gravesend.

Mirth. *That's but one gossip's opinion, and my gossip Tattle's too! but what says Expectation here? She sits sullen and silent.*

Expect. *Troth, I expect their office, their great office, the Staple, what it will be! they have talk'd on't, but we see it not open yet.—Would Butter would come in,[5] and spread itself a little to us!*

Mirth. *Or the butter-box, Buz, the emissary.*

Tat. *When it is churn'd and dish'd we shall hear of it.*

Expect. *If it be fresh and sweet butter; but say it be sour and wheyish?*

Mirth. *Then it is worth nothing, mere pot butter, fit to be spent in suppositories, or greasing coachwheels, stale stinking butter, and such, I fear, it is, by the being barrelled up so long.*

Expect. *Or rank Irish butter.*

Cen. *Have patience, gossip; say that, contrary to our expectation, it prove right, seasonable, salt butter?*

Mirth. *Or to the time of year, in Lent, delicate almond butter! I have a sweet tooth yet, and I will hope the best, and sit down as quiet and calm as butter, look as smooth and soft as butter, be merry and melt like butter, laugh and be fat like butter: so butter answer my expectation, and be not mad butter;*[6]

———————— "if it be,
It shall both July and December see!"
I say no more, but——Dixi.

---

[5] *Would* Butter *would come in.*] See p. 173. Enough has now been said on this subject. *Buz, the emissary,* was evidently a Dutchman.

[6] "Something too much of this"—but the allusion is to the old proverb, *butter is mad twice a year,* i. e. in *July,* when it is too soft, and in *December,* when it is too hard.

ACT III.[1]

SCENE I. *The Office of the Staple.*

Enter FITTON, CYMBAL, REGISTER, Clerk, *and*
THO. Barber.

Fitton.

YOU hunt upon a wrong scent still, and think
    The air of things will carry them; but it
       must
    Be reason and proportion, not fine sounds,
My cousin Cymbal, must get you this lady.
You have entertain'd a pettyfogger here,
Picklock, with trust of an emissary's place,
And he is all for the young prodigal;
You see he has left us.

---

[1] This Act, it appears, gave offence, and therefore Jonson thought
proper to prefix the following notice to it, before the play was given
to the press.

                " TO **THE** READER.

*In this following act the Office is open'd, and shewn to the Prodigal
and his princess Pecunia, wherein the allegory and purpose of the
author hath hitherto been wholly mistaken, and so sinister an interpretation been made, as if the souls of most of the spectators had lived in
the eyes and ears of these ridiculous gossips that tattle between the acts.
But he prays you thus to mend it. To consider the news here vented
to be none of his news, or any reasonable man's; but news made like
the time's news, (a weekly cheat to draw money) and could not be fitter
reprehended, than in raising this ridiculous office of the Staple, wherein
the age may see her own folly, or hunger and thirst after published
pamphlets of news, set out every Saturday, but made all at home, and
no syllable of truth in them; than which there cannot be a greater disease*

Cym. Come, you do not know him,
That speak thus of him : he will have a trick
To open us a gap by a trap-door,
When they least dream on't. Here he comes.

Enter PICKLOCK.

What news ?
　Pick. Where is my brother Buz, my brother
　　Ambler ?
The register, examiner, and the clerks ?
Appear, and let us muster all in pomp,
For here will be the rich Infanta presently,
To make her visit. Pennyboy the heir,
My patron, has got leave for her to play
With all her train, of the old churl her guardian.
Now is your time to make all court unto her,
That she may first but know, then love the place,
And shew it by her frequent visits here :
And afterwards get her to sojourn with you.
She will be weary of the prodigal quickly.
　Cym. Excellent news !
　Fit. And counsel of an oracle !
　Cym. How say you, cousin Fitton ?
　Fit. Brother Picklock,
I shall adore thee for this parcel of tidings,
It will cry up the credit of our office
Eternally, and make our Staple immortal !

*in nature, or a fouler scorn put upon the times. And so apprehending
it, you shall do the author and your own judgment a courtesy, and perceive the trick of alluring money to the office, and there cozening the
people. If you have the truth, rest quiet, and consider that*
　　　' Ficta, voluptatis causâ, sint proxima veris.' "

It argues very little for the good sense of the audience to take
offence at a piece of satire so just and well timed, as this evidently
was. Not one part in a thousand of the ridiculous stories fabricated, and propagated in the poet's time as authentic news, is come
down to us; and yet more than enough remains to prove that the
public credulity was imposed upon by the Fittons of the day, in the
most gross and shameless manner.

Pick. Look your addresses then be fair and fit,
And entertain her and her creatures too,
With all the migniardise, and quaint caresses
You can put on them.
    Fit. Thou seem'st by thy language,
No less a courtier² than a man of law.
I must embrace thee.
    Pick. Tut, I am Vertumnus,
On every change, or chance, upon occasion,
A true camelion, I can colour for it.
I move upon my axle like a turnpike,³
Fit my face to the parties, and become
Straight one of them.

    Enter NATHANIEL, THO. Barber, *and* REGISTER.

Cym. Sirs, up into your desks,
And spread the rolls upon the table,—so!
Is the examiner set ?
    Reg. Yes, sir.
    Cym. Ambler and Buz
Are both abroad now.
    Pick. We'll sustain their parts.
No matter, let them ply the affairs without,
Let us alone within, I like that well.
On with the cloke, and you with the Staple gown,
    [FIT. *puts on the office cloke, and* CYM. *the gown.*
And keep your state, stoop only to the Infanta ;
We'll have a flight at Mortgage, Statute, Band,

---

² *Thou seem'st by thy* language
    No less a courtier, *&c.*] Alluding to Picklock's use of the
French word *migniardise,* (affected delicacy of speech or behaviour,)
which was probably one of the *perfumed terms* of the time.
    ³ ——————————— *like a* turnpike,] i. e. a turnstile. It is pro-
bable that, in Jonson's time, the roads, or rather lanes, had no
other barriers than these, which every one opened for himself—
they have resigned their name (picca) to the noble public roads of
the present day, and modestly assumed another better adapted to
their humble office.

And hard but we'll bring Wax to the retrieve :[4]
Each know his several province, and discharge it.
        [*They take their seats.*
 Fit. I do admire this nimble engine, Picklock.
 Cym. Coz, what did I say ?
 Fit. You have rectified my error.

Enter PENNYBOY, jun., P. Canter, PECUNIA, STATUTE,
  BAND, MORTGAGE, WAX, *and* BROKER.

 P. jun. By your leave, gentlemen, what news ?
  good, good still,
In your new office ? Princess, here's the Staple !
This is the governor, kiss him, noble princess,
For my sake.—Tom, how is it, honest Tom ?
How does thy place, and thou ?—My creature,
  princess,
This is my creature, give him your hand to kiss,
He was my barber, now he writes clericus !
I bought this place for him, and gave it him.
 P. Can. He should have spoke of that, sir, and not
  you :
Two do not do one office well.
 P. jun. 'Tis true,
But I am loth to lose my courtesies.
 P. Can. So are all they that do them to vain
  ends ;
And yet you do lose when you pay yourselves.
 P. jun. No more of your sentences, Canter, they
  are stale ;
We come for news, remember where you are.
I pray thee let my princess hear some news,
Good master Cymbal.

 [4] *But we'll bring Wax to the* retrieve.] A term in falconry ; to
make the hawk return to the lure. WHAL.
 "*Retrieve* is when partridges, having been sprung, are to find
again." *Gent. Recreat. I'll take the ghost's word for a thousand
pound.* For Cymbal's allusion just below, see p. 220.

Cym. What news would she hear ?
Or of what kind, sir ?
   P. jun. Any, any kind,
So it be news, the newest that thou hast,
Some news of state for a princess.
   Cym. Read from Rome there.
   Tho. *They write, the king of Spain is chosen pope.*
   P. jun. How !
   Tho. *And emperor too, the thirtieth of February.*
   P. jun. Is the emperor dead ?
   Cym. No, but he has resign'd,
And trails a pike now under Tilly.
   Fit. For penance.
   P. jun. These will beget strange turns in Chris-
      tendom !
   Tho. *And Spinola is made general of the Jesuits.*
   P. jun. Stranger !
   Fit. Sir, all are alike true and certain.
   Cym. All the pretence to the fifth monarchy
Was held but vain, until the ecclesiastic
And secular powers were united thus,
Both in one person.
   Fit. It has been long the aim
Of the house of Austria.
   Cym. See but Maximilian
His letters to the baron of Bouttersheim.
Or Scheiter-huyssen.
   Fit. No, of Leichtenstein,
Lord Paul, I think.
   P. jun. I have heard of some such thing.
Don Spinola made general of the Jesuits !
A priest !
   Cym. O, no, he is dispens'd withal——
And the whole society, who do now appear
The only enginers of Christendom.
   P. jun. They have been thought so long, and
      rightly too.

Fit. Witness the engine that they have presented
          him,
To wind himself with up into the moon,
And thence make all his discoveries!
    Cym. Read on.
    Tho. *And Vitellesco, he that was last general,*
Being now turn'd cook to the society,
Has drest his excellence such a dish of eggs——
    P. jun. What, potch'd?
    Tho. No, powder'd.
    Cym. All the yolk is wild-fire,
As he shall need beleaguer no more towns,
But throw his egg in.
    Fit. It shall clear consume
Palace and place; demolish and bear down
All strengths before it!
    Cym. Never be extinguish'd,
Till all become one ruin!
    Fit. And from Florence.
    Tho. *They write was found in Galilæo's study.*
A burning glass, which they have sent him too,
To fire any fleet that's out at sea.——
    Cym. By moonshine, is't not so?
    Tho. Yes sir, in the water.
    P. jun. His strengths will be unresistible, if this
          hold.
Have you no news against him, on the contrary?
    Nath. Yes, sir. *They write here, one Cornelius-Son,*
Hath made the Hollanders an invisible eel
To swim the haven at Dunkirk, and sink all
The shipping there.
    P. jun. Why have not you this, Tom?
    Cym. Because he keeps the pontificial side.
    P. jun. How! Change sides, Tom, 'twas never in
          my thought
To put thee up against our selves. Come down,
Quickly.

Cym. Why, sir?

P. jun. I ventured not my money
Upon those terms: if he may change, why so!
I'll have him keep his own side, sure.

    Fit. Why, let him,
It is but writing so much over again.

    P. jun. For that I'll bear the charges: there's two
        pieces.

    Fit. Come, do not stick with the gentleman.

    Cym. I'll take none, sir,
And yet he shall have the place.

    P. jun. They shall be ten then.
Up, Tom, and the office shall take them. Keep your
        side, Tom.   [THO. *changes his side.*
Know your own side, do not forsake your side, Tom.

    Cym. Read.

    Tho. *They write here one Cornelius-Son*
Hath made the Hollanders an invisible eel
To swim the haven at Dunkirk, and sink all
The shipping there.

    P. jun. But how is't done?

    Cym. I'll shew you, sir.
It is an automa, runs under water,
With a snug nose, and has a nimble tail
Made like an auger, with which tail she wriggles
Betwixt the costs of a ship,[5] and sinks it straight.

    P. jun. Whence have you this news?

    Fit. From a right hand, I assure you,
The eel boats here, that lie before Queen-hythe,
Came out of Holland.

    P. jun. A most brave device,
To murder their flat bottoms.

    Fit. I do grant you:
But what if Spinola have a new project,

5 —————————— *She wriggles*
    Betwixt the costs of a ship,] i. e. the ribs; from the Latin *cost.e.*
WHAL.

5   Q

To bring an army over in cork-shoes,
And land them here at Harwich ? all his horse
Are shod with cork, and fourscore pieces of ordnance,
Mounted upon cork-carriages, with bladders
Instead of wheels, to run the passage over
At a spring tide.
    P. jun. Is't true ?
    Fit. As true as the rest.
    P. jun. He'll never leave his engines : I would
        hear now
Some curious news.
    Cym. As what ?
    P. jun. Magic or alchemy,
Or flying in the air, I care not what.
    Nath. *They write from Libtzig* (reverence to your
        ears)
The art of drawing farts out of dead bodies,
Is by the brotherhood of the Rosie Cross
Produced unto perfection, in so sweet
And rich a tincture——
    Fit. As there is no princess
But may perfume her chamber with the extraction.
    P. jun. There's for you, princess !
    P. Can. What, a fart for her ?
    P. jun. I mean the spirit.
    P. Can. Beware how she resents it.
    P. jun. And what hast thou, Tom ?
    Tho. *The perpetual motion*
Is here found out by an ale-wife in Saint Katherine's,
At the sign of the Dancing Bears.
    P. jun. What, from her tap ?
I'll go see that, or else I'll send old Canter :
He can make that discovery.
    P. Can. Yes, in ale.   [*Noise without.*
    P. jun. Let me have all this news made up and
        seal'd.
    Reg. The people press upon us.   Please you, sir,

Withdraw with your fair princess : there's a room
Within, sir, to retire to.

P. jun. No, good register,
We'll stand it out here, and observe your office ;
What news it issues.

Reg. 'Tis the House of Fame, sir,
Where both the curious and the negligent,
The scrupulous and careless, wild and stay'd,
The idle and laborious, all do meet,
To taste the cornu-copiæ of her rumours,
Which she, the mother of sport, pleaseth to scatter
Among the vulgar : baits, sir, for the people !
And they will bite like fishes.

Enter a crowd of Customers.

P. jun. Let us see it.

1 *Cust.*[6] Have you in your profane shop any news
Of the saints at Amsterdam ?

Reg. Yes ; how much would you ?

1 *Cust.* Six penny-worth.

Reg. Lay your money down.—Read, Thomas.

Tho. *The saints do write, they expect a prophet
          shortly,*
The prophet Baal, to be sent over to them,
To calculate a time, and half a time,
And the whole time,[1] *according to Naometry.*

---

[6] 1 *Cust.*] A marginal note describes this first customer as " a
dopper (dipper) or she-Baptist."

[1] *The prophet* Baal, *to be sent over to them,*
      To calculate a time, *and* half a time,
      And the whole time.] This was intended to ridicule the fanatics
of those days, who dealt much in expounding the prophecies contained in the Revelations, and applied them to themselves.   We
read, that the woman fled from the face of the serpent into the
wilderness, where she was nourished for a *time*, and *times*, and *half
a time*, Revel. xii. 14.   By the prophet *Baal*, is meant any factious
leader, like *John Baal*, a Kentish minister, and fomenter of the rebellion by Wat Tyler in Richard the IId's time.   WHAL.

This Baal was, as Whalley says, a principal mover in the rebel-

P. jun. What's that ?

Tho. The measuring of the temple ; a cabal
Found out but lately, and set out by Archie,
Or some such head, of whose long coat they have
      heard,
And, being black, desire it.[8]

lion, and by his pretended prophecies kept up the seditious spirit of
the people.   He was an excommunicated priest, and called himself chaplain to the insurrectionary army.

    Gower, like Jonson, terms him a *prophet,*

> Balle propheta *docet quem spiritus ante malignus*
>   *Edocuitque, sua tunc fuit alta schola.*

Some of the lines in which the agents of the pseudo-prophet instigate one another to fury, are curious from the muster-roll of names.

> *Watte vocat cui Thome venit, neque Simme retardat,*
>   *Batteque Gibbe simul Hykke venire jubent.*
> *Colle furit, quem Gibbe juvat nocumenta parantes,*
>   *Cum quibus ad damnum Wille coire vovet.*
> *Hudde ferit quos Judde terit, dum Tibbe juvatur,*
>   *Jakke domosque viros vellit et ense necat.*   Vox Clam.

    After all, it was not necessary for the poet to have recourse to
the times of Richard II. for a fanatic ; his own age furnished them
in abundance ; Osborne says that many of the Puritans believed
prince Henry to be prefigured in the Apocalypse, and boldly pro-
phesied that he should overthrow the beast ; and that one *Ball*, a
tailor, (and not improbably, the person whom Jonson had in view)
was so far over-run with this *lunacy,* "as to put out money on adventure, i. e. to receive it back, double or treble, when James himself should be elected Pope !"   *Traditional Memoires of James I.*
sec. 38.

    Ball (be he who he may) is again mentioned by Jonson in the
Execration of Vulcan, together with Butter's rival, the indefatigable
Captain.

> " Or captain Pamphlet's horse and foot that salley
>   Upon the Exchange, still out of Pope's Head alley ;
>   The weekly courants, with Paul's seal, and all
>   The admired discourses of the prophet *Ball."*

  [8] *And being* black *desire it.*]   The old copy has a marginal note
here—*Archie mourn'd then.*   This was Archibald Armstrong, jester
to James and Charles I.   Why he was in black, does not appear.
The court was then in mourning, indeed, for the death of James :—
but Archy might also be in disgrace, and condemned to sable for

1 *Cust.* Peace be with them !

Reg. So there had need, for they are still by the ears
One with another.

1 *Cust.* It is their zeal.

Reg. Most likely.

1 *Cust.* Have you no other of that species ?

some act of impertinence.   This licentious buffoon was something
of a fool, more of a knave, and altogether a meddling and mischievous agent of the factious in church and state.   James contrived to keep him in some order by means of the whip, which was
frequently exercised upon him to advantage ; but the unfortunate
Charles, with whom he was a favourite, gave a loose to his scurrility,
which he had more than one occasion to regret.   The great object of Archy's malignity were the bishops, and of them, more particularly Laud, who has been blamed for noticing his attacks.   "As
Laud was at the head of the state, says the author of the *Discourse
on Irony*, p. 71, "he should have despised the jests of a *fool*, and not
have been hurried on to speak against him, (in the Privy Council,)
but left it to others who would have been glad, upon the least inti-
mation, to pay their court, by sacrificing a *fool* to his resentment."
This has been repeated a thousand times ; but there is neither truth
nor wisdom in the observation.   Archy was a rancorous bigot to
the discipline of the Church of Scotland ; this was quickly per-
ceived by the favourers of the Puritans about the court, and they
hastened to avail themselves of his prejudices, by secretly instiga-
ting him to scurrilous jests upon Laud, as the readiest means of
bringing the hierarchy into contempt.   Not to know this, argues a
very imperfect acquaintance with the history of those disastrous
times.   Even Osborn, who neither loved Laud nor his cause, has
the candour to acknowledge that Archy not only " carried on the
contention against the prelates for divers years, but received such
encouragement, that he often, in his own hearing, belched in his
face such miscarriages as he was really guilty of, and might, but for
this *foul-mouth'd Scot*, have been forgotten : adding such other re-
proaches of his own, as the dignity of the Archbishop's calling and
greatnesse of his parts could not in reason or manners admit."   *Advice to a Son*, Pt. ii. p. 12.   That Osborn, after this, should reprove
Laud for appealing to the Council, appears not very creditable to
his judgment, especially as he immediately adds, that " all the *Fool*
did, was but a symptom of the strong and inveterate distemper in
the hearts of his countrymen against the calling of bishops, out of
whose ruins, the major part of the Scottish nobility had feathered
their nests."—But enough of Archy.

Reg. Yes,
But dearer ; it will cost you a shilling.
  1 *Cust.* Verily,
There is a nine-pence, I will shed no more.
  Reg. Not to the good of the saints ?
  1 *Cust.* I am not sure
That man is good.
  Reg. Read from Constantinople
Nine penn'orth.
  Tho. *They give out here, the grand signior*
Is certainly turn'd Christian ; and to clear
The controversy 'twixt the pope and him,
Which is the Antichrist, he means to visit
The church at Amsterdam this very summer,
And quit all marks of the beast.
  1 *Cust.* Now joyful tidings !
Who brought in this ! which emissary ?
  Reg. Buz,
Your countryman.
  1 *Cust.* Now, blessed be the man,
And his whole family, with the nation !
  Reg. Yes, for Amboyna, and the justice there ![9]—
This is a Dopper, a she Anabaptist !
Seal and deliver her her news, dispatch.
  2 *Cust.* Have you any news from the Indies ? any
    miracle

---

[9] *Yes, for Amboyna, and the justice there !*] The massacre of
Amboyna took place in 1622 ; but the news of it did not reach this
country till the commencement of 1624, so that the horror of it
was in all its freshness. If nations could ever profit by experience ;
if they could perceive the danger as well as the guilt of wantonly
venturing on deeds of inhumanity and injustice, this *bloody tragedie,*
as Wilson calls it, would not be acted wholly in vain.   Two centuries have elapsed since it took place, yet the remembrance of it
is recent in the breast of every Englishman, while the Dutch have
not ceased for a moment to labour under the curse of their bar-
barity, and to suffer in every possible mode, for a transaction, which
no degree of punishment will ever be thought to expiate, no time
erase from the public mind.

Done in Japan by the Jesuits, or in China?
    Nath. No, but *we hear of a colony of cooks*
To be set ashore on the coast of America,
For the conversion of the cannibals,
And making them good eating Christians.
Here comes the colonel that undertakes it.

Enter LICKFINGER.

    3 *Cust.* Who, captain Lickfinger?
    Lick. News, news, my boys!
I am to furnish a great feast to-day,
And I would have what news the office affords.
    Nath. We were venting some of you, of your new
        project.
    Reg. Afore 'twas paid for! you were somewhat
        too hasty.
    P. jun. What, Lickfinger! wilt thou convert the
        cannibals
With spit and pan divinity?
    Lick. Sir, for that
I will not urge, but for the fire and zeal
To the true cause; thus I have undertaken:
With two lay-brethren, to myself, no more,
One of the broach, the other of the boiler,
In one six months, and by plain cookery,
No magic to it, but old Japhet's physic,
The father of the European arts,
To make such sauces for the savages,
And cook their meats with those enticing steams,
As it would make our cannibal-christians
Forbear the mutual eating one another,
Which they do do more cunningly than the wild
Anthropophági, that snatch only strangers,
Like my old patron's dogs there.
    P. jun. O, my uncle's!
Is dinner ready, Lickfinger?
    Lick. When you please, sir,

I was bespeaking but a parcel of news,
To strew out the long meal withal, but it seems
You are furnish'd here already.
　　P. jun. O, not half.
　　Lick. What court news is there? any proclama-
　　　　tions,
Or edicts to come forth?
　　Tho. Yes, there is one,
That the king's barber has got, for aid of our trade,
Whereof there is a manifest decay.
A precept for the wearing of long hair,
To run to seed, to sow bald pates withal,
And the preserving fruitful heads and chins
To help a mystery almost antiquated.
Such as are bald and barren beyond hope,
Are to be separated and set by
For ushers to old countesses: and coachmen [10]
To mount their boxes reverently, and drive,
Like lapwings, with a shell upon their heads,
Thorough the streets.
　　Lick. Have you no news of the stage?
They'll ask me about new plays at dinner-time,
And I should be as dumb as a fish.
　　Tho. O, yes.
There is a legacy left to the king's players,
Both for their various shifting of their scene,
And dextrous change of their persons to all shapes,
And all disguises, by the right reverend

---

[10] Lick. ――――――――――――― *And coachmen*
　　　　To mount their boxes reverently.] This seems to be a part
of Tom's speech: I imagine that Lickfinger ought not to speak till
he asks the question,
　　　　　　Have you no news of the stage?
and I have accordingly reformed the speeches in that manner.
WHAL.
　　There was no need of change: but I have not disturbed Whalley's reformation, as he calls it.

Archbishop of Spalato.[1]

   Lick. He is dead

That play'd him !

   Tho. Then he has lost his share of the legacy.

   Lick. What news of Gondomar ?

   Tho. *A second fistula,*

Or an excoriation, at the least,

For putting the poor English play, was writ of him,[2]

---

   [1] ————————— *the right reverend*

   Archbishop of Spalato.] Antonio de Dominis, archbishop of Spalato, in Dalmatia, and the prototype of Archibald Bowyer, came into this country about 1622.   Under the pretence of having re-nounced the errors of popery, he obtained considerable preferment in the church, and was for some time dean of Windsor. Gondomar, who suspected his sincerity, set all his engines to work, and at length discovered the imposture.   Antonio then fled from Eng-land, and read a second recantation at Rome: he was however abandoned to neglect, and died miserably.   The reader now sees the drift of the satire in noticing his bequest to the players, for their dexterity in *shifting the scene*, which does not, as Mr. Malone supposes, allude to the use of what is now called *scenery*, but simply to a change of place.

   [2] *For putting the poor English play, was writ of him, &c.*] This play, as the margin of the old folio tells us, was the *Game at Chess.* The game is played, as Langbaine says, between one of the church of England, and one of the church of Rome, in the presence of Igna-tius Loyola. It does not promise much amusement, and yet a MS. note taken by Capell from an old copy of this play, describes it as exceedingly popular. "After nine days (the writer adds) wherein I have heard the actors say they took fifteen hundred pounds, (this is an incredible sum) the Spanish faction got the play suppressed, and the author, master Thomas Middleton, committed to prison, where he lay some time, and at last got out upon this petition to king James:

    " A harmless Game coyned only for delight,

      Was play'd betwixt the black house and the white ;

      The white house won.   Yet still the black doth brag,

      They had the power to put me in the bag.

      Use but your royal hand, 'twill set me free,

      'Tis but removing of a man—that's ME."

   From the MS. notes to Langbaine, it appears that Gondomar (*the black house*) had other motives of complaint besides his defeat ;

To such a sordid use, as, is said, he did,
Of cleansing his posteriors.
    Lick. Justice! justice!
    Tho. Since when, he lives condemn'd to his share at
        Bruxels,
And there sits filing certain politic hinges,
To hang the states on he has heaved off the hooks.
    Lick. What must you have for these?
    P. jun. Thou shalt pay nothing,
But reckon them in the bill. [*Exit* LICK.]   There's
        twenty pieces,
Her grace bestows upon the office, Tom:
Write thou that down for news.
    Reg. We may well do't,
We have not many such.
    P. jun. There's twenty more,
If you say so; my princess is a princess!
And put that too under the office seal.
    Cym. [*Takes* PECUNIA *aside, while* FITTON *courts*
        the Waiting-women.]   If it will please your
        grace to sojourn here,
And take my roof for covert, you shall know
The rites belonging to your blood and birth,
Which few can apprehend: these sordid servants,
Which rather are your keepers, than attendants,
Should not come near your presence.   I would have
You waited on by ladies, and your train
Borne up by persons of quality and honour;
Your meat should be serv'd in with curious dances,

for the play was embellished with an engraved frontispiece, where
he was introduced in *propria persona*, in no very friendly conversation with Loyola.
    Gondomar's *second* fistula must be set down to the poet's account;
his first is mentioned in all the histories of the time.   The allusion
of the whole passage, as well as the exclamation of Lickfinger which
follows it, is taken from Rabelais' inimitable description of the trans-
actions which took place with the good bishop Homenas, at the
blessed Island of Papimania.

And set upon the board with virgin hands,
Tuned to their voices ; not a dish removed,
But to the music, nor a drop of wine
Mixt with his water, without harmony.

    Pec. You are a courtier, sir, or somewhat more,
That have this tempting language.

    Cym. I am your servant,
Excellent princess, and would have you appear
That which you are : come forth the state and wonder
Of these our times, dazzle the vulgar eyes,
And strike the people blind with admiration.

    P. Can. Why that's the end of wealth ! thrust
        riches outward,
And remain beggars within ; contemplate nothing
But the vile sordid things of time, place, money,
And let the noble and the precious go :
Virtue and honesty ; hang them, poor thin mem-
        branes
Of honour ! who respects them ? O, the fates,
How hath all just true reputation fallen,
Since money, this base money 'gan to have any !
                                      [*Aside.*

    Band. Pity the gentleman is not immortal.

    Wax. As he gives out the place is by description.

    Fit. A very paradise, if you saw all, lady.

    Wax. I am the chamber-maid, sir, you mistake,
My lady may see all.

    Fit. Sweet mistress Statute, gentle mistress Band,
And mother Mortgage, do but get her grace
To sojourn here.

    Pick. I thank you, gentle Wax.

    Mor. If it were a chattel, I would try my credit.

    Pick. So it is, for term of life, we count it so.

    Sta. She means inheritance to him and his heirs :
Or that he could assure a state of years ;
I'll be his Statute staple, Statute-merchant,
Or what he please.

Pick. He can expect no more.

Band. His cousin, alderman Security,
That he did talk of so, e'en now———

Sta. Who is
The very brooch of the bench, gem of the city.

Band. He and his deputy, but assure his life
For one seven years—

Sta. And see what we'll do for him,
Upon his scarlet motion.

Band. And old chain,
That draws the city ears.

Wax. When he says nothing,
But twirls it thus.

Sta. A moving oratory !

Band. Dumb rhetoric, and silent eloquence !
As the fine poet says.[3]

Fit. Come, they all scorn us ;

---

[3] Ban. Dumb rhetoric, *and* silent eloquence !
    As the fine poet says.] A sneering allusion to these lines
of Daniel :

> " Ah ! beauty, siren, fair inchanting good,
>   Sweet silent rhetoric of persuading eyes ;
>   Dumb eloquence, whose power doth move the blood,
>   More than the words, or wisdom of the wise."   WHAL.

It is but fair to give the remainder of this stanza, in which the
thought is woefully wire-drawn :

> " Still harmony, whose diapason lies
>   Within a brow, the key which passions move
>   To ravish sense, and play a world in love."

There was no great kindness between Daniel and our poet ; but I
know not the cause of their mutual dislike. Both were patronized
by Lucy, countess of Bedford, and Jonson tells her noble friend,
the countess of Rutland, that Daniel " envied him, though he bore
him no ill will on his part." He could not have hazarded this to
such a personage, unless the fact had been notorious ; and this circumstance may serve to admonish us, when we find an occasional
reflection in Jonson, not to set it down immediately to the score of
malignity, and conclude with Messrs. Chalmers, Steevens, Malone,
&c. that he is, in every case, a wanton and unprovoked aggressor.

Do you not see't? the family of scorn!

Bro. Do not believe him : gentle master Picklock,
They understood you not ; the gentlewomen,
They thought you would have my lady sojourn with
    you,
And you desire but now and then a visit.

    Pick. Yes, if she pleased, sir, it would much
        advance
Unto the office, her continual residence :
I speak but as a member.

    Bro. 'Tis enough.
I apprehend you : and it shall go hard,
But I'll so work, as somebody shall work her.

    Pick. Pray you change with our master but a word
        about it.

    P. jun. Well, Lickfinger, see that our meat be ready.
Thou hast news enough.

    Lick. Something of Bethlem Gabor,[4]
And then I am gone.

    Tho. We hear he has devised
A drum, to fill all Christendom with the sound :
But that he cannot draw his forces near it,
To march yet, for the violence of the noise.
And therefore he is fain, by a design,
To carry them in the air, and at some distance,
'Till he be married, then they shall appear.

    Lick. Or never ; well, God be wi' you ! stay, who's
        here ?

---

[4] *Something of* Bethlem Gabor.] This person, who is sometimes
called Beth Gabriel, was prince of Transilvania. He had interest
enough to get himself declared king of Hungary ; but being shortly
afterwards suspected of meditating an alliance with the Turks, and
forming designs hostile to Christendom, he was abandoned by his
new subjects. His exploits were of the romantic kind, and he is
said to have been in forty general battles : so that the Mercuries,
foreign and domestic, rang with his achievements, about this time.
He died in 1629. Godwin has taken the name for the military
hero of his *St. Leon.*

A little of the Duke of Bavier, and then—

    Nath. He has taken a grey habit, and is turn'd
The church's miller, grinds the catholic grist
With every wind; and Tilly takes the toll.

    4 *Cust.* Have you any news of the pageants to
        send down
Into the several counties? All the country
Expected from the city most brave speeches,
Now, at the coronation.[5]

    Lick. It expected
More than it understood; for they stand mute,
Poor innocent dumb things; they are but wood,
As is the bench, and blocks they were wrought on: yet
If May-day come, and the sun shine, perhaps,
They'll sing like Memnon's statue, and be vocal.[6]

    5 *Cust.* Have you any forest news?

    Tho. None very wild, sir,
Some tame there is, out of the forest of fools.
A new park is a making there, to sever
Cuckolds of antler, from the rascals. Such

---

    [5] *Now at the coronation.*] James died on the 27th of March,
1625; this play therefore appears to have been brought out in the
interval between that day and the first of May. Whoever wishes to
become acquainted with the nature of those *brave speeches* expected
by the country, must turn to those which were introduced into the
city pageants, on the accession of James, by our poet, among many
others, and of which enough and more than enough is to be found
in the Chronicles of the times.

    [6] *If May-day come, and the sun shine, perhaps*
      They'll sing like Memnon's statue, and be vocal.] May-day was
a day of general festivity, and more especially with the good citizens
of London, who had the happiness of enjoying some of their favourite
processions on it. The trite allusion in the next line may be best
explained by a quotation from Akenside:

        " As Memnon's marble *form*, renown'd of old
           By fabling Nilus, at the potent touch
           Of morning, uttered from its inmost frame
           Unbidden music."   *Pleasures of Imag.*

Whose wives are dead, and have since cast their heads,
Shall remain cuckolds pollard.

   Lick. I'll have that news.

   1 *Cust.* And I.

   2 *Cust.* And I.

   3 *Cust.* And I.

   4 *Cust.* And I.

   5 *Cust.* And I.

   Cym. Sir, I desire to be excused ; [*to* P. jun.] and, madam,
I cannot leave my office the first day.
My cousin Fitton here shall wait upon you,
And emissary Picklock.

   P. jun. And Tom Clericus?

   Cym. I cannot spare him yet, but he shall follow you,
When they have order'd the rolls. Shut up the office,
When you have done, till two o'clock.

            [*Exeunt all but* THOMAS *and* NATH.

   Enter SHUNFIELD, ALMANAC, *and* MADRIGAL.

   Shun. By your leave, clerks,
Where shall we dine to-day? do you know?

   Nath. The jeerers !⁷

   Alm. Where is my fellow Fitton?

   Tho. New gone forth.

   Shun. Cannot your office tell us, what brave fellows
Do eat together to-day, in town, and where?

   Tho. Yes, there's a gentleman, the brave heir, young Pennyboy,
Dines in Apollo.

   Mad. Come, let's thither then,
I have supt in Apollo.

   Alm. With the Muses?

---

⁷ *The jeerers !*] The old folio, which is miserably incorrect, gives this to Shunfield. It must be as it now stands, unless the reader choose rather to give the exclamation to Tho. Barber.

Mad. No,
But with two gentlewomen, call'd the Graces.
   Alm. They were ever three in *poetry*.
   Mad. This was *truth*, sir.[8]
   Tho. Sir, master Fitton's there too.
   Shun. All the better.
   Alm. We may have a jeer, perhaps.
   Shun. Yes, you'll drink, doctor,
If there be any good meat, as much good wine now,
As would lay up a Dutch ambassador.
   Tho. If he dine there, he's sure to have good meat,
For Lickfinger provides the dinner.
   Alm. Who!
The glory of the kitchen! that holds cookery
A trade from Adam, quotes his broths and sallads,
And swears he is not dead yet, but translated

   [8] *This was truth, sir.*] It appears from the elegant rules drawn
up by Jonson for the regulation of his Club, that women of character were not excluded from attending the meetings.
             "*Probæ feminæ non repudiantor.*"
so that we have an allusion to a fact well known at the time; though
the names of the "two Graces" were not mentioned. From the
manner in which Marmion (an enthusiastic admirer of Jonson,)
speaks of his entertainment there, it may be safely concluded that
an admission to it was a favour of no ordinary kind. The " boon
Delphic god " was our poet.

   Careless. "I am full
     Of oracles, I am come from Apollo—
  Emilia. From Apollo!
  Careless. From the heaven
     Of my delight, where the boon Delphic god
     Drinks sack, and keeps his Bacchanalia,
     And has his incense, and his altars smoking,
     And speaks in sparkling prophecies; thence I come,
     My braines perfumed with the rich Indian vapour,
     And heighten'd with conceits. From *tempting beauties*,
     From dainty music, and poetic strains,
     From bowls of nectar, and ambrosiac dishes;
     From witty varlets, fine companions,
     And from a mighty continent of pleasure
     Sails thy brave Careless."   *Fine Companion.*

In some immortal crust, the paste of almonds!

Mad. The same. He holds no man can be a poet,
That is not a good cook,[9] to know the palates,
And several tastes of the time. He draws all arts
Out of the kitchen, but the art of poetry,
Which he concludes the same with cookery.

Shun. Tut, he maintains more heresies than that.
He'll draw the magisterium from a minced-pie,
And prefer jellies to your julaps, doctor.

Alm. I was at an olla podrida of his making,
Was a brave piece of cookery : at a funeral!
But opening the pot-lid, he made us laugh,
Who had wept all day, and sent us such a tickling
Into our nostrils, as the funeral feast
Had been a wedding-dinner!

Shun. Give him allowance,
And that but a moderate, he will make a syren
Sing in the kettle, send in an Arion,
In a brave broth, and of a watery green,
Just the sea-colour, mounted on the back
Of a grown conger, but in such a posture,
As all the world would take him for a dolphin.

Mad. He's a rare fellow, without question! but
He holds some paradoxes.

Alm. Ay, and pseudodoxes.
Marry for most, he's orthodox in the kitchen.

Mad. And knows the clergy's taste!

Alm. Ay, and the laity's!

Shun. You think not of your time; we shall come
    too late,
If we go not presently.

Mad. Away then.

Shun. Sirs,
You must get of this news, to store your office,

---

[9] *He holds no man can be a poet,*
    That is not a good cook.] This is literally from Athenæus, of
which more hereafter.

5   R

Who dines and sups in the town; where, and with
      whom;
It will be beneficial: when you are stored,
And as we like our fare, we shall reward you.
    Nath. A hungry trade, 'twill be.
    Tho. Much like duke Humphry's,
But, now and then, as the wholesome proverb says,
'Twill *obsonare famem ambulando.*
    Nath. Shut up the office, gentle brother Thomas.
    Tho. Brother Nathaniel, I have the wine for you.[10]
I hope to see us, one day, emissaries.
    Nath. Why not? 'Slid, I despair not to be master!
                              [*Exeunt.*

SCENE II. *A Room in* PENNYBOY senior's *House.*

Enter PENNYBOY sen. *and* BROKER, *at different doors.*

              Pennyboy sen.

OW now! I think I was born under Hercules'
        star,
    Nothing but trouble and tumult to oppress me!
Why come you back? where is your charge?
    Bro. I have brought
A gentleman to speak with you.
    P. sen. To speak with me!
You know 'tis death for me to speak with any man.
What is he? set me a chair.
    Bro. He is the master
Of the great office.
    P. sen. What?
    Bro. The Staple of News,
A mighty thing, they talk six thousand a year.

---

[10] *I have the wine for you.*] A proverbial expression. I have the
perquisites (of the office) which you are to share.

P. sen. Well, bring your six in. Where have you
    left Pecunia?
Bro. Sir, in Apollo, they are scarce set.
P. sen. Bring six.
           [*Exit* BROKER, *and returns with* CYMBAL.
Bro. Here is the gentleman.
P. sen. He must pardon me,
I cannot rise, a diseased man.
    Cym. By no means, sir;
Respect your health and ease.
    P. sen. It is no pride in me,
But pain, pain: What's your errand, sir, to me?
Broker, return to your charge, be Argus-eyed,
Awake to the affair you have in hand,
Serve in Apollo, but take heed of Bacchus.
                      [*Exit* BROKER.
Go on, sir.
    Cym. I am come to speak with you.
    P. sen. 'Tis pain for me to speak, a very death;
But I will hear you.
    Cym. Sir, you have a lady,
That sojourns with you.
    P. sen. Ha! I am somewhat short
In my sense too——
    Cym. Pecunia.
    P. sen. O' that side
Very imperfect; on——
    Cym. Whom I would draw
Oftener to a poor office, I am master of——
    P. sen. My hearing is very dead, you must speak
    quicker.
    Cym. Or, if it please you, sir, to let her sojourn,
In part with me; I have a moiety
We will divide, half of the profits.
    P. sen. Ha!
I hear you better now. How come they in?
Is it a certain business, or a casual?

For I am loth to seek out doubtful courses,
Run any hazardous paths ; I love straight ways,
A just and upright man ! now all trade totters ;
The trade of money is fall'n two in the hundred :
That was a certain trade, while the age was thrifty,
And men good husbands, look'd unto their stocks,
Had their minds bounded ; now the public riot
Prostitutes all, scatters away in coaches,
In footmen's coats, and waiting women's gowns,
They must have velvet haunches, with a pox !
Now taken up, and yet not pay the use ;
Bate of the use ! I am mad with this time's manners.
                              [*Vehemently and loud.*
 Cym. You said e'en now, it was death for you to
  speak.
 P. sen. Ay, but an anger, a just anger, as this is,
Puts life in man. Who can endure to see
                              [*Starts from his chair.*
The fury of men's gullets, and their groins ?
What fires, what cooks, what kitchens might be spared ?
What stews, ponds, parks, coops, garners, magazines ?
What velvets, tissues, scarfs, embroideries,
And laces they might lack ? They covet things
Superfluous still ; when it were much more honour
They could want necessary : what need hath nature
Of silver dishes, or gold chamber-pots ?
Of perfumed napkins, or a numerous family
To see her eat ? poor, and wise, she requires
Meat only ; hunger is not ambitious :
Say, that you were the emperor of pleasures,
The great dictator of fashions, for all Europe,
And had the pomp of all the courts, and kingdoms,
Laid forth unto the shew, to make yourself
Gazed and admired at ; you must go to bed,
And take your natural rest : then all this vanisheth.
Your bravery was but shown ; 'twas not possest :
While it did boast itself, it was then perishing.

Cym. This man has healthful lungs.   [*Aside.*
  P. sen. All that excess
Appear'd as little yours, as the spectator's :
It scarce fills up the expectation
Of a few hours, that entertains men's lives.
  Cym. He has the monopoly of sole-speaking.
                            [*Aside.*

Why, good sir, you talk all.
  P. sen. [*angrily.*] Why should I not?
Is it not under mine own roof, my cieling ?
  Cym. But I came here to talk with you.
  P. sen. Why, an I will not
Talk with you, sir! you are answer'd; who sent for you?
  Cym. No body sent for me——
  P. sen. But you came ; why then
Go as you came, here's no man holds you ; there,
There lies your way, you see the door.
  Cym. This is strange !
  P. sen. 'Tis my civility, when I do not relish
The party, or his business. Pray you be gone, sir,
I'll have no venture in your shop, the office,
Your bark of six, if 'twere sixteen, good sir.
  Cym. You are a rogue.
  P. sen. I think I am, sir, truly.
  Cym. A rascal, and a money-bawd.
  P. sen. My surnames.
  Cym. A wretched rascal——
  P. sen. You will overflow,
And spill all.
  Cym. Caterpillar, moth,
Horse-leech, and dung-worm——
  P. sen. Still you lose your labour.
I am a broken vessel, all runs out :
A shrunk old dryfat. Fare you well, good six !
                            [*Exeunt.*
  Cen. A notable tough rascal, this old Pennyboy !
right city-bred!

Mirth. *In Silver-street, the region of money, a good seat for an usurer.*

Tat. *He has rich ingredients in him, I warrant you, if they were extracted; a true receipt to make an alderman, an he were well wrought upon, according to art.*

Expect. *I would fain see an alderman in* chimia, *that is, a treatise of aldermanity truly written!*

Cen. *To shew how much it differs from urbanity.*

Mirth. *Ay, or humanity. Either would appear in this Pennyboy, an he were rightly distill'd. But how like you the news? you are gone from that.*

Cen. *O, they are monstrous! scurvy, and stale, and too exotic! ill cook'd and ill-dish'd!*

Expect. *They were as good, yet, as butter could make them!*

Tat. *In a word, they were beastly butter'd: he shall never come on my bread more, nor in my mouth, if I can help it. I have better news from the bakehouse, by ten thousand parts, in a morning; or the conduits in Westminster: all the news of Tuttle-street, and both the Alm'ries, the two Sanctuaries, long and round Wool-staple, with King's-street, and Canon-row to boot.*

Mirth. *Ay, my gossip Tattle knew what fine slips grew in Gardener's-lane; who kist the butcher's wife with the cow's breath; what matches were made in the Bowling-alley, and what bets were won and lost; how much grist went to the mill, and what besides: who conjured in Tuttle-fields, and how many, when they never came there; and which boy rode upon doctor Lamb in the likeness of a roaring lion, that run away with him in his teeth, and has not devour'd him yet.*

Tat. *Why, I had it from my maid Joan Hearsay; and she had it from a limb o' the school, she says, a little limb of nine year old; who told her, the master left out his conjuring book one day, and he found it, and so the fable came about. But whether it were true or*

*no, we gossips are bound to believe it, an't be once out,
and a-foot: how should we entertain the time else, or
find ourselves in fashionable discourse, for all companies, if we do not credit all, and make more of it in
the reporting?*

Cen. *For my part, I believe it: an there were no
wiser than I, I would have ne'er a cunning school-
master in England. I mean, a cunning man a school-
master; that is, a conjurer, or a poet, or that had
any acquaintance with a poet. They make all their
scholars play-boys! Is't not a fine sight, to see all our
children made interluders? Do we pay our money for
this? we send them to learn their grammar and their
Terence, and they learn their play-books! Well, they
talk we shall have no more parliaments,[1] God bless
us! but an we have, I hope, Zeal-of-the-land-Busy
and my gossip Rabbi Troubletruth will start up, and
see we shall have painful good ministers to keep school,
and catechise our youth, and not teach them to speak
plays, and act fables of false news, in this manner, to
the super-vexation of town and country, with a wannion!*

[1] *Well, they talk we shall have no more parliaments, &c.*] These
" ridiculous gossips," as the author calls them, tattle the cant of the
times: their language, however, was fearfully ominous; and actors
and spectators were unconsciously sporting on the verge of a precipice, which no long time after, betrayed their feet, and plunged
them into the abyss together.

ACT IV.

SCENE I. *The Devil Tavern. The Apollo.*

PENNYBOY jun. FITTON, SHUNFIELD, ALMANAC, MAD-
RIGAL, PENNYBOY Canter, *and* PICKLOCK, *discovered
at table.*

Pennyboy jun.

OME, gentlemen, let's breathe from healths
awhile.
This Lickfinger has made us a good dinner,
For our Pecunia : what shall's do with our-
selves,
While the women water, and the fidlers eat ?
Fit. Let's jeer a little.[2]
P. jun. Jeer ! what's that ?
Shun. Expect, sir.
Alm. We first begin with ourselves, and then at
you.
Shun. A game we use.
Mad. We jeer all kind of persons
We meet withal, of any rank or quality,

---

[2] *Let's jeer a little.*] This JEERING, has scarcely more to interest
the reader than the *vapouring,* in *Bartholomew Fair.* Jonson's object was to expose to scorn and ridicule the pestilent *humour* of a
set of bullies then in vogue. As the chief characteristics of this
game were dullness and impudence, and as it did not enter into the
poet's plan to change its nature by the admixture of any quality
less odious, he has contented himself with merely playing it as it
was unquestionably played in society, by the Shunfields and Madrigals of the day.

And if we cannot jeer them, we jeer ourselves.

P. Can. A pretty sweet society, and a grateful!

Pick. Pray let's see some.

Shun. Have at you then, lawyer.

They say there was one of your coat in Bethlem
  lately.

Alm. I wonder all his clients were not there.

Mad. They were the madder sort.

Pick. Except, sir, one

Like you, and he made verses.

Fit. Madrigal,

A jeer!

Mad. I know.

Shun. But what did you do, lawyer,

When you made love to mistress Band, at dinner?

Mad. Why, of an advocate, he grew the client.

P. jun. Well play'd, my poet.

Mad. And shew'd the law of nature

Was there above the common-law.

Shun. Quit, quit!

P. jun. Call you this jeering! I can play at this,

'Tis like a ball at tennis.

Fit. Very like;

But we were not well in.

Alm. It is indeed, sir,

When we do speak at volley,[3] all the ill

We can one of another.

Shun. As this morning,

(I would you had heard us,) of the rogue your uncle.

Alm. That money-bawd.

Mad. We call'd him a coat-card,

---

[3] *When we do speak* at volley.] *A la volée,* Fr. heedlessly, without due consideration, &c. The phrase occurs again in the *New
Inn.*

    ——— "You must not give credit
  To all that ladies publicly profess,
  Or talk o' *the volée,* unto their servants."

Of the last order.

P. jun. What is that, a knave?

Mad. Some readings have it so, my manuscript
Doth speak it varlet.

P. Can. And yourself a fool
Of the first rank, and one shall have the leading
Of the right-hand file, under this brave commander.

P. jun. What say'st thou, Canter?

P. Can. Sir, I say this is
A very wholesome exercise, and comely.
Like lepers shewing one another their scabs,
Or flies feeding on ulcers.

P. jun. What news, gentlemen,
Have you any news for after dinner? methinks
We should not spend our time unprofitably.

P. Can. They never lie, sir, between meals; 'gainst
    supper
You may have a bale or two brought in.

Fit. This Canter
Is an old envious knave!

Alm. A very rascal!

Fit. I have mark'd him all this meal, he has done
    nothing
But mock, with scurvy faces, all we said.

Alm. A supercilious rogue! he looks as if
He were the patrico——

Mad. Or arch-priest of Canters.

Shun. He is some primate metropolitan rascal,
Our shot-clog⁴ makes so much of him.

Alm. The law,
And he does govern him.

---

⁴ *Our shot-clog, &c.*] Whalley's explanation of this term, (vol.
ii. p. 191.) is incorrect. Instead of "an incumbrance on the reckoning," it appears to mean both here, and in the passage referred to,
one who is pledged for the reckoning; a simpleton, a gull, in short,
who discharges the shot for the whole party. By the *law*, Picklock
is meant.

P. jun. What say you, gentlemen ?

Fit. We say, we wonder not, your man of law
Should be so gracious with you ; but how it comes,
This rogue, this Canter——

P. jun. O, good words.

Fit. A fellow
That speaks no language——

Alm. But what jingling gypsies,
And pedlars trade in——

Fit. And no honest Christian
Can understand——

P. Can. Why, by that argument
You are all Canters, you, and you, and you :
All the whole world are Canters, I will prove it
In your professions.

P. jun. I would fain hear this :
But stay, my princess comes ; provide the while,
I'll call for it anon.

Enter LICKFINGER, PECUNIA, STATUTE, BAND, WAX,
and MORTGAGE.

How fares your grace ?

Lick. I hope the fare was good.

Pec. Yes, Lickfinger,
And we shall thank you for it, and reward you.

Mad. Nay, I'll not lose my argument, Lickfinger ;
Before these gentlewomen,[5] I affirm,
The perfect and true strain of poetry
Is rather to be given the quick cellar,
Than the fat kitchen.

          [P. jun. *takes* PECUNIA *aside, and courts her.*

---

[5] *Before these* gentlewomen.] The old copies read "gentlemen,"
which destroys at once the metre and the poet's meaning. Madrigal alludes to what had already passed *before the gentlemen* (p. 186) ;
and he now resumes the subject on the entrance of the ladies. The
Oracle of the Bottle, (see the next speech,) Ben found in Rabelais,
with whom he was apparently familiar.

Lick. Heretic, I see
Thou art for the vain Oracle of the Bottle.
The hogshead, Trismegistus, is thy Pegasus.
Thence flows thy muse's spring, from that hard hoof.
Seduced poet, I do say to thee,
A boiler, range, and dresser were the fountains
Of all the knowledge in the universe.
And they're the kitchens, where the master-cook——
Thou dost not know the man, nor can'st thou know
      him,
Till thou hast serv'd some years in that deep school,
That's both the nurse and mother of the arts,
And hear'st him read, interpret, and demonstrate—
A master-cook! why, he's the man of men,
For a professor! he designs, he draws,
He paints, he carves, he builds, he fortifies,
Makes citadels of curious fowl and fish,
Some he dry-dishes, some motes round with broths;
Mounts marrow-bones, cuts fifty-angled custards,
Rears bulwark pies, and for his outer works,
He raiseth ramparts of immortal crust;
And teacheth all the tactics, at one dinner:[6]
What ranks, what files, to put his dishes in;
The whole art military.   Then he knows
The influence of the stars upon his meats,
And all their seasons, tempers, qualities,
And so to fit his relishes and sauces.
He has nature in a pot, 'bove all the chymists,
Or airy brethren of the Rosie-cross.
He is an architect, an enginer,
A soldier, a physician, a philosopher,

---

[6] *And teacheth all the tactics, at one dinner.*] We have all this in
the Masque called *Neptune's Triumph:* our poet seems so pleased
with his conceit, that he was willing the good people of the city
should share in it, as well as the finer gentlemen about court. The
reader will find the original of this description, in a note on the
Masque above mentioned. WHAL.

A general mathematician.

 Mad. It is granted.

 Lick. And that you may not doubt him for a
  poet——

 Alm. This fury shews, if there were nothing else,
And 'tis divine! I shall for ever hereafter
Admire the wisdom of a cook.

 Band. And we, sir.

 P. jun. O, how my princess draws me with her
  looks,
And hales me in, as eddies draw in boats,
Or strong Charybdis ships, that sail too near
The shelves of love! The tides of your two eyes,
Wind of your breath, are such as suck in all
That do approach you.

 Pec. Who hath changed my servant?

 P. jun. Yourself, who drink my blood up with
  your beams,
As doth the sun the sea! Pecunia shines
More in the world than he; and makes it spring
Where'er she favours! please her but to show
Her melting wrists, or bare her ivory hands,
She catches still! her smiles they are love's fetters!
Her breasts his apples! her teats strawberries!
Where Cupid, were he present now, would cry,
Farewell my mother's milk, here's sweeter nectar!
Help me to praise Pecunia, gentlemen;
She is your princess, lend your wits.

 Fit. A lady
The Graces taught to move!

 Alm. The Hours did nurse!

 Fit. Whose lips are the instructions of all lovers!

 Alm. Her eyes their lights, and rivals to the stars!

 Fit. A voice, as if that harmony still spake!

 Alm. And polish'd skin, whiter than Venus' foot!

 Fit. Young Hebe's neck, or Juno's arms!

 Alm. A hair,

Large as the morning's, and her breath as sweet
As meadows after rain, and but new mown !
   Fit. Leda might yield unto her for a face !
   Alm. Hermione for breasts !
   Fit. Flora for cheeks !
   Alm. And Helen for a mouth !
   P. jun. Kiss, kiss 'em, princess.

                              [PECUNIA *kisses them.*

   Fit. The pearl doth strive in whiteness with her
      neck——
   Alm. But loseth by it : here the snow thaws snow ;
One frost resolves another !
   Fit. O, she has
A front too slippery to be look'd upon ! [7]
   Alm. And glances that beguile the seer's eyes !
   P. jun. Kiss, kiss again. [PECUNIA *kisses* ALM. *and*
      FIT.] What says my man of war ?
   Shun. I say, she's more than fame can promise of
      her,
A theme that's overcome with her own matter !
Praise is struck blind and deaf and dumb with her,
She doth astonish commendation !
   P. jun. Well pump'd, i'faith, old sailor ; kiss him too,
Though he be a slug. [*She kisses him.*] What says my
      poet-sucker ?
He's chewing his muse's cud, I do see by him.
   Mad. I have almost done, I want but e'en to finish.
   Fit. That's the ill luck of all his works still.
   P. jun. What ?
   Fit. To begin many works, but finish none.
   P. jun. How does he do his mistress' work ?

---

  [7] Fit. *O, she has*
      A front too slippery to be look'd upon.] Literally from
Horace :

        " *Urit me Glyceræ nitor*
      Splendentis Pario marmore purius,
      Et vultus nimium lubricus aspici." WHAL.

Fit. Imperfect.

Alm. I cannot think he finisheth that.

P. jun. Let's hear.

Mad. It is a madrigal ; I affect that kind
Of poem much.

P. jun. And thence you have the name.

Fit. It is his rose, he can make nothing else.[8]

Mad. I made it to the tune the fidlers play'd,
That we all liked so well.

P. jun. Good ! read it, read it.

Mad. The sun is father of all metals, you know,
Silver and gold.

P. jun. Ay, leave your prologues, say.

Mad. *As bright as is the sun her sire,*
   Or earth her mother, in her best attire,
   Or Mint, the midwife, with her fire,
      Comes forth her grace!

P. jun. That Mint, the midwife, does well.
   The splendour of the wealthiest mines,
   The stamp and strength of all imperial lines,
   Both majesty and beauty shines,
      In her sweet face!

Fit. That's fairly said of money.
   Look how a torch of taper light,
   Or of that torch's flame, a beacon bright ;

P. jun. Good !

Mad. Now there, I want a line to finish, sir.

P. jun. *Or of that beacon's fire, moon-light :*

Mad. *So takes she place!*

Fit. 'Tis good.

Mad. And then I have a saraband——
   She makes good cheer, she keeps full boards,
   She holds a fair of knights and lords,
   A market of all offices,
   And shops of honours, more or less.

---

[8] *It is his* rose, *he can make nothing else.*] Alluding to the painter,
who could paint nothing but that flower. Whal.

According to Pecunia's grace,
The bride hath beauty, blood, and place;
The bridegroom virtue, valour, wit,
And wisdom, as he stands for it.
P. jun. Call in the fidlers.

Enter the Fidlers, *and* NICHOLAS.

Nick the boy shall sing it.
Sweet princess, kiss him, kiss them all, dear madam,
[PEC. *kisses them.*
And at the close, vouchsafe to call them cousins.
    Pec. Sweet cousin Madrigal and cousin Fitton,
My cousin Shunfield and my learned cousin——
    Pick. Al-manach, though they call him Almanac.
    P. Can. Why, here's the prodigal prostitutes his
        mistress!⁹   [*Aside.*
    P. jun. And Picklock, he must be a kinsman too.
My man of law will teach us all to win,
And keep our own.—Old founder!
    P. Can. Nothing, I, sir.
I am a wretch, a beggar: She the fortunate,
Can want no kindred; we the poor know none.
    Fit. Nor none shall know, by my consent.
    Alm. Nor mine.
    P. jun. Sing, boy, stand here.
    Nich. [*sings.*] *As bright, &c.*   [*Music.*
    P. Can. Look, look, how all their eyes
Dance in their heads, observe, scatter'd with lust,
At sight of their brave idol! how they are tickled
With a light air, the bawdy saraband!
They are a kind of dancing engines all,
And set by nature, thus to run alone
To every sound! all things within, without them,

---

⁹ P. Can. *Why, here's the prodigal, &c.*] The names of the
speakers are miserably out of place in the old folio. The author
assuredly never revised, probably never saw, a line of this publication.

Move, but their brain, and that stands still! mere
    monsters,
Here in a chamber, of most subtile feet,
And make their legs in tune, passing the streets!
These are the gallant spirits of the age,
The miracles of the time! that can cry up
And down men's wits, and set what rate on things
Their half-brain'd fancies please! now pox upon them!
See how solicitously he learns the jig,
As if it were a mystery of his faith.   [*Aside.*
   Shun. A dainty ditty!
   Fit. O, he's a dainty poet,
When he sets to it!
   P. jun. And a dainty scholar!
   Alm. No, no great scholar; he writes like a
    gentleman. .
   Shun. Pox o' your scholar!
   P. Can. Pox o' your distinction!
As if a scholar were no gentleman.
With these, to write like a gentleman, will in time
Become all one, as to write like an ass.[1]
These gentlemen! these rascals; I am sick
Of indignation at them.   [*Aside.*
   P. jun. How do you like't, sir?
   Fit. 'Tis excellent!
   Alm. 'Twas excellently sung!
   Fit. A dainty air!
   P. jun. What says my Lickfinger?
   Lick. I am telling mistress Band and mistress
    Statute,
What a brave gentleman you are, and Wax, here!

---

[1] *With these to* write like a gentleman, *will in time,*
   Become all one, as to write like an ass.] Old Canter was right;
"the mob of *gentlemen* who wrote with ease," about half a century
later, verified his observation. "The phrase (*a person of quality*)
is a *little variations*," as captain Fluellin says, "but the meaning is
all one reckoning."

5   S

How much 'twere better, that my lady's grace
Would here take up, sir, and keep house with you.
 P. jun. What say they?
 Sta. We could consent, sir, willingly.
 Band. Ay, if we knew her grace had the least liking.
 Wax. We must obey her grace's will and pleasure.
 P. jun. I thank you, gentlewomen.—Ply them,
  Lickfinger.
Give mother Mortgage, there——
 Lick. Her dose of sack.
I have it for her, and her distance of hum.[2]
 Pec. Indeed therein, I must confess, dear cousin,
I am a most unfortunate princess.
 Alm. And
You still will be so, when your grace may help it!
   [*The gallants gather all about* PECUNIA.
 Mad. Who'd lie in a room with a close-stool, and
  garlic,
And kennel with his dogs, that had a prince,
Like this young Pennyboy, to sojourn with!
 Shun. He'll let you have your liberty——
 Alm. Go forth,
Whither you please, and to what company——
 Mad. Scatter yourself amongst us——
 P. jun. Hope of Parnassus!
Thy ivy shall not wither, nor thy bays;

---

[2] ——— *and her distance of* hum.] Hum has been already
noticed as a kind of spirituous liquor. (p. 15.) It is mentioned by
Shirley:
 "*Lod.* They say that canary sack must dance again
  To the apothecary's, and be sold for
 Physic in *hum*-glasses and thimbles." *The Wedding*, Act. ii.
I cannot pretend to give the meaning of a *distance* of hum. As it
was drank in *small glasses*, it was probably of considerable strength,
and the expression in the text may therefore allude to some division,
either real or imaginary, in the ordinary vessels, by which the
draughts of it were regulated, and below which it was not allowable
to go. That such rules once existed, is well-known. But this is
merely conjecture.

Thou shalt be had into her grace's cellar,
And there know sack and claret, all December :
Thy vein is rich, and we must cherish it.
Poets and bees swarm now a days ; but yet
There are not those good taverns, for the one sort,
As there are flowery fields to feed the other.
Though bees be pleased with dew, ask little Wax,
That brings the honey to her lady's hive :
The poet must have wine ; and he shall have it.

Enter PENNYBOY sen. *hastily.*

P. sen. Broker ! what, Broker !
P. jun. Who's that, my uncle ?
P. sen. I am abused ; where is my knave, my
      Broker ?
Lick. Your Broker is laid out upon a bench, yonder ;
Sack hath seized on him, in the shape of sleep.
  Pick. He hath been dead to us almost this hour.
  P. sen. This hour !
  P. Can. Why sigh you, sir ? 'cause he's at rest ?
  P. sen. It breeds my unrest.
  Lick. Will you take a cup,
And try if you can sleep ?
  P. sen. No, cogging Jack,
Thou and thy cups too, perish.
                    [*Strikes the cup out of his hand.*
  Shun. O, the sack !
  Mad. The sack, the sack !
  P. Can. A madrigal on sack !
  Pick. Or rather an elegy, for the sack is gone.
  Pec. Why do you this, sir ? spill the wine, and rave,
For Broker's sleeping ?
  P. sen. What through sleep and sack,
My trust is wrong'd : but I am still awake,
To wait upon your grace, please you to quit
This strange lewd company, they are not for you
  Pec. No, guardian, I do like them very well.

P. sen. Your grace's pleasure be observ'd; but you,
Statute, and Band, and Wax will go with me?
  Sta. Truly, we will not.
  Band. We will stay, and wait here
Upon her grace, and this your noble kinsman.
  P. sen. Noble! how noble! who hath made him
    noble?
  P. jun. Why, my most noble Money hath, or shall.
My princess here; she that, had you but kept
And treated kindly, would have made you noble,
And wise too : nay, perhaps have done that for you,
An act of parliament could not, made you honest.
The truth is, uncle, that her grace dislikes
Her entertainment, 'specially her lodging.
  Pec. Nay, say her jail : never unfortunate princess
Was used so by a jailor.   Ask my women :
Band, you can tell, and Statute, how he has used me,
Kept me close prisoner, under twenty bolts——
  Sta. And forty padlocks——
  Band. All malicious engines
A wicked smith could forge out of his iron ;
As locks and keys, shackles and manacles,
To torture a great lady.
  Sta. He has abused
Your grace's body.
  Pec. No, he would have done ;
That lay not in his power : he had the use
Of our bodies, Band and Wax and sometimes
    Statute's :
But once he would have smother'd me in a chest.[3]

  [3] *But once he would have smother'd me, &c.*]   This is from Aristophanes :

Αλλ' αχθομαι μεν εισων νη τους θεους,
Ες οικιαν ἑκαστοτ' αλλοτριαν πανυ·
Αγαθον γαρ απελαυσ' ουδεν αυτου πωποτε.
Ην μεν γαρ ες φειδωλον εισελθων τυχω,
Ευθυς κατωρυξεν με κατα της γης κατω.

It is amusing to contemplate the manner in which these two great

And strangled me in leather, but that you
Came to my rescue then, and gave me air.
   Sta. For which he cramm'd us up in a close box,
All three together, where we saw no sun ˄
In one six months.
   Wax. A cruel man he is !
   Band. He has left my fellow Wax out in the cold—
   Sta. Till she was stiff as any frost, and crumbled
Away to dust, and almost lost her form.
   Wax. Much ado to recover me.
   P. sen. Women jeerers !
Have you learn'd too the subtle faculty ?
Come, I will shew you the way home, if drink
Or too full diet have disguised you.
   Band. Troth,
We have not any mind, sir, of return——
   Sta. To be bound back to back——
   Band. And have our legs
Turn'd in, or writh'd about——
   Wax. Or else display'd——
   Sta. Be lodged with dust and fleas, as we were
       wont——
   Band. And dieted with dogs'-dung.
   P. sen. Why, you whores,
My bawds, my instruments, what should I call you,
Man may think base enough for you ?
   P. jun. Hear you, uncle :
I must not hear this of my princess' servants,
And in Apollo, in Pecunia's room.
Go, get you down the stairs ; home, to your kennel,
As swiftly as you can.   Consult your dogs,
The Lares of your family ; or believe it,

masters of comic humour have treated a nearly similar subject.
The strictness of the ancient drama would not admit the boundless
variety with which Jonson has diversified and enriched his scenes ;
but Aristophanes has nevertheless made his simple plot the vehicle
of much exquisite mirth, and much powerful satire.

The fury of a footman and a drawer
Hangs over you.
   Shun. Cudgel and pot do threaten
A kind of vengeance.
   Mad. Barbers are at hand.
   Alm. Washing and shaving will ensue.
   Fit. The pump
Is not far off ; if 'twere, the sink is near,
Or a good jordan.
   Mad. You have now no money.
   Shun. But are a rascal.
   P. sen. I am cheated, robb'd,
Jeer'd by confederacy.
   Fit. No, you are kick'd,
And used kindly, as you should be.
   Shun. Spurn'd
From all commerce of men, who are a cur.
                    [They kick him.
   Alm. A stinking dog in a doublet, with foul linen.
   Mad. A snarling rascal, hence !
   Shun. Out!
   P. sen. Well, remember,
I am cozen'd by my cousin, and his whore.
Bane o' these meetings in Apollo !
   Lick. Go, sir,
You will be tost like Block in a blanket, else.
   P. jun. Down with him, Lickfinger.
   P. sen. Saucy Jack, away :
Pecunia is a whore.
   P. jun. Play him down, fidlers,
And drown his noise. [*Exeunt* P. sen. *and* LICK-
     FINGER.]—Who's this ?

   Enter PIEDMANTLE *with* PECUNIA's *pedigree.*

   Fit. O, master Piedmantle !
   Pie. By your leave, gentlemen.
   Fit. Her grace's herald ?

Alm. No herald yet, a heraldet.

P. jun. What's that ?

P. Can. A canter.

P. jun. O, thou saidst thou'dst prove us all so !

P. Can. Sir, here is one will prove himself so,
　　straight ;
So shall the rest, in time.

Pec. My pedigree ?
I tell you, friend, he must be a good scholar
Can my descent : I am of princely race ;
And as good blood as any is in the mines
Runs through my veins.　I am, every limb, a prin-
　　cess !
Dutchess of mines was my great grandmother ;
And by the father's side, I come from Sol :
My grandfather was duke of Or, and match'd
In the blood-royal of Ophir.

Pie. Here is his coat.

Pec. I know it, if I hear the blazon.

Pie. He bears
In a field azure, a sun proper, beamy,
Twelve of the second.

P. Can. How far is this from canting ?

P. jun. Her grace doth understand it.

P. Can. She can cant, sir.

Pec. What be these, bezants ?

Pie. Yes, an't please your grace.

Pec. That is our coat too, as we come from Or.
What line is this ?

Pie. The rich mines of Potosi,
The Spanish mines in the West Indies.

Pec. This ?

Pie. The mines of Hungary, this of Barbary.

Pec. But this, this little branch ?

Pie. The Welsh mine, that.

Pec. I have Welsh blood in me too ; blaze, sir,
　　that coat.

Pie. She bears, an't please you, argent, three leeks
vert,
In canton or, and tassell'd of the first.

P. Can. Is not this canting ? do you understand
him ? [4]

P. jun. Not I ; but it sounds well, and the whole
thing
Is rarely painted : I will have such a scroll,
Whate'er it cost me.

Pec. Well, at better leisure
We'll take a view of it, and so reward you.

P. jun. Kiss him, sweet princess, and style him a
cousin.

Pec. I will, if you will have it.—Cousin Piedmantle.   [*She kisses him.*

P. jun. I love all men of virtue, from my princess,
Unto my beggar here, old Canter.   On,
On to thy proof ; whom prove you the next canter ?

P. Can. The doctor here ; I will proceed with the
learned.
When he discourseth of dissection,
Or any point of anatomy ; that he tells you

---

[4] *Is not this canting? Do you understand him ?*] Here, as was
observed in a similar case, (p. 105,) it would not have been a matter of difficulty, though of considerable labour, to furnish some kind
of explanation of all the technical terms which occur in the remainder of this scene; but it would still be a thankless office. No
one, I should suppose, would even dwell for a moment on such an
uninteresting muster-roll of hard words ; and, in fact, if any prodigy
of patience and curiosity should enquire after their sense, and learn
that *tassell'd of the first,* means of the first colour, " because heraldry
abhors to repeat the name ;" that *trine* is " the aspect of one star
with regard to another, when they are distant 120 degrees," &c., &c.,
he would not, I suspect, find himself very far advanced in the
sciences of heraldry and astronomy.   Jonson, who was not only
possessed of as much learning, but of as much general knowledge
as any man of his time, undoubtedly understood them all: the
general reader, however, will do well to content himself (like the
Prodigal) with saying " they sound well," and pass on.

Of vena cava, and of vena porta,
The meseraics, and the mesenterium :
What does he else but cant ? or if he run
To his judicial astrology,
And trowl the Trine, the Quartile, and the Sextile,
Platic aspect, and Partile, with his Hyleg,
Or Alchochoden, Cuspes, and Horoscope ;
Does not he cant? who here does understand him ?
   Alm. This is no canter, though !
   P. Can. Or when my muster-master
Talks of his tactics, and his ranks and files,
His bringers-up, his leaders-on, and cries
Faces about to the right hand, the left,
Now, *as you were;* then tells you of redoubts,
Of cats, and cortines : doth not he cant?
   P. jun. Yes, faith.
   P. Can. My egg-chin'd laureat here, when he
      comes forth
With dimeters, and trimeters, tetrameters,
Pentameters, hexameters, catalectics,
His hyper and his brachy-catalectics,
His pyrrhics, epitrites, and choriambics ;
What is all this, but canting ?
   Mad. A rare fellow !
   Shun. Some begging scholar !
   Fit. A decay'd doctor, at least !
   P. jun. Nay, I do cherish virtue, though in rags.
   P. Can. And you, mas courtier—   [*To* FITTON.
   P. jun. Now he treats of you,
Stand forth to him fair.
   P. Can. With all your fly-blown projects,
And looks-out of the politics, your shut faces,
And reserv'd questions and answers, that you game
      with ; as,
Is't a clear business? will it manage well?
My name must not be used else.   Here'twill dash—
Your business has receiv'd a taint,—give off,

I may not prostitute myself.   Tut, tut,
That little dust I can blow off at pleasure.—
Here's no such mountain, yet, in the whole work,
But a light purse may level.—I will tide
This affair for you ; give it freight, and passage :—
And such mint phrase, as 'tis the worst of canting,
By how much it affects the sense it has not.
　Fit. This is some other than he seems !
　P. jun. How like you him ?
　Fit. This cannot be a canter !
　P. jun. But he is, sir,
And shall be still, and so shall you be too :
We'll all be canters.　Now I think of it,
A noble whimsy's come into my brain :
I'll build a college, I and my Pecunia,
And call it CANTERS COLLEGE : sounds it well ?
　Alm. Excellent !
　P. jun. And here stands my father rector,
And you professors ; you shall all profess
Something, and live there, with her grace and me,
Your founders : I'll endow it with lands and means,
And Lickfinger shall be my master-cook.
What, is he gone ?
　P. Can. And a professor ?
　P. jun. Yes.
　P. Can. And read Apicius *de re culinaria*
To your brave doxy and you !
　P. jun. You, cousin Fitton,
Shall, as a courtier, read the politics ;
Doctor Almanac he shall read astrology ;
Shunfield shall read the military arts.
　P. Can. As carving and assaulting the cold custard.
　P. jun. And Horace here, the art of poetry.
His lyrics, and his madrigals ; fine songs,
Which we will have at dinner, steep'd in claret,
And against supper, soused in sack.
　Mad. In troth,

A divine whimsy !
Shun. And a worthy work,
Fit for a chronicle !
　P. jun. Is it not ?
　Shun. To all ages.
　P. jun. And Piedmantle shall give us all our arms :
But Picklock, what wouldst thou be ? thou canst
　　　cant too.
　Pick. In all the languages in Westminster-hall,
Pleas, Bench, or Chancery.   Fee-farm, fee-tail,
Tenant in dower, at will, for term of life,
By copy of court-roll, knights' service, homage,
Fealty, escuage, soccage, or frank almoigne,
Grand serjeantry, or burgage.
　P. jun. Thou appear'st,
Κατ' ἐξοχὴν, a canter.   Thou shalt read
All Littleton's Tenures to me, and, indeed,
All my conveyances.
　Pick. And make them too, sir :
Keep all your courts, be steward of your lands,
Let all your leases, keep your evidences.
But first, I must procure and pass your mortmain,
You must have license from above, sir.
　P. jun. Fear not,
Pecunia's friends shall do it.
　P. Can. But I shall stop it.
　　　　　　　[Throws off his patched cloke, &c., and
　　　　　　　　　　　discovers himself.
Your worship's *loving and obedient father*,
Your *painful steward*, and *lost officer* !
Who have done this, to try how you would use
Pecunia when you had her ; which since I see,
I will take home the lady to my charge,
And these her servants, and leave you my cloke,
To travel in to Beggars-bush !   A seat
Is built already, furnish'd too, worth twenty
Of your imagined structures, Canters College.

Fit. It is his father!

Mad. He's alive, methinks.

Alm. I knew he was no rogue.[5]

P. Can. Thou prodigal,
Was I so careful for thee, to procure
And plot with my learn'd counsel, master Picklock,
This noble match for thee, and dost thou prostitute,
Scatter thy mistress' favours, throw away
Her bounties, as they were red-burning coals,
Too hot for thee to handle, on such rascals,
Who are the scum and excrements of men!
If thou hadst sought out good and virtuous persons
Of these professions, I had loved thee and them:
For these shall never have that plea against me,
Or colour of advantage, that I hate
Their callings, but their manners and their vices.
A worthy courtier is the ornament
Of a king's palace, his great master's honour;
This is a moth, a rascal, a court-rat,

                              [*Points to* FITTON.

That gnaws the commonwealth with broking suits,
And eating grievances! so, a true soldier,
He is his country's strength, his sovereign's safety,
And to secure his peace, he makes himself
The heir of danger, nay the subject of it,
And runs those virtuous hazards that this scarecrow
Cannot endure to hear of.

Shun. You are pleasant, sir.

P. Can. With you I dare be! here is Piedmantle;
'Cause he's an ass, do not I love a herald,
Who is the pure preserver of descents,

---

[5] *I knew he was no rogue,*] i. e. no beggar by profession: see
p. 209. *Beggars-bush,* which occurs just above, "is (as Fuller tells
us) a tree notoriously known, on the left hand of the London road
from Huntington to Coxton. It is spoken of such who use disso-
lute and improvident courses, which tend to poverty." *Hunting-
tonshire Prov.*

The keeper fair of all nobility,
Without which all would run into confusion?
Were he a learned herald, I would tell him
He can give arms and marks, he cannot honour;
No more than money can make noble: it may
Give place, and rank, but it can give no virtue:
And he would thank me for this truth. This dog-
     leach,
You style him doctor, 'cause he can compile
An almanac, perhaps erect a scheme
For my great madam's monkey, when't has ta'en
A glyster, and bewray'd the Ephemerides.
Do I despise a learn'd physician,
In calling him a quacksalver? or blast
The ever-living garland, always green,
Of a good poet, when I say his wreath
Is pieced and patch'd of dirty wither'd flowers?—
Away! I am impatient of these ulcers,
That I not call you worse. There is no sore
Or plague but you to infect the times: I abhor
Your very scent.—Come, lady, since my prodigal
Knew not to entertain you to your worth,
I'll see if I have learn'd how to receive you,
With more respect to you, and your fair train here.
Farewell, my beggar in velvet, for to-day;
To-morrow you may put on that grave robe,
                          [Points to his patch'd cloke.
And enter your great work of *Canters College,*
Your work, and worthy of a chronicle!   *[Exeunt.*

    Tat. *Why, this was the worst of all, the catastrophe!*
    Cen. *The matter began to be good but now; and he
has spoil'd it all with his beggar there!*
    Mirth. *A beggarly Jack it is, I warrant him, and
akin to the poet.*
    Tat. *Like enough, for he had the chiefest part in his
play, if you mark it.*

Expect. *Absurdity on him, for a huge overgrown play-maker! why should he make him live again, when they and we all thought him dead? if he had left him to his rags, there had been an end of him.*

Tat. *Ay, but set a beggar on horseback, he'll never lin till he be a gallop.*

Cen. *The young heir grew a fine gentleman in this last act.*

Expect. *So he did, gossip, and kept the best company.*

Cen. *And feasted them, and his mistress.*

Tat. *And shew'd her to them all: was not jealous!*

Mirth. *But very communicative and liberal, and began to be magnificent, if the churl his father would have let him alone.*

Cen. *It was spitefully done of the poet, to make the chuff take him off in his height, when he was going to do all his brave deeds.*

Expect. *To found an academy.*

Tat. *Erect a college.*

Expect. *Plant his professors, and water his lectures.*

Mirth. *With wine, gossips, as he meant to do;—and then to defraud his purposes!*

Expect. *Kill the hopes of so many towardly young spirits.—*

Tat. *As the doctors—*

Cen. *And the courtiers! I protest I was in love with master Fitton: he did wear all he had, from the hatband to the shoe-tie, so politically, and would stoop, and leer!*

Mirth. *And lie so in wait for a piece of wit, like a mouse-trap!*

Expect. *Indeed, gossip, so would the little doctor; all his behaviour was mere glyster. O' my conscience, he would make any party's physic in the world work with his discourse.*

Mirth. *I wonder they would suffer it; a foolish old fornicating father to ravish away his son's mistress.*

Cen. And all her women at once, as he did.

Tat. I would have flown in his gypsy's face, i'faith.

Mirth. It was a plain piece of political incest, and worthy to be brought afore the high commission of wit. Suppose we were to censure him; you are the youngest voice, gossip Tattle, begin.

Tat. Marry, I would have the old coney-catcher cozen'd of all he has, in the young heir's defence, by his learned counsel, master Picklock!

Cen. I would rather the courtier had found out some trick to beg him for his estate!

Expect. Or the captain had courage enough to beat him!

Cen. Or the fine Madrigal-man in rhyme, to have run him out of the country, like an Irish rat.

Tat. No, I would have master Piedmantle, her grace's herald, to pluck down his hatchments, reverse his coat-armour, and nullify him for no gentleman.

Expect. Nay, then, let master doctor dissect him, have him opened, and his tripes translated to Lick-finger, to make a probation-dish of.

Cen. Tat. Agreed, agreed!

Mirth. Faith, I would have him flat disinherited by a decree of court, bound to make restitution of the lady Pecunia, and the use of her body, to his son.

Expect. And her train to the gentlemen.

Cen. And both the poet, and himself, to ask them all forgiveness!

Tat. And us too.

Cen. In two large sheets of paper——

Expect. Or to stand in a skin of parchment, which the court please.

Cen. And those fill'd with news!

Mirth. And dedicated to the sustaining of the Staple!

Expect. Which their poet hath let fall most abruptly.

Mirth. Bankruptly indeed.

Cen. *You say wittily, gossip ; and therefore let a protest go out against him.*

Mirth. *A mournival of protests, or a gleek,*[6] *at least.*

Expect. *In all our names.*

Cen. *For a decay'd wit*——

Expect. *Broken*——

Tat. *Non-solvent*——

Cen. *And for ever forfeit*——

Mirth. *To scorn of Mirth !*

Cen. *Censure !*

Expect. *Expectation !*

Tat. *Subsign'd, Tattle.   Stay, they come again.*

ACT V.

SCENE I.   PENNYBOY's *Lodgings.*

Enter PENNYBOY jun. *in the patched and ragged cloke his father left him.*

Pennyboy jun.

NAY, they are fit, as they had been made for me,
And I am now a thing worth looking at,
The same I said I would be in the morning !
No rogue, at a comitia of the canters,
Did ever there become his parent's robes
Better than I do these.   Great fool, and beggar !

---

[6] *A mournival of protests, or a* gleek, *at least.*]   " A *mournival* is either *all* the aces, the *four* kings, queens, or knaves ; and a *gleek* is *three* of any of the aforesaid."   *Complete Gamester,* p. 94.

Why do not all that are of those societies
Come forth, and gratulate me one of theirs ?
Methinks I should be on every side saluted,
Dauphin of beggars, prince of prodigals !
That have so fallen under the ears, and eyes,
And tongues of all, the fable of the time,
Matter of scorn, and mark of reprehension !
I now begin to see my vanity
Shine in this glass, reflected by the foil !—
Where is my fashioner, my feather-man,
My linener, perfumer, barber, all
That tail of riot follow'd me this morning ?
Not one ! but a dark solitude about me,
Worthy my cloke and patches ; as I had
The epidemical disease upon me ;
And I'll sit down with it.   [*Seats himself on the floor.*

Enter THO. Barber.

   Tho. My master, maker !
How do you ? why do you sit thus on the ground, sir ?
Hear you the news ?
   P. jun. No, nor I care to hear none.
Would I could here sit still, and slip away
The other one and twenty, to have this
Forgotten, and the day razed out, expunged
In every ephemerides, or almanac !
Or if it must be in, that time and nature
Have decreëd ; still let it be a day
Of tickling prodigals about the gills,
Deluding gaping heirs, losing their loves,
And their discretions, falling from the favours
Of their best friends and parents, their own hopes,
And entering the society of canters.
   Tho. A doleful day it is, and dismal times
Are come upon us ! I am clear undone.
   P. jun. How, Tom ?
   Tho. Why, broke, broke ; wretchedly broke.

5   T

P. jun. Ha!

Tho. Our Staple is all to pieces, quite dissolv'd.

P. jun. Ha!

Tho. Shiver'd, as in an earthquake! heard you not
The crack and ruins? we are all blown up!
Soon as they heard the Infanta was got from them,
Whom they had so devoured in their hopes,
To be their patroness, and sojourn with them,
Our emissaries, register, examiner,
Flew into vapour: our grave governor
Into a subtler air, and is return'd,[7]
As we do hear, grand captain of the jeerers.
I and my fellow melted into butter,
And spoil'd our ink, and so the office vanish'd.
The last hum that it made, was, that your father
And Picklock are fall'n out, the man of law.

    P. jun. [*starting up.*] How! this awakes me from
        my lethargy.

    Tho. And a great suit is like to be between them:
Picklock denies the feoffment, and the trust,
Your father says, he made of the whole estate
Unto him, as respecting his mortality,
When he first laid his late device, to try you.

    P. jun. Has Picklock then a trust?

    Tho. I cannot tell,
Here comes the worshipful——

              [P. jun. *makes a sign to* THO. *who retires*
                    behind the hangings.

Enter PICKLOCK.

    Pick. What, my velvet heir
Turn'd beggar in mind, as robes!

    P. jun. You see what case
Your, and my father's plots have brought me to.

    Pick. Your father's, you may say, indeed, not mine.

---

    [7] ——— *and is* return'd, *&c.*] i. e. gone back to his former
situation, &c. This is sufficiently harsh.

He's a hard-hearted gentleman ; I am sorry
To see his rigid resolution !
That any man should so put off affection,
And human nature, to destroy his own,
And triumph in a victory so cruel !
He's fallen out with me, for being yours,
And calls me knave, and traitor to his trust ;
Says he will have me thrown over the bar——

    P. jun. Have you deserv'd it ?

    Pick. O, good heaven knows
My conscience, and the silly latitude of it ;
A narrow-minded man ! my thoughts do dwell
All in a lane, or line indeed ; no turning,
Nor scarce obliquity in them.   I still look
Right forward, to the intent and scope of that
Which he would go from now.

    P. jun. Had you a trust then ?

    Pick. Sir, I had somewhat will keep you still lord
Of all the estate, if I be honest, as
I hope I shall.   My tender scrupulous breast
Will not permit me see the heir defrauded,
And like an alien thrust out of the blood.
The laws forbid that I should give consent
To such a civil slaughter of a son !

    P. jun. Where is the deed ? hast thou it with thee ?

    Pick. No.
It is a thing of greater consequence,
Than to be borne about in a black box,
Like a Low-Country vorloffe,[8] or Welsh brief.

---

[8] *Like a Low-Country* vorloffe.] One of the terms picked up by the poet in his Flemish campaign.   He gives it indeed, as an exotic ; but it has long since been naturalized among us, as *furlough*, by which it has lost nothing but its pristine sense and sound.

It is greatly to the credit of the gentlemen of the army, that they have contrived to obviate the miserable poverty of the English tongue, by adopting the military vocabulary of almost all the nations of Europe.   This gives a richness to their language, which is scarcely surpassed by its idiomatic pureness and intelligibility.

It is at Lickfinger's, under lock and key.
 P. jun. O, fetch it hither.
 Pick. I have bid him bring it,
That you might see it.
 P. jun. Knows he what he brings?
 Pick. No more than a gardener's ass, what roots
  he carries.
 P. jun. I was a sending my father, like an ass,
A penitent epistle; but I am glad
I did not now.
 Pick. Hang him, an austere grape,
That has no juice, but what is verjuice in him!
 P. jun. I'll shew you my letter.[9]   [*Exit.*
 Pick. Shew me a defiance!
If I can now commit father and son,
And make my profits out of both; commence
A suit with the old man for his whole state,
And go to law with the son's credit, undo
Both, both with their own money, it were a piece
Worthy my night-cap, and the gown I wear,
A Picklock's name in law.—Where are you, sir?
What do you do so long?

Re-enter PENNYBOY jun.

 P. jun. I cannot find
Where I have laid it; but I have laid it safe.
 Pick. No matter, sir; trust you unto my Trust,
'Tis that that shall secure you, an absolute deed!
And I confess it was in trust for you,
Lest any thing might have happen'd mortal to him:
But there must be a gratitude thought on,
And aid, sir, for the charges of the suit,
Which will be great, 'gainst such a mighty man
As is your father, and a man possest

---

 [9] Here the margin says, *Pennyboy runs out to fetch his letter.*
This is merely a pretence. He runs out to dispatch a ticket-porter
to meet Lickfinger, and take the deed of trust from him.

Of so much land, Pecunia and her friends.
I am not able to wage law with him,[1]
Yet must maintain the thing, as my own right,
Still for your good, and therefore must be bold
To use your credit for moneys.
    P. jun. What thou wilt,
So we be safe, and the trust bear it.
    Pick. Fear not,
'Tis he must pay arrearages in the end.
We'll milk him and Pecunia, draw their cream down,
Before he get the deed into his hands.
My name is Picklock, but he'll find me a padlock.

        Enter PENNYBOY Canter.

    P. Can. How now! conferring with your learned
        counsel
Upon the cheat! Are you of the plot to cozen me?
    P. jun. What plot?
    P. Can. Your counsel knows there, master Pick-
        lock,
Will you restore the trust yet?
    Pick. Sir, take patience
And memory unto you, and bethink you,
What trust? where does't appear? I have your
        deed;
Doth your deed specify any trust? Is it not
A perfect act, and absolute in law,
Seal'd and deliver'd before witnesses,
The day and date emergent?
    P. Can. But what conference,

---

[1] *Wage law.*] "When an action is brought for money or chattles left or lent to the defendant, he may *wage his law;* that is, swear, and certain persons with him, that he owes nothing to the plaintiff, in manner as he hath disclosed." *Law Dict.*

Perhaps, I have shot beyond the author in this grave quotation; the meaning of which may, after all, be—"I am not rich enough to *contend* with him."

What oaths and vows preceded ?
  Pick. I will tell you, sir,
Since I am urged of those ; as I remember,
You told me you had got a grown estate,
By griping means, sinisterly——
  P. Can. How !
  Pick. And were
Even weary of it ; if the parties lived
From whom you had wrested it——
  P. Can. Ha !
  Pick. You could be glad
To part with all, for satisfaction :
But since they had yielded to humanity,
And that just heaven had sent you for a punishment,
You did acknowledge it, this riotous heir,
That would bring all to beggary in the end,
And daily sow'd consumption where he went——
  P. Can. You would cozen both then ? your con-
    federate too ?
  Pick. After a long mature deliberation,
You could not think where better how to place it——
  P. Can. Than on you, rascal ?
  Pick. What you please, in your passion ;
But with your reason, you will come about,
And think a faithful and a frugal friend
To be preferr'd.
  P. Can. Before a son ?
  Pick. A prodigal,
A tub without a bottom, as you term'd him !
For which I might return you a vow or two,
And seal it with an oath of thankfulness,
I not repent it, neither have I cause ; yet——
  P. Can. Forehead of steel, and mouth of brass !
    hath impudence
Polish'd so gross a lie, and dar'st thou vent it ?
Engine, composed of all mixt metals ! hence,
I will not change a syllable with thee more,

Till I may meet thee at a bar in court,
Before thy judges.
    Pick. Thither it must come,
Before I part with it to you, or you, sir.
    P. Can. I will not hear thee.
    P. jun. Sir, your ear to me though—
Not that I see through his perplexed plots,
And hidden ends; nor that my parts depend
Upon the unwinding this so knotted skean,
Do I beseech your patience.   Unto me,
He hath confest the trust.
    Pick. How! I confess it?
    P. jun. Ay, thou false man.
    P. Can. Stand up to him, and confront him.
    Pick. Where, when, to whom?
    P. jun. To me, even now, and here:
Canst thou deny it?
    Pick. Can I eat or drink,
Sleep, wake, or dream, arise, sit, go, or stand,
Do any thing that's natural?
    P. jun. Yes, lie
It seems thou canst, and perjure; that is natural.
    Pick. O me, what times are these of frontless
        carriage!
An egg of the same nest! the father's bird!
It runs in a blood, I see.
    P. jun. I'll stop your mouth.
    Pick. With what?
    P. jun. With truth.
    Pick. With noise; I must have witness:
Where is your witness? you can produce witness?
    P. jun. As if my testimony were not twenty,
Balanced with thine!
    Pick. So say all prodigals,
Sick of self-love; but that's not law, young Scatter-
        good:
I live by law.

P. jun. Why, if thou hast a conscience,
That is a thousand witnesses.
    Pick. No court
Grants out a writ of summons for the conscience,
That I know, nor subpœna, nor attachment.
I must have witness, and of your producing,
Ere this can come to hearing, and it must
Be heard on oath and witness.
    P. jun. Come forth, Tom!

        Re-enter THO. Barber.

Speak what thou heard'st, the truth, and the whole
    truth,
And nothing but the truth.　What said this varlet?
    Pick. A rat behind the hangings?
    Tho. Sir, he said,
It was a trust! an act, the which your father
Had will to alter; but *his tender breast*
Would not permit to see the heir defrauded,
And, like an alien, thrust out of the blood.
The laws forbid that he should give consent
To such a civil slaughter of a son——
    P. jun. And talk'd of a gratuity to be given,
And aid unto the charges of the suit;
Which he was to maintain in his own name,
But for my use, he said.
    P. Can. It is enough.
    Tho. And he *would milk Pecunia, and draw down*
Her cream, before you got the trust again.
    P. Can. Your ears are in my pocket, knave, go
    shake 'em
The little while you have them.
    Pick. You do trust
To your great purse.
    P. Can. I have you in a purse-net,
Good master Picklock, with your worming brain,

And wriggling engine-head of maintenance,[2]
Which I shall see you hole with very shortly!
A fine round head, when those two lugs are off,
To trundle through a pillory! You are sure
You heard him speak this?

    P. jun. Ay, and more.

    Tho. Much more.

    Pick. I'll prove yours maintenance and combina-
        tion,

And sue you all.

    P. Can. Do, do, my gowned vulture,

Crop in reversion! I shall see you quoited
Over the bar, as bargemen do their billets.

    Pick. This 'tis, when men repent of their good
        deeds,

And would have 'em in again—They are almost mad:
But I forgive their *lucida intervalla.*

Enter LICKFINGER.

O, Lickfinger! come hither.

        Comes forward with LICKFINGER; *while* P.
          jun. *discovers the plot, aside, to his father,*
          and that he is in possession of the deed.

Where's my writing?

    Lick. I sent it you, together with your keys.

    Pick. How?

    Lick. By the porter that came for it from you,

And by the token, you had given me the keys,
And bade me bring it.

    Pick. And why did you not?

    Lick. Why did you send a countermand?

    Pick. Who, I?

---

  [2] *And wriggling engine-head of* maintenance.] "*Maintenance* signifies the supporting a cause or person by any kind of countenance
or encouragement, and is generally taken in a bad sense. The writ
that lies against a man for this offence, is also called *maintenance.*"
Law Dict.

Lick. You, or some other you, you put in trust.
Pick. In trust!
Lick. Your trust's another self, you know;
And without trust, and your trust, how should he
Take notice of your keys, or of my charge?
Pick. Know you the man?
Lick. I know he was a porter,
And a seal'd porter; for he bore the badge
On his breast, I am sure.
Pick. I am lost: a plot! I scent it.
Lick. Why, and I sent it by the man you sent,
Whom else I had not trusted.
Pick. Plague on your trust!
I am truss'd up among you——
P. jun. Or you may be.
Pick. In mine own halter; I have made the noose.
[*Exit.*

P. jun. What was it, Lickfinger?
Lick. A writing, sir,
He sent for't by a token; I was bringing it,
But that he sent a porter, and he seem'd
A man of decent carriage.
P. Can. 'Twas good fortune!
To cheat the cheater, was no cheat, but justice.
Put off your rags, and be yourself again:
This act of piety and good affection
Hath partly reconciled me to you.
P. jun. Sir——
P. Can. No vows, no promises; too much protes-
        tation
Makes that suspected oft, we would persuade.
Lick. Hear you the news?
P. jun. The office is down, how should we?
Lick. But of your uncle?
P. jun. No.
Lick. He is run mad, sir.
P. Can. How, Lickfinger?

Lick. Stark staring mad, your brother,
He has almost kill'd his maid——
    P. Can. Now heaven forbid!
    Lick. But that she is cat-lived and squirrel-limb'd,
With throwing bed-staves at her : he has set wide
His outer doors, and now keeps open house
For all the passers by to see his justice.
First, he has apprehended his two dogs,
As being of the plot to cozen him ;
And there he sits like an old worm of the peace,
Wrapp'd up in furs, at a square table, screwing,
Examining, and committing the poor curs
To two old cases of close stools, as prisons ;
The one of which he calls his Lollard's tower,
T'other his Block-house, 'cause his two dogs' names
Are Block and Lollard.
    P. jun. This would be brave matter
Unto the jeerers.
    P. Can. Ay, if so the subject
Were not so wretched.
    Lick. Sure I met them all,
I think, upon that quest.
    P. Can. 'Faith, like enough :
The vicious still are swift to shew their natures.
I'll thither too, but with another aim,
If all succeed well, and my simples take.   [*Exeunt.*

SCENE II. *A Room in* PENNYBOY senior's *House.*

PENNYBOY sen. *discovered sitting at table with papers, &c., before him;* Porter, *and* Block *and* Lollard *(two dogs.)*

Pennyboy senior.

WHERE are the prisoners?
 Por. They are forth-coming, sir,
Or coming forth, at least.
 P. sen. The rogue is drunk,
Since I committed them to his charge.—Come hither,
Near me, yet nearer; breathe upon me. [*He smells
  him.*] Wine!
Wine o' my worship! sack, Canary sack!
Could not your badge have been drunk with fulsom
  ale,
Or beer, the porters' element? but sack!
 Por. I am not drunk; we had, sir, but one pint,
An honest carrier and myself.
 P. sen. Who paid for't?
 Por. Sir, I did give it him.
 P. sen. What, and spend sixpence!
A frock spend sixpence! sixpence!
 Por. Once in a year, sir.
 P. sen. In seven years, varlet! know'st thou what
  thou hast done,
What a consumption thou hast made of a state?
It might please heav'n (a lusty knave and young)
To let thee live some seventy years longer,
Till thou art fourscore and ten, perhaps a hundred.
Say seventy years; how many times seven in seventy?
Why seven times ten, is ten times seven, mark me,
I will demonstrate to thee on my fingers.
Sixpence in seven year, use upon use,

Grows in that first seven year to be a twelve-pence ;
That, in the next, two shillings ; the third, four shil-
        lings ;
The fourth seven year, eight shillings ; the fifth, six-
        teen ;
The sixth, two and thirty; the seventh, three pound
        four ;
The eighth, six pound and eight; the ninth, twelve
        pound sixteen ;
And the tenth seven, five and twenty pound
Twelve shillings. This thou art fall'n from by thy riot,
Should'st thou live seventy years, by spending sixpence
Once in the seven : but in a day to waste it !
There is a sum that number cannot reach !
Out of my house, thou pest of prodigality,
Seed of consumption, hence ! a wicked keeper
Is oft worse than the prisoners. There's thy penny,
Four tokens for thee. Out, away ! [*Exit* Por.] My
        dogs
May yet be innocent and honest : if not,
I have an entrapping question or two more,
To put unto them, a cross intergatory,
And I shall catch them. Lollard ! Peace :
                        [*He calls forth* Lollard.
What whispering was that you had with Mortgage,
When you last lick'd her feet ? the truth now. Ha !
Did you smell she was going ? Put down that. *And
        not,*
Not to return? You are silent : good ! And when
Leap'd you on Statute ? *As she went forth?* Consent!
There was consent, as she was going forth.
'Twould have been fitter at her coming home,
But you knew *that she would not?* To your tower :
You are cunning, are you ? I will meet your craft.
                        [*Commits him again.*
Block, shew your face ; leave your caresses ; tell me,
                        [*Calls forth* Block.

And tell me truly, what affronts do you know
Were done Pecunia, that she left my house?
None, say you so? *not that you know?* or *will know?*
I fear me, I shall find you an obstinate cur.
Why did your fellow Lollard cry this morning?
'Cause Broker kick'd him? Why did Broker kick him?
Because he pist against my lady's gown?
Why, that was no affront, no, no distaste.
You knew of none? you are a dissembling tyke,
To your hole again, your Block-house. [*Commits
    him.*] Lollard, arise.
Where did you lift your leg up last, 'gainst what?
Are you struck dummerer now, and whine for mercy?
Whose kirtle was't you gnaw'd too, mistress Band's?
And Wax's stockings? Who? *Did Block bescumber
Statute's white suit, with the parchment lace there;
And Broker's satin doublet?* All will out.
They had offence, offence enough to quit me.
Appear, Block, foh! 'tis manifest; he shews it,
Should he forswear't, make all the affidavits
Against it, that he could afore the bench,
And twenty juries, he would be convinced.[3]
He bears an air about him doth confess it.

    Enter CYMBAL, FITTON, SHUNFIELD, ALMANAC,
        and MADRIGAL *behind.*

To prison again, close prison. Not you, Lollard;
You may enjoy the liberty of the house:
And yet there is a quirk come in my head,
For which I must commit you too, and close.
Do not repine, it will be better for you——
  Cym. This is enough to make the dogs mad too:
Let's in upon him.   [*They come forward.*
  P. sen. How now, what's the matter?
Come you to force the prisoners? make a rescue?
  Fit. We come to bail your dogs.

    [3] *Convinced,*] i. e. overcome, by the evidence, convicted.

P. sen. They are not bailable,
They stand committed without bail or mainprise,
Your bail cannot be taken.
    Shun. Then the truth is,
We come to vex you.
    Alm. Jeer you.
    Mad. Bait you, rather.
    Cym. A baited usurer will be good flesh.
    Fit. And tender, we are told.
    P. sen. Who is the butcher,
Amongst you, that is come to cut my throat?
    Shun. You would die a calf's death fain; but 'tis
        an ox's
Is meant you.
    Fit. To be fairly knock'd o' the head.
    Shun. With a good jeer or two.
    P. sen. And from your jaw-bone,
Don Assinigo?
    Cym. Shunfield, a jeer! you have it.
    Shun. I do confess, a swashing blow; but, Snarl,
You that might play the third dog, for your teeth,
You have no money now?
    Fit. No, nor no Mortgage.
    Alm. Nor Band.
    Mad. Nor Statute.
    Cym. No, nor blushet Wax.
    P. sen. Nor you no office, as I take it.
    Shun. Cymbal,
A mighty jeer!
    Fit. Pox o' these true jests, I say!
    Mad. He'll turn the better jeerer.
    Alm. Let's upon him,
And if we cannot jeer him down in wit——
    Mad. Let's do't in noise.
    Shun. Content.
    Mad. Charge, man of war.
    Alm. Lay him aboard.

Shun. We'll give him a broadside first.
Fit. Where is your venison now?
Cym. Your red-deer pies?
Shun. With your baked turkeys?
Alm. And your partridges?
Mad. Your pheasants and fat swans!
P. sen. Like you, turn'd geese.
Mad. But such as will not keep your Capitol.
Shun. You were wont to have your breams—
Alm. And trouts sent in.
Cym. Fat carps and salmons.
Fit. Ay, and now and then,
An emblem of yourself, an o'ergrown pike.
P. sen. You are a jack, sir.
Fit. You have made a shift
To swallow twenty such poor jacks ere now.
Alm. If he should come to feed upon poor John—
Mad. Or turn pure Jack-a-lent after all this?
Fit. Tut, he will live like a grasshopper——
Mad. On dew.
Shun. Or like a bear, with licking his own claws.
Cym. Ay, if his dogs were away.
Alm. He'll eat them first,
While they are fat.
Fit. Faith, and when they are gone,
Here's nothing to be seen beyond.
Cym. Except
His kindred spiders, natives of the soil.
Alm. Dust he will have enough here, to breed fleas.
Mad. But by that time he'll have no blood to rear
     them.
Shun. He will be as thin as a lanthorn, we shall
     see through him.
Alm. And his gut colon tell his *intestina.*
P. sen. Rogues! rascals!
                    [*The dogs bark.* [Bow, wow!]
Fit. He calls his dogs to his aid.

Alm. O, they but rise at mention of his tripes.
Cym. Let them alone, they do it not for him.
Mad. They bark *se defendendo*.
Shun. Or for custom,
As commonly curs do, one for another.

Enter LICKFINGER.

Lick. Arm, arm you, gentlemen jeerers! the old
        Canter
Is coming in upon you with his forces,
The gentleman that was the Canter.
Shun. Hence!
Fit. Away!
Cym. What is he?
Alm. Stay not to ask questions.
Fit. He is a flame.
Shun. A furnace.
Alm. A consumption,
Kills where he goes.
        [CYM. FIT. MAD. ALM. *and* SHUN. *run off.*
Lick. See! the whole covey is scatter'd;
'Ware, 'ware the hawks! I love to see them fly.

Enter PENNYBOY Canter, PENNYBOY jun. PECUNIA,
    STATUTE, BAND, WAX, *and* MORTGAGE.

P. Can. You see by this amazement and distraction,
What your companions were, a poor, affrighted,
And guilty race of men, that dare to stand
No breath of truth; but conscious to themselves
Of their no-wit, or honesty, ran routed
At every pannic terror themselves bred.
Where else, as confident as sounding brass,
Their tinkling captain, Cymbal, and the rest,
Dare put on any visor, to deride
The wretched, or with buffoon license jest
At whatsoe'er is serious, if not sacred.

5   U

P. sen. Who's this ? my brother ! and restored to
    life !

P. Can. Yes, and sent hither to restore your wits ;
If your short madness be not more than anger
Conceived for your loss ! which I return you.
See here, your mortgage, Statute, Band, and Wax,
Without your Broker, come to abide with you,
And vindicate the prodigal from stealing
Away the lady. Nay, Pecunia herself
Is come to free him fairly, and discharge
All ties, but those of love unto her person,
To use her like a friend, not like a slave,
Or like an idol. Superstition
Doth violate the deity it worships,
No less than scorn doth ; and believe it, brother,
The use of things is all, and not the store :
Surfeit and fulness have kill'd more than famine.
The sparrow with his little plumage, flies,
While the proud peacock, overcharg'd with pens,
Is fain to sweep the ground with his grown train,
And load of feathers.

P. sen. Wise and honour'd brother !
None but a brother, and sent from the dead,
As you are to me, could have alter'd me :
I thank my destiny, that is so gracious.
Are there no pains, no penalties decreed
From whence you come, to us that smother money
In chests, and strangle her in bags ?

P. Can. O, mighty,
Intolerable fines, and mulcts imposed,
Of which I come to warn you : forfeitures
Of whole estates, if they be known and taken.

P. sen. I thank you, brother, for the light you have
    given me ;
I will prevent them all. First, free my dogs,
Lest what I have done to them, and against law,
Be a præmunire ; for by magna charta

They could not be committed as close prisoners,
My learned counsel tells me here, my cook :
And yet he shew'd me the way first.

    Lick. Who did ? I !
I trench the liberty of the subjects !

    P. Can. Peace,
Picklock, your guest, that Stentor, hath infected you,
Whom I have safe enough in a wooden collar.

    P. sen. Next, I restore these servants to their lady,
With freedom, heart of cheer, and countenance ;
It is their year and day of jubilee.

    Omnes. We thank you, sir.

    P. sen. And lastly, to my nephew
I give my house, goods, lands, all but my vices,
And those I go to cleanse ; kissing this lady,
Whom I do give him too, and join their hands.

    P. Can. If the spectators will join theirs, we
        thank 'em.

    P. jun. And wish they may, as I, enjoy Pecunia.

    Pec. And so Pecunia herself doth wish,
That she may still be aid unto their uses,
Not slave unto their pleasures, or a tyrant
Over their fair desires ; but teach them all
The golden mean ; the prodigal how to live ;
The sordid and the covetous how to die :
That, with sound mind ; this, safe frugality. [*Exeunt.*

The Epilogue.

Thus have you seen the maker's double scope,
To profit and delight ; wherein our hope
Is, though the clout we do not always hit,[4]

    [4] *Though the* clout *we do not always hit.*] The metaphor is taken
from archery : the *clout* is the white mark in the butts, which the
archers aimed at.   And so it is used by Shakspeare.   WHAL.

    Clout is merely the French *clou*, the wooden pin by which the
target is fastened to the butt.   As the head of this pin was com-

It will not be imputed to his wit :—
A tree so tried, and bent, as 'twill not start :
Nor doth he often crack a string of art ;
Though there may other accidents as strange
Happen, the weather of your looks may change,
Or some high wind of misconceit arise,
To cause an alteration in our skies :
If so, we are sorry, that have so misspent
Our time and tackle ; yet he's confident,
And vows, the next fair day he'll have us shoot
The same match o'er for him, if you'll come to't.

monly painted *white*, to hit the *white* and hit the *clout*, were of
course synonymous : both phrases expressed perfection in art, or
success of any kind.   In pursuing his metaphor, Jonson mentions
the accidents by which the highest skill in archery was occasionally
defeated ; humidity, which affected the elasticity of the string, and
high winds which diverted the course of the shaft.

There are few of Jonson's dramatic works which exhibit stronger
marks of his peculiar talents than this play.   The language is for-
cible, and in some places highly poetical ; the satire is powerful
and well directed, and the moral pointed and just.   Its plot indeed,
labours under the same difficulties and defects as that of the *Plutus*,
which the poet had in view, namely, an occasional confusion of the
allegorical and real character.   Queen Pecunia, like the Deity of
Aristophanes, is *nearly strangled in leather, smothered in a chest*, &c.,
and subjected to other accidents, which cannot be properly predi-
cated of an existing personage.   Jonson, however, offends less frequently in this matter than his great prototype, whom he also sur-
passes in the moral purpose of his satire.   The use and abuse of
riches are delineated with great force and discrimination, and the
prodigal and the miser corrected in a strain of serious monition
that would not misbecome the sacredness of the closet.   Aristophanes had no such object in view.   If the history of his own time
may be trusted, every statesman had his orator, and every orator
had his price ; thus politics were rendered subservient to money,
and the destiny of Athens waited on a bribe.   To expose this
general venality, he wrote his *Plutus*.   In wit of the brightest kind,
in satire of the most poignant and overwhelming quality, it stands
pre-eminent, not only over the *Staple of News*, but over every other
drama, ancient or modern : here however its praise must end ; it
teaches nothing, but that gold is omnipotent, (a pernicious lesson,)

and it concludes with involving the *dramatis personæ* in one mass of corruption: the whole, without distinction, conspiring to pull down the gods, and raise Plutus to the vacant seat.

In the introduction of the dogs during the transient fit of insanity brought upon the miser by the sudden defection of his treasure, Jonson had again Aristophanes in view; but he has not imitated him with much dexterity. The short episode of Block and Lollard contributes little to the advancement of the story, since the derangement of Pennyboy sen. might easily have been communicated through the ordinary characters of the play; while the trial of the dog *Labes*, in the *Wasps*, which must have been irresistibly comic, is highly illustrative of the litigious disposition of Philocleo, and opens, at the same time, a masked battery, against the peculations of the noted Laches.

It would not be doing justice to Jonson to pass over this division of his plot without noticing the judgment manifested in the trifling parts of Pecunia's attendants, who invariably maintain a correct and close adherence to the relative characters which they support under their principal.

The *Staple* is well conceived and happily executed. Credulity, which was then at its height, was irritated rather than fed by impositions of every kind; and the country kept in a feverish state of deceitful expectation by stories of wonderful events, *gross and palpable*, to use the words of Shakspeare, *as the father of lies, who begat them*. On the whole, the *Staple of News* is one of those compositions which the admirer of Jonson may contemplate with "delight," and from the perusal of which the impartial reader can scarcely rise without "profit."

THE NEW INN;

OR,

THE LIGHT HEART.

THE NEW INN.] This Comedy was brought on the stage on the 19th of January, 1629, and in the technical language of the Green-room, "completely damn'd," not being heard to the conclusion. Whatever indignation Jonson might have felt at this treatment, he appears to have made no public manifestation of it at the time: but Ben was now the sick lion, and his enemies had too little respect for his enfeebled condition to forego so good an opportunity of insulting him with impunity. Forbearance was at no time our poet's peculiar virtue, and the jealousy of reputation so natural to age and infirmity, co-operated with the taunts of his ungenerous critics, to force him upon the publication of the *New Inn*, two years after its condemnation. It was printed in 8vo. with this angry title-page:

The New Inn: or, the Light Heart, a Comedy. As it was never Acted, but most negligently Played by some, the KING'S SERVANTS; and more squeamishly beheld and censur'd by others, the KING'S SUBJECTS, 1629. *Now at last set at Liberty to the Readers, his MAJESTY'S Servants and Subjects, to be judg'd of.* 1631.

―― *Me lectori credere mallem,*
Quàm spectatoris fastidia ferre superbi. HOR.

This unfortunate Play not only brought a cloud over the dramatic fame of Jonson, at its first appearance, but furnished a pretence for calumniating his memory even within our own times. About the middle of the last century, Macklin the player brought forward an indifferent piece of Ford's, called the *Lover's Melancholy*, for his daughter's benefit. To excite the curiosity of the town to this performance, he fabricated a most ignorant and impudent tissue of malicious charges against Jonson, whom he chose to represent as the declared enemy of Ford, as well as of Shakspeare. This atrocious libel, which seems to have been composed *à pure perte*, lay, with a thousand other forgotten falsehoods, among a pile of old newspapers, till it was discovered by Steevens, who with triumphant malice dragged it again to light, and reprinted it at the end of Jonson's eulogium on Shakspeare, as the true key to that celebrated piece! Not content with the obloquy with which Macklin had so liberally furnished him, he had the incredible baseness to subjoin the following stanza from Shirley, which he declared to be also addressed to Jonson, upon the appearance of Ford's play :—

> " Look here *thou* that hast *malice* to the stage,
>   And *impudence* enough for the whole age ;
>   *Voluminously* [1] *ignorant !* be vext,
>   To read this *tragedy*, and *thy own* [2] be next "—

though he well knew that the lines were directly pointed at Prynne, and that Shirley regarded the talents and learning of Jonson with a degree of respect bordering on idolatry. This vile fabrication, in which all the creative powers of malignity are set to work to destroy the character of an unoffending man, who had been more than a century in his grave, in the hope of effecting the sale of a few tickets, Mr. Malone styles "*an innocent forgery,*" "*a sportive and ingenious fabrication,*" "*a mere jeu d'esprit, for a harmless purpose,*" [3] &c. He however sets about its confutation, and with the assistance of Whalley, [4] whom he condescends not once to mention, easily effects his object. In fact, a simple reference to dates, of which Macklin happened to be wholly ignorant, was amply sufficient to destroy the whole fabric. [5]

A rejoinder was made by Steevens, in which there is not one syllable to the purpose, though Mr. Weber, with proper gravity,

---

[1] *Voluminously.*] Prynne was known to the writers of his time by the name of *Voluminous* Prynne, under which title he is mentioned by Wood and others.

[2] *Thy own tragedy,*] i. e. according to Steevens and his followers, the " *Comedy* of the New Inn !"

[3] This gentleman thus indulgent to the unprincipled calumniator of Jonson, is the same Mr. Malone, be it observed, who taxes Jonson every instant with the blackest ingratitude, with the most rooted and rancorous malice towards Shakspeare because he uses the word "tempestuous," or "chorus," or "target," or some other of equal rarity, which bears a fancied resemblance to the name of a play, or to a stage direction in the works of the latter.

[4] In Whalley's corrected copy, which Malone as well as Steevens had seen, as I find by their letters, most of Macklin's ridiculous blunders in his dates, of which Malone afterwards made such good use, are distinctly pointed out.

[5] It is quite amusing to follow the enemies of Jonson through this most contemptible forgery. The prose part of it they in some measure give up ; but there is a little poem with which they are all enraptured, and which is pronounced to be as much beyond the powers of Macklin, as the composition of a Greek Chorus, &c. This "uncommonly elegant," this " exquisite," this "first and best

observes, that it renders the affair very doubtful. In fact, Steevens, as is noticed above, knew the story to be a falsehood from the beginning; and Mr. Malone, of whom I enquired the reason of his coadjutor's disgraceful pertinacity, wrote to me in reply that Steevens merely held out "because the discovery of the *forgery* had been made by another." That Steevens believed a word of it, he never thought for a moment.

After the complete detection of this clumsy fabrication, by Mr. Malone, it might reasonably be hoped that the public would have heard no more of it: but who can sound the depths of folly ! Mr. Weber, the editor of Ford, has thought proper to repeat it, and with an hardihood of assertion which his profound ignorance cannot excuse, to affirm, in addition, that the enmity of Jonson to Ford, (on which Macklin's forgery is built,) is "corroborated by indisputable documents !" One of them (the only one, indeed, with which he condescends to favour his readers) is the quotation produced from Shirley by Steevens, (for the mischievous purpose of misleading some heedless gull,) which Mr. Weber pronounces, on his own knowledge, "to be *evidently* pointed at our author's insulting ode."

To attempt to convince a person, who has not understanding enough for reason to operate upon, is, as *learned authors utter, to wash a tile;* to others it may be just sufficient to say, that the "ode" was published near two years *after* the verses to which it is here affirmed to have given birth !—This is going beyond Mr. Steevens, and may serve to shew how dangerous it is for stupidity to meddle with cunning, or to venture on gratuitous falsehoods to recover the credit of an exploded slander.

---

of all fictions," is a miserable piece of doggrel, a wretched cento, which would not at this time be admitted into the corner of a newspaper. Will the reader have a specimen of this "combined effort of taste and learning," to which the talents of the author of the *Man of the World* were "so unequal ?" Let him take, then, the first stanza :—

> "Says Ben to Tom, the *Lover's* stole,
> 'Tis Shakspeare's every word ;
> Indeed, says Tom, upon the whole
> 'Tis much too good for Ford !"

Euge Poeta! The splendour of the composition so effectually dazzled the critics, that the compliment paid to Shakspeare by "the envious Ben" luckily escaped their notice. It would have made Mr. Malone miserable.

TO THE READER.

*I*F thou be such, I make thee my patron, and dedicate the piece to thee: if not so much, would I had been at the charge of thy better literature. Howsoever, if thou canst but spell, and join my sense, there is more hope of thee, than of a hundred fastidious impertinents, who were there present the first day, yet never made piece of their prospect the right way. What did they come for, then? thou wilt ask me. I will as punctually answer: To see, and to be seen: to make a general muster of themselves in their clothes of credit; and possess the stage against the play: to dislike all, but mark nothing. And by their confidence of rising between the acts, in oblique lines, make affidavit to the whole house, of their not understanding one scene. Armed with this prejudice, as the stage-furniture, or arras-clothes, they were there, as spectators, away: for the faces in the hangings, and they, beheld alike. So I wish they may do ever; and do trust myself and my book, rather to thy rustic candour, than all the pomp of their pride, and solemn ignorance to boot. Fare thee well, and fall to. Read.

BEN JONSON.

But first,

THE ARGUMENT.

*T*HE *lord Frampul, a noble gentleman, well educated, and bred a scholar in Oxford, was married young, to a virtuous gentlewoman, Sylly's daughter of the South, whose worth, though he truly enjoyed, he never could rightly value; but, as many green husbands, (given over to their extravagant delights, and some peccant humours of their own,) occasioned in his over loving wife so deep a melancholy, by his leaving her in the time of her lying-in of her second daughter, she having brought him only two daughters, Frances and Lætitia: and (out of her hurt fancy) interpreting that to be a cause of her husband's coldness in affection, her not being blest with a son, took a resolution with herself, after her month's time, and thanksgiving rightly in the church, to quit her home, with a vow never to return, till by reducing her lord, she could bring a wished happiness to the family.*

He in the mean time returning, and hearing of this departure of his lady, began, though over-late, to resent the injury he had done her: and out of his cock-brain'd resolution, entered into as solemn a quest of her. Since when, neither of them had been heard of. But the eldest daughter, Frances, by the title of lady Frampul, enjoyed the estate, her sister being lost young, and is the sole relict of the family. Here begins our Comedy.

ACT I.

This lady, being a brave, bountiful lady, and enjoying this free and plentiful estate, hath an ambitious disposition to be esteemed the mistress of many servants, but loves none. And hearing of a famous New-inn, that is kept by a merry host, call'd Goodstock, in Barnet, invites some lords and gentlemen to wait on her thither, as well to see the fashions of the place, as to make themselves merry, with the accidents on the by. It happens there is a melancholy gentleman, one master Lovel, hath been lodged there some days before in the inn, who (unwilling to be seen) is surprised by the lady, and invited by Prudence, the lady's chamber-maid, who is elected governess of the sports in the inn for that day, and install'd their sovereign. Lovel is persuaded by the host, and yields to the lady's invitation, which concludes the first act. Having revealed his quality before to the host.

Act II.

In this, Prudence and her lady express their anger conceiv'd at the tailor, who had promised to make Prudence a new suit, and bring it home, as on the eve, against this day. But he failing of his word, the lady had commanded a standard of her own best apparel to be brought down; and Prudence is so fitted. The lady being put in mind, that she is there alone without other company of women, borrows, by the advice of Prue, the host's son of the house, whom they dress, with the host's consent, like a lady, and send out the coachman with the empty coach, as for a kinswoman of her ladyship's, mistress Lætitia Sylly, to bear her company: who attended with his nurse, an old chare-woman in the inn, drest odly by the host's counsel, is believed to be a lady of quality, and so receiv'd, entertain'd, and love made to her by the young lord Beaufort, &c. In the mean time the Fly of the inn is discover'd to colonel Glorious, with the militia of the house, below the stairs, in the drawer, tapster, chamberlain, and hostler, inferior officers; with the coachman Trundle, Ferret, &c. And the preparation is made to the lady's design upon Lovel, his upon her, and the sovereign's upon both.

Act III.

Here begins the Epitasis, or business of the play.

Lovel, by the dexterity and wit of the sovereign of the sports, Prudence, having two hours assign'd him of free colloquy, and love-making to his mistress, one after dinner, the other after supper, the court being set, is demanded by the lady Frampul, what love is: as doubting if there were any such power, or no. To whom he, first by definition, and after by argument, answers; proving and describing the effects of love so vively, as she who had derided the name of love before, hearing his discourse, is now so taken both with the man and his matter, as she confesseth herself enamour'd of him, and, but for the ambition she hath to enjoy the other hour, had presently declared herself: which gives both him and the spectators occasion to think she yet dissembles, notwithstanding the payment of her kiss, which he celebrates. And the court dissolves, upon news brought of a new lady, a newer coach, and a new coachman call'd Barnaby.

Act IV.

The house being put into a noise, with the rumour of this new lady, and there being drinking below in the court, the colonel, sir Glorious, with Bat Burst, a broken citizen, and Hodge Huffle, his champion; she falls into their hands, and being attended but with one footman, is uncivilly entreated by them, and a quarrel commenced, but is rescued by the valour of Lovel; which beheld by the lady Frampul, from the window, she is invited up for safety, where coming, and conducted by the host, her gown is first discovered to be the same with the whole suit, which was bespoken for Prue, and she herself, upon examination, found to be Pinnacia Stuff, the tailor's wife, who was wont to be preoccupied in all his customers' best clothes, by the footman her husband. They are both condemned and censured, she stript like a doxey, and sent home a-foot. In the interim, the second hour goes on, and the question, at suit of the lady Frampul, is changed from love to valour; which ended, he receives his second kiss, and, by the rigour of the sovereign, falls into a fit of melancholy, worse, or more desperate than the first.

ACT V.

Is the catastrophe, or knitting up of all, where Fly brings word to the host of the lord Beaufort's being married privately in the New Stable, to the supposed lady, his son; which the host receives as an omen of mirth; but complains that Lovel is gone to bed melancholic, when Prudence appears drest in the new suit, applauded by her lady. and employed to retrieve Lovel. The host encounters them, with this relation of Lord Beaufort's marriage, which is seconded by the lord Latimer, and all the servants of the house. In this while, lord Beaufort comes in, and professes it, calls for his bed and bride-bowl to be made ready; the host forbids both, shews whom he hath married, and discovers him to be his son, a boy. The lord bridegroom confounded, the nurse enters like a frantic bedlamite, cries out on Fly, says she is undone in her daughter, who is confessed to be the lord Frampul's child, sister to the other lady, the host to be their father, she his wife. He finding his children, bestows them one on Lovel, the other on the lord Beaufort, the inn upon Fly, who had been a gypsy with him; offers a portion with Prudence, for her wit, which is refused; and she taken by the lord Latimer, to wife; for the crown of her virtue and goodness. And all are contented.

DRAMATIS PERSONÆ.

With some short Characterism of the chief Actors.

GOODSTOCK,

the host, (play'd well,) alias the lord FRAMPUL. *He pretends to be a gentleman and a scholar, neglected by the times, turns host, and keeps an inn, the sign of the Light-Heart in Barnet: is supposed to have one only son, but is found to have none, but two daughters, Frances and Lætitia, who was lost young, &c.*

LOVEL,

a complete gentleman, a soldier and a scholar, is a melancholy guest in the Inn: first quarrell'd, after much honoured and beloved by the host. He is known to have been page to the old lord Beaufort, follow'd him in the French wars, after a companion of his studies, and left guardian to his son. He is assisted in his love to the lady Frampul, by the host and the chambermaid Prudence. He was one that acted well too.

FERRET,

who is called STOTE *and* VERMIN, *is Lovel's servant, a fellow of a quick, nimble wit, knows the manners and affections of people, and can make profitable and timely discoveries of them.*

FRANK,

supposed a boy, and the host's son, borrowed to be drest for a lady, and set up as a stale by Prudence, to catch Beaufort or Latimer, proves to be Lætitia, sister to Frances, and lord Frampul's younger daughter, stolen by a beggar-woman, shorn, put into boy's apparel, sold to the host, and brought up by him as his son.

NURSE,

a poor chare-woman in the Inn, with one eye, that tends the boy, is thought the Irish beggar that sold him, but is truly the lady Frampul, who left her home melancholic, and jealous that her lord loved her not, because she brought him none but daughters ; and lives unknown to her husband, as he to her.

FRANCES,

*supposed the lady Frampul, being reputed his sole daughter and heir,
the barony descending upon her, is a lady of great fortune, and beauty,
but phantastical: thinks nothing a felicity, but to have a multitude of
servants, and be call'd mistress by them, comes to the Inn to be merry,
with a chambermaid only, and her servants her guests, &c.*

PRUDENCE,

*the chambermaid, is elected sovereign of the sports in the Inn, governs
all, commands, and so orders, as the lord Latimer is exceedingly taken
with her, and takes her to his wife, in conclusion.*

Lord LATIMER *and* Lord BEAUFORT,

*are a pair of young lords, servants and guests to the lady Frampul;
but as Latimer falls enamour'd of Prudence, so doth Beaufort on the
boy, the host's son, set up for Lætitia, the younger sister, which she
proves to be indeed.*

Sir GLORIOUS TIPTO,

*a knight, and colonel, hath the luck to think well of himself, without a
rival, talks gloriously of any thing, but very seldom is in the right.
He is the lady's guest, and her servant too; but this day utterly neglects
his service, or that him. For he is so enamour'd on the Fly of the Inn,
and the militia below stairs, with Hodge-Huffle and Bat Burst, guests
that come in, and Trundle, Barnaby, &c., as no other society relisheth
with him.*

FLY,

*is the parasite of the Inn, visitor general of the house, one that had
been a strolling gypsy, but now is reclaim'd, to be inflamer of the
reckonings.*

PIERCE,

*the drawer, knighted by the colonel, styled sir Pierce, and young Anon,
one of the chief of the infantry.*

JORDAN,

*the chamberlain, another of the militia, and an officer, commands the
tertia of the beds.*

JUG, *the tapster, a thoroughfare of news.*
PECK, *the hostler.*
BAT BURST, *a broken citizen, an in-and-in man.*[6]

---

[6] *An* in-and-in *man.*]   *In-and-in* was a game played by two or
three persons, with four dice: it was the usual diversion at ordinaries, and places of the like resort. WHAL.

HODGE HUFFLE, *a cheater, his champion.*
NICK STUFF, *the ladies' tailor.*
PINNACIA STUFF, *his wife.*
TRUNDLE, *a coachman.*
BARNABY, *a hired coachman.*
STAGGERS, *the smith,* } *only talked on.*
TREE, *the sadler,*

The SCENE, Barnet.

THE PROLOGUE.

YOU are welcome, welcome all to the New Inn :
Though the old house, we hope our cheer
will win
Your acceptation : we have the same cook
Still, and the fat, who says, you shall not look
Long for your bill of fare, but every dish
Be serv'd in i' the time, and to your wish :
If any thing be set to a wrong taste,
'Tis not the meat there, but the mouth's displaced,
Remove but that sick palate, all is well.
For this the secure dresser bade me tell,
Nothing more hurts just meetings, than a crowd ;
Or, when the expectation's grown too loud :
That the nice stomach would have this or that,
And being ask'd, or urged, it knows not what :
When sharp or sweet, have been too much a feast,
And both outlived the palate of the guest.
Beware to bring such appetites to the stage,
They do confess a weak, sick, queasy age ;
And a shrewd grudging too of ignorance,
When clothes and faces 'bove the men advance :
Hear for your health, then, but at any hand,
Before you judge, vouchsafe to understand,
Concoct, digest : if then, it do not hit,
Some are in a consumption of wit,
Deep, he dares say, he will not think, that all—
For hectics are not epidemical.

THE NEW INN.

ACT I.

SCENE I. *A Room in the Inn.*

Enter HOST, *followed by* FERRET.

Host.

I AM not pleased, indeed, you are in the right;
Nor is my house pleased, if my sign could speak,
The sign of the LIGHT HEART. There you may read it;
So may your master too, if he look on it.
A heart weigh'd with a feather, and outweigh'd too:
A brain-child of my own, and I am proud on't!
And if his worship think, here, to be melancholy,
In spite of me or my wit, he is deceived;
I will maintain the rebus against all humours,
And all complexions in the body of man,
That is my word, or in the isle of Britain!
    Fer. You have reason, good mine host.
    Host. Sir, I have rhyme too.
Whether it be by chance or art,
A heavy purse makes a light heart.

There 'tis exprest : first, by a purse of gold,
A heavy purse, and then two turtles, makes,[7]
A heart with a light stuck in it, a Light Heart
Old abbot Islip could not invent better,
Or prior Bolton with his bolt and ton.[8]
I am an inn-keeper, and know my grounds,
And study them ; brain o' man ! I study them.
I must have jovial guests to drive my ploughs,
And whistling boys to bring my harvest home,
Or I shall hear no flails thwack.   Here, your master
And you have been this fortnight, drawing fleas
Out of my mats, and pounding them in cages
Cut out of cards, and those roped round with pack
        thread
Drawn thorough birdlime, a fine subtility !
Or poring through a multiplying-glass,
Upon a captived crab-louse, or a cheese-mite
To be dissected, as the sports of nature,
With a neat Spanish needle ! speculations
That do become the age, I do confess !
As measuring an ant's eggs with the silk-worm's,

[7] *Two turtles*, makes.] The old term for *mates.* " The turtle-
doves have such love one to another, being *makes*, that when one
of them is dead, the other will never after have any other *make*."
Book of notable Things.   1627.

[8] *Old abbot Islip could not invent better,*
    Or prior Bolton with his bolt *and* ton.]   The reader may find
in *Camden's Remains*, the rebus made use of by these ecclesiastics
to express their names on the several buildings erected by them,
or belonging to them.   The *bolt* and *ton*, is a ton pierced through
with an *arrow*, for which *bolt* was anciently used.   WHAL.

   One of " old abbot Islip's " conundrums was *an eye* with a *slip*
of a tree !   There is not much to be said for the ingenuity of either ;
but such was the wisdom of the times.   Both these men, however,
had other and better claims to the notice of posterity than those
puerile devices, and Islip in particular (who was abbot of Westminster) is entitled to our commendation for the stand which he
made against Wolsey in the height of his power, and the generous
firmness with which he protected the proscribed Skelton, from his
resentment.

By a phantastic instrument of thread,
Shall give you their just difference to a hair!
Or else recovering of dead flies with crumbs,
Another quaint conclusion in the physics,
Which I have seen you busy at, through the key
      hole——
But never had the fate to see a fly

Enter LOVEL.

Alive in your cups, or once heard, *Drink, mine host!*
Or such a cheerful chirping charm come from you.
    Lov. What's that, what's that?
    Fer. A buzzing of mine host
About a fly; a murmur that he has.
    Host. Sir, I am telling your Stote here, monsieur
      Ferret,
For that I hear's his name, and dare tell you, sir,
If you have a mind to be melancholy, and musty,
There's Footman's inn at the town's end, the stocks,
Or Carrier's place, at sign of the Broken Wain,
Mansions of state! take up your harbour there,
There are both flies and fleas, and all variety
Of vermin, for inspection or dissection.
    Lov. We have set our rest up here, sir, in your
      Heart.
    Host. Sir, set your heart at rest, you shall not do it,
Unless you can be jovial.   Brain of man!
Be jovial first, and drink, and dance, and drink.
Your lodging here, and with your daily dumps,
Is a mere libel 'gain my house and me;
And, then, your scandalous commons——
    Lov. How, mine host!
    Host. Sir, they do scandal me upon the road here.
A poor quotidian rack of mutton, roasted
Dry to be grated! and that driven down
With beer and butter-milk, mingled together,
Or clarified whey instead of claret!

It is against my freehold, my inheritance,
My Magna Charta, *cor lætificat,*
To drink such balderdash, or bonny-clabber!⁹
Give me good wine, or catholic, or christian,
Wine is the word that glads the heart of man :
And mine's the house of wine : Sack, says my bush,
Be merry, and *drink sherry ;* that's my posie !
For I shall never joy in my light heart,
So long as I conceive a sullen guest,
Or any thing that's earthy.
   Lov. Humorous host !
   Host. I care not if I be.
   Lov. But airy also !
Not to defraud you of your rights, or trench
Upon your privileges, or great charter,
For those are every hostler's language now,
Say, you were born beneath those smiling stars,
Have made you lord, and owner of the Heart,
Of the Light Heart in Barnet ; suffer us,
Who are more saturnine, to enjoy the shade

---

⁹ ——— *bonny-clabber !*] "We scorn," says Swift—

> "We scorn, for want of talk, to jabber
> Of parties, o'er our bonny-clabber."

The word also occurs in Ford, (as, indeed, it does in a hundred other writers,)

> ——— "The feasts, the manly stomachs,
> The healths in usquebaugh, and *bonny-clabber.*"

Upon which Mr. Weber remarks—" I have *not been able to discover* what particular kind of liquor was thus denominated, never having met with the *phrase* before." Vol. ii. 53. *Phrase call you it !* He had not far to go for it, as the reader sees ; but as it was not pointed out to him in the index to *Shakspeare,* or Reed's *Old Plays,* the *discovery* of the word in any other place never came within his scope of possibility. Let it not however be forgotten, that this wretched reviler of Jonson, who has devoted several pages to a stale repetition of abuse on the *New Inn,* could not discover a particular term in it, which must have stared him in the face if he had ever turned the first leaf of it !

  Bonny-clabber, to which it is time to return, is *sour buttermilk.*

Of your round roof yet.

Host. Sir, I keep no shades
Nor shelters, I, for either owls or rere-mice.

Enter FRANK.

Fer. He'll make you a bird of night, sir.

Host. Bless you child !—   *[Aside to* FRANK.
You'll make your selves such.

Lov. That your son, mine host ?

Host. He's all the sons I have, sir.

Lov. Pretty boy !
Goes he to school ?

Fer. O lord, sir, he prates Latin,
An it were a parrot, or a play-boy.

Lov. Thou
Commend'st him fitly !

Fer. To the pitch he flies, sir.
He'll tell you what is Latin for a looking-glass,
A beard-brush, rubber, or quick-warming pan.

Lov. What's that ?

Fer. A wench, in the inn-phrase, is all these ;

> *A looking glass in her eye,*
> *A beard-brush with her lips,*
> *A rubber with her hand,*
> *And a warming pan with her hips.*

Host. This, in your scurril dialect : but my inn
Knows no such language.

Fer. That's because, mine host,
You do profess the teaching him your self.

Host. Sir, I do teach him somewhat : by degrees,
And with a funnel, I make shift to fill
The narrow vessel ; he is but yet a bottle.

Lov. O let him lose no time though.

Host. Sir, he does not.

Lov. And less his manners.

Host. I provide for those, too.—
Come hither, Frank, speak to the gentleman

In Latin; he is melancholy: say,
I long to see him merry, and so would treat him.
    Fra. *Subtristis visu' es esse aliquantulùm patri, qui
te lautè excipere, etiam ac tractare gestit.*
    Lov. *Pulchrè.*
    Host. Tell him, I fear it bodes us some ill luck,
His too reservedness.
    Fra. *Veretur pater, ne quid nobis mali ominis
apportet iste nimis præclusus vultus.*
    Lov. *Bellè.* A fine child!
You will not part with him, mine host?
    Host. Who told you
I would not?
    Lov. I but ask you.
    Host. And I answer
To whom? for what?
    Lov. To me, to be my page.
    Host. I know no mischief yet the child hath done,
To deserve such a destiny.
    Lov. Why?
    Host. Go down, boy,
And get your breakfast. [*Exeunt* FRANK *and*
        FERRET.]—Trust me, I had rather
Take a fair halter, wash my hands, and hang him
My self, make a clean riddance of him, than——
    Lov. What?
    Host. Than damn him to that desperate course of
        life.
    Lov. Call you that desperate, which by a line
Of institution, from our ancestors,
Hath been derived down to us, and received
In a succession, for the noblest way
Of breeding up our youth,[1] in letters, arms,

---

    [1] —— *the noblest way
    Of breeding up our youth, &c.*] It is unnecessary to repeat
what is advanced upon this subject in the Introduction to Massinger, (p. xxxviii.) but the following passage, which has a direct bear-

Fair mien, discourses, civil exercise,
And all the blazon of a gentleman?
Where can he learn to vault, to ride, to fence,
To move his body gracefuller, to speak
His language purer, or to tune his mind,
Or manners, more to the harmony of nature,
Than in these nurseries of nobility?

   Host. Ay, that was when the nursery's self was
       noble,
And only virtue made it, not the market,
That titles were not vented at the drum,
Or common out-cry; goodness gave the greatness,
And greatness worship: every house became
An academy of honour, and those parts——
We see departed, in the practice now
Quite from the institution.

   Lov. Why do you say so,
Or think so enviously? do they not still
Learn there the Centaur's skill, the art of Thrace,
To ride? or Pollux' mystery, to fence?
The Pyrrhic gestures, both to dance and spring
In armour, to be active for the wars?
To study figures, numbers, and proportions,
May yield them great in counsels, and the arts
Grave Nestor and the wise Ulysses practised,
To make their English sweet upon their tongue,
As reverend Chaucer says?[2]

ing upon it, may not improperly be added here. "The next thing
in a family is the entertainment of servants, which this honourable
person knew best to chuse, because himselfe had been a servant.
Though he was born of a most noble family, yet being a younger
brother, as the usual custome of our countrie is, he was compelled
by necessitie to serve in a noble familie, but after was preferred to
the service of the late queene of happie memorie." *Sermon at the
Funerall of Henrie (Grey, 7th) Earl of Kent,* 1614.

   [2] *As reverend Chaucer says?*] In his character of the *Frere.*

    " Somwhat he lisped for his wantonnesse,
      To make his English swete upon his tonge." v. 266.

Host. Sir, you mistake ;
To play sir Pandarus, my copy hath it,
And carry messages to madam Cressid,
Instead of backing the brave steed, o' mornings,
To mount the chambermaid ; and for a leap
Of the vaulting horse, to ply the vaulting-house :
For exercise of arms, a bale of dice,[3]
Or two or three packs of cards to shew the cheat,
And nimbleness of hand ; mistake a cloak
From my lord's back, and pawn it ; ease his pockets
Of a superfluous watch, or geld a jewel
Of an odd stone or so ; twinge three or four buttons
From off my lady's gown : these are the arts,
Or seven liberal deadly sciences
Of pagery, or rather paganism,
As the tides run ! to which, if he apply him,
He may, perhaps, take a degree at Tyburn,
A year the earlier ; come, to read a lecture
Upon Aquinas at St. Thomas à Waterings,[4]
And so go forth a laureat in hemp circle !
   Lov. You are tart, mine host, and talk above your
      seasoning,

---

[3] Bale of dice,] i. e. a pair of dice ; the expression is common to the writers of Jonson's age, as well as the preceding. Thus Skelton :

> "What lo man, se here of *dyce a bale.*"   *Bouge of Court.*
> WHAL.

Again—
    "*Item*, to my son, Mat Flowerdale, I bequeath two *bale* of false dice." *The London Prodigal.*
    [4] ———— *come to read a lecture*
    Upon Aquinas at St. Thomas à Waterings.] Anciently the place where criminals were executed, in the county of Surrey. WHAL.
   It lies on the road to Deptford. This elegant translation of Thomas *Aquinas* is of old date. It occurs in Chaucer :

> "And forth we riden all a little space,
> Unto the *Watering* of St. Thomàs."

And appropriately in the ancient Morality of *Hycke Scorner.*

> "For at *Saynt Thomas* of Watrynge, and they strike a sayle
> Then must they ryde in the haven of *hempe* without fayle."

O'er what you seem : it should not come, methinks,
Under your cap, this vein of salt and sharpness,
These strikings upon learning, now and then.
How long have you, if your dull guest may ask it,
Drove this quick trade, of keeping the Light Heart,
Your mansion, palace, here, or hostelry ?

    Host. Troth, I was born to somewhat, sir, above it.
    Lov. I easily suspect that: mine host, your name?
    Host. They call me Goodstock,
    Lov. Sir, and you confess it,
Both in your language, treaty, and your bearing.

    Host. Yet all, sir, are not sons of the white hen :
Nor can we, as the songster says, come all
To be wrapt soft and warm in fortune's smock.
When she is pleas'd to trick or tromp mankind,
Some may be coats, as in the cards ; but, then
Some must be knaves, some varlets, bawds, and ostlers,
As aces, duces, cards of ten, to face it
Out in the game, which all the world is.—

    Lov. But,
It being in your free-will (as 'twas) to choose
What parts you would sustain, methinks a man
Of your sagacity, and clear nostril, should
Have made another choice, than of a place
So sordid, as the keeping of an inn :
Where every jovial tinker, for his chink,
May cry, " Mine host, to crambe !⁵ *Give us drink ;*
And do not slink, but skink, or else you stink."
Rogue, bawd, and cheater, call you by the surnames,
And known synonyma of your profession.

    Host. But if I be no such, who then's the rogue,
In understanding, sir, I mean ? who errs,
Who tinkles then, or personates Tom Tinker ?
Your weazle here may tell you I talk bawdy,

    ⁵ *Crambe /*] or Crambo, " a play at short verses, in which a word
is given, and the parties contend who can find most rhymes to it."
Dict. *Clear nostril*, is from the *naris emunctæ* of Horace.

And teach my boy it; and you may believe him :
But, sir, at your own peril, if I do not;
And at his too, if he do lie, and affirm it.
No slander strikes, less hurts, the innocent.
If I be honest, and that all the cheat
Be of my self, in keeping this Light Heart,
Where, I imagine all the world's a play ;
The state, and men's affairs, all passages
Of life, to spring new scenes ; come in, go out,
And shift, and vanish ; and if I have got
A seat to sit at ease here, in mine inn,
To see the comedy ; and laugh, and chuck
At the variety and throng of humours
And dispositions, that come justling in
And out still, as they one drove hence another ;
Why will you envy me my happiness ?
Because you are sad and lumpish ; carry a loadstone
In your pocket, to hang knives on ; or jet rings,
To entice young straws to leap at them ; are not
          taken
With the alacrities of an host ! 'Tis more,
And justlier, sir, my wonder, why you took
My house up, Fidlers-hall, the seat of noise
And mirth, an inn here, to be drowsy in,
And lodge your lethargy in the Light Heart ;
As if some cloud from court had been your harbinger,
Or Cheapside debt-books, or some mistress' charge,
Seeing your love grow corpulent, gave it a diet,
By absence, some such mouldy passion !
 Lov. 'Tis guess'd unhappily.   [*Aside.*

    Re-enter FERRET.

 Fer. Mine host, you're call'd.
 Host. I come, boys.   [*Exit.*
 Lov. Ferret, have not you been ploughing
With this mad ox, mine host, nor he with you ?
 Fer. For what, sir ?

Lov. Why, to find my riddle out.[6]

Fer. I hope you do believe, sir, I can find
Other discourse to be at, than my master,
With hosts and hostlers.

Lov. If you can, 'tis well :
Go down, and see, who they are come in, what guests ;
And bring me word.   [*Exit* FERRET.

Lov. O love, what passion art thou !
So tyrannous and treacherous ! first to enslave,
And then betray all that in truth do serve thee !
That not the wisest, nor the wariest creature,
Can more dissemble thee, than he can bear
Hot burning coals, in his bare palm, or bosom :
And less conceal or hide thee, than a flash
Of enflamed powder, whose whole light doth lay it
Open to all discovery, even of those
Who have but half an eye, and less of nose.
An host, to find me ! who is, commonly,
The log, a little of this side the sign-post ;
Or at the best some round-grown thing, a jug
Faced with a beard,[7] that fills out to the guests,
And takes in from the fragments of their jests !

[6] Lovel alludes to the proverbial expression of Samson, "If ye
had not ploughed with my heifer," &c. *Judges*, c. xiv. It signifies
to obtain information by a breach of confidence.

[7] ———— *a jug,*
  Faced with a beard, &c.]   Thus Cartwright :

  " The greater sort, they say,
    Are like stone pots, with *beards* that do reach down
    Even to their knees."   *Lady Errant.*

And again, more pleasantly, in the *Ordinary :*

  " Thou'rt like the larger jug, that some men call
    A Bellarmine, but we a Conscience ;
    Whereon the lewder hand of pagan workman,
    Over the proud ambitious head, hath carv'd
    An idol huge, with beard episcopal,
    Making the vessel look like tyrant Eglon,"

See vol. iv. p. 460.

But I may wrong this out of sullenness,
Or my mistaking humour : pray thee, phant'sy,
Be laid again : and, gentle melancholy,
Do not oppress me ; I will be as silent
As the tame lover should be, and as foolish.

Re-enter HOST.

Host. My guest, my guest, be jovial, I beseech thee.
I have fresh golden guests, guests of the game,
Three coachful! lords! and ladies! new come in.
And I will cry them to thee, and thee to them,
So I can spring a smile but in this brow,
That, like the rugged Roman alderman,
Old master Gross, surnam'd Ἀγέλαστος,
Was never seen to laugh, but at an ass.[8]

Re-enter FERRET.

Fer. Sir, here's the lady Frampul.
Lov. How!
Fer. And her train,
Lord Beaufort, and lord Latimer, the colonel
Tipto, with mistress Prue, the chambermaid,
Trundle, the coachman——
Lov. Stop—discharge the house,
And get my horses ready ; bid the groom
Bring them to the back gate.   [*Exit* FERRET.
Host. What mean you, sir ?
Lov. To take fair leave, mine host.
Host. I hope, my guest,
Though I have talk'd somewhat above my share,

---

[8] *That, like the rugged Roman alderman,*
  Old master Gross, *surnam'd* Ἀγέλαστος,
  Was never seen to laugh, but at an ass.] The Roman alluded
to, and here called master *Gross*, was Crassus, the grandfather of
Crassus the rich. And, as Pliny tells us, he was never seen to
laugh but once, and that was at an ass mumbling a thistle. WHAL.
  It may here be observed, once for all, that Jonson invariably read
Greek not by quantity, but accent.

At large, and been in the altitudes, the extravagants,
Neither my self, nor any of mine have given you
The cause to quit my house thus on the sudden.

Lov. No, I affirm it on my faith. Excuse me
From such a rudeness ; I was now beginning
To taste and love you : and am heartily sorry,
Any occasion should be so compelling,
To urge my abrupt departure thus.   But——
Necessity's a tyrant, and commands it.

Host. She shall command me first to fire my bush ;
Then break up house : or, if that will not serve,
To break with all the world ; turn country bankrupt,
In mine own town, upon the market-day,
And be protested for my butter and eggs,
To the last bodge of oats, and bottle of hay.
Ere you shall leave me I will break my Heart ;
Coach and coach-horses, lords and ladies pack :
All my fresh guests shall stink. I'll pull my sign down,
Convert mine Inn to an alms-house, or a spittle
For lazars, or switch-sellers ; turn it to
An academy of rogues ; or give it away
For a free-school to breed up beggars in,
And send them to the canting universities,
Before you leave me !

Lov. Troth, and I confess
I am loth, mine host, to leave you: your expressions
Both take and hold me.   But, in case I stay,
I must enjoin you and your whole family
To privacy, and to conceal me ; for,
The secret is, I would not willingly
See, or be seen, to any of this ging,
Especially the lady.

Host. Brain o' man !
What monster is she, or cockatrice in velvet,
That kills thus ?

Lov. O good words, mine host.   She is
A noble lady, great in blood and fortune,

Fair and a wit! but of so bent a phant'sy,
As she thinks nought a happiness, but to have
A multitude of servants ; and to get them,
Though she be very honest, yet she ventures
Upon these precipices, that would make her
Not seem so, to some prying narrow natures.
We call her, sir, the lady Frances Frampul,
Daughter and heir to the lord Frampul.

 Host. Who!
He that did live in Oxford, first a student,
And after, married with the daughter of——

 Lov. Sylly.

 Host. Right.
Of whom the tale went, to turn puppet-master.

 Lov. And travel with young Goose, the motion-
  man.

 Host. And lie and live with the gipsies half a year
Together, from his wife.

 Lov. The very same :
The mad lord Frampul! and this same is his daughter,
But as cock-brain'd as e'er the father was!
There were two of them, Frances and Lætitia,
But Lætitia was lost young ; and, as the rumour
Flew then, the mother upon it lost herself ;
A fond weak woman, went away in a melancholy.
Because she brought him none but girls, she thought
Her husband loved her not : and he as foolish,
Too late resenting the cause given, went after,
In quest of her, and was not heard of since.

 Host. A strange division of a family !

 Lov. And scattered as in the great confusion !

 Host. But yet the lady, the heir, enjoys the land ?

 Lov. And takes all lordly ways how to consume it
As nobly as she can ; if clothes, and feasting,
And the authorised means of riot will do it.

 Host. She shews her extract, and I honour her
  for it.

Re-enter FERRET.

Fer. Your horses, sir, are ready ; and the house
Dis——

Lov. —Pleased, thou think'st ?

Fer. I cannot tell ; discharged
I am sure it is.

Lov. Charge it again, good Ferret,
And make unready the horses ; thou know'st how.
Chalk, and renew the rondels, I am now
Resolved to stay.

Fer. I easily thought so,
When you should hear what's purposed.   .

Lov. What ?

Fer. To throw
The house out of the window.

Host. Brain o' man,
I shall have the worst of that ! will they not throw
My houschold-stuff out first, cushions, and carpet,
Chairs, stools, and bedding ? is not their sport my
          ruin ?

Lov. Fear not, mine host, I am not of the fellow-
          ship.

Fer. I cannot see, sir, how you will avoid it ;
They know already, all, you are in the house.

Lov. Who know ?

Fer. The lords : they have seen me, and enquired it.

Lov. Why were you seen ?

Fer. Because indeed I had
No medicine, sir, to go invisible :
No fern-seed in my pocket ; nor an opal
Wrapt in bay-leaf, in my left fist, to charm
Their eyes with.

Host. He does give you reasons, [sir,]
As round as Gyges' ring ; which, say the ancients,
Was a hoop ring ; and that is, round as a hoop.

Lov. You will have your rebus still, mine host.

5   Y

Host. I must.

Fer. My lady too look'd out of the window, and
　　call'd me.
And see where secretary Prue comes from her,
Employ'd upon some embassy unto you.

　　Host. I'll meet her if she come upon employment :—

Enter PRUDENCE.

Fair lady, welcome, as your host can make you !

　　Pru. Forbear, sir, I am first to have mine audience,
Before the compliment.　This gentleman
Is my address to.

　　Host. And it is in state.

　　Pru. My lady, sir, as glad of the encounter
To find a servant here, and such a servant,
Whom she so values ; with her best respects,
Desires to be remember'd ; and invites
Your nobleness to be a part, to-day,
Of the society, and mirth intended
By her, and the young lords, your fellow-servants.
Who are alike ambitious of enjoying
The fair request ; and to that end have sent
Me, their imperfect orator, to obtain it :
Which if I may, they have elected me,
And crown'd me, with the title of a sovereign
Of the day's sports devised in the Inn,
So you be pleased to add your suffrage to it.

　　Lov. So I be pleased, my gentle mistress Pru-
　　dence !
You cannot think me of that coarse disposition,
To envý you any thing.

　　Host. That's nobly said,
And like my guest !

　　Lov. I gratulate your honour,
And should, with cheer, lay hold on any handle
That could advance it : but for me to think,
I can be any rag or particle

Of your lady's care, more than to fill her list,
She being the lady, that professeth still
To love no soul or body, but for ends,
Which are her sports ; and is not nice to speak this,
But doth proclaim it, in all companies——
Her ladyship must pardon my weak counsels,
And weaker will, if I decline to obey her.

   Pru. O, master Lovel, you must not give credit
To all that ladies publicly profess,
Or talk o' the volée,⁹ unto their servants.
Their tongues and thoughts oft-times lie far asunder.
Yet when they please, they have their cabinet-
     counsels,
And reserv'd thoughts, and can retire themselves
As well as others.

   Host. Ay, the subtlest of us.
All that is born within a lady's lips——

   Pru. Is not the issue of their hearts, mine host.

   Host. Or kiss or drink afore me.¹

   Pru. Stay, excuse me ;
Mine errand is not done. Yet, if her ladyship's
Slighting, or disesteem, sir, of your service,
Hath formerly begot any distaste,
Which I not know of; here I vow unto you,
Upon a chambermaid's simplicity,
Reserving still the honour of my lady,
I will be bold to hold the glass up to her,
To shew her ladyship where she hath err'd,
And how to tender satisfaction ;
So you vouchsafe to prove but the day's venture.

   Host. What say you, sir ? where are you, are you
     within ?   [*Strikes* LOVEL *on the breast.*

   Lov. Yes, I will wait upon her and the company.

---

⁹ *O' the* volée,] i. e. at random. See p. 249.
¹ *Or kiss or drink afore me.*] This is a familiar expression, employed when what the speaker is just about to say is anticipated
by another of the company.

Host. It is enough, queen Prudence ; I will bring
    him :
And on this kiss.—[*kisses her. Exit* PRUDENCE.]   I
    long'd to kiss a queen.
Lov. There is no life on earth, but being in love!
There are no studies, no delights, no business,
No intercourse, or trade of sense, or soul,
But what is love ! I was the laziest creature,
The most unprofitable sign of nothing,
The veriest drone, and slept away my life
Beyond the dormouse, till I was in love !
And now, I can outwake the nightingale,
Out-watch an usurer, and out-walk him too ;
Stalk like a ghost, that haunted 'bout a treasure,
And all that phant'sied treasure, it is love.
    Host. But is your name Love-ill, sir, or Love-well ?
I would know that.
    Lov. I do not know't myself,
Whether it is ; but it is love hath been
The hereditary passion of our house,
My gentle host, and, as I guess, my friend :
The truth is, I have loved this lady long,
And impotently,[2] with desire enough,
But no success : for I have still forborne
To express it, in my person, to her.
    Host. How then ?
    Lov. I have sent her toys, verses, and anagrams,
Trials of wit, mere trifles she has commended,
But knew not whence they came, nor could she guess.
    Host. This was a pretty riddling way of wooing !
    Lov. I oft have been too in her company ;
And look'd upon her a whole day ; admired her ;
Loved her, and did not tell her so ; loved still.
Look'd still, and loved ; and loved, and look'd, and
    sigh d :
But, as a man neglected, I came off,

---

[2] *And* impotently,] i. e. madly, without the control of reason, &c.

And unregarded——
  Host. Could you blame her, sir,
When you were silent, and not said a word ?
    Lov. O but I loved the more ; and she might
          read it
Best in my silence, had she been——
  Host. As melancholic
As you are ! Pray you, why would you stand mute,
        sir ?
    Lov. O, thereon hangs a history, mine host.
Did you e'er know, or hear of the lord Beaufort,
Who serv'd so bravely in France ? I was his page,
And ere he died, his friend : I follow'd him,
First, in the wars, and, in the times of peace,
I waited on his studies ; which were right.
He had no Arthurs, nor no Rosicleers,
No knights o' the Sun, nor Amadis de Gauls,
Primalions, Pantagruels, public nothings ;
Abortives of the fabulous dark cloyster,
Sent out to poison courts and infest manners :
But great Achilles, Agamemnon's acts,
Sage Nestor's counsels, and Ulysses' slights,
Tydides' fortitude, as Homer wrought them
In his immortal phant'sy, for examples
Of the heroic virtue. Or, as Virgil,
That master of the epic poem, limn'd
Pious Æneas, his religious prince,
Bearing his aged parent on his shoulders,
Rapt from the flames of Troy, with his young son :
And these he brought to practice, and to use.
He gave me first my breeding, I acknowledge,
Then shower'd his bounties on me, like the Hours,
That open-handed sit upon the clouds,
And press the liberality of heaven
Down to the laps of thankful men ! But then
The trust committed to me at his death,
Was above all, and left so strong a tie

On all my powers, as time shall not dissolve,
Till it dissolve itself, and bury all !
The care of his brave heir, and only son :
Who being a virtuous, sweet, young, hopeful lord,
Hath cast his first affections on this lady.
And though I know, and may presume her such,
As, out of humour, will return no love ;
And therefore might indifferently be made
The courting-stock, for all to practise on,
As she doth practise on all us, to scorn :
Yet, out of a religion to my charge,
And debt profess'd, I have made a self-decree,
Ne'er to express my person, though my passion
Burn me to cinders.

 Host. Then you are not so subtle
Or half so read in love-craft, as I took you ;
Come, come, you are no phœnix ; an you were,
I should expect no miracle from your ashes.
Take some advice. Be still that rag of love,
You are : burn on till you turn tinder.
This chamber-maid may hap to prove the steel,
To strike a sparkle out of the flint, your mistress,
May beget bonfires yet ; you do not know,
What light may be forced out, and from what dark-
  ness.

 Lov. Nay, I am so resolv'd, as still I'll love
Though not confess it.

 Host. That's, sir, as it chances ;
We'll throw the dice for it : cheer up.

 Lov. I do.   [*Exeunt.*

ACT II.

SCENE I. *A Room in the Inn.*

Enter lady FRAMPUL, *and* PRUDENCE *pinning on her lady's gown.*

Lady Frampul.

COME, wench, this suit will serve; dispatch,
    make ready :
    It was a great deal with the biggest for me,
    Which made me leave it off after once
      wearing.
How does it fit ? will it come together ?
   Pru. Hardly.
   Lady F. Thou must make shift with it ; pride feels
    no pain.
Girt thee hard, Prue.   Pox o' this errant tailor,
He angers me beyond all mark of patience !
These base mechanics never keep their word,
In any thing they promise.
   Pru. 'Tis their trade, madam,
To swear and break ; they all grow rich by breaking
More than their words ; their honesties, and credits,
Are still the first commodity they put off.
   Lady F. And worst, it seems ; which makes them
    do it so often.
If he had but broke with me, I had not cared,
But with the company ! the body politic !——
   Pru. Frustrate our whole design, having that time,
And the materials in, so long before !

Lady F. And he to fail in all, and disappoint us !
The rogue deserves a torture——
    Pru. To be cropp'd
With his own scissars.
    Lady F. Let's devise him one.
    Pru. And have the stumps sear'd up with his own
        searing candle.
    Lady F. Close to his head, to trundle on his
        pillow.——
I'll have the lease of his house cut out in measures.
    Pru. And he be strangled with them.
    Lady F. No, no life
I would have touch'd, but stretch'd on his own yard
He should be a little, have the strappado——
    Pru. Or an ell of taffata
Drawn through his guts, by way of glyster, and fired
With aqua vitæ.
    Lady F. Burning in the hand
With the pressing-iron, cannot save him.
    Pru. Yes,
Now I have got this on ; I do forgive him,
What robes he should have brought.
    Lady F. Thou art not cruel,
Although strait-laced, I see, Prue.
    Pru. This is well.
    Lady F. 'Tis rich enough, but 'tis not what I meant
        thee.
I would have had thee braver than myself,
And brighter far. 'Twill fit the players yet,
When thou hast done with it, and yield thee some-
        what.
    Pru. That were illiberal, madam, and mere sordid
In me, to let a suit of yours come there.
    Lady F. Tut, all are players, and but serve the
        scene, Prue :
Dispatch ; I fear thou dost not like the province,
Thou art so long a fitting thyself for it.

Here is a scarf to make thee a knot finer.

 Pru. You send me a-feasting, madam.

 Lady F. Wear it, wench.

 Pru. Yes; but with leave of your ladyship, I
  would tell you,

This can but bear the face of an odd journey.

 Lady F. Why, Prue?

 Pru. A lady of your rank and quality,

To come to a public inn, so many men,

Young lords and others, in your company,

And not a woman but myself, a chambermaid!

 Lady F. Thou doubt'st to be o'erlaid, Prue! fear
  it not,

I'll bear my part, and share with thee in the venture.

 Pru. O but the censure, madam, is the main.

What will they say of you, or judge of me,

To be translated thus, above all the bound

Of fitness or decorum?

 Lady F. How now, Prue!

Turn'd fool upon the sudden, and talk idly

In thy best clothes! shoot bolts and sentences

To affright babies with! as if I lived

To any other scale than what's my own,

Or sought myself, without myself, from home![3]

 Pru. Your ladyship will pardon me my fault;

If I have over-shot, I'll shoot no more.

 Lady F. Yes, shoot again, good Prue; I'll have thee
  shoot,

And aim, and hit; I know 'tis love in thee,

And so I do interpret it.

 Pru. Then, madam,

I'd crave a farther leave.

 Lady F. Be it to license,

---

 [3] *Or sought myself, without myself, &c.*] The lady has her
"bolts and sentences" as well as the maid. The present is from
Persius:

   Ne te quæsiveris extra.

It shall not want an ear, Prue.   Say, what is it ?

Pru. A toy I have, to raise a little mirth
To the design in hand.

Lady F. Out with it, Prue,
If it but chime of mirth.

Pru. Mine host has, madam,
A pretty boy in the house, a dainty child,
His son, and is of your ladyship's name, too, Francis,
Whom if your ladyship would borrow of him,
And give me leave to dress him as I would,
Should make the finest lady and kinswoman,
To keep you company, and deceive my lords,
Upon the matter, with a fountain of sport.

Lady F. I apprehend thee, and the source of mirth
That it may breed ; but is he bold enough,
The child, and well assured ?

Pru. As I am, madam :
Have him in no suspicion, more than me.
Here comes mine host ; will you but please to ask him,
Or let me make the motion ?

Lady F. Which thou wilt, Prue.

Enter Host.

Host. Your ladyship, and all your train are welcome.

Lady F. I thank my hearty host.

Host. So is your sovereignty,[4]

---

[4] *So is your* sovereignty.] In Horatio's adjuration to Hamlet
not to follow the ghost, he urges, among other dissuasives,

> " What if it tempt you toward the flood, my lord,
>   Or to the dreadful summit of the cliff,
>   And then assume some other horrible form,
>   Which might deprive your sovereignty of reason,
>   And draw you into madness ! "

This passage has proved a perpetual torment to the commentators.—" Your sovereignty of reason," Steevens says, " is, your ruling
power of reason !" And then he proceeds with matchless gravity :
"When poets wish to invest any quality or virtue with uncommon
splendor, they do it by some allusion to regal eminence."—War-

Madam, I wish you joy of your new gown.

    Lady F. It should have been, my host ; but Stuff,
        our tailor,

Has broke with us ; you shall be of the counsel.

    Pru. He will deserve it, madam.   My lady has
        heard

You have a pretty son, mine host, she'll see him.

    Lady F. Ay, very fain ; I pray thee let me see
        him, host.

    Host. Your ladyship shall presently.——

                                  [Goes to the door.

Bid Frank come hither anon, unto my lady.——
It is a bashful child, homely brought up,
In a rude hostelry : but the Light Heart
Is now his father's, and it may be his.
Here he comes.——

          Enter FRANK.

        Frank, salute my lady.

    Frank. I do

What, madam, I am design'd to do, by my birthright,
As heir of the Light Heart, bid you most welcome.

    Lady F. And I believe your *most*, my pretty boy,
Being so emphased by you.

    Frank. Your ladyship, madam,
If you believe it such, are sure to make it.

    Lady F. Prettily answered ! Is your name Francis ?

---

burton would read, *deprave* your sovereignty of reason—but it would
be idle to produce more of this nature. The critics have stumbled
over a difficulty raised by themselves : *sovereignty* here, as in the
text, is merely a title of respect ; and to deprive your sovereignty
of reason, means neither more nor less, than to deprive your lordship, or your honour, or your highness of reason.   As if this was
not enough, on a passage which it seems almost impossible to mistake, Dr. Johnson and Steevens disagree about the word *deprive:* the
former " conceiving it to mean simply, *take away*," and the latter
stoutly " affirming it to signify *disinherit !*"   Is not this to turn
criticism into the *line of children !*

Frank. Yes, madam.

Lady F. I love mine own the better.

Frank. If I knew yours,
I should make haste to do so too, good madam.

Lady F. It is the same with yours.

Frank. Mine then acknowledges
The lustre it receives, by being named after.

Lady F. You will win upon me in compliment.

Frank. By silence.

Lady F. A modest and a fair well-spoken child.

Host. Her ladyship shall have him, sovereign Prue,
Or what I have beside ; divide my Heart
Between you and your lady ; make your use of it :
My house is yours, my son is yours.   Behold,
I tender him to your service ; Frank, become
What these brave ladies would have you. Only this,
There is a chare-woman in the house, his nurse,
An Irish woman, I took in a beggar,
That waits upon him, a poor, silly fool,
But an impertinent and sedulous one
As ever was ; will vex you on all occasions,
Never be off, or from you, but in her sleep ;
Or drink which makes it ; she doth love him so,
Or rather doat on him.   Now, for her, a shape,[5]
And we may dress her, and I'll help to fit her,
With a tuft-taffata cloke, an old French hood,
And other pieces, heterogene enough.

Pru. We have brought a standard of apparel down,
Because this tailor fail'd us in the main.

Host. She shall advance the game.

Pru. About it then.
And send but Trundle hither, the coachman, to me.

Host. I shall : but, Prue, let Lovel have fair
      quarter.   [*Aside.*

---

[5] *Now for her a* shape,] i. e. as has been already observed, a suit
by way of disguise. It is a theatrical term still in use, for a foreign
dress.

Pru. The best.   [*Exit* Host.

Lady F. Our host, methinks, is very gamesome.

Pru. How like you the boy?

Lady F. A miracle!

Pru. Good madam,
But take him in, and sort a suit for him.
I'll give our Trundle his instructions;
And wait upon your ladyship in the instant.

Lady F. But, Prue, what shall we call him, when
     we have drest him?

Pru. My lady Nobody, any thing, what you will.

Lady F. Call him Lætitia, by my sister's name,
And so 'twill mend our mirth too we have in hand.
                              [*Exit.*

Enter TRUNDLE.

Pru. Good Trundle, you must straight make ready
     the coach,
And lead the horses out but half a mile,
Into the fields, whither you will, and then
Drive in again, with the coach-leaves put down,
At the back gate, and so to the back stairs,
As if you brought in some body to my lady,
A kinswoman that she sent for.   Make that answer,
If you be ask'd; and give it out in the house so.

Trun. What trick is this, good mistress secretary,
You'd put upon us?

Pru. Us! do you speak plural?

Trun. Me and my mares are us.

Pru. If you so join them,
Elegant Trundle, you may use your figures:
I can but urge, it is my lady's service.

Trun. Good mistress Prudence, you can urge
     enough;
I know you are secretary to my lady,
And mistress steward.

Pru. You will still be trundling,

And have your wages stopt now at the audit.
　　Trun. 'Tis true, you are gentlewoman o' the horse
　　　　too ;
Or what you will beside, Prue.　I do think it
My best t'obey you.
　　Pru. And I think so too, Trundle.　　[*Exeunt.*

SCENE II.　*Another Room in the Same.*

Enter lord BEAUFORT *and* lord LATIMER.

Lord Beaufort.

WHY, here's return enough of both our ventures,
　　If we do make no more discovery.
　　　　Lord L. What ?
Than of this parasite ?
　　Lord B. O, he's a dainty one,
The parasite of the house.
　　Lord L. Here comes mine host.

Enter Host.

　　Host. My lords, you both are welcome to the
　　　　Heart.
　　Lord B. To the Light Heart, we hope.
　　Lord L. And merry, I swear.
We never yet felt such a fit of laughter,
As your glad Heart hath offered us since we enter'd.
　　Lord B. How came you by this property ?
　　Host. Who, my Fly ?
　　Lord B. Your Fly, if you call him so.
　　Host. Nay, he is that,
And will be still.
　　Lord B. In every dish and pot ?
　　Host. In every cup and company, my lords,
A creature of all liquors, all complexions,
Be the drink what it will, he'll have his sip.

Lord L. He's fitted with a name.

Host. And he joys in it.
I had him when I came to take the Inn here,
Assign'd me over in the inventory,
As an old implement, a piece of household stuff,
And so he doth remain.

Lord B. Just such a thing
We thought him.

Lord L. Is he a scholar ?

Host. Nothing less ;
But colours for it, as you see ; wears black,
And speaks a little tainted, fly-blown Latin,
After the school.

Lord B. Of Stratford o' the Bow :
For Lillie's Latin is to him unknown.[6]

Lord L. What calling has he ?

Host. Only to call in still,
Enflame the reckoning, bold to charge a bill,
Bring up the shot in the rear, as his own word is.

Lord B. And does it in the discipline of the house,
As corporal of the field, maestro del campo ?

Host. And visitor general of all the rooms :
He has form'd a fine militia for the Inn too.

Lord B. And means to publish it ?

Host. With all his titles ;
Some call him deacon Fly, some doctor Fly ;
Some captain, some lieutenant : but my folks
Do call him quarter-master Fly, which he is.

Enter colonel T IPTO *and* F LY.

Tip. Come, quarter-master Fly.

---

[6] *Of* Stratford o' the Bow :
For Lillie's Latin is to him unknown.] Alluding to the following
lines in Chaucer's *Character of the Prioress :*

" And French she spake full fayr and fetisly,
After the school of *Stratford attè Bowe,*
For French of Paris was to her unknowe." W HAL.

Host. Here's one already
Hath got his titles.
   Tip. Doctor.
   Fly. Noble colonel,
No doctor, yet a poor professor of ceremony,
Here in the Inn, retainer to the host,
I discipline the house.
   Tip. Thou read'st a lecture
Unto the family here : when is the day ?
   Fly. This is the day.
   Tip. I'll hear thee, and I'll have thee a doctor;
Thou shalt be one, thou hast a doctor's look,
A face disputative, of Salamanca.
   Host. Who's this ?
   Lord L. The glorious colonel Tipto, host.
   Lord B. One talks upon his tiptoes, if you'll hear
     him.
   Tip. Thou hast good learning in thee ; *macte*, Fly.
   Fly. And I say *macte* to my colonel.
   Host. Well *macted* of them both.
   Lord B. They are match'd, i' faith.
   Tip. But, Fly, why *macte?*
   Fly. *Quasi magis aucte,*
My honourable colonel.
   Tip. What, a critic !
   Host. There is another accession, critic Fly.
   Lord L. I fear a taint here in the mathematics.
They say, lines parallel do never meet ;
He has met his parallel in wit and school-craft.
   Lord B. They side, not meet, man ; mend your
     metaphor,
And save the credit of your mathematics.
   Tip. But Fly, how cam'st thou to be here, com-
     mitted
Unto this Inn ?
   Fly. Upon suspicion of drink, sir.
I was taken late one night here with the tapster,

And the under-officers, and so deposited.

Tip. I will redeem thee, Fly, and place thee better,
With a fair lady.

Fly. A lady, sweet sir Glorious!

Tip. A sovereign lady. Thou shalt be the bird
To sovereign Prue, queen of our sports, her Fly,
The Fly in household and in ordinary;
Bird of her ear, and she shall wear thee there,
A Fly of gold, enamell'd, and a school-fly.

Host. The school then, are my stables, or the
    cellar,
Where he doth study deeply, at his hours,
Cases of cups, I do not know how spiced
With conscience, for the tapster and the hostler; as
Whose horses may be cosen'd, or what jugs
Fill'd up with froth? that is his way of learning.

Tip. What antiquated feather's that that talks?

Fly. The worshipful host, my patron, master Good-
    stock,
A merry Greek, and cants in Latin comely,
Spins like the parish top.

Tip. I'll set him up then.—
Art thou the Dominus?

Host. Fac-totum here, sir.

Tip. Host real of the house, and cap of mainten-
    ance?

Host. The lord of the Light Heart, sir, cap-a-pie;
Whereof the feather is the emblem, colonel,
Put up with the ace of hearts.

Tip. But why in cuerpo?
I hate to see an host, and old, in cuerpo.

Host. Cuerpo! what's that?

Tip. Light-skipping hose and doublet,
The horse-boy's garb! poor blank and half blank
    cuerpo,
They relish not the gravity of an host,
Who should be king at arms, and ceremonies,

5   z

In his own house ; know all, to the gold weights.[7]

Lord B. Why that his Fly doth for him here, your
     bird.

Tip. But I would do it myself were I my host,
I would not speak unto a cook of quality,
Your lordship's footman, or my lady's Trundle,
In cuerpo : if a dog but stay'd below,[8]
That were a dog of fashion, and well nosed,
And could present himself ; I would put on
The Savoy chain about my neck, the ruff
And cuffs of Flanders, then the Naples hat,
With the Rome hatband, and the Florentine agat,
The Milan sword, the cloke of Genoa, set
With Brabant buttons ; all my given pieces,
Except my gloves, the natives of Madrid,
To entertain him in ; and compliment
With a tame coney, as with a prince that sent it.

Host. The same deeds, though, become not every
     man ;
That fits a colonel will not fit an host.

Tip. Your Spanish host is never seen in cuerpo,
Without his paramentos, cloke and sword.

Fly. Sir,
He has the father of swords within, a long sword ;

---

[7] *Know all, to the* gold weights,] i. e. every minute particular
with great exactness. The weights made use of in weighing gold,
being reducible to very small quantities, such as carats, grains, &c.
WHAL.

The expression seems proverbial. Thus in Beaumont and
Fletcher :

      " She's one that weighs her words and her behaviour
         In the *gold-weights* of discretion."   *Wild Goose Chase.*
Again :

      " A man, believe it,
         That knows his place, to the *gold-weight.*"
                                        Love's Pilgrimage.

[8] This and the following speech, as Whalley observes, occur
almost *verbatim* in the play just quoted.

Blade Cornish styled of sir Rud Hughdebras.

> *Tip.* And why a long sword,[9] bully bird? thy
> sense?
>
> *Fly.* To note him a tall man, and a master of fence.
>
> *Tip.* But doth he teach the Spanish way of don
> Lewis?
>
> *Fly.* No, the Greek master he.
>
> *Tip.* What call you him?
>
> *Fly.* Euclid.
>
> *Tip.* Fart upon Euclid, he is stale and antic!

Give me the moderns.

> *Fly.* Sir, he minds no moderns,

Go by, Hieronimo!

> *Tip.* What was he?
>
> *Fly.* The Italian,

That play'd with abbot Antony in the Friars,
And Blinkinsops the bold.[1]

> *Tip.* Ay, marry, those

Had fencing names; What is become of them?

> *Host.* They had their times, and we can say, they
> were.

So had Caranza his; so had don Lewis.

> *Tip.* Don Lewis of Madrid is the sole master

Now of the world.

> *Host.* But this of the other world,

---

[9] *And why a long sword?*] This is Whalley's reading for *with*,
that of the 8vo. Rud Hughdebras, who is mentioned just above,
was, as Milton tells us, the son of Leil, who built Caerliel, and I
know not how many more cities. He seems to have been a peace-
ful monarch, so that his *blade Cornish* was not, perhaps, much the
worse for use.

[1] *The Italian,*
   That play'd with abbot Antony in the Friars,
   And Blinkinsops the bold.] The Italian is mentioned again in
the *Epigrams:* he was a master of legerdemain, as well as fencing.
Abbot Antony is, I believe, Antony Monday, who might have learned
the "noble science of fencing" in Italy: of Blinkinsops I know
nothing, nor is the enquiry worth pursuit. This part of the dialogue
is intolerably dull.

Euclid, demonstrates.   He ! he is for all :
The only fencer of name, now in Elysium.
  Fly. He does it all by lines and angles, colonel ;
By parallels and sections, has his diagrams.
  Lord B. Wilt thou be flying, Fly ?
  Lord L. At all, why not ?
The air's as free for a fly as for an eagle.
  Lord B. A buzzard ! he is in his contemplation.
  Tip. Euclid a fencer, and in the Elysium !
  Host. He play'd a prize last week with Archimedes,
And beat him, I assure you.
  Tip. Do you assure me ?
For what ?
  Host. For four i' the hundred.   Give me five,
And I assure you again.
  Tip. Host peremptory,
You may be ta'en. But where, whence had you this ?
  Host. Upon the road.   A post that came from
          thence,
Three days ago, here, left it with the tapster.
  Fly. Who is indeed a thoroughfare of news,
Jack Jug with the broken belly, a witty fellow !
  Host. Your bird here heard him.
  Tip. Did you hear him, bird ?
  Host. Speak in the faith of a Fly.   [*Exit.*
  Fly. Yes, and he told us
Of one that was the prince of Orange' fencer.
  Tip. Stevinus ?
  Fly. Sir, the same had challenged Euclid
At thirty weapons more than Archimedes
E'er saw, and engines ; most of his own invention.
  Tip. This may have credit, and chimes reason, this!
If any man endanger Euclid, bird,
Observe, that had the honour to quit Europe
This forty year, 'tis he.   He put down Scaliger.
  Fly. And he was a great master.
  Lord B. Not of fence, Fly.

Tip. Excuse him, lord, he went on the same
    grounds.
Lord B. On the same earth, I think, with other
    mortals.
Tip. I mean, sweet lord, the mathematics. Basta!
When thou know'st more, thou wilt take less green
    honour.
He had his circles, semicircles, quadrants——
Fly. He writ a book of the quadrature of the
    circle——
Tip. Cyclometria, I read——
Lord B. The title only.
Lord L. And indice.
Lord B. If it had one ; of that, quære ?—
What insolent, half-witted things these are !
Lord L. So are all smatterers, insolent and im-
    pudent.
Lord B. They lightly go together.
Lord L. 'Tis my wonder
Two animals should hawk at all discourse thus,
Fly every subject to the mark, or retrieve——
Lord B. And never have the luck to be in the right !
Lord L. 'Tis some folks' fortune.
Lord B. Fortune is a bawd,
And a blind beggar : 'tis their vanity,
And shews most vilely.
Tip. I could take the heart now
To write unto don Lewis into Spain,
To make a progress to the Elysian fields
Next summer——
Lord B. And persuade him die for fame,
Of fencing with a shadow ! Where's mine host ?
I would he had heard this bubble break, i'faith.

Re-enter Host, *with* PRUDENCE *richly dressed,* FRANK
    as a lady, Nurse, *and lady* FRAMPUL.

Host. Make place, stand by, for the queen-regent,
    gentlemen !

Tip. This is thy queen that shall be, bird, our
  sovereign.
Lord B. Translated Prudence !
Pru. Sweet my lord, hand off;
It is not now, as when plain Prudence lived,
And reach'd her ladyship——
  Host. The chamber-pot.
  Pru. The looking-glass, mine host : lose your
  house metaphor !
You have a negligent memory indeed.
Speak the host's language. Here is a young lord
Will make't a precedent else.
  Lord L. Well acted, Prue.
  Host. First minute of her reign ! What will
  she do
Forty years hence, God bless her !
  Pru. If you'll kiss,
Or compliment, my lord, behold a lady,
A stranger, and my lady's kinswoman.
  Lord B. I do confess my rudeness, that had need
To have mine eye directed to this beauty.
  Frank. It was so little, as it ask'd a perspicil.
  Lord B. Lady, your name ?
  Frank. My lord, it is Lætitia.
  Lord B. Lætitia ! a fair omen, and I take it :
Let me have still such Lettice for my lips.
But that of your family, lady ?
  Frank. Sylly, sir.
  Lord B. My lady's kinswoman ?
  Frank. I am so honour'd.
  Host. Already it takes.   [*Aside to* lady F.
  Lady F. An excellent fine boy.
  Nurse. He is descended of a right good stock, sir.
  Lord B. What's this, an antiquary ?
  Host. An antiquity,
By the dress, you'd swear ! an old Welsh herald's
  widow :

She's a wild Irish born, sir, and a hybride,[2]
That lives with this young lady a mile off here,
And studies Vincent against York.[3]
    Lord B. She'll conquer
If she read Vincent. Let me study her.
    Host. She's perfect in most pedigrees, most descents.
    Lord B. A bawd, I hope, and knows to blaze a
      coat.   *[Aside.*
    Host. And judgeth all things with a single eye.
Fly, come you hither ; no discovery
Of what you see, to your colonel Toe, or Tip, here,
But keep all close ; though you stand in the way o'
    preferment,
Seek it off from the road ; no flattery for't,
No lick-foot, pain of losing your proboscis,
My liquorish Fly.   *[Aside to* FLY.
    Tip. What says old velvet-head ?
    Fly. He will present me himself, sir, if you will not.
    Tip. Who, he present ! what ? whom ? an host, a
      groom,
Divide the thanks with me ? share in my glories ?
Lay up : I say no more.
    Host. Then silence, sir,
And hear the sovereign.
    Tip. Hostlers to usurp
Upon my Sparta or province, as they say !
No broom but mine![4]
    Host. Still, colonel, you mutter.
    Tip. I dare speak out, as cuerpo.

    [2] *And a* hybride.] Latin, a mongrel.
    [3] *And studies* Vincent *against* York.] There was a dispute on
foot about this time between two heralds at arms ; one was *Vincent*
and the other *Brook*, who was *York* herald. *Vincent* published a
book, entituled, *A Discovery of Errors in two editions of the Catalogue of Nobility, written by Ralph Brook.* WHAL.
    [4] *No* broom *but mine.*] Col. Tipto's allusions are scarcely worth
explaining : but the present is to *Sparta*, in the preceding line,
which in Span. means *broom*, or brush-wood.

Fly. Noble colonel——

Tip. And carry what I ask——

Host. Ask what you can, sir,
So it be in the house.

Tip. I ask my rights and privileges;
And though for form I please to call't a suit,
I have not been accustomed to repulse.

Pru. No, sweet sir Glorious, you may still command——

Host. And go without.

Pru. But yet, sir, being the first,
And call'd a suit, you'll look it shall be such
As we may grant.

Lady F. It else denies itself.

Pru. You hear the opinion of the court.

Tip. I mind no court opinions.

Pru. 'Tis my lady's, though.

Tip. My lady is a spinster at the law,
And my petition is of right.

Pru. What is it?

Tip. It is for this poor learned bird.

Host. The fly.

Tip. Professor in the Inn, here, of small matters.

Lord L. How he commends him!

Host. As to save himself in him.

Lady F. So do all politics in their commendations.

Host. This is a state-bird, and the verier fly.

Tip. Hear him problematize.

Pru. Bless us, what's that?

Tip. Or syllogize, elenchize.

Lady F. Sure, petards
To blow us up.

Lord L. Some enginous strong words.

Host. He means to erect a castle in the air,
And make his fly an elephant to carry it.

Tip. Bird of the arts he is, and Fly by name.

Pru. Buz!

Host. Blow him off, good Prue, they'll mar all else.

Tip. The sovereign's honour is to cherish learning.

Pru. What in a fly?

Tip. In any thing industrious.

Pru. But flies are busy.

Lady F. Nothing more troublesome,
Or importune.

Tip. There's nothing more domestic,
Tame or familiar, than your fly in cuerpo.

Host. That is when his wings are cut, he is tame
     indeed, else
Nothing more impudent and greedy; licking——

Lady F. Or saucy, good sir Glorious.

Pru. Leave your advocateship,
Except that we shall call you orator Fly,
And send you down to the dresser and the dishes.

Host. A good flap that!

Pru. Commit you to the steam.

Lady F. Or else condemn you to the bottles.

Pru. And pots.
There is his quarry.

Host. He will chirp far better,
Your bird, below.

Lady F. And make you finer music.

Pru. His buz will there become him.

Tip. Come away,
Buz, in their faces: give them all the buz,
Dor in their ears and eyes, hum, dor, and buz!
I will statuminate and under-prop thee.
If they scorn us, let us scorn them—We'll find
The thoroughfare below,[5] and quære him;
Leave these relicts, buz; they shall see that I,
Spite of their jeers, dare drink, and with a fly.

                    [*Exeunt* TIPTO *and* FLY.

---

[5] *We'll find*
     The thoroughfare *below,*] i. e. Jug.   Statuminate is pure Latin.
Statuminibus firmare occurs in Pliny, and means to support vines
by poles or stakes, as is still done in Italy.

Lord L. A fair remove at once of two impertinents!
Excellent Prue, I love thee for thy wit,
No less than state.

Pru. One must preserve the other.

Enter LOVEL.

Lady F. Who's here?

Pru. O Lovel, madam, your sad servant.

Lady F. Sad! he is sullen still, and wears a cloud
About his brows; I know not how to approach him.

Pru. I will instruct you, madam, if that be all,
Go to him, and kiss him.

Lady F. How, Prue!

Pru. Go, and kiss him,
I do command it.

Lady F. Thou art not wild, wench.

Pru. No,
Tame, and exceeding tame, but still your sovereign.

Lady F. Hath too much bravery made thee mad?

Pru. Nor proud.
Do what I do enjoin you. No disputing
Of my prerogative, with a front, or frown;
Do not detract; you know the authority
Is mine, and I will exercise it swiftly,
If you provoke me.

Lady F. I have woven a net
To snare myself in!—[*To* LOVEL.] Sir, I am enjoin'd
To tender you a kiss: but do not know
Why, or wherefore, only the pleasure royal
Will have it so, and urges——Do not you
Triumph on my obedience, seeing it forced thus.
There 'tis. ·   [*Kisses him.*

Lov. And welcome.—Was there ever kiss
That relish'd thus! or had a sting like this,
Of so much nectar, but with aloes mixt!   [*Aside.*

Pru. No murmuring nor repining, I am fixt.

Lov. It had, methinks, a quintessence of either.

But that which was the better, drown'd the bitter.
How soon it pass'd away, how unrecover'd !
The distillation of another soul
Was not so sweet; and till I meet again
That kiss, those lips, like relish, and this taste,
Let me turn all consumption, and here waste. [*Aside.*
 Pru. The royal assent is past and cannot alter.
 Lady F. You'll turn a tyrant.
 Pru. Be not you a rebel.
It is a name is alike odious.
 Lady F. You'll hear me ?
 Pru. No, not on this argument.
Would you make laws, and be the first that break them ?
The example is pernicious in a subject,
And of your quality, most.
 Lord L. Excellent princess !
 Host. Just queen!
 Lord L. Brave sovereign !
 Host. A she Trajan, this !
 Lord B. What is't ? proceed, incomparable Prue ;
I am glad I am scarce at leisure to applaud thee.
 Lord L. It's well for you, you have so happy ex-
  pressions.
 Lady F. Yes, cry her up with acclamations, do,
And cry me down ; run all with sovereignty :
Prince Power will never want her parasites.
 Pru. Nor murmur her pretences : master Lovel,
For so your libel here, or bill of complaint,
Exhibited, in our high court of sovereignty,
At this first hour of our reign, declares
Against this noble lady, a disrespect
You have conceived, if not received, from her.
 Host. Received ; so the charge lies in our bill.
 Pru. We see it, his learned council, leave your
  planing.
We that do love our justice above all
Our other attributes, and have the nearness,

To know your extraordinary merit,
As also to discern this lady's goodness,
And find how loth she'd be to lose the honour
And reputation she hath had, in having
So worthy a servant, tho' but for few minutes;
Do here enjoin——
    Host. Good!
    Pru. Charge, will, and command
Her ladyship, pain of our high displeasure,
And the committing an extreme contempt
Unto the court, our crown, and dignity——
    Host. Excellent sovereign, and egregious Prue!
    Pru. To entertain you for a pair of hours,
Choose, when you please, this day, with all respects,
And valuation of a principal servant,
To give you all the titles, all the privileges,
The freedoms, favours, rights, she can bestow——
    Host. Large ample words, of a brave latitude!
    Pru. Or can be expected, from a lady of honour,
Or quality, in discourse, access, address——
    Host. Good!
    Pru. Not to give ear, or admit conference
With any person but yourself : nor there,
Of any other argument but LOVE,
And the companion of it, gentle courtship.
For which your two hours' service, you shall take
Two kisses.
    Host. Noble!
    Pru. For each hour a kiss,
To be ta'en freely, fully, and legally,
Before us; in the court here, and our presence.
    Host. Rare!
    Pru. But those hours past, and the two kisses paid,
The binding caution is, never to hope
Renewing of the time, or of the suit,
On any circumstance.
    Host. A hard condition!

Lord L. Had it been easier, I should have suspected
The sovereign's justice.

Host. O you are [a] servant,
My lord, unto the lady, and a rival :
In point of law, my lord, you may be challenged.

Lord L. I am not jealous.

Host. Of so short a time
Your lordship needs not, and being done *in foro.*

Pru. What is the answer ?

Host. He craves respite, madam,
To advise with his learned council.

Pru. Be you he,
And go together quickly.

                        [LOVEL *and* Host *walk aside.*

Lady F. You are no tyrant !

Pru. If I be, madam, you were best appeal me.

Lord L. Beaufort——

Lord B. I am busy, prithee let me alone ;[6]
I have a cause in hearing too.

Lord L. At what bar ?

Lord B. Love's court of Requests.

Lord L. Bring it into the sovereignty,
It is the nobler court, afore judge Prue ;
The only learned mother of the law,
And lady of conscience, too !

Lord B. 'Tis well enough
Before this mistress of requests, where it is.

Host. Let them not scorn you : bear up, master
     Lovel,
And take your hours and kisses, they are a fortune.

Lov. Which I cannot approve, and less make use of.

Host. Still in this cloud ! why cannot you make use of?

Lov. Who would be rich to be so soon undone ?
The beggar's best is wealth he doth not know ;
And, but to shew it him, inflames his want.

---

[6] Beau. *I am busy, &c.*] It should be observed that throughout this scene Beaufort is employed in privately making love to Frank, apart from the nurse.

Host. Two hours at height!

Lov. That joy is too, too narrow,
Would bound a love so infinite as mine;
And being past, leaves an eternal loss.
Who so prodigiously affects a feast,
To forfeit health and appetite, to see it?
Or but to taste a spoonful, would forego
All gust of delicacy ever after?

Host. These, yet, are hours of hope.

Lov. But all hours following
Years of despair, ages of misery!
Nor can so short a happiness, but spring
A world of fear, with thought of losing it;
Better be never happy, than to feel
A little of it, and then lose it ever.

Host. I do confess, it is a strict injunction;
But then the hope is, it may not be kept.
A thousand things may intervene; we see
The wind shift often, thrice a day sometimes:
Decrees may alter upon better motion,
And riper hearing. The best bow may start,
And the hand vary. Prue may be a sage
In law, and yet not sour; sweet Prue, smooth Prue,
Soft, debonaire, and amiable Prue,
May do as well as rough and rigid Prue;
And yet maintain her, venerable Prue,
Majestic Prue, and serenissimous Prue.
Try but one hour first, and as you like
The loose of that, draw home and prove the other.

Lov. If one hour could the other happy make,
I should attempt it.

Host. Put it on; and do.

Lov. Or in the blest attempt that I might die!

Host. Ay, marry, there were happiness indeed!
Transcendent to the melancholy, meant.
It were a fate above a monument,
And all inscription, to die so! A death
For emperors to enjoy, and the kings

Of the rich East to pawn their regions for ;
To sow their treasure, open all their mines,
Spend all their spices to embalm their corps,
And wrap the inches up in sheets of gold,
That fell by such a noble destiny !
And for the wrong to your friend, that fear's away,
He rather wrongs himself, following fresh light,
New eyes to swear by.   If lord Beaufort change,
It is no crime in you to remain constant,
And upon these conditions, at a game
So urg'd upon you.
   Pru. Sir, your resolution ?
   Host. How is the lady affected ?
   Pru. Sovereigns use not
To ask their subjects' suffrage where 'tis due,
But where conditional.
   Host. A royal sovereign !
   Lord L. And a rare stateswoman ! I admire her
      bearing
In her new regiment.[7]
   Host. Come, choose your hours,
Better be happy for a part of time,
Than not the whole ; and a short part, than never.
Shall I appoint them, pronounce for you ?
   Lov. Your pleasure.
   Host. Then he designs his first hour after dinner ;
His second after supper.   Say ye, content ?
   Pru. Content.
   Lady F. I am content.
   Host. Content.
   Frank. Content.
   Lord B. What's that ? I am content too.
   Lord L. You have reason,

---

[7] *In her new* regiment,] i. e. government.   The word is so common to our old writers in this sense, that one example of its ues
will be sufficient.   " After he had recovered the kingdom, he continued in the *regiment* thereof three years."   Holinshed's *Descript.*
of Scotland.

You had it on the bye, and we observed it.
    Nurse. Trot' I am not content : in fait' I am not.
    Host. Why art not thou content, good Sheleenien ?
    Nurse. He tauk so desperate, and so debausht,
So baudy like a courtier and a lord,
God bless him, one that tak'th tobacco.
    Host. Very well mixt !
What did he say ?
    Nurse. Nay, nothing to the purposh,
Or very little, nothing at all to purposh.
    Host. Let him alone, Nurse.
    Nurse. I did tell him of Serly
Was a great family come out of Ireland,
Descended of O Neal, Mac Con, Mac Dermot,
Mac Murrogh, but he mark'd not.
    Host. Nor do I ;
Good queen of heralds, ply the bottle, and sleep.
                                                    [*Exeunt.*

ACT III.

Scene I.   *A Lower Room in the Inn.*

Enter col. Tipto, Fly, *and* Jug.

Tipto.

LIKE the plot of your militia well.
It is a fine militia, and well order'd,
And the division's neat ! 'twill be desired
Only, the expressions were a little more
    Spanish ;
For there's the best militia of the world.

To call them tertias[8]—tertia of the kitchen,
Tertia of the cellar, tertia of the chamber,
And tertia of the stables.
    Fly. That I can, sir ;
And find out very able, fit commanders
In every tertia.
    Tip. Now you are in the right.
As in the tertia of the kitchen, yourself,
Being a person elegant in sauces,
There to command, as prime maestro del campo,
Chief master of the palate, for that tertia,
Or the cook under you ; 'cause you are the mar-
        shal,
And the next officer in the field, to the host.
Then for the cellar, you have young Anon,
Is a rare fellow—what's his other name ?
    Fly. Pierce, sir.
    Tip. Sir Pierce, I'll have him a cavalier.
Sir Pierce Anon will pierce us a new hogshead.
And then your thoroughfare, Jug here, his alfarez :
An able officer, give me thy beard, round Jug,
I take thee by this handle, and do love
One of thy inches.   In the chambers, Jordan here ;
He is the don del campo of the beds.
And for the stables, what's his name ?
    Fly. Old Peck.
    Tip. Maestro del campo, Peck! his name is curt,
A monosyllable, but commands the horse well.
    Fly. O, in an inn, sir, we have other horse,
Let those troops rest a while.   Wine is the horse,
That we must charge with here.
    Tip. Bring up the troops,
Or call, sweet Fly ; 'tis an exact militia,

---

    [8] *To call them* tertias.]   Tertia (Span.) is that portion of an army
which is levied out of one particular district, or division of a country.   *Alfarez* is an ensign, or standard-bearer.

And thou an exact professor ; Lipsius Fly [9]
Thou shalt be call'd, and Jouse :—

Enter Ferret *and* Trundle.

                              Jack Ferret, welcome.
Old trench-master, and colonel of the pioneers,
What canst thou bolt us now ? a coney or two
Out of Tom Trundle's burrow, here, the coach ?
This is the master of the carriages.
How is thy driving, Tom, good, as it was ?
   Trun. It serves my lady, and our officer Prue.
Twelve miles an hour ! Tom has the old trundle still.
   Tip. I am taken with the family here, fine fellows !
Viewing the muster-roll.
   Trun. They are brave men.
   Fer. And of the Fly-blown discipline all, the quar-
       ter-master.
   Tip. The Fly is a rare bird in his profession.
Let's sip a private pint with him : I would have him
Quit this light sign of the Light Heart, my bird,
And lighter house.   It is not for his tall
And growing gravity, so cedar-like,
To be the second to an host in cuerpo,
That knows no elegances : use his own

   [9] *And thou an exact professor*, Lipsius Fly.] *Lipsius* wrote a
treatise upon the Roman militia ; so that the allusion is evident :
but what is the meaning of the following,

       ———— " *Lipsius Fly*
       Thou shalt be call'd, and *Jouse?*"

The Christian name of *Lipsius*, as he wrote it in Latin, was *Justus ;*
of which *Jouse* perhaps is the original.   Whal.
   Whalley has overlooked one part of the allusion.   Lipsius' Fly
(for so it should be printed) refers to the description given by Lipsius of a celebrated automaton, a steel *fly*, made by a German artist,
which would fly round the table.   " Quæ ex artificis manu egressa,
convivas circumvolitavit, tandemque veluti defessa, in domini manus
reversa est."   The artist's name was (Müller) Regiomontanus.

Dictamen, and his genius ; I would have him
Fly high, and strike at all.—

Enter PIERCE.

Here's young Anon, too.

Pierce. What wine is't gentlemen, white or claret ?

Tip. White,
My brisk Anon.

Pierce. I'll draw you Juno's milk
That dyed the lilies, colonel.   [*Exit.*

Tip. Do so, Pierce.

Enter PECK.

Peck. [1]A plague of all jades, what a clap he has
    gi'en me !

Fly. Why, how now, cousin ?

Tip. Who's that ?

Fer. The hostler.

Fly. What ail'st thou, cousin Peck ?

[*Takes him aside.*

Peck. O me, my hanches ![2]
As sure as you live, sir, he knew perfectly
I meant to cozen him.   He did leer so on me,

---

[1] Peck. *A plague of all jades, &c.*] Here should have been a
stage-direction, *Enter Peck.* WHAL.
  This is excellent. We are almost got to the end of Jonson's
plays, and Whalley has just discovered that an *entrance* is wanting !
I have supplied thousands ; and not a few in what has already
passed of the present drama.

[2] Peck. *O me, &c.*] What follows, about the tricks of ostlers,
occurs likewise in the first act of Fletcher's *Love's Pilgrimage ;* and
perhaps there may be some difficulty in accounting for this coin-
cidence. We are told that some plays of Beaumont and Fletcher
being left imperfect, were fitted for the stage by Shirley, who added
what he thought necessary to complete them : and that it is probable
he here borrowed from our author's *New Inn,* what passes between
Lazaro and Diego in *Love's Pilgrimage :* and this he thought, perhaps, might be done with safety enough, as the *New Inn* met with
ill success in the representation.   It will not, I believe, be said

And then he sneer'd, as who would say, take heed,
　　sirrah ;
And when he saw our half-peck, which you know
Was but an old court-dish,[3] lord, how he stamp'd,
I thought 't had been for joy : when suddenly
He cuts me a back-caper with his heels,
And takes me just o' the crupper.　Down come I
And my whole ounce of oats!　Then he neigh'd out,
As if he had a mare by the tail.
　　Fly. Troth, cousin,
You are to blame to use the poor dumb Christians
So cruelly, defraud 'em of their *dimensum.*[4]
Yonder's the colonel's horse (there I look'd in)
Keeping our Lady's eve! the devil a bit
He has got, since he came in yet! there he stands,
And looks and looks, but 'tis your pleasure, coz,
He should look lean enough.

that Jonson was the borrower; for the whole scene is entirely in
his manner : and we have an instance in *Sejanus,* how extremely
scrupulous he was in claiming the production of another person.
WHAL.

　Love's Pilgrimage did not appear until 1647, when it was com-
pleted and given to the world by Shirley.　He therefore is accountable for the introduction of this scene into Fletcher's fragment;
and he might insert it with the less scruple, as the practice was not
much of a novelty, and the plundered play was, perhaps, as little
known as esteemed.　Mr. Stephen Jones observes with that perspicacity and good sense for which he is so deservedly famous,
that, "as the New Inn miscarried, (in 1629) it is very *probable* that
Jonson gave Beaumont and Fletcher his consent to make use of
this dialogue." *Biograph. Dramat.*　There can be no doubt of it ;
since Fletcher had then been in his grave only four, and Beaumont
fourteen years!

　[3] *Was but an old* court-dish.]　Whalley could not explain this
term ; neither can I; though I have met with the expression elsewhere in the sense of *short allowance.*　Perhaps it is a misprint for
curt-dish, a shallow, or rather broken dish : this, however, would be
more in the style of colonel Tipto than of cousin Peck.

　[4] *Defraud them of their* dimensum,]　i. e. of their full measure.
Dimensum was the term used by the Romans for the stated allowance of provisions periodically delivered out to their slaves.

Peck. He has hay before him.

Fly. Yes, but as gross as hemp, and as soon will
  choke him,
Unless he eat it butter'd. He had four shoes,
And good ones, when he came in : it is a wonder,
With standing still, he should cast three.

Peck. Troth, quarter-master,
This trade is a kind of mystery, that corrupts
Our standing manners quickly : once a week,
I meet with such a brush to mollify me,
Sometimes a brace, to awake my conscience,
Yet still I sleep securely.

Fly. Cousin Peck,
You must use better dealing, faith, you must.

Peck. Troth, to give good example to my suc-
  cessors,
I could be well content to steal but two girths,
And now and then a saddle-cloth, change a bridle,
For exercise ; and stay there.

Fly. If you could,
There were some hope on you, coz : but the fate is,
You are drunk so early, you mistake whole saddles ;
Sometimes a horse.

Peck. Ay, there's——

Re-enter PIERCE *with wine.*

Fly. The wine ! come, coz,
I'll talk with you anon.   [*They come forward.*

Peck. Do, lose no time,
Good quarter-master.

Tip. There are the horse, come, Fly.

Fly. Charge, in boys, in——

Enter JORDAN.
                  Lieutenant of the ordnance,
Tobacco and pipes.

Tip. Who's that ? Old Jordan ! good.

A comely vessel, and a necessary.
New scour'd he is : Here's to thee, marshal Fly ;
In milk, my young Anon says.   [*Drinks.*
    Pierce. Cream of the grape,
That dropt from Juno's breasts and sprung the lily !
I can recite your fables, Fly. Here is, too,
The blood of Venus, mother of the rose !
                                    [*Music within.*
    Jor. The dinner is gone up.
    Jug. I hear the whistle.
    Jor. Ay, and the fidlers : We must all go wait.
    Pierce. Pox o' this waiting, quarter-master Fly.
    Fly. When chambermaids are sovereigns, wait
        their ladies ;
Fly scorns to breathe.—
    Peck. Or blow upon them, he.
    Pierce. Old parcel Peck, art thou there ? how now,
        lame !
    Peck. Yes faith : it is ill halting afore cripples ;
I have got a dash of a jade here, will stick by me.
    Pierce. O you have had some phant'sy, fellow Peck,
Some revelation——
    Peck. What ?
    Pierce. To steal the hay
Out of the racks again.
    Fly. I told him so,
When the guests' backs were turn'd.
    Pierce. Or bring his peck,
The bottom upwards, heap'd with oats ; and cry,
Here's the best measure upon all the road ! when,
You know, the guest put in his hand to feel,
And smell to the oats, that grated all his fingers
Upon the wood——
    Peck. Mum !
    Pierce. And found out your cheat.
    Peck. I have been in the cellar, Pierce.
    Pierce. You were then there,

Upon your knees, I do remember it,
To have the fact conceal'd.   I could tell more,
Soaping of saddles, cutting of horse-tails,
And cropping—pranks of ale, and hostelry——
   Fly. Which he cannot forget, he says, young knight,
No more than you can other deeds of darkness,
Done in the cellar.
   Tip. Well said, bold professor.
   Fer. We shall have some truth explain'd.
   Pierce. We are all mortal,
And have our visions.
   Peck. Truly, it seems to me,
That every horse has his whole peck, and tumbles
Up to the ears in litter.
   Fly. When, indeed,
There's no such matter, not a smell of provender.
   Fer. Not so much straw as would tie up a horse-
      tail.
   Fly. Nor any thing in the rack but two old cob-
      webs,
And so much rotten hay as had been a hen's nest.
   Trun. And yet he's ever apt to sweep the
      mangers !
   Fer. But puts in nothing.
   Pierce. These are fits and fancies.
Which you must leave, good Peck.
   Fly. And you must pray
It may be reveal'd to you at some times,
Whose horse you ought to cozen ; with what con-
      science ;
The how, and when : a parson's horse may suffer—
   Pierce. Whose master's double beneficed ; put in
      that.
   Fly. A little greasing in the teeth ; 'tis wholesome ;
And keeps him in a sober shuffle.
   Pierce. His saddle too
May want a stirrup.

Fly. And, it may be sworn,
His learning lay o' one side, and so broke it.
    Peck. They have ever oats in their cloke-bags, to
        affront us.
    Fly. And therefore 'tis an office meritorious,
To tithe such soundly.
    Pierce. And a grazier's may——
    Fer. O, they are pinching puckfists!
    Trun. And suspicious.
    Pierce. Suffer before the master's face, sometimes.
    Fly. He shall think he sees his horse eat half a
        bushel——
    Pierce. When the slight is, rubbing his gums with
        salt
Till all the skin come off, he shall but mumble,
Like an old woman that were chewing brawn,
And drop them out again.
    Tip. Well argued, cavalier.
    Fly. It may do well; and go for an example.
But, coz, have a care of understanding horses,
Horses with angry heels, nobility horses,
Horses that know the world; let them have meat
Till their teeth ake, and rubbing till their ribs
Shine like a wench's forehead: they are devils else,
Will look into your dealings.
    Peck. For mine own part,
The next I cozen of the pamper'd breed,
I wish he may be foundred.
    Fly. Foun-der-ed.
Prolate it right.
    Peck. And of all four, I wish it,
I love no crupper-compliments.
    Pierce. Whose horse was it?
    Peck. Why, master Burst's.
    Pierce. Is Bat Burst come?
    Peck. An hour
He has been here.

Tip. What Burst?

Pierce. Mas Bartolmew Burst.
One that hath been a citizen, since a courtier,
And now a gamester : hath had all his whirls,
And bouts of fortune, as a man would say,
Once a bat and ever a bat! a rere-mouse,
And bird of twilight, he has broken thrice.

Tip. Your better man, the Genoway proverb says:
Men are not made of steel.

Pierce. Nor are they bound
Always to hold.

Fly. Thrice honourable colonel,
Hinges will crack.

Tip. Though they be Spanish iron.

Pierce. He is a merchant still, adventurer,
At in-and-in; and is our thoroughfare's friend.

Tip. Who, Jug's?

Pierce. The same : and a fine gentleman
Was with him.

Peck. Master Huffle.

Pierce. Who, Hodge Huffle!

Tip. What's he?

Pierce. A cheater, and another fine gentleman,
A friend o' the chamberlain's, Jordan's.   Master
          Huffle,
He's Burst's protection.

Fly. Fights and vapours for him.

Pierce. He will be drunk so civilly——

Fly. So discreetly——

Pierce. And punctually! just at this hour.

Fly. And then
Call for his Jordan with that hum and state,
As if he piss'd the politics.

Pierce. And sup
With his tuft-taffata night gear, here, so silently!

Fly. Nothing but music.

Pierce. A dozen of bawdy songs.

Tip. And knows the general this?

Fly. O no, sir; *dormit,*
Dormit patronus still, the master sleeps.
They'll steal to bed.

Pierce. In private, sir, and pay
The fidlers with that modesty, next morning.

Fly. Take a *dejeune* of muskadel and eggs.

Pierce. And pack away in their trundling cheats,[5]
like gipsies.

Trun. Mysteries, mysteries, Ferret.

Fer. Ay, we see, Trundle,
What the great officers in an inn may do;
I do not say the officers of the Crown,
But the Light Heart.

Tip. I'll see the Bat and Huffle.

Fer. I have some business, sir, I crave your
pardon——

Tip. What?

Fer. To be sober.   [*Exit.*

Tip. Pox, go get you gone then.
Trundle shall stay.

Trun. No, I beseech you, colonel.
Your lordship has a mind to be drunk private,
With these brave gallants; I will step aside
Into the stables, and salute my mares.   [*Exit.*

Pierce. Yes, do, and sleep with them.—Let him
go, base whip-stock;
He is as drunk as a fish now, almost as dead.

Tip. Come, I will see the flicker-mouse, my Fly.
[*Exeunt.*

---

[5] *Trundling cheats.*] Among gypsies and professed beggars, the
cant term for carts or coaches.

SCENE II.   *Another Room in the Same, furnished
as a Tribunal, &c.*

Music.   Enter the Host, *ushering* PRUDENCE, *who
takes her seat of judicature, assisted by* lord BEAU-
FORT *and* lord LATIMER; *the* Nurse, FRANK, JUG,
JORDAN, TRUNDLE, *and* FERRET.

Prudence.

HERE set the hour ; but first produce the
parties ;
And clear the court: the time is now of price.
  Host. Jug, get you down, and, Trundle, get you up,
You shall be crier ; Ferret here, the clerk.
Jordan, smell you without, till the ladies call you ;
Take down the fidlers too, silence that noise,
Deep in the cellar, safe.
                    [*Exeunt* JUG, JORDAN, *and* Musicians.
  Pru. Who keeps the watch ?
  Host. Old Sheelinin, here, is the madam Tell-clock.
  Nurse. No fait' and trot', sweet maister, I shall
            sleep ;
I' fait', I shall.
  Lord B. I prithee do then, screech-owl.
She brings to mind the fable of the dragon,
That kept the Hesperian fruit.   Would I could
            charm her !
  Host. Trundle will do it with his hum.   Come,
            Trundle :
Precede him Ferret, in the form.
  Fer. Oyez, oyez, oyez.
  Trun. Oyez, oyez, oyez.
  Fer. Whereas there hath been awarded,——
  Trun. Whereas there hath, &c.

[*As* FERRET *proclaims,* TRUNDLE *repeats after
    him, at the breaks here, and through the
    rest of this scene.*

Fer. By the queen regent of love,——
In this high court of sovereignty,——
Two special hours of address,——
To Herbert Lovel, appellant,——
Against the lady Frampul, defendant.——
Herbert Lovel, come into the court,——
Make challenge to thy first hour,——
And save thee and thy bail,——
    Trun. And save thee, &c.

Enter LOVEL, *and ranges himself on the one side.*

Host. Lo, louting, where he comes into the court!
Clerk of the sovereignty, take his appearance,
And how accoutred, how design'd he comes!
    Fer. 'Tis done. Now, crier, call the lady Frampul,
And by the name of
        Frances, lady Frampul, defendant,——
    Trun. Frances, lady Frampul, &c.
    Fer. Come into the court,——
Make answer to the award,——
And save thee and thy bail,——
    Trun. And save thee, &c.

Enter lady FRAMPUL, *and takes her place on the
        other side.*

Host. She makes a noble and a just appearance.
Set it down likewise, and how arm'd she comes.
    Pru. Usher of Love's court, give them [both] their
        oath,
According to the form, upon Love's missal.
    Host. Arise, and lay your hands upon the book.

Herbert **Lovel**, *appellant,* **and lady** *Frances Frampul, defendant,* **you** *shall* **swear** *upon the liturgy of*

Love, Ovid de arte amandi, *that you neither have, ne will have, nor in any wise bear about you, thing, or things, pointed, or blunt, within these lists, other than what are natural and allow'd by the court: no in-chanted arms, or weapons, stones of virtue, herb of grace, charm, character, spell, philtre, or other power than Love's only, and the justness of your cause. So help you Love, his mother, and the contents of this book: kiss it.*[6]   [Lov. kisses the book.

Return unto your seats.—Crier, bid silence.

    Trun. Oyez, oyez, oyez, oyez.

    Fer. In the name of the sovereign of Love,—

    Trun. In the name of the, &c.

    Fer. Notice is given by the court,——

To the appellant, and defendant,——

That the first hour of address proceeds,——

And Love save the sovereign,——

    Trun. And Love save, &c.

Every man or woman keep silence, pain of imprison-
    ment.

    Pru. Do your endeavours in the name of Love.

    Lov. To make my first approaches, then, in love.

    Lady F. Tell us what love is, that we may be sure
There's such a thing, and that it is in nature.

    Lov. Excellent lady, I did not expect
To meet an infidel, much less an atheist,
Here in Love's list! of so much unbelief
To raise a question of his being!

    Host. Well charged!

    Lov. I rather thought, and with religion think,
Had all the characters of Love been lost,
His lines, dimensions, and whole signature
Razed and defaced, with dull humanity,

---

[6] This is a pretty correct copy (*mutatis mutandis*) of the oath taken in the lists, before the combatants were permitted to join battle.

That both his nature, and his essence, might
Have found their mighty instauration here ;
Here, where the confluence of fair and good
Meets to make up all beauty. For what else
Is love, but the most noble, pure affection
Of what is truly beautiful and fair,
Desire of union with the thing beloved ?

 Lord B. Have the assistants of the court their votes,
And writ of privilege, to speak them freely ?
 Pru. Yes, to assist, but not to interrupt.
 Lord B. Then I have read somewhere, that man
  and woman
Were, in the first creation, both one piece,
And being cleft asunder, ever since
Love was an appetite to be rejoin'd.
As for example——   [*Kisses* FRANK.
 Nurse. Cramo-cree! what mean'sh tou ?
 Lord B. Only to kiss and part.
 Host. So much is lawful.
 Lord L. And stands with the prerogative of Love's
  court.
 Lov. It is a fable of Plato's, in his banquet,
And utter'd there by Aristophanes.
 Host. 'Twas well remember'd here, and to good use.
But on with your description, what love is :
Desire of union with the thing beloved.
 Lov. I meant a definition. For I make
The efficient cause, what's beautiful and fair ;
The formal cause, the appetite of union :
The final cause, the union itself.
But larger if you'll have it ; by description,
It is a flame and ardour of the mind,
Dead, in the proper corps, quick in another's ;
Transfers the lover into the be-loved.
The he or she that loves, engraves or stamps
The idea of what they love, first in themselves :
Or like to glasses, so their minds take in

The forms of their beloved, and then reflect.
It is the likeness of affections,
Is both the parent and the nurse of love.
Love is a spiritual coupling of two souls,
So much more excellent, as it least relates
Unto the body; circular, eternal,
Not feign'd, or made, but born; and then so precious,
As nought can value it but itself; so free,
As nothing can command it but itself;
And in itself so round and liberal,
As where it favours, it bestows itself.

Lord B. And that do I; here my whole self I tender,
According to the practice of the court.

[*To* FRANK.

Nurse. Ay, 'tish a naughty practish, a lewd practish,
Be quiet man, dou shalt not leip her here.

Lord B. Leap her! I lip her, foolish queen at arms,
Thy blazon's false : wilt thou blaspheme thine office?

Lov. But we must take and understand this love,
Along still, as a name of dignity;
Not pleasure.

Host. Mark you that, my light young lord?

[*To* lord B.

Lov. True love hath no unworthy thought, no light,
Loose, unbecoming appetite, or strain,
But fixed, constant, pure, immutable.

Lord B. I relish not these philosophical feasts;
Give me a banquet of sense, like that of Ovid :
A form to take the eye; a voice mine ear;
Pure aromatic to my scent : a soft,
Smooth, dainty hand to touch; and for my taste,
Ambrosiac kisses to melt down the palate.

Lov. They are the earthly, lower form of lovers,
Are only taken with what strikes the senses;
And love by that loose scale. Although I grant,
We like what's fair and graceful in an object,
And, true, would use it, in the all we tend to,

Both of our civil and domestic deeds;
In ordering of an army, in our style,
Apparel, gesture, building, or what not:
All arts and actions do affect their beauty.
But put the case, in travel I may meet
Some gorgeous structure, a brave frontispiece,
Shall I stay captive in the outer court,
Surprised with that, and not advance to know
Who dwells there, and inhabiteth the house?
There is my friendship to be made, within,
With what can love me again: not with the walls,
Doors, windows, architraves, the frieze, and cornice.
My end is lost in loving of a face,
An eye, lip, nose, hand, foot, or other part,
Whose all is but a statue, if the mind
Move not, which only can make the return.
The end of love, is to have two made one
In will, and in affection, that the minds
Be first inoculated, not the bodies.

    Lord B. Give me the body, if it be a good one.
                           [*Kisses* FRANK.
    Frank. Nay, sweet, my lord, I must appeal the
        sovereign
For better quarter, if you hold your practice.
    Trun. Silence, pain of imprisonment! hear the court.
    Lov. The body's love is frail, subject to change,
And alters still with it; the mind's is firm,
One and the same, proceedeth first from weighing,
And well examining what is fair and good;
Then what is like in reason, fit in manners;
That breeds good-will: good-will desire of union.
So knowledge first begets benevolence,
Benevolence breeds friendship, friendship love:
And where it starts or steps aside from this,
It is a mere degenerous appetite,
A lost, oblique, depraved affection,
And bears no mark or character of love.

Lady F. How am I changed! by what alchemy
Of love, or language, am I thus translated!
His tongue is tipt with the philosopher's stone,
And that hath touched me through every vein!
I feel that transmutation of my blood,
As I were quite become another creature,
And all he speaks it is projection.
    Pru. Well feign'd, my lady: now her parts begin.
    Lord L. And she will act them subtily.
    Pru. She fails me else.
    Lov. Nor do they trespass within bounds of
        pardon,
That giving way, and license to their love,
Divest him of his noblest ornaments,
Which are his modesty and shamefacedness :
And so they do, that have unfit designs
Upon the parties they pretend to love.
For what's more monstrous, more a prodigy,
Than to hear me protest truth of affection
Unto a person that I would dishonour ?
And what's a more dishonour, than defacing
Another's good with forfeiting mine own ;
And drawing on a fellowship of sin ?
From note of which, though for a while, we may
Be both kept safe by caution, yet the conscience
Cannot be cleans'd : for what was hitherto
Call'd by the name of love, becomes destroy'd
Then, with the fact ; the innocency lost,
The bateing of affection soon will follow ;
And love is never true that is not lasting :
No more than any can be pure or perfect,
That entertains more than one object. *Dixi.*
    Lady F. O speak, and speak for ever! let mine
        ear
Be feasted still, and filled with this banquet !
No sense can ever surfeit on such truth,
It is the marrow of all lovers' tenets !

5   B B

Who hath read Plato, Heliodore, or Tatius,[7]
Sidney, D'Urfé, or all Love's fathers, like him?
He's there the Master of the Sentences,
Their school, their commentary, text, and gloss,
And breathes the true divinity of love!

 Pru. Excellent actor, how she hits this passion!
 Lady F. Where have I lived, in heresy, so long
Out of the congregation of Love,
And stood irregular, by all his canons?
 Lord L. But do you think she plays?
 Pru. Upon my sovereignty;
Mark her anon.
 Lord L. I shake, and am half jealous.
 Lady F. What penance shall I do to be received,
And reconciled to the church of Love?
Go on procession, barefoot, to his image,
And say some hundred penitential verses,
There, out of Chaucer's Troilus and Cressid?

---

[7] *Who hath read Heliodore or Tatius, &c.*] Heliodorus was bishop of Tricca, in Thessaly, and author of the *Loves of Theagenes and Chariclea*, a romance in Greek, and the parent of a countless family. Achilles Tatius is known as the writer of the *Loves of Clitipho and Leucippe*, an imitation of the former, not altogether without merit, though far inferior to it. The *Master of the Sentences* (mentioned in the next line) is Peter Lombard, scholar of the celebrated Abelard, and once little less celebrated himself for a work called *Four Books of Sentences*, containing the very essence of Theology, &c. *D'Urfé* was a voluminous pastoral and amatory writer; but is, or rather was, better known as the author of the "Divine Astrea." Honoré d'Urfé was born at Marseilles about the middle of the 16th century. He was of a noble family and seems to have been intended for the church. A marriage, unfortunate in all its circumstances, drove him into retirement, where he found leisure, and what was less to be expected, inclination, to compose his *Astrée.* This pastoral romance, in five huge volumes, which once formed the delight of our grandmothers, and which bears a remote or allegorical allusion to the gallantries of the court of Hen. IV. is now never heard of, and would, in fact, exhaust the patience and weary the curiosity of the most ardent and indefatigable devourer of novels, at a watering-place or a boarding-school. D'Urfé died in 1625. Sidney's *Arcadia* has been noticed before.

Or to his mother's shrine, vow a wax-candle
As large as the town May-pole is, and pay it?
Enjoin me any thing this court thinks fit,
For I have trespass'd, and blasphemed Love:
I have, indeed, despised his deity,
Whom (till this miracle wrought on me) I knew not.
Now I adore Love, and would kiss the rushes
That bear this reverend gentleman, his priest,
If that would expiate——but I fear it will not.
For, though he be somewhat struck in years, and old
Enough to be my father, he is wise,
And only wise men love, the other covet.
I could begin to be in love with him,[8]
But will not tell him yet, because I hope
To enjoy the other hour with more delight,
And prove him farther.
   Pru. Most Socratic lady,
Or, if you will ironic! give you joy
Of your Platonic love here, master Lovel!
But pay him his first kiss yet, in the court,
Which is a debt, and due: for the hour's run.
   Lady F. How swift is time, and slily steals away
From them would hug it, value it, embrace it!
I should have thought it scarce had run ten minutes,
When the whole hour is fled. Here, take your kiss, sir,
Which I most willingly tender you in court.
                        [Kisses Lov.
   Lord B. And we do imitate.   *[Kisses* FRANK.
   Lady F. And I could wish,
It had been twenty—so the sovereign's
Poor narrow nature had decreed it so——
But that is past, irrevocable, now:
She did her kind, according to her latitude——
   Pru. Beware you do not conjure up a spirit

----

[8] I could begin to be in love with *him*,] i. e. with Lovel; she had
been speaking before, of the host. All this is said aside.

You cannot lay.

Lady F. I dare you, do your worst :
Shew me but such an injustice ; I would thank you
To alter your award.

Lord L. Sure she is serious !
I shall have another fit of jealousy,
I feel a grudging.

Host. Cheer up, noble guest,
We cannot guess what this may come to yet ;
The brain of man or woman is uncertain.

Lov. Tut, she dissembles ; all is personated,
And counterfeit comes from her ! if it were not,
The Spanish monarchy, with both the Indies,
Could not buy off the treasure of this kiss,
Or half give balance for my happiness.

Host. Why, as it is yet, it glads my Light Heart
To see you rouzed thus from a sleepy humour
Of drowsy, accidental melancholy ;
And all those brave parts of your soul awake,
That did before seem drown'd, and buried in you.
That you express yourself, as you had back'd
The Muses' horse, or got Bellerophon's arms—

Enter FLY.

What news with Fly ?

Fly. News of a newer lady,
A finer, fresher, braver, bonnier beauty,
A very bona-roba, and a bouncer,
In yellow, glistering, golden satin.

Lady F. Prue,
Adjourn the court.

Pru. Cry, Trundle.

Trun. Oyez,
Any man, or woman, that hath any personal attend-
        ance
To give unto the court; keep the second hour,
And Love save the sovereign !   [*Exeunt.*

ACT IV.

Scene I. *A Room in the Inn.*

Enter Jug, Barnaby, *and* Jordan.

Jug.

BARNABY!

Jor. Welcome, Barnaby! where hast thou
    been?

Bar. In the foul weather.

Jug. Which has wet thee, Barnaby.

Bar. As dry as a chip! Good Jug, a cast of thy
    name,

As well as thy office : two jugs.

Jug. By and by.   *[Exit.*

Jor. What lady's this thou hast brought here?

Bar. A great lady!

I know no more; one that will try you, Jordan;

She'll find your gage, your circle, your capacity.

How does old Staggers the smith, and Tree the
    sadler?

Keep they their penny club still?

Jor. And the old catch too,

Of *Whoop-Barnaby!*

Bar. Do they sing at me?

Jor. They are reeling at it in the parlour now.

Re-enter Jug *with wine.*

Bar. I'll to them : give me a drink first. [*Drinks.*

Jor. Where's thy hat?

Bar. I lost it by the way—Give me another.

Jug. A hat!

Bar. A drink.   [*Drinks.*

Jug. Take heed of taking cold, Bar——

Bar. The wind blew't off at Highgate, and my lady
Would not endure me light to take it up;
But made me drive bareheaded in the rain.

Jor. That she might be mistaken for a countess? [9]

Bar. Troth, like enough: she might be an o'er-
        grown dutchess,
For aught I know.

Jug. What, with one man!

Bar. At a time,
They carry no more, the best of them.

Jor. Nor the bravest.

Bar. And she is very brave.

Jor. A stately gown
And petticoat, she has on!

Bar. Have you spied that, Jordan?
You are a notable peerer, an old rabbi,
At a smock's hem, boy.

Jug. As he is chamberlain,
He may do that by his place.

Jor. What is her squire?

Bar. A toy, that she allows eight-pence a day,
A slight mannet, to port her up and down:
Come, shew me to my play-fellows, old Staggers,
And father Tree.

Jor. Here, this way, Barnaby.   [*Exeunt.*

---

[9]   *But made me drive* bareheaded *in the rain.*
          That she might be mistaken for a countess.] See p. 55.

SCENE II. *The Court of the Inn.*

Enter TIPTO, BURST, HUFFLE, *and* FLY.

Tipto.

COME, let us take in fresco, here, one quart.
    Burst. Two quarts, my man of war, let's not
        be stinted.
    Huf. Advance three Jordans, varlet of the house.
    Tip. I do not like your Burst, bird; he is saucy:
Some shop-keeper he was?
    Fly. Yes, sir.
    Tip. I knew it,
A broke-wing'd shop-keeper? I nose them straight.
He had no father, I warrant him, that durst own him;
Some foundling in a stall, or the church-porch;
Brought up in the hospital;[1] and so bound prentice;
Then master of a shop; then one o' the inquest;
Then breaks out bankrupt, or starts alderman:
The original of both is a church-porch——
    Fly. Of some, my colonel.
    Tip. Good faith, of most
Of your shop citizens: they are rude animals!
And let them get but ten mile out of town,
They out-swagger all the wapentake.
    Fly. What's that?
    Tip. A Saxon word to signify the hundred.
    Burst. Come, let us drink, sir Glorious, some brave
        health
Upon our tip-toes.
    Tip. To the health of the Bursts.

----

[1] *Some foundling*
    Brought up in the hospital, *&c.*] i. e. in Christ's hospital. See
vol. i. p. 39.

Burst. Why Bursts?
Tip. Why Tiptos?
Burst. O, I cry you mercy!
Tip. It is sufficient.
Huf. What is so sufficient?
Tip. To drink to you is sufficient.
Huf. On what terms?
Tip. That you shall give security to pledge me.
Huf. So you will name no Spaniard, I will pledge
 you.
Tip. I rather choose to thirst, and will thirst ever,
Than leave that cream of nations uncried up.
Perish all wine, and gust of wine!

 [*Throws the wine at him.*

Huf. How! spill it?
Spill it at me? [2]
Tip. I reck not; but I spilt it.
Fly. Nay, pray you be quiet, noble bloods.
Burst. No Spaniards,
I cry, with my cousin Huffle.
Huf. Spaniards! pilchers.

---

 [2] *Spill it at me?*] This vapour of a drunken bully, is set down
by the commentators as a *sneer* at Shakspeare. That Shakspeare
meant to raise a laugh at the practice of biting the thumb as an in-
citement to quarrel (which is noticed by many of our old writers)
is clear; but who, that is not warped by prejudice can see any propensity to "ridicule" the incident here. One drunkard flings his
glass in the face of another, and when questioned whether the insult was designed, professes that it was, and that he is indifferent
as to the consequences. In *Romeo and Juliet*, the dialogue is purely
comic; in this place it is serious. As well might the critics maintain that, when Barnaby in the preceding page says, "Do they
sing at me?" he intended a burlesque upon the same passage.
"*Vixere fortes ante Agamemnona*," and others, besides Shakspeare,
had undoubtedly eyes and ears for the fantastic and apish humours
of the times. Whalley, whose copy of this play is full of errors,
reads above, "I reck not, but I *spill* it:" and Steevens and Malone
gladly follow him, as the corruption is in favour of the imaginary
allusion to Shakspeare.

Tip. Do not provoke my patient blade ; it sleeps,
And would not hear thee : Huffle, thou art rude,
And dost not know the Spanish composition.
   Burst. What is the recipe ? name the ingredients.
   Tip. Valour.
   Burst. Two ounces !
   Tip. Prudence.
   Burst. Half a dram !
   Tip. Justice.
   Burst. A pennyweight !
   Tip. Religion.
   Burst. Three scruples !
   Tip. And of gravidàd.
   Burst. A face-full.
   Tip. He carries such a dose of it in his looks,
Actions and gestures, as it breeds respect
To him from savages, and reputation
With all the sons of men.
   Burst. Will it give him credit
With gamesters, courtiers, citizens, or tradesmen ?
   Tip. He'll borrow money on the stroke of his beard,
Or turn of his mustaccio ! his mere cuello,
Or ruff about his neck, is a bill of exchange
In any bank in Europe : not a merchant
That sees his gait, but straight will furnish him
Upon his pace.
   Huf. I have heard the Spanish name
Is terrible to children in some countries ;
And used to make them eat their bread and butter,
Or take their worm-seed.
   Tip. Huffle, you do shuffle.

Enter STUFF, *and* PINNACIA *his wife richly habited.*

   Burst. 'Slid, here's a lady !
   Huf. *And a lady gay !*
   Tip. A well-trimm'd lady !
   Huf. Let us lay her aboard.

Burst. Let's hail her first.

Tip. By your sweet favour, lady.

Stuff. Good gentlemen be civil, we are strangers.

Burst. An you were Flemings, sir——

Huf. Or Spaniards——

Tip. They are here, have been at Sevil in their
    days,
And at Madrid too.

Pin. He is a foolish fellow,
I pray you mind him not, he is my Protection.

Tip. In your protection he is safe, sweet lady.
So shall you be in mine.

Huf. A share, good colonel.

Tip. Of what?

Huf. Of your fine lady: I am Hodge,
My name is Huffle.

Tip. Huffling Hodge, be quiet.

Burst. And I pray you, be you so, glorious colonel;
Hodge Huffle shall be quiet.

Huf. [singing.] *A lady, gay, gay:*
For she is a lady gay, gay, gay. For she is a lady gay.

Tip. Bird of the vespers, vespertilio Burst,
You are a gentleman of the first head;
But that head may be broke, as all the body is—
Burst, if you tie not up your Huffle quickly.

Huf. Tie dogs, not men.

Burst. Nay, pray thee, Hodge, be still.

Tip. This steel here rides not on this thigh in vain.

Huf. Shew'st thou thy steel and thigh, thou
    glorious dirt!
Then Hodge sings Samson, and no ties shall hold.

[*They fight.*

Enter PIERCE, JUG, *and* JORDAN.

Pierce. Keep the peace, gentlemen: what do you
    mean?

Tip. I will not discompose myself for Huffle.

[*Exeunt all (but* STUFF *and* PIN.) *fighting.*

Pin. You see what your entreaty and pressure still
Of gentlemen, to be civil, doth bring on :
A quarrel, and perhaps man-slaughter.   You
Will carry your goose about you still, your planing-
      iron !
Your tongue to smooth all ! is not here fine stuff !
    Stuff.. Why, wife ?
    Pin. Your wife ! have not I forbidden you that ?
Do you think I'll call you husband in this gown,
Or any thing, in that jacket, but Protection ?
Here, tie my shoe, and shew my velvet petticoat,
And my silk stocking.   Why do you make me a lady,
If I may not do like a lady in fine clothes ?
    Stuff. Sweet heart, you may do what you will with
      me.
    Pin. Ay, I knew that at home ; what to do with
      you ;
But why was I brought hither ? to see fashions ?
    Stuff. And wear them too, sweet heart ; but this
      wild company——
    Pin. Why do you bring me in wild company ?
You'd have me tame and civil, in wild company !
I hope I know wild company are fine company,
And in fine company, where I am fine myself,
A lady may do any thing, deny nothing
To a fine party, I have heard you say it.

Re-enter PIERCE.

    Pierce. There are a company of ladies above
Desire your ladyship's company, and to take
The surety of their lodgings from the affront
Of these half beasts were here e'en now, the Centaurs.
    Pin. Are they fine ladies ?
    Pierce. Some very fine ladies.
    Pin. As fine as I ?
    Pierce. I dare use no comparisons,
Being a servant, sent——

Pin. Spoke like a fine fellow!
I would thou wert one; I'd not then deny thee :
But, thank thy lady.   [*Exit* PIERCE.

Enter Host.

Host. Madam, I must crave you
To afford a lady a visit, would excuse
Some harshness of the house, you have received
From the brute guests.
    Pin. This is a fine old man!
I'd go with him an he were a little finer.
    Stuff. You may, sweet heart, it is mine host.
    Pin. Mine host!
    Host. Yes, madam, I must bid you welcome.
    Pin. Do then.
    Stuff. But do not stay.
    Pin. I'll be advised by you! yes.   [*Exeunt.*

SCENE III.—*A Room in the same.*

Enter lord LATIMER, lord BEAUFORT, lady FRAMPUL,
    PRUDENCE, FRANK, *and* Nurse.

Lord Latimer.

WHAT more than Thracian barbarism was this?
        Lord B. The battle of the Centaurs with
            the Lapithes!
    Lady F. There is no taming of the monster, Drink.
    Lord L. But what a glorious beast our Tipto
        shew'd!
He would not discompose himself, the don!
Your Spaniard ne'er doth discompose himself.
        Lord B. Yet, how he talk'd, and roar'd in the
            beginning!
        Pru. And ran as fast as a knock'd marrow-bone.

Lord B. So they did all at last, when Lovel went
    down,
And chased them 'bout the court.
    Lord L. For all's don Lewis,
Or fencing after Euclid.
    Lady F. I ne'er saw
A lightning shoot so, as my servant did,
His rapier was a meteor, and he waved it
Over them, like a comet, as they fled him.
I mark'd his manhood ! every stoop he made
Was like an eagle's at a flight of cranes :
As I have read somewhere.
    Lord B. Bravely exprest.
    Lord L. And like a lover.
    Lady F. Of his valour, I am.
He seem'd a body rarified to air ;
Or that his sword, and arm were of a piece,
They went together so !—Here comes the lady.

Enter Host, *with* PINNACIA.

    Lord B. A bouncing bona-roba! as the Fly said.
    Frank. She is some giantess : I will stand off,
For fear she swallow me.
    Lady F. Is not this our gown, Prue,
That I bespoke of Stuff?
    Pru. It is the fashion.
    Lady F. Ay, and the silk; feel: sure it is the same!
    Pru. And the same petticoat, lace and all!
    Lady F. I'll swear it.
How came it hither ? make a bill of enquiry.
    Pru. You have a fine suit on, madam, and a rich
    one.
    Lady F. And of a curious making.
    Pru. And a new.
    Pin. As new as day.
    Lord L. She answers like a fish-wife.
    Pin. I put it on since noon, I do assure you.

Pru. Who is your tailor?

Lady F. Pray you, your fashioner's name?

Pin. My fashioner is a certain man of mine own;
He is in the house : no matter for his name.

Host. O, but to satisfy this bevy of ladies,
Of which a brace, here, long'd to bid you welcome.

Pin. He is one, in truth, I title my Protection :
Bid him come up.

Host. [*calls.*] Our new lady's Protection!
What is your ladyship's style?

Pin. Countess Pinnacia.

Host. Countess Pinnacia's man, come to your lady!

Enter STUFF.

Pru. Your ladyship's tailor! master Stuff!

Lady F. How, Stuff!
He the Protection!

Host. Stuff looks like a remnant.

Stuff. I am undone, discover'd. [*Falls on his knees.*

Pru. 'Tis the suit, madam,
Now, without scruple : and this some device
To bring it home with.

Pin. Why upon your knees?
Is this your lady godmother?

Stuff. Mum, Pinnacia.
It is the lady Frampul ; my best customer.

Lady F. What shew is this that you present us
　　with?

Stuff. I do beseech your ladyship, forgive me ;
She did but say the suit on.

Lady F. Who? which she?

Stuff. My wife, forsooth.

Lady F. How! mistress Stuff, your wife!
Is that the riddle?

Pru. We all look'd for a lady,
A dutchess, or a countess at the least.

Stuff. She's my own lawfully begotten wife,

In wedlock : we have been coupled now seven years.
   Lady F. And why thus mask'd ? you like a foot-
      man, ha !
And she your countess !
   Pin. To make a fool of himself,
And of me too.
   Stuff. I pray thee, Pinnace, peace.
   Pin. Nay, it shall out, since you have call'd me
      wife,
And openly dis-ladied me : Though I am dis-
      countess'd
I am not yet dis-countenanced.   These shall see.
   Host. Silence !
   Pin. It is a foolish trick, madam, he has ;
For though he be your tailor, he is my beast :
I may be bold with him, and tell his story.
When he makes any fine garment will fit me,
Or any rich thing that he thinks of price,
Then must I put it on, and be his countess,
Before he carry it home unto the owners.
A coach is hired, and four horse ; he runs
In his velvet jacket thus, to Rumford, Croydon,
Hounslow, or Barnet, the next bawdy road :
And takes me out, carries me up, and throws me
Upon a bed——
   Lady F. Peace, thou immodest woman !—
She glories in the bravery of the vice.
   Lord L. It is a quaint one.
   Lord B. A fine species
Of fornicating with a man's own wife,
Found out by—what's his name ?
   Lord L. Master Nic. Stuff.
   Host. The very figure of pre-occupation
In all his customers' best clothes.
   Lord L. He lies
With his own succuba, in all your names.
   Lord B. And all your credits.

Host. Ay, and at all their costs.

Lord L. This gown was then bespoken for the
    sovereign ?

Lord B. Ay, marry was it.

Lord L. And a main offence
Committed 'gainst the sovereignty ; being not brought
Home in the time : beside, the profanation
Which may call on the censure of the court.

Host. Let him be blanketted. Call up the
    quarter-master.
Deliver him o'er to Fly.

Enter FLY.

Stuff. O good, my lord.

Host. Pillage the Pinnace.

Lady F. Let his wife be stript.

Lord B. Blow off her upper deck.

Lord L. Tear all her tackle.

Lady F. Pluck the polluted robes over her ears ;
Or cut them all to pieces, make a fire of them.

Pru. To rags and cinders burn th' idolatrous
    vestures.

Host. Fly, and your fellows, see that the whole
    censure
Be thoroughly executed.

Fly. We'll toss him bravely,
Till the Stuff stink again.

Host. And send her home,
Divested to her flannel, in a cart.

Lord L. And let her footman beat the bason afore
    her.[3]

---

[3] *And let her footman* beat the bason *afore her.*] When bawds and
other infamous persons were carted, a mob of people used to precede them *beating basons*, and other utensils of the same kind, to
make the noise and tumult the bigger. Thus in the *Silent Woman*,
Morose, amongst other execrations on the barber Cutbeard, says,
"Let there be no bawd carted that year, to employ a *bason* of his."
WHAL.

Fly. The court shall be obey'd.
Host. Fly, and his officers,
Will do it fiercely.
Stuff. Merciful queen Prue!
Pru. I cannot help you.
          [*Exit* FLY, *with* STUFF *and* PINNACIA.
Lord B. Go thy ways, Nic. Stuff,
Thou hast nickt it for a fashioner of venery.
Lord L. For his own hell! though he run ten
          mile for it.
Pru. O, here comes Lovel, for his second hour.
Lord B. And after him the type of Spanish valour.

Enter LOVEL *with a paper, followed by* TIPTO.

Lady F. Servant, what have you there?
Lov. A meditation,
Or rather a vision, madam, and of beauty,
Our former subject.
Lady F. Pray you let us hear it.

> Lov. *It was a beauty that I saw*
> *So pure, so perfect, as the frame*
> *Of all the universe was lame,*
> *To that one figure, could I draw,*
> *Or give least line of it a law!*
>
> *A skein of silk without a knot,*
> *A fair march made without a halt,*
> *A curious form without a fault,*
> *A printed book without a blot,*
> *All beauty, and without a spot!*

Lady F. They are gentle words, and would deserve
          a note,
Set to them, as gentle.
Lov. I have tried my skill,
To close the second hour, if you will hear them;

5   C C

My boy by that time will have got it perfect.
    Lady F. Yes, gentle servant. In what calm he
        speaks,
After this noise and tumult, so unmoved,
With that serenity of countenance,
As if his thoughts did acquiesce in that
Which is the object of the second hour,
And nothing else.
    Pru. Well then, summon the court.
    Lady F. I have a suit to the sovereign of Love,
If it may stand with the honour of the court,
To change the question but from love to valour,
To hear it said, but what true valour is,
Which oft begets true love.
    Lord L. It is a question
Fit for the court to take true knowledge of,
And hath my just assent.
    Pru. Content.
    Lord B. Content.
    Frank. Content. I am content, give him his oath.

    Host. *Herbert Lovel, Thou shalt swear upon the Testament of Love,*[4] *to make answer to this question propounded to thee by the court. What true valour is? and therein to tell the truth, the whole truth, and nothing but the truth. So help thee Love, and thy bright sword at need.*

    Lov. So help me, Love, and my good sword at need.
It is the greatest virtue, and the safety
Of all mankind, the object of it is danger.
A certain mean 'twixt fear and confidence :
No inconsiderate rashness, or vain appetite
Of false encountering formidable things ;
But a true science of distinguishing

---

    [4] *The* Testament of Love.] A treatise in three books, written by Chaucer, in imitation of *Boetius de Consolatione Philosophiæ.*

What's good or evil.   It springs out of reason,
And tends to perfect honesty, the scope
Is always honour, and the public good :
It is no valour for a private cause.
    Lord B. No! not for reputation?
    Lov. That's man's idol,
Set up 'gainst God, the maker of all laws,
Who hath commanded us we should not kill ;
And yet we say, we must for reputation.
What honest man can either fear his own,
Or else will hurt another's reputation?
Fear to do base unworthy things, is valour ;
If they be done to us, to suffer them,
Is valour too.   The office of a man
That's truly valiant, is considerable,
Three ways : the first is in respect of matter,
Which still is danger ; in respect of form,
Wherein he must preserve his dignity ;
And in the end, which must be ever lawful.
    Lord L. But men, when they are heated, and in
        passion,
Cannot consider.
    Lov. Then it is not valour.
I never thought an angry person valiant :
Virtue is never aided by a vice.
What need is there of anger and of tumult ;
When reason can do the same things, or more?
    Lord B. O yes, 'tis profitable, and of use ;
It makes us fierce, and fit to undertake.
    Lov. Why, so will drink make us both bold and
        rash,
Or phrensy if you will : do these make valiant?
They are poor helps, and virtue needs them not.
No man is valianter by being angry,
But he that could not valiant be without :
So that it comes not in the aid of virtue,
But in the stead of it.

Lord L. He holds the right.

Lov. And 'tis an odious kind of remedy,
To owe our health to a disease.

Tip. If man
Should follow the *dictamen* of his passion,
He could not 'scape——

Lord B. To discompose himself.

Lord L. According to don Lewis!

Host. Or Caranza!

Lov. Good colonel Glorious, whilst we treat of
    valour,
Dismiss yourself.

Lord L. You are not concern'd.

Lov. Go drink,
And congregate the hostlers and the tapsters,
The under-officers of your regiment;
Compose with them, and be not angry valiant.
                                    [*Exit* TIPTO.

Lord B. How does that differ from true valour?

Lov. Thus.
In the efficient, or that which makes it:
For it proceeds from passion, not from judgment:
Then brute beasts have it, wicked persons; there
It differs in the subject; in the form,
'Tis carried rashly, and with violence:
Then in the end, where it respects not truth,
Or public honesty, but mere revenge.
Now confident, and undertaking valour,
Sways from the true, two other ways, as being
A trust in our own faculties, skill, or strength,
And not the right, or conscience of the cause,
That works it: then in the end, which is the victory,
And not the honour.

Lord B. But the ignorant valour,
That knows not why it undertakes, but doth it
To escape the infamy merely——

Lov. Is worst of all:

That valour lies in the eyes o' the lookers on ;
And is call'd valour with a witness.
   Lord B. Right.
   Lov. The things true valour's exercised about,
Are poverty, restraint, captivity,
Banishment, loss of children, long disease :
The least is death.   Here valour is beheld,
Properly seen ; about these it is present :
Not trivial things, which but require our confidence.
And yet to those we must object ourselves,
Only for honesty ; if any other
Respects be mixt, we quite put out her light.
And as all knowledge, when it is removed,
Or separate from justice, is call'd craft,
Rather than wisdom ; so a mind affecting,
Or undertaking dangers, for ambition,
Or any self-pretext, not for the public,
Deserves the name of daring, not of valour.
And over-daring is as great a vice,
As over-fearing.
   Lord L. Yes, and often greater.
   Lov. But as it is not the mere punishment,
But cause that makes a martyr, so it is not
Fighting, or dying, but the manner of it,
Renders a man himself.   A valiant man
Ought not to undergo, or tempt a danger,
But worthily, and by selected ways :
He undertakes with reason, not by chance.
His valour is the salt to his other virtues,
They are all unseason'd without it.   The waiting-
      maids,
Or the concomitants of it, are his patience,
His magnanimity, his confidence,
His constancy, security, and quiet ;
He can assure himself against all rumour,
Despairs of nothing, laughs at contumelies,
As knowing himself advanced in a height

Where injury cannot reach him, nor aspersion
Touch him with soil!
 Lady F. Most manly utter'd all!
As if Achilles had the chair in valour,
And Hercules were but a lecturer.
Who would not hang upon those lips for ever,
That strike such music! I could run on them;
But modesty is such a school-mistress
To keep our sex in awe——
 Pru. Or you can feign;
My subtle and dissembling lady mistress.
 Lord L. I fear she means it, Prue, in too good
  earnest.
 Lov. The purpose of an injury 'tis to vex
And trouble me; now nothing can do that
To him that's valiant. He that is affected
With the least injury, is less than it.
It is but reasonable to conclude
That should be stronger still which hurts, than that
Which is hurt. Now no wickedness is stronger
Than what opposeth it: not Fortune's self,
When she encounters virtue, but comes off
Both lame and less! why should a wise man then
Confess himself the weaker, by the feeling
Of a fool's wrong? There may an injury
Be meant me. I may choose, if I will take it.
But we are now come to that delicacy,
And tenderness of sense, we think an insolence
Worse than an injury, bear words worse than deeds;
We are not so much troubled with the wrong,
As with the opinion of the wrong; like children,
We are made afraid with visors: such poor sounds
As is the lie, or common words of spite,
Wise laws thought never worthy a revenge;
And 'tis the narrowness of human nature,
Our poverty, and beggary of spirit,
To take exception at these things. He laugh'd at me!

He broke a jest ! a third took place of me !
How most ridiculous quarrels are all these ?[5]
Notes of a queasy and sick stomach, labouring
With want of a true injury : the main part
Of the wrong, is our vice of taking it.
   Lord L. Or our interpreting it to be such.
   Lov. You take it rightly. If a woman, or child
Give me the lie, would I be angry ? no,
Not if I were in my wits, sure, I should think it
No spice of a disgrace. No more is theirs,
If I will think it, who are to be held
In as contemptible a rank, or worse.
I am kept out a masque, sometime thrust out,
Made wait a day, two, three, for a great word,
Which, when it comes forth, is all frown and forehead :
What laughter should this breed, rather than anger !
Out of the tumult of so many errors,
To feel with contemplation, mine own quiet !
If a great person do me an affront,
A giant of the time, sure I will bear it

   [5] *How most ridiculous quarrels are all these?*] It is not impro-
bable, that the zeal and good sense our author hath expressed
against the senseless and impious mode of duelling, so prevalent at
that time, might contribute to raise a party against him in order to
damn his play, which accounts for its want of success, when represented on the stage. WHAL.
   I am not of Whalley's mind. The play probably never reached
this scene on the stage ; as it seems scarcely possible that it should
have outlived the tedious uninteresting squabbles of colonel Tipto,
and his maudlin associates. With respect to the present debate,
indeed, too much cannot easily be said in its favour as a moral
dialogue, replete with the purest principles, and the most cogent
and convincing arguments: all however is glaringly out of time
and place, and when we consider the composition of the "court,"
in which it is produced, it is natural to ask, with one of the author's
acutest antagonists,

     " When was there ever laid
       Before a chambermaid,
       Discourse so weigh'd, as might have serv'd of old,
       For schools, when they of love and valour told ?"

Or out of patience, or necessity :
Shall I do more for fear, than for my judgment ?
For me now to be angry with Hodge Huffle,
Or Burst, his broken charge, if he be saucy,
Or our own type of Spanish valour, Tipto,
Who were he now necessitated to beg,
Would ask an alms, like Conde Olivares,[6]
Were just to make myself such a vain animal
As one of them.   If light wrongs touch me not,
No more shall great ; if not a few, not many.
There's nought so sacred with us but may find
A sacrilegious person, yet the thing is
No less divine, 'cause the profane can reach it.
He is shot-free, in battle, is not hurt,
Not he that is not hit : so he is valiant,
That yields not unto wrongs ; not he that 'scapes
        them.
They that do pull down churches, and deface
The holiest altars, cannot hurt the Godhead.
A calm wise man may shew as much true valour,
Amidst these popular provocations,
As can an able captain shew security
By his brave conduct, through an enemy's country.
A wise man never goes the people's way :
But as the planets still move contrary
To the world's motion ; so doth he, to opinion.
He will examine, if those accidents
Which common fame calls injuries, happen to him
Deservedly, or no ? Come they deservedly,
They are no wrongs then, but his punishments:
If undeservedly, and he not guilty,
The doer of them, first, should blush, not he.
    Lord L. Excellent !
    Lord B. Truth, and right !

    [6] *Would ask an alms like Conde Olivares.*]   This is character-
istic, and well expressed. Olivares was, at this time, prime minister
of Spain.

Frank. An oracle
Could not have spoken more !
    Lady F. Been more believed !
    Pru. The whole court runs into your sentence, sir :
And see your second hour is almost ended.
    Lady F. It cannot be ! O clip the wings of time,
Good Prue, or make him stand still with a charm.
Distil the gout into it, cramps, all diseases
To arrest him in the foot, and fix him here :
O, for an engine, to keep back all clocks,
Or make the sun forget his motion !—
If I but knew what drink the time now loved,
To set my Trundle at him, mine own Barnaby !
    Pru. Why, I'll consult our Shelee-nien Thomas.
                                 [Shakes her.

    Nurse. *Er grae Chreest.*
    Lord B. Wake her not.
    Nurse. *Tower cen cuppaw*
D'usque-bagh, doone.[7]
    Pru. Usquebaugh's her drink,
But 'twill not make the time drunk.
    Host. As it hath her.
Away with her, my lord, but marry her first.
                      [Exit Lord B. *with* FRANK.
    Pru. Ay,
That will be sport anon too for my lady,
But she hath other game to fly at yet.—
The hour is come, your kiss.
    Lady F. My servant's song, first.
    Pru. I say the kiss, first ; and I so enjoin'd it :
At your own peril, do, make the contempt.
    Lady F. Well, sir, you must be pay'd, and legally.
                            [Kisses LOVEL.
    Pru. Nay, nothing, sir, beyond.
    Lov. One more——I except.

---

    [7] *Tower, &c.*] " Hand me a cup of usquebaugh, man."

This was but half a kiss, and I would change it.
    Pru. The court's dissolv'd, removed, and the play
      ended,
No sound, or air of love more, I decree it.
    Lov. From what a happiness hath that one word
Thrown me into the gulph of misery!
To what a bottomless despair! how like
A court removing, or an ended play,
Shews my abrupt precipitate estate,
By how much more my vain hopes were increased
By these false hours of conversation!
Did not I prophesy this of myself,
And gave the true prognostics? O my brain,
How art thou turned! and my blood congeal'd,
My sinews slacken'd, and my marrow melted,
That I remember not where I have been,
Or what I am! only my tongue's on fire;
And burning downward, hurls forth coals and cinders,
To tell, this temple of love will soon be ashes!
Come, indignation, now, and be my mistress.
No more of Love's ungrateful tyranny;
His wheel of torture, and his pits of birdlime,
His nets of nooses, whirlpools of vexation,
His mills to grind his servants into powder——
I will go catch the wind first in a sieve,
Weigh smoak, and measure shadows; plough the
    water,
And sow my hopes there, ere I stay in love.
    Lord L. My jealousy is off, I am now secure.
                        [*Aside and exit.*
    Lov. Farewell the craft of crocodiles, women's piety,
And practice of it, in this art of flattering,
And fooling men! I have not lost my reason,
Though I have lent myself out for two hours,
Thus to be baffled by a chambermaid,
And the good actor, her lady, afore mine host
Of the Light Heart, here, that hath laugh'd at all—

Host. Who, I ?

Lov. Laugh on, sir, I'll to bed and sleep,
And dream away the vapour of love, if the house
And your leer drunkards let me.[8]

    [*Exeunt all but* lady F. PRUDENCE, *and* Nurse.

Lady F. Prue !

Pru. Sweet madam.

Lady F. Why would you let him go thus ?

Pru. In whose power
Was it to stay him, properer than my lady's ?

Lady F. Why, in your lady's ? are not you the
      sovereign ?

Pru. Would you in conscience, madam, have me vex
His patience more ?

Lady F. Not, but apply the cure,
Now it is vext.

Pru. That's but one body's work ;

---

[8] Lov. *I'll to bed and sleep,*
    If the house and your leer drunkards *let me.*] Though the
meaning of *leer* cannot very easily be settled, the expression seems
here, as well as in vol. iv. p. 349, to denote *noisy, laughing, roaring
drunkards.* WHAL.

I subjoin a further explanation of this word, by my learned friend,
Mr. Archdeacon Nares.

"*Leer* is used in the sense of *empty*, and particularly applied to
a horse without a rider, in which sense Skinner derives it from
Ɖelæn, Sax. Coles (Dict.) has *a leer horse*, Vacuus :

    ' But at the first encounter down he lay,
    The horse runs *leere* (empty) away, without the man.'
                    Harringt. Ariosto, 35, 64.

Hence *leer* horse meant also a *led* horse. In this sense, Ben
Jonson has applied it to a drunkard, as being *led* in the train of
another. *Bartholomew Fair, Induction,* and *New Inn*, Act iv. sc. 3."

The word is sufficiently common in every part of Devonshire, in
the sense of empty, as a "*leer* stomach," &c. In the *Exmoor
Courtship*, the *leer* is properly explained as "the *hollow* under the
ribs :" but I suspect that there is yet a sense of the word with which
we are not acquainted, and which chance or a wider scope of reading may one day bring to light. Meanwhile enough has been done
to render the poet at least intelligible.

Two cannot do the same thing handsomely.

    Lady F. But had not you the authority absolute?

    Pru. And were not you in rebellion, lady Frampul,
From the beginning?

    Lady F. I was somewhat froward,
I must confess, but frowardness sometime
Becomes a beauty, being but a visor
Put on. You'll let a lady wear her mask, Prue!

    Pru. But how do I know, when her ladyship is
        pleased
To leave it off, except she tell me so?

    Lady F. You might have known that by my looks,
        and language,
Had you been or regardant, or observant.
One woman reads another's character
Without the tedious trouble of deciphering,
If she but give her mind to't; you knew well,
It could not sort with any reputation
Of mine, to come in first, having stood out
So long, without conditions for mine honour.

    Pru. I thought you did expect none, you so jeer'd
        him,
And put him off with scorn.

    Lady F. Who, I, with scorn?
I did express my love to idolatry rather,
And so am justly plagued, not understood.

    Pru. I swear I thought you had dissembled, madam,
And doubt you do so yet.

    Lady F. Dull, stupid wench!
Stay in thy state of ignorance still, be damn'd,
An idiot chambermaid! Hath all my care,
My breeding thee in fashion, thy rich clothes,
Honour, and titles wrought no brighter effects
On thy dark soul, than thus? Well! go thy ways;
Were not the tailor's wife to be demolish'd,
Ruin'd, uncased, thou should'st be she, I vow.

    Pru. Why, take your spangled properties, your gown

And scarfs.   *[Tearing off her gown.*

    Lady F. Prue, Prue, what dost thou mean ?

    Pru. I will not buy this play-boy's bravery

At such a price, to be upbraided for it,

Thus, every minute.

    Lady F. Take it not to heart so.

    Pru. The tailor's wife ! there was a word of scorn !

    Lady F. It was a word fell from me, Prue, by

        chance.

    Pru. Good madam, please to undeceive yourself,

I know when words do slip, and when they are

        darted

With all their bitterness : *uncased, demolish'd !*

An *idiot chambermaid, stupid,* and *dull !*

Be *damn'd for ignorance !* I will be so ;

And think I do deserve it, that, and more,

Much more I do.

    Lady F. Here comes mine host : no crying,

Good Prue !—

                Re-enter Host.

              Where is my servant Lovel, host ?

    Host. You have sent him up to bed, would you

        would follow him,

And make my house amends !

    Lady F. Would you advise it ?

    Host. I would I could command it ! My light heart

Should leap till midnight.

    Lady F. Pray thee be not sullen,

I yet must have thy counsel. Thou shalt wear, Prue,

The new gown yet.

    Pru. After the tailor's wife !

    Lady F. Come, be not angry or grieved : I have

        a project.   *[Exeunt* lady F. *and* PRU.

    Host. Wake Shelee-nien Thomas ! is this your

        heraldry,

And keeping of records, to lose the main ?

Where is your charge ?
  Nurse. *Grae Chreest !*
  Host. Go ask the oracle
Of the bottle, at your girdle, there you lost it :
You are a sober setter of the watch !   [*Exeunt.*

ACT V.

Scene I. *A Room in the Inn.*

Enter Host *and* Fly.

Host.

OME, Fly and Legacy, the bird o' the
    Heart :
    Prime insect of the Inn, professor, quarter-
    master,
As ever thou deserved'st thy daily drink,
Padling in sack, and licking in the same,
Now shew thyself an implement of price,
And help to raise a nap to us out of nothing.—
Thou saw'st them married ?
  Fly. I do think I did,
And heard the words, *I Philip, take thee Lætice.*
I gave her too, was then the father Fly,
And heard the priest do his part, far as five nobles
Would lead him in the lines of matrimony.
  Host. Where were they married ?
  Fly. In the new stable.
  Host. Ominous !
I have known many a church been made a stable,
But not a stable made a church till now :

I wish them joy. Fly, was he a full priest?

Fly. He belly'd for it, had his velvet sleeves,
And his branch'd cassock, a side sweeping gown,[9]
All his formalities, a good cramm'd divine!
I went not far to fetch him, the next inn,
Where he was lodged, for the action.

Host. Had they a license?

Fly. License of love; I saw no other; and purse
To pay the duties both of church and house:
The angels flew about.

Host. Those birds send luck;
And mirth will follow. I had thought to have sacri-
    ficed
To merriment to-night in my Light Heart, Fly,
And like a noble poet, to have had
My last act best; but all fails in the plot.
Lovel is gone to bed; the lady Frampul
And sovereign Prue fall'n out: Tipto and his regi-
    ment
Of mine-men, all drunk dumb, from his whoop
    Barnaby,
To his hoop Trundle: they are his two tropics.
No project to rear laughter on, but this,
The marriage of lord Beaufort with Lætitia.
Stay, what is here? the satin gown redeem'd,
And Prue restored in't to her lady's grace!

Fly. She is set forth in't, rigg'd for some employ-
    ment!

Host. An embassy at least.

Fly. Some treaty of state.

Host. 'Tis a fine tack about; and worth the ob-
    serving.   [*They stand aside.*

---

[9] *And his* branch'd *cassock, a* side *sweeping gown,*] i. e. detached
sleeve ornaments, projecting from the shoulders of the gown. *Side*
is long, trailing, in which sense it often occurs in our old writers.
Lyndsay has a furious satire against the *side* tails of the ladies'
gowns, in Scotland.

Enter lady Frampul, *and* Prudence *magnificently dressed.*

Lady F. Sweet Prue, ay, now thou art a queen
    indeed !
These robes do royally, and thou becom'st them !
So they do thee ! rich garments only fit
The parties they are made for ; they shame others.
How did they shew on goody tailor's back ?
Like a caparison for a sow, God save us !
Thy putting 'em on hath purged and hallow'd them
From all pollution meant by the mechanics.
    Pru. Hang him, poor snip, a secular shop-wit !
He hath nought but his sheers to claim by, and his
        measures :
His prentice may as well put in for his needle,
And plead a stitch.
    Lady F. They have no taint in them
Now of the tailor.
    Pru. Yes, of his wife's hanches,
Thus thick of fat ; I smell them, of the say.
    Lady F. It is restorative, Prue : with thy but
        chafing it,
A barren hind's grease may work miracles.—
Find but his chamber-door, and he will rise
To thee ; or if thou pleasest, feign to be
The wretched party herself, and com'st unto him
In forma pauperis, to crave the aid
Of his knight-errant valour, to the rescue
Of thy distressed robes : name but thy gown,
And he will rise to that.
    Pru. I'll fire the charm first,
I had rather die in a ditch with mistress Shore,
Without a smock, as the pitiful matter has it,
Than owe my wit to clothes, or have it beholden.
    Host. Still spirit of Prue !
    Fly. And smelling of the sovereign !

Pru. No, I will tell him, as it is indeed ;
I come from the fine, froward, frampul lady,
One was run mad with pride, wild with self-love,
But late encountering a wise man who scorn'd her,
And knew the way to his own bed, without
Borrowing her warming-pan, she hath recover'd
Part of her wits ; so much as to consider
How far she hath trespass'd, upon whom, and how,
And now sits penitent and solitary,
Like the forsaken turtle, in the volary
Of the Light Heart, the cage, she hath abused,
Mourning her folly, weeping at the height
She measures with her eyes, from whence she is
      fall'n,
Since she did branch it on the top o' the wood.
    Lady F. I prithee, Prue, abuse me enough, that's
      use me
As thou think'st fit, any coarse way, to humble me,
Or bring me home again, or Lovel on :
Thou dost not know my sufferings, what I feel,
My fires and fears are met; I burn and freeze,
My liver's one great coal, my heart shrunk up
With all the fibres, and the mass of blood
Within me, is a standing lake of fire,
Curl'd with the cold wind of my gelid sighs,
That drive a drift of sleet through all my body,
And shoot a February through my veins.
Until I see him, I am drunk with thirst,
And surfeited with hunger of his presence.
I know not whêr I am, or no ;[1] or speak,
Or whether thou dost hear me.

---

[1] *I know not whêr I am, or no.*] A contraction of *whether ;* it occurs again in the *Epigrams :*

      " Who shall doubt, Donne, *whêr* I a poet be,
        When I dare send my epigrams to thee." *Epig.* 96.
                         WHAL.

It is frequently found thus contracted in Shakspeare.

5   D D

Pru. Spare expressions.
I'll once more venture for your ladyship,
So you will use your fortunes reverently.
　　Lady F. Religiously, dear Prue : Love and his
　　　　mother,
I'll build them several churches, shrines, and altars,
And over head, I'll have, in the glass windows,
The story of this day be painted, round,
For the poor laity of love to read :
I'll make myself their book, nay, their example,
To bid them take occasion by the forelock,
And play no after-games of love hereafter.
　　Host. [*coming forward with* Fly.] And here your
　　　　host and's Fly witness your vows,
And like two lucky birds, bring the presage
Of a loud jest ; lord Beaufort's married.
　　Lady F. Ha !
　　Fly. All to-be-married.
　　Pru. To whom, not your son ?
　　Host. The same, Prue.　If her ladyship could take
　　　　truce
A little with her passion, and give way
To their mirth now running——
　　Lady F. Runs it mirth ! let it come,
It shall be well received, and much made of it.
　　Pru. We must of this, it was our own conception.

　　　　Enter lord Latimer.

　　Lord L. Room for green rushes, raise the fidlers,
　　　　chamberlain,
Call up the house in arms !
　　Host. This will rouse Lovel.
　　Fly. And bring him on too.
　　Lord L. Sheelee-nien Thomas
Runs like a heifer bitten with the brize,
About the court, crying on Fly, and cursing.
　　Fly. For what, my lord ?

Lord L. You were best hear that from her,
It is no office, Fly, fits my relation.
Here come the happy couple !—

Enter lord BEAUFORT, FRANK, FERRET, JORDAN *and*
JUG, Fiddlers, Servants, *&c.*

Joy, lord Beaufort !
Fly. And my young lady too.
Host. Much joy, my lord !
Lord B. I thank you all ; I thank thee, father Fly.
Madam, my cousin, you look discomposed,
I have been bold with a sallad after supper,
Of your own lettice here.
Lady F. You have, my lord :
But laws of hospitality, and fair rites,
Would have made me acquainted.
Lord B. In your own house,
I do acknowledge ; else I much had trespass'd.
But in an inn, and public, where there is license
Of all community ; a pardon of course
May be sued out.
Lord L. It will, my lord, and carry it.
I do not see, how any storm or tempest
Can help it now.
Pru. The thing being done and past,
You bear it wisely, and like a lady of judgment.
Lord B. She is that, secretary Prue.
Pru. Why secretary,
My wise lord ? is your brain [too] lately married !
Lord B. Your reign is ended, Prue, no sovereign
    now :
Your date is out, and dignity expired.
Pru. I am annull'd ; how can I treat with Lovel,
Without a new commission ?
Lady F. Thy gown's commission.
Host. Have patience, Prue, expect, bid the lord joy.
Pru. And this brave lady too.   I wish them joy !

Pierce. Joy!

Jor. Joy!

Jug. All joy!

Host. Ay, the house full of joy.

Fly. Play the bells, fidlers, crack your strings with
  joy.   [*Music.*

Pru. But, lady Lætice, you shew'd a neglect
Un-to-be-pardon'd, to'ards my lady, your kinswoman,
Not to advise with her.

Lord B. Good politic Prue,
Urge not your state-advice, your after-wit;
'Tis near upbraiding. Get our bed ready, chamber-
  lain,
And host, a bride-cup; you have rare conceits,
And good ingredients; ever an old host,
Upon the road, has his provocative drinks.

Lord L. He is either a good bawd, or a physician.

Lord B. 'Twas well he heard you not, his back was
  turn'd.
A bed, the genial bed! a brace of boys,
To-night, I play for.

Pru. Give us points, my lord.[2]

Lord B. Here take them, Prue, my cod-piece point,
  and all.
I have clasps, my Lætice' arms; here take them,
  boys.   [*Throws off his doublet, &c.*
What, is the chamber ready? Speak, why stare you
On one another.

Jor. No, sir.

Lord B. And why no?

  [2] *Give us points.*] The fringe, or tagged laces with which the
breeches were fastened, or trussed (as the expression was) to the
doublet. These tags, which supplied the place of buttons, were
sometimes very costly, being formed of silver, gold, and occasionally
of precious stones, cornelians, agats, &c. To shew the impatience
of a bridegroom, it was a custom (not indeed of the most delicate
nature,) to tear them off, instead of untying them, and throw them,
to be scrambled for, amongst the guests.

Jor. My master has forbid it : he yet doubts,
That you are married.

Lord B. Ask his vicar-general,
His Fly, here.

Fly. I must make that good ; they are married.

Host. But I must make it bad, my hot young
  lord.—
Give him his doublet again, the air is piercing;
You may take cold, my lord. See whom you have
  married,
Your host's son, and a boy !

      [*Pulls off* FRANK'S *head-dress.*

Fly. You are abused.

Lady F. Much joy, my lord !

Pru. If this be your Lætitia,
She'll prove a counterfeit mirth, and a clipp'd lady.

Ser. A boy, a boy, my lord has married a boy !

Lord L. Raise all the house in shout and laughter,
  a boy !

Host. Stay, what is here ! peace, rascals, stop your
  throats.—

    Enter Nurse *hastily.*

Nurse. That maggot, worm, that insect ! O my
  child,
My daughter ! where's that Fly ? I'll fly in his face,
The vermin, let me come to him.

Fly. Why, nurse Sheelee ?

Nurse. Hang thee, thou parasite, thou son of
  crumbs
And orts, thou hast undone me, and my child,
My daughter, my dear daughter !

Host. What means this ?

Nurse. O sir, my daughter, my dear child is ruin'd,
By this your Fly, here, married in a stable,
And sold unto a husband.

Host. Stint thy cry,

Harlot, if that be all ; didst thou not sell him
To me for a boy, and brought'st him in boy's rags
Here to my door, to beg an alms of me ?
  Nurse. I did, good master, and I crave your pardon :
But 'tis my daughter, and a girl.
  Host. Why saidst thou
It was a boy, and sold'st him then to me
With such entreaty, for ten shillings, carlin ?
  Nurse. Because you were a charitable man,
I heard, good master, and would breed him well ;
I would have given him you for nothing gladly.
Forgive the lie of my mouth, it was to save
The fruit of my womb. A parent's needs are urgent,
And few do know that tyrant o'er good natures :
But you relieved her, and me too, the mother,
And took me into your house to be the nurse,
For which heaven heap all blessings on your head,
Whilst there can one be added.
  Host. Sure thou speak'st
Quite like another creature than thou hast lived
Here, in the house, a Sheelee-nien Thomas,
An Irish beggar.
  Nurse. So I am, God help me.
  Host. What art thou ? tell : the match is a good
        match,[3]
For aught I see ; ring the bells once again. [*Music.*
  Lord B. Stint, I say, fidlers.
  Lady F. No going off, my lord.

---

[3] *The match is a good match, &c.*] Something like this occurs
in the *Widow*, a comedy, said to be written by Fletcher, Middleton,
and our poet in conjunction: there, as here, a supposed male in
female habiliments is wooed and won, and much good mirth is
spoiled by the instantaneous discovery of the bride's sex.

  " *Vide.* Ha ! ha ! here they come, one man married to another,
    Val. How ! man to man?
    Muck. Why, this is my *daughter*, Martha."

  The *Widow* was not published during Jonson's life, though it appeared on the stage so early as 1618.

Lord B. Nor coming on, sweet lady, things thus
    standing.
Fly. But what's the heinousness of my offence,
Or the degrees of wrong you suffer'd by it?
In having your daughter match'd thus happily,
Into a noble house, a brave young blood,
And a prime peer of the realm?
Lord B. Was that your plot, Fly?
Give me a cloke, take her again among you.
I'll none of your Light Heart fosterlings, no inmates,
Supposititious fruits of an host's brain,
And his Fly's hatching, to be put upon me.
There is a royal court of the Star-chamber,
Will scatter all these mists, disperse these vapours,
And clear the truth: Let beggars match with
    beggars——
That shall decide it; I will try it there.
Nurse. Nay then, my lord, it's not enough, I see,
You are licentious, but you will be wicked.
You are not alone content to take my daughter,
Against the law; but having taken her,
You would repudiate and cast her off,
Now at your pleasure, like a beast of power,
Without all cause, or colour of a cause,
That, or a noble, or an honest man,
Should dare to except against, her poverty;
Is poverty a vice?
Lord B. The age counts it so.
Nurse. God help your lordship, and your peers
    that think so,
If any be: if not, God bless them all,
And help the number of the virtuous,
If poverty be a crime! You may object
Our beggary to us, as an accident,
But never deeper, no inherent baseness.
And I must tell you now, young lord of dirt,
As an incensed mother, she hath more,

And better blood, running in those small veins,
Than all the race of Beauforts [4] have in mass,
Though they distil their drops from the left rib
Of John o' Gaunt.

    Host. Old mother of records,
Thou know'st her pedigree then : whose daughter is
      she ?

    Nurse. The daughter and co-heir to the lord Frampul,
This lady's sister.

    Lady F. Mine ! what is her name ?

    Nurse. Lætitia.

    Lady F. That was lost !

    Nurse. The true Lætitia.

    Lady F. Sister, O gladness ! Then you are our
      mother ?

    Nurse. I am, dear daughter.

    Lady F. On my knees I bless
The light I see you by.

    Nurse. And to the author
Of that blest light, I ope my other eye,
Which hath almost, now, seven years been shut,
Dark as my vow was, never to see light,
Till such a light restored it, as my children,
Or your dear father, who, I hear, is not.

    Lord B. Give me my wife, I own her now, and
      will have her.

    Host. But you must ask my leave first, my young
      lord.
Leave is but light.—Ferret, go bolt your master,
Here's gear will startle him. [*Exit* FERRET.]—I
    cannot keep

---

    [4] *Than all the race of Beauforts, &c.*] " The children of John o'
Gaunt, by his third wife, Catherine Swinford, widow of sir Hugh
Swinford, Bt. and daughter to sir Paen Roet, Kt. Guyen king at
arms, took their name from the castle of *Beaufort* in France, which
came to the house of Lancaster by Blanch of Artois, wife to Edmund Crouchback, the first earl of Lancaster. They were legiti-
mated by Act of Parliament in the 20th of Richard II."

The passion in me, I am e'en turn'd child,
And I must weep.—Fly, take away mine host,
                    [*Pulls off his disguise.*
My beard and cap here from me, and fetch my
      lord.—   [*Exit* FLY.
I am her father, sir, and you shall now
Ask my consent, before you have her.—Wife!
My dear and loving wife! my honour'd wife!
Who here hath gain'd but I? I am lord Frampul,
The cause of all this trouble; I am he
Have measured all the shires of England over,
Wales, and her mountains, seen those wilder nations,
Of people in the Peak, and Lancashire;
Their pipers, fidlers, rushers, puppet-masters,
Juglers, and gipsies, all the sorts of canters,
And colonies of beggars, tumblers, ape-carriers;
For to these savages I was addicted,
To search their natures, and make odd discoveries:
And here my wife, like a she-Mandevile,
Ventured in disquisition after me.

      Re-enter FLY *with* lord FRAMPUL'S *robes.*

   Nurse. I may look up, admire, I cannot speak
Yet to my lord.
   Host. Take heart, and breathe, recover,
Thou hast recover'd me, who here had coffin'd
Myself alive, in a poor hostelry,
In penance of my wrongs done unto thee,
Whom I long since gave lost.
   Nurse. So did I you,
Till stealing mine own daughter from her sister,
I lighted on this error hath cured all.
   Lord B. And in that cure, include my trespass,
      mother,
And father, for my wife——
   Host. No, the *Star-chamber.*

Lord B. Away with that, you sour the sweetest
　　lettice
Was ever tasted.
　　Host. Give you joy, my son,
Cast her not off again.—

　　　　　　　Enter LOVEL.

　　　　　　　　　　　O call me father,
Lovel, and this your mother, if you like.
But take your mistress, first, my child; I have power
To give her now, with her consent; her sister
Is given already to your brother Beaufort.
　　Lov. Is this a dream now, after my first sleep,
Or are these phant'sies, made in the Light Heart,
And sold in the New Inn?
　　Host. Best go to bed,
And dream it over all. Let's all go sleep,
Each with his turtle. Fly, provide us lodgings,
Get beds prepared; you are master now of the inn,
The lord of the Light Heart, I give it you.
Fly was my fellow-gipsy. All my family,
Indeed, were gipsies, tapsters, ostlers, chamberlains,
Reduced vessels of civility.—
But here stands Prue, neglected, best deserving
Of all that are in the house, or in my Heart,
Whom though I cannot help to a fit husband,
I'll help to that will bring one, a just portion:
I have two thousand pound in bank for Prue,
Call for it when she will.
　　Lord B. And I as much.
　　Host. There's somewhat yet, four thousand pound!
　　　　that's better,
Than sounds the proverb,[5] *four bare legs in a bed.*
　　Lov. Me and her mistress, she hath power to coin
Up into what she will.

　　[5] *Than sounds the proverb.*] The proverb, at full is, "There goes
more to matrimony than *four bare legs,*" &c.

Lady F. Indefinite Prue!

Lord L. But I must do the crowning act of bounty.

Host. What's that, my lord?

Lord L. Give her myself, which here
By all the holy vows of love I do.
Spare all your promised portions; she's a dowry
So all-sufficient in her virtue and manners,
That fortune cannot add to her.

Pru. My lord,
Your praises are instructions to mine ears,
Whence you have made your wife to live your servant

Host. Lights! get us several lights!

Lov. Stay, let my mistress
But hear my vision sung, my dream of beauty,
Which I have brought, prepared, to bid us joy,
And light us all to bed, 'twill be instead
Of airing of the sheets with a sweet odour.

Host. 'Twill be an incense to our sacrifice
Of love to-night, where I will woo afresh,
And like Mæcenas, having but one wife,
I'll marry her every hour of life hereafter.[6]

[Exeunt with a song.

EPILOGUE.

Plays in themselves have neither hopes nor fears;
Their fate is only in their hearers' ears:
If you expect more than you had to-night,
The maker is sick, and sad. But do him right;

---

[6] *And like* Mæcenas, *having but* one wife,
I'll marry her every hour of life hereafter.] Terentia, the wife
of Mæcenas, is reported to have been not of the most gentle and
complying manners, which necessarily produced many quarrels and
reconcilements between her and her husband: this gave occasion
to those words of Seneca, to which our poet alludes: *Hunc esse, qui
uxorem millies duxit, cum unam habuerit.* Epist. 114. WHAL.

He meant to please you : for he sent things fit,
In all the numbers both of sense and wit ;
If they have not miscarried ! if they have,
All that his faint and faltering tongue doth crave,
Is, that you not impute it to his brain,
That's yet unhurt, although, set round with pain,
It cannot long hold out. All strength must yield ;
Yet judgment would the last be in the field,
With a true poet. He could have haled in
The drunkards, and the noises of the Inn,
In his last act ; if he had thought it fit
To vent you vapours in the place of wit :
But better 'twas that they should sleep, or spue,
Than in the scene to offend or him or you.
This he did think ; and this do you forgive :
Whene'er the carcass dies, this art will live.
And had he lived the care of king and queen,[7]
His art in something more yet had been seen ;
But mayors and shrieves may yearly fill the stage :
A king's, or poet's birth doth ask an age.

Another Epilogue there was, made for the Play,
in the Poet's defence, but the play lived not, in
opinion, to have it spoken.

A jovial host, and lord of the New Inn,
'Clept the Light Heart, with all that past therein,

---

[7] *And had he lived the care of king and queen, &c.*] This pathetic
appeal (of which more elsewhere) though it never probably reached
the ears of the audience, did not escape those of the *king* and *queen*.
Charles hastened to atone for his neglect of the "sick and sorrow-
ing bard," and sent him a hundred pounds, a noble present in those
days ; for which Jonson returned him thanks in an " Epigram " full
of gratitude, and dutiful affection. But the king's kindness did not
stop here : he increased the poet's salary from a hundred marks to
a hundred pounds, to take place from this very period, (the beginning of the year,) and to cheer his " old servant's " heart still more,
added an annual butt of canary to his other favours.

Hath been the subject of our play to-night,
To give the king, and queen, and court delight.
But then we mean the court above the stairs,
And past the guard; men that have more of ears,
Than eyes to judge us: such as will not hiss,
Because the chambermaid was named Cis.
We think it would have serv'd our scene as true,
If, as it is, at first we had call'd her Prue,[8]
For any mystery we there have found,
Or magic in the letters, or the sound.
She only meant was for a girl of wit,
To whom her lady did a province fit :
Which she would have discharged, and done as well,
Had she been christen'd Joyce, Grace, Doll, or Nell.[9]

Would it be believed, (unless in Jonson's case) that in defiance of his own words, (still existing) his enemies should have the confidence to reduce this sum to ten pounds, and to fabricate an insolent answer for the poet, patched up from a broken sentence in the *Staple of News !*

[8] *If, as it is, at first we had call'd her* Prue.] In the first draught of the play, the chambermaid's name was *Cicely,* which, it seems, was not approved of by the audience, and therefore altered by the poet to *Prudence.* In the 8vo. of 1631, she is called *Cis,* through the first and second act. WHAL.

[9] The author has entered so fully into the characters and conduct of this unfortunate comedy, that little remains to be said on either. The first act is very well written, and many passages in it might be pointed out, not only marked with spirit, but elegance, and poetic feeling : even the disquisitions of Lovel, though intolerable in a drama of action, are, yet, as scholastic theses, possessed of no inconsiderable degree of merit. The characters are, as usual, correctly maintained ; but the inferior ones are so ill conceived, that more disgust than pleasure is generated by the poet's rigid attention to the *suum cuique.*

With respect to the conduct of the piece, it seems very extraordinary that Jonson, during his elaborate detail of it should not have been once struck with its palpable absurdities. To pass over the episode of *Nick Stuff and his Pinnacia,* which is merely ridiculous, what must we think of a lord who abandons his family, turns travelling tinker, show-man, and finally inn-keeper, because his wife had brought him two daughters ! of a lady, who runs away from her home, leaves her title and estate to her eldest daughter, steals her youngest, and sells her, in the disguise of a boy, to her own husband, whom she does not recognize, and continues to live with him, under the appearance of a drunken Irish nurse, with a patch over one eye (as an effectual screen) and a bottle of usquebaugh at her girdle !—But it is needless to proceed—the fact seems to be, that poor Jonson, though his *faint and faltering tongue* could scarcely shake out a few lines by way of apology, yet clung, with a pertinacity, which those who cannot pity and forgive, have no touch of human kindness, no knowledge of human feeling, to the fond hope that *judgment* was still "in the field," and that the palsy, which had long *chilled his blood,* and *beset his enfeebled limbs with pain,* had not seized the nobler parts, nor injured the pristine sanity and vigour of his mind :

Hæc cura et cineri vixit inusta suo !

O D E [1]

(TO HIMSELF.)

COME leave the loathed stage,
   And the more loathsome age;
Where pride and impudence, in faction
      knit,
   Usurp the chair of wit!
Indicting and arraigning every day,
   Something they call a play.
   Let their fastidious, vain
   Commission of the brain
Run on and rage, sweat, censure and condemn;
They were not made for thee, less thou for them.

   Say that thou pour'st them wheat,
   And they will acorns eat;
'Twere simple fury still thyself to waste
   On such as have no taste!
To offer them a surfeit of pure bread,
   Whose appetites are dead!
   No, give them grains their fill,
   Husks, draff to drink and swill:
If they love lees, and leave the lusty wine,
Envy them not, their palate's with the swine.

   No doubt some mouldy tale,
   Like Pericles, and stale

[1] This Ode is prefaced with the following explanatory notice:

"The just indignation the author took at the vulgar censure of his play, by some malicious spectators, begat this following Ode to himself."

As the shrieve's crusts, and nasty as his fish—
  Scraps, out of every dish
Thrown forth, and raked into the common tub,
  May keep up the Play-club :
  There, sweepings do as well
  As the best-order'd meal ;
For who the relish of these guests will fit,
Needs set them but the alms-basket of wit.

  And much good do't you then :
  Brave plush and velvet-men,
Can feed on orts ; and, safe in your stage-clothes,
  Dare quit, upon your oaths,
The stagers and the stage-wrights too, your peers,
  Of larding your large ears
  With their foul comic socks,
  Wrought upon twenty blocks ;
Which if they are torn, and turn'd, and patch'd
  enough,
The gamesters share your gilt, and you their stuff.

  Leave things so prostitute,
  And take the Alcaic lute ;
Or thine own Horace, or Anacreon's lyre ;
  Warm thee by Pindar's fire :
And though thy nerves be shrunk, and blood be cold
  Ere years have made thee old,
  Strike that disdainful heat,
  Throughout, to their defeat,
As curious fools, and envious of thy strain,
May, blushing, swear no palsy's in thy brain.

  But when they hear thee sing
  The glories of thy king,
His zeal to God, and his just awe o'er men :
  They may, blood-shaken then,
Feel such a flesh-quake to possess their powers
  As they shall cry, " Like ours,

In sound of peace or wars,
No harp e'er hit the stars,
In tuning forth the acts of his sweet reign ;
And raising Charles his chariot 'bove his Wain." [2]

[2] This " strain of defiance," which is both vigorous and poetical, was not heard without impatience by *some* of the minor critics of the day, who took offence at its " arrogance," and retorted on the poet with more justice (it must be said) than humanity. The only piece on the subject, which is come down to us, is a kind of parody of the style and measure of the ode, by Owen Feltham, the author of the *Resolves*.

Several of the first scholars of the time amused themselves with putting this ode into Latin verse. There is a translation by Randolph ; and another by W. Strode, whom Oldys, in his MS. notes to Langbaine, calls, how correctly I know not, " the University Orator of Cambridge," is now before me, in the hand-writing of sir Kenelm Digby. The reader may take the two last stanzas as specimens of its latinity.

Hæc conamina prostituta mitte,
Alcæumque manu resume plectrum,
Anacreonta, tuum Flaccum, simul igne calescas
Pindaricæ musæ :
Contractusque licet nervis, et sanguine lentus,
Ante dies canos,
Indignante lyrâ cie calorem :
Sic tenta modulos ubique Victor,
Ut stolide percontatrix ac invida turba,
Hoc cerebrum juret nullum quassare tremorem.

At quando audierint lyræ accinentem
Te magnalia Cæsaris Britanni,
Quâ pietate Deum, quâ majestate popellum
Et colit et terret ;
Sanguine stent quassi, carnis tremor occupet artus,
Quod lyra sic nulla
Seu pacem resonat, vel arma clangat,
Vere sidera perforare posset,
Quando gesta legent Caroli, currumque videbunt
Alterius Caroli plaustrum superare triumpho.

E E

AN ANSWER TO THE ODE,

Come leave the loathed Stage, &c.

(By Owen Feltham.)

COME leave this saucy way
  Of baiting those that pay
Dear for the sight of your declining wit :
   'Tis known it is not fit,
That a sale poet, just contempt once thrown,
   Should cry up thus his own.
  I wonder by what dower,
  Or patent, you had power
From all to rape a judgment. Let 't suffice,
Had you been modest, you'd been granted wise.

  'Tis known you can do well,
  And that you do excell,
As a Translator : But when things require
   A genius, and fire,
Not kindled heretofore by others pains ;
   As oft you've wanted brains
  And art to strike the white,
  As you have levell'd right :
Yet if men vouch not things apocryphal,
You bellow, rave, and spatter round your gall.

  Jug, Pierce, Peck, Fly, and all
  Your jests so nominal,
Are things so far beneath an able brain,
   As they do throw a stain
Through all th' unlikely plot, and do displease
   As deep as Pericles,
  Where, yet, there is not laid
  Before a chambermaid

Discourse so weigh'd as might have serv'd of old
For schools, when they of love and valour told.

Why rage then ! when the show
Should judgment be and know-
ledge, there are in plush who scorn to drudge
For stages, yet can judge
Not only poets looser lines, but wits,
And all their perquisits.
A gift as rich, as high
Is noble poesie :
Yet though in sport it be for kings a play,
'Tis next mechanics, when it works for pay.

Alcæus lute had none,
Nor loose Anacreon
Ere taught so bold assuming of the bays,
When they deserv'd no praise.
To rail men into approbation,
Is new to yours alone ;
And prospers not : for know,
Fame is as coy, as you
Can be disdainful ; and who dares to prove
A rape on her, shall gather scorn, not love.

Leave then this humour vain,
And this more humorous strain,
Where self-conceit, and choler of the blood
Eclipse what else is good :
Then if you please those raptures high to touch,
Whereof you boast so much ;
And but forbear your crown,
Till the world puts it on :
No doubt from all you may amazement draw,
Since braver theme no Phœbus ever saw.[3]

[3] Whalley speaks somewhat slightly of Feltham : but his parody
appears to me to have a considerable degree of merit, and its good
sense and pertinacity cannot be denied. A little more mercy to
the sick and sorrowful state of the declining poet would not have

AN ANSWER TO BEN JONSON'S ODE,

to persuade him not to leave the Stage.

(By T. Randolph.)

BEN, do not leave the stage,
  'Cause 'tis a loathsome age:
For pride and impudence will grow too bold,
  When they shall hear it told
They frighted thee; stand high as is thy cause,
  Their hiss is thy applause:
  More just were thy disdain,
  Had they approved thy vein:
So thou for them, and they for thee were born,
They to incense, and thou as much to scorn.

  Will't thou engross thy store
  Of wheat, and pour no more,
Because their bacon-brains have such a taste,
  As more delight in mast:
No! set them forth a board of dainties, full
  As thy best Muse can cull;

been discreditable to him: but the times were savage, and unfeeling, and Feltham found a ready apology for his severity in the authorized language of controversy, and crimination. It does not appear that he entertained any personal hostility against Jonson, as his name is found among those who lamented his death;—unless we apply to him the trite observation,

Extinctus amabitur, &c.

Jonson, however, was not abandoned to his enemies. Randolph Carew (a poet whose merits are not sufficiently understood,) Cleveland, and many others came forward in his defence, and strove to temper and compose his irritated feelings. Randolph's Ode, which, like Feltham's, is a kind of parody upon the original, is too severe on the public, and somewhat too complimentary to the discarded play: Carew's little poem is at once kind and critical, and will be read with pleasure.

Whilst they the while do pine
And thirst, midst all their wine.
What greater plague can hell itself devise,
Than to be willing thus to tantalize ?

Thou canst not find them stuff,
That will be bad enough
To please their palates : let 'em them refuse,
For some Pye-Corner Muse ;
She is too fair an hostess, 'twere a sin
For them to like thine *Inn :*
'Twas made to entertain
Guests of a nobler strain ;
Yet if they will have any of thy store,
Give them some scraps, and send them from thy door.

And let those things in plush,
Till they be taught to blush,
Like what they will, and more contented be
With what Brome swept from thee.[4]

[4] *With what Broome swept from thee.*] There seems to have existed a wish among the poet's friends to embroil him with his old servant, Richard Brome : it was, however, without effect, for the "envious Ben" continued to esteem him to the close of his life. Very shortly after the condemnation of the *New Inn*, Brome produced a successful piece—this, if ever printed, is lost ; but a second comedy, (*The Northern Lass*,) still more successful perhaps, which he brought forward in the same year, has an excellent commendatory copy of verses by our poet prefixed to it, in which he terms the author "his old and faithful servant, and, by his *continued virtue,* his loving friend, Richard Brome."

In a duodecimo edition of Jonson's minor poems, published about three years after his death, the *Ode to Himself* is given with several variations for the worse, and among the rest, the 7th and 8th lines of the third stanza are thus impudently converted into personal satire, probably to bolster up the passage quoted in this note :

"*Broome's* sweepings do as well,
There, as his master's meal."

It is needless to repeat that this could not come from Jonson. The Ode is here given as printed under his own eye, and he is accountable for nothing beyond it.

I know thy worth, and that thy lofty strains
    Write not to clothes, but brains ;
    But thy great spleen doth rise,
    'Cause moles will have no eyes :
This only in my Ben I faulty find,
He's angry, they'll not see him that are blind.

    Why should the scene be mute,
    'Cause thou canst touch thy lute,
And string thy Horace ? let each Muse of nine
    Claim thee, and say, Thou'rt mine.
'Twere fond to let all other flames expire,
    To sit by Pindar's fire :
    For by so strange neglect,
    I should myself suspect,
The palsy were as well thy brain's disease,
If they could shake thy Muse which way they please.

    And though thou well canst sing
    The glories of thy King ;
And on the wings of verse his chariot bear,
    To heaven, and fix it there ;
Yet let thy Muse as well some raptures raise,
    To please him, as to praise.
    I would not have thee choose
    Only a treble Muse ;
But have this envious, ignorant age to know,
Thou that canst sing so high, canst reach as low.

TO BEN JONSON,

Upon occasion of his Ode of defiance annexed to his Play of the New Inn.

(By T. Carew.)

'TIS true, dear Ben, thy just chastizing hand
　　Hath fix'd upon the sotted age a brand
　　To their swoln pride, and empty scribbling due;
It can nor judge, nor write : and yet 'tis true,
Thy comic Muse from the exalted line
Touch'd by the Alchemist, doth since decline
From that her zenith, and foretels a red
And blushing evening, when she goes to bed ;
Yet such, as shall outshine the glimmering light,
With which all stars shall gild the following night.
Nor think it much (since all thy eaglets may
Endure the sunny trial) if we say
This hath the stronger wing, or that doth shine,
Trick'd up in fairer plumes, since all are thine :
Who hath his flock of cackling geese compared
With thy tuned quire of swans ? or else who dared
To call thy births deform'd ? but if thou bind,
By city custom, or by gavel-kind,
In equal shares thy love on all thy race,
We may distinguish of their sex, and place ;
Though one hand form them, and though one brain
　　　　strike
Souls into all, they are not all alike.
Why should the follies then of this dull age
Draw from thy pen such an immodest rage,
As seems to blast thy else-immortal bays,
When thine own tongue proclaims thy itch of praise ?
Such thirst will argue drought.　No, let be hurl'd

Upon thy works, by the detracting world,
What malice can suggest: let the rout say,
" The running sands, that, ere thou make a play,
Count the slow minutes, might a Godwin frame,
To swallow, when thou hast done, thy shipwreck'd
     name."
Let them the dear expense of oil upbraid,
Suck'd by thy watchful lamp, " that hath betray'd
To theft the blood of martyr'd authors, spilt
Into thy ink, whilst thou grow'st pale with guilt." [5]
Repine not at the taper's thrifty waste,
That sleeks thy terser poems ; nor is haste
Praise, but excuse ; and if thou overcome
A knotty writer, bring the booty home :
Nor think it theft if the rich spoils, so torn
From conquer'd authors, be as trophies worn.
Let others glut on the extorted praise
Of vulgar breath, trust thou to after days:
Thy labour'd works shall live, when Time devours
The abortive offspring of their hasty hours.
Thou art not of their rank ; the quarrel lies
Within thine own verge : then let this suffice,
The wiser world doth greater thee confess
Than all men else, than thyself only less.

[5] These are the old accusations against Jonson. His enemies
had apparently more malice than invention, since they merely repeat what Decker and his party had urged against him thirty years
before. This threadbare ribaldry was thought too valuable to be
kept from the readers of Shakspeare, and therefore they are treated
with it by Messrs. Steevens and Malone in a hundred different
places.

ODE TO BEN JONSON,

upon his Ode *to Himself.*

(By J. Cleveland.)

PROCEED in thy brave rage,
 Which hath rais'd up our stage
Unto that height, as Rome in all her state,
 Or Greece might emulate ;
Whose greatest senators did silent sit,
 Hear and applaud the wit,
 Which those more temperate times,
 Used when it tax'd their crimes:
Socrates stood, and heard with true delight,
All that the sharp Athenian Muse could write

 Against his supposed fault ;
 And did digest the salt
That from that full vein did so freely flow :
 And though that we do know
The Graces jointly strove to make that breast
 A temple for their rest,[6]
 We must not make thee less
 Than Aristophanes :
He got the start of thee in time and place,
But thou hast gain'd the goal in art and grace.

 But if thou make thy feasts
 For the high-relish'd guests,
And that a cloud of shadows shall break in,
 It were almost a sin

---

[6] This alludes to the well known distich of Plato, which is thus
rendered by Scaliger :

  " *Ut templum Charites quod non labatur haberent,*
   Invenêre tuum pectus, Aristophanes."

To think that thou shouldst equally delight
  Each several appetite;
  Though Art and Nature strive
  Thy banquets to contrive:
Thou art our whole Menander,[7] and dost look[8]
Like the old Greek; think, then, but on his Cook.[9]

If thou thy full cups bring
  Out of the Muses' spring,
And there are some foul mouths had rather drink
  Out of the common sink;
There let them seek to quench th' hydropic thirst,
  Till the swoln humour burst.
  Let him who daily steals
  From thy most precious meals,
Since thy strange plenty finds no loss by it,
Feed himself with the fragments of thy wit.

  And let those silken men
  That know not how, or when
To spend their money, or their time, maintain
  With their consumed no-brain,
Their barbarous feeding on such gross base stuff
  As only serves to puff

[7] " *Cæsar* called *Terence Menander* halfed, because he wanted so much of his grace and sharpness. *Ben Jonson* may well be call'd our *Menander*, whole, or more: exceeding him as much in sharpness and grace, as *Terence* wanted of him." I. C.

[8] " *Ben Jonson* is said to be very like the picture we have of *Menander*, taken from an ancient medal." I. C.

[9] " *Menander* in a fragment of one of his Comedies, makes his Cook speak after this manner of the diversity of tastes, viz.:

  ' What is his usual fare?
  What countryman is he?
  These things 'tis meet the cook should scan:
For such nice guests as in the isles are bred,
With various sorts of fresh-fish nourished,
In salt meat take little or no delight,
But taste them with fastidious appetite.' " I. C.

Up the weak empty mind,
Like bubbles, full with wind,
And strive t' engage the scene with their damn'd oaths,
As they do with the privilege of their clothes.

Whilst thou tak'st that high spirit,
Well purchas'd by thy merit :
Great Prince of Poets, though thy head be gray,
Crown it with Delphic bay,
And from the chief [pin] in Apollo's quire,
Take down thy best tuned lyre,
Whose sound shall pierce so far
It shall strike out the star,
Which fabulous Greece durst fix in heaven, whilst
thine,
With all due glory, here on earth shall shine.

Sing, English Horace, sing
The wonders of thy King ;
Whilst his triumphant chariot runs his whole
Bright course about each pole :
Sing down the Roman harper ; he shall rain
His bounties on thy vein ;
And with his golden rays,
So gild thy glorious bays,
That Fame shall bear on her unwearied wing,
What the best Poet sung of the best King.

ADDITIONAL NOTES.

NOTES TO THE DEVIL IS AN ASS.

Page 1.

THE DEVIL IS AN ASS.] Jonson's own title for the play is THE DIVELL IS AN ASS, and I regret it was not retained. It appears to me much more in accordance with the spirit of playful satire which pervades the piece, than the grim hard name which the modern editors have substituted. The letter misprinted by Gifford at p. cxxxviii. of the *Memoirs* establishes the fact that the 1631 edition of this play was printed under the author's auspices. It must be admitted, however, that the marginal directions are not given with Jonson's customary brevity and perspicacity, and that for the most part they may very well be spared. The motto is from the *Ars Poetica*, and was thus translated by Jonson himself:

> "Let what thou feign'st for pleasure's sake be near
>   The truth."

In speaking of the piece to Drummond (vol. ix. p. 400), he told him that he had been "accused" about it, which is not to be wondered at, as there are many hard and clever hits at some of the projects which tended so much to lower the court in the eyes of the country. With regard to the literary conduct of the play itself, he says that "according to *Comœdia Vetus*, in England the Divell was brought in either with one Vice or other: the Play done, the Divell carried away the Vice." Jonson's improvement upon this was to represent "the Divell so overcome with the wickedness of this age, that he thought himself an ass. Παρεργους is discoursed of the Duke of Drounland : the King desired him to conceal it."

P. 4. *Or were* Muscovy glass.] Muscovy glass is talc. So in Marston's *Malcontent*, 1604 : "She were an excellent lady but that her face pealeth like Muscovy glass."

P. 5. *If this play do not like, the Devil is in't.*] Dekker's play is entitled : *If it be not good, the Divel is in it.*   Gifford's note is calculated to make a reader search for it under the name of *Belphegor*, whereas it is only built upon a plot taken from Machiavelli's novel of the " Marriage of Belphegor."   Dekker's Epilogue commences :

> " If't be not good, the Divell is in't (they say),
>   The Divell was in't, this then 's no good play."

Nares points out that *like* in the sense of *please* is preserved in the old court phrase, " And like your majesty," which has been corrupted from " An it like your majesty."

P. 7. *Hoh, hoh, hoh, &c.*] I cannot join in Gifford's condemnation of Whalley's note.   Jonson tells us himself that he had the English *Vetus Comœdia* in his eye, and this was the mode in which, in the old Moralities, the Divell introduced himself.   In Dekker's play, above referred to, the " Divell" generally comes on with " Oooh, oooh !" " Ooooh."   It may be that Jonson's " Hoh " was shouted in a tone of sarcastic merriment, but it was derived from the custom Whalley refers to.

P. 9. *Stay in your place, know your own* strength, *and put not*
          Beyond the sphere of your activity.]   By changing the *strengths* of Jonson into *strength*, Gifford has sadly damaged the meaning of this passage.   *Strengths* were *strong places, strong-holds,* and *Satan* sagaciously advises *Pug* to " put not beyond " ground that he's sure of.   In *Sejanus* the word is used metaphorically :

> " Make mine own *strengths* by giving suits and places,
>   Conferring dignities and offices."   Vol. iii. p. 84.

P. 10.   Pug. *Why any : Fraud,*
          Or Covetousness, or lady Vanity,
          Or old Iniquity.
              Sat. I'll call him hither.]   In the folio the words " I'll call him hither," are *Pug's,* and it is perfectly plain, from Iniquity's opening speech, that *he* understood them to be so.   Since writing the above, I have found that Coleridge, who was not aware of the folio reading, had arrived at the same conclusion.   " That [the uttering of the words by Satan] is against all probability, and with a (for Jonson) impossible violation of character.   The words plainly belong to *Pug,* and mark at once his simpleness and his impatience."

P. 12. *To spend it in* pies *at the* Dagger.]   For notices of the Dagger and its pies, see vol. iv. pp. 24, 165.   In *Satiromastix*, Dekker makes Tucca say to Horace (i. e. Jonson), " Out bench whistler, out, ile not take thy word for a Dagger pye."

P. 13. *Where* Vennor *comes.*] Gifford tells us afterwards in a note, vol. vii. p. 414, that when he wrote this he was ignorant of the true history of Vennor or Fenner. In Richard Brome's *Covent Garden Weeded* (*circ.* 1638), we have: "Sure 'tis Fenner or his ghost. He was a riming souldier." (p. 42.)

P. 13. *And take his* Almain-leap *into a custard.*] An Almain leap was a dancing leap. "*Allemands,*" says Nares, who was born in 1753, "were danced here a few years back;" and Mr. Dyce, I find, has a MS. note in his copy: "Rabelais tells us that Gargantua ' wrestled, ran, jumped, not at three steps and a leap, called the hops, nor at clokepied, called the hare's leap, nor yet at the Almane's, for, said Gymnast, these jumps are for the wars altogether unprofitable and of no use.' *Rabelais,* book i. c. xxiii."

P. 14.   *Strong waters,* Hum,
          Meath and Obarni.] Gifford afterwards discovered (see his note vol. vii. p. 226) that Obarni was a preparation of meath, not of usquebagh, and he also adds a better definition of Hum, from Heywood's *Drunkard.* At *post,* p. 258, we read of a "distance of hum," which Gifford is unable to explain. It was evidently a potent liquor.

P. 16. *There is a* handsome cut-purse *hang'd at Tyburn.*] On this Mr. Dyce has noted in his copy: "It would seem as if the highwaymen of Jonson's days, as well as those of the last century, prided themselves on riding to Tyburn in grand costume. Rogues die now in dishabille."

P. 16. *Franklin, and* Fiske, *and Savory.*] Fiske has also been fortunate enough to obtain a niche in *Hudibras,* part ii. c. iii. v. 403 :

          " And high an ancient obelisk
          Was rais'd by him, found out by Fisk."

The lines from Beaumont and Fletcher ought to be quoted :

          " Oh I shall bring you wonders ! There's a friar
          Russe, an admirable man ; another
          De Bube, a gentleman ; and then La Fiske,
          The mirror of his time, 'twas he that set it."
                    *The Bloody Brother ; or, Rollo, Duke of
                    Normandy,* vol. x. p. 437.

P. 17. Pentacles *with characters.*] Pentacle (from low Latin *pentaculum*) was the name given to three triangles intersecting each other, and made up of five lines. It was considered a charm against demons, and, when delineated upon the body of a man, was supposed to point out the five wounds of the Saviour. Its origin, however, is of a much earlier date. My brother, General A. Cunningham, tells me that he has seen the pentacle on a coin of Tarsus of about 300 B. C. He has also in his own possession an Indian seal of about A. D. 200, in which the device is cut over the word " Ko-ma-dâ-ra." It has in fact been a favourite mystic symbol from a very early age, and is still cherished by the Freemasons. See Marlowe's *Works*, p. 348.

P. 17. *An ancient gentleman, of* [*as*] *good a house*
    As most are now in England.] According to my ear, if a pause is made after *gentleman*, there is no necessity for making any change in the first line, as Jonson printed it :

> " An ancient gentleman—of a good house
>   As most are now in England."

Coleridge was greatly charmed with this soliloquy of Fitzdottrel's. He says : " Compare this exquisite piece of sense, satire, and sound philosophy in 1616 with sir M. Hale's speech from the bench in a trial of a witch many years afterwards."

P. 19. *To keep me upright*, while *things be reconciled.*] Of *while* in the sense of *until*, Nares says, " *Even* Jonson so uses it ;" but it was recognized by the greatest scholars, as witness sir John Cheke : " Joseph took her to his wife, and lay not with her *while* she had brought forth her first begotten son." *St. Matthew*, p. 29.

P. 19. *'Till I had view'd his shoes well : for those* roses
    Were big enough to hide a cloven foot.] Chapman in his *Cæsar and Pompey* (*Works*, vol. iii. p. 145) has exactly the same idea, which appears sufficiently ridiculous when applied to an ancient Roman :

> " *Fro.* Yet you cannot change the old fashion (they say)
>   And hide your cloven feet.
> *Oph.* No ! I can wear roses that shall spread quite
>   Over them."

Mr. Dyce also noted in his copy of Jonson : " The present play was first acted in 1616." In Webster's *White Devil*, which was printed in 1612, we find :

> " Why 'tis the devil ;
> I know him by a great rose he wears on 's shoe
> To hide his cloven foot."

P. 19. *He is my wardrobe-man, my* cater, *cook.*] This word *cater* is generally written *acater*, in the same way as *cates* and *acates*. In the dramatis personæ of the *Sad Shepherd* (vol. vi. p. 236), Much is described as Robin Hood's " bailiff, or *acater*."

P. 20. *And save four pound a year.*] This we may suppose to have been the customary wages of a domestic servant, *circa* 1616. I have already alluded to this in my note to " livery-three-pound-thrum " in the *Alchemist*, vol. iv. p. 12.

P. 21. *Yes, that's a* hired *suit he now has on.*] According to Gifford's system of elision, *hired* should have been printed *hir'd*, as in the folio, for, although a dissyllable, the added sound was gained before the *r*, not after it. Two lines higher up, " *doth* study," should be " *does* study."

P. 22. *After* saying on *the cloke.*] To *say on* for to *try on* is of constant recurrence in Jonson. See note *post*, p. 163, and vol. ii. p. 128.

P. 24. *My right I have* departed with.] "To part and *depart* with anything were synonymous expressions." See Gifford's note, vol. ii. p. 151, and *Cynthia's Revels*, p. 208.

P. 24. *Nor takings by the arms, nor tender circles*
    Cast 'bout the waste.] *Waist* and *waste* were alike spelt *waste* or *wast*, and modern editors must choose between them. I presume there can be no doubt which Gifford ought to have fixed upon here. Oddly enough in this same play (*post*, p. 111), where the word occurs again, he falls into the opposite error ! The ignorance of the recent editors of D'Avenant as to this word has led them into the penning of one of the most ludicrously blundering notes I remember to have fallen in with.

P. 24. *Those soft* migniard *handlings.*] Cotgrave has in his dictionary, " *Mignard*—migniard, prettie, quaint, neat, feat, wanton, daintie, delicate." In the *Staple of News*, *post*, p. 221, it will be seen that Jonson tries to introduce the substantive *migniardise*, but happily without success.

P. 29. *I must obey* [aside.] There is no mark of *aside* in the original, nor any conceivable reason why there should be.

P. 29. *As wise as a court-parliament.*] Massinger's *Parliament of Love* was not produced for many years after this.

P. 30. *I did look for this* jeer.] In the original it is *geere*, and so it ought still to stand. *Gear* was a word with a most extended signification. Nares defines it, " matter, subject, or business in general !" When Jonson uses the word *jeer* he spells it quite differently. The *Staple of News* was first printed at the same time as the present play, and in the beginning of Act iv. Sc. 1 I find :

" *Fit.* Let's *ieere* a little. *Pen.* Ieere ? what's that ? "

P. 31. *I cannot be so false to* my own *thoughts.*] The original has "*mine own* thoughts."

P. 32. *Since your* cautelous *jailer.*] Gifford is quite justified in saying that *cautelous* is distinguished from *cautious* by having the sense of "artful and insidious ingrafted upon it." This is perfectly evident with the substantive *cautel* from which the adjective was formed. Shakspeare in *Hamlet* speaks of "soil and cautel" as "besmirching," and in an old statute of 24 Henry VIII., quoted by Mr. Froude, I find "compassed and practised by cautill, and subtle means." Vol. i. p. 60.

P. 32. Man. *Sir, what do you mean?*
(And again four lines lower down)
Man. *You must play fair, sir.*] I am not certain about the latter of these two speeches, but it is perfectly unquestionable that the former *must* have been spoken by the husband Fitzdottrel.

P. 35. *I'll go bespeak me straight a gilt* caroch.] There was some distinction apparently between *caroch* and *coach*. I find in Lord Bacon's will, in which he disposed of so much imaginary wealth, the following bequest : "I give also to my wife my four coach geld-ings, and my best caroache, and her own coach mares and caroache."

P. 35. *And thence into Blackfriars,*
Visit the painters, where you may see pictures.] Vandyck did not come to England till 1632, sixteen years after this play was produced, but when he did come Charles lodged him in Blackfriars, which would appear to have been the recognized quarter for artists, just as Newman Street was sixty years ago.

P. 35. *I have kept the contract, and the* cloke's mine own.] I suppose this ending was considered an *improvement* on what Jonson himself wrote :
"I've kept the contract, and the *cloake is mine*."
May I be allowed to prefer the genuine reading ?

P. 35. *Wife, your face this way ; look on me, and think*
You had a wicked dream, wife, and forget it.] Here is more *improvement*. Jonson wrote the last line :
" *You've had* a wicked dream, wife, and forget it."

P. 38. *Sir,* money is *a whore, a bawd, a drudge.*] Jonson printed this line :
" Sir, *money's* a whore, a bawd, a drudge."
Gifford saw there were only nine syllables in this arrangement, and printed *is* at full length. Coleridge also marked the deficiency and proposed a different remedy. "I doubt not that *money* was the first word of the line, and has dropped out :
' Money, sir, money's a whore, a bawd, a drudge.'"

It is presumptuous in me to differ from two such authorities, but I cannot help thinking that the nine-syllable arrangement is quite in Jonson's manner, and will be found, if tried upon the tongue, to force an emphasis on every word, which would have a particularly good effect in the opening utterances of an act.

P. 38. *Via, pecunia !*] *Via* being the Latin word for *a way*, some light-hearted student must have raised a laugh by employing it for *away*—"Begone! dull care! via! dull care!" or "Via Pecunia!" Shakspeare, Chapman, Beaumont and Fletcher all alike make use of it, and in precisely the same sense. This is Nares' explanation, and is something more than plausible. Steevens, on the other hand, says it is an Italian exclamation, signifying, *Courage, come on*, which does not agree with "Via! Pecunia!" but is confirmed by old Florio, who says it is "an adverbe of encouragement much used by commanders, as also by riders to their horses." Nares' story may easily have grown out of the use of the word in the riding school.

P. 38. *Yes, I will* take *no less, and do* it *too.*] Gifford would have found it difficult to explain this line as he has chosen to print it, but had he turned to the original he would have seen that it stands:

> "Yes, I will *talke* no less and doe it too,"

being the natural rejoinder to Fitzdottrel's wondering interrogatory two lines above of, "*How talks* he? Millions!"

P. 39. *As I set down, out of true* reasons *of state.*] Jonson wrote, "true *reason* of state."

P. 40. *Whereof the crown's to have a moiety.*] Jonson wrote, "the crown's to have *his* moiety."

P. 40. In the note in this page the long passage from Brome should be called a misquotation rather than a quotation. Take, for instance, the fifth and sixth lines:

> "It may be looked into ; and so may yours,
> Against the multiplicity of watches."

So Gifford prints, but in the only known edition of the play, Brome wrote:

> "It may be looked into: And yours against
> The multiplicity of pocket-watches."

Here the elision of the word *pocket* is no improvement, any more than the changing the last line:

> "To stop the growth of witchcraft,"

from what Brome wrote:

> "To *prevent* witchcraft *and contagion*."

P. 41. *I have computed all, and made my survey*
 Unto my acre. I'll begin at the pan,
 Not at the skirts.] Jonson wrote " unto *an* acre," which is sense. The *pan* is evidently the deepest part of the swamp, which continues to hold water when the *skirts* dry up, like the hole in the middle of the tray under a joint when roasting, which collects all the dripping. Meercraft proposed to grapple with the main difficulty at once.

P. 41. *Will not be sold for the earldom of Pancridge.*] Pancridge was St. Pancras. Jonson has this earldom again in the *Tale of a Tub*, vol. vi. p. 175. The project which Trains would not exchange for this title is called by Jonson *Dog-skins* (not Dogs' skins) just as we now speak of hare-skins and rabbit-skins. These points are certainly very trifling, but still not without interest in a small way.

P. 42. *I will not bate a* Harrington.] At this period there was a similar token in Scotland, which I find mentioned in *A Nest of Ninnies*, 1608 (Shak. Soc. Reprint, p. 19): " Jemy thinks it was much to give a crowne for that, for which shee did demand but an *atchison*, which in our money is but three farthings." In his note on this passage Gifford mentions *Drunken Barnaby*, against which Mr. Dyce wrote in his copy, " We now know that Brathwait wrote the Journal, and perhaps there is cause to regret that Haslewood's curiosity discovered the author, for it has much lessened the pleasure of reading the work, which is no longer a genuine memorial by some poor rattling scholar, but a piece of mere fancy."—MS.

P. 45. *As I protest I will, out of my* dividend.] This word had not yet assumed a fixed form, and Jonson both here and at p. 83, when he has occasion to use it again, spells it *dividend*.

P. 46. *In the* Bermudas.] See note *post*, p. 81, also vol. iv. p. 407, and vol. viii. p. 348.

P. 47. *I will not have Good Fortune, or God's Blessing*
 Let in.] Gifford's story is very pretty, but the whining " *Good fortune* will attend you, Miss," " *God's blessing* will attend you, Miss," may be heard daily in half the areas in London, when the tramps come to beg the cook for leavings. I do not suppose that Jonson intended anything more.

P. 52. *We will make a* Cokes *of this Wise Master.*] For Ford's excellent definition of a *cokes*, see my note to vol. iv. p. 408.

P. 52. *Or of that truth of Picardil, in clothes.*] Jonson mentions this article of dress twice again. In the *Challenge at Tilt* (vol.

vii. p. 217), he spells it *pickardil;* and in the same manner, but with an additional *l*, in the *Epistle to a Friend*, vol. viii. p. 356. In this place he printed *picardill.* It has always been asserted, on the strength of a passage in Gerarde's *Herball*, about the small buglose growing "upon the dry ditch bankes about Piccadilla," that the locality bore this name as early as 1596, when Gerarde's volume was published; the fact being, however, that the notice does not make its appearance till the second edition came out in 1633.

P. 54. *Upon the point of trust ! in your first charge,*
The very day of your probation,
To tempt your mistress !] This mode of punctuation makes the passage read very tame. Jonson printed it:

"Upon the point of trust !   In your first charge !
The very day of your probation !"

which makes you fancy you hear the blows coming down.

P. 54. *Were you* tentiginous, *ha ?*]   I hardly expected to find this word in Samuel Johnson's *Dictionary*.   It is from the Latin *tentigo*.

P. 55.   *To the utmost* bounds in *Lincolnshire.*]   Jonson printed "the utmost *bound of* Lincolnshire," which seems to me better English and better sense than the *improved* version.   Five lines higher up "engine" is " *Ingine,*" with a capital *I*, and in italics, for both of which there was a reason.

P. 56. *'Tis fatal,*] i. e. the title of *Gloucester* is fatal, whereas at p. 45, to which Gifford refers the reader, it was the title of Duke in general that was said to be so.   When Jonson wrote, there was a nobleman who is always called "the duke" in the letters of the period.   This was a Scotch peer, the duke of Lennox.   The dukedom of Norfolk had been forfeited in 1572, and was not restored till 1660.   The Buckinghams, Somersets, and Northumberlands had all gone down in blood, and a new Buckingham was not made till 1623.   Is it possible that this could have been the title which Meercraft *whispers* in the next page, which leads Fitz-dottrel to say, " No, a noble house pretends to that," for we know that the next dukes of Buckingham were apprehensive of some ancient claim, and called themselves from the shire, not the town. This whole subject of titles must have been very distasteful to James, and this year, 1616, was the very one in which Villiers was first made *earl* of *Buckingham.*

P. 56. *No, I confess I have it from the play-books.*]   And so did the great duke of Marlborough.   At this place in his copy, Mr.

Dyce notes that bishop Corbet says the same of his host at Bosworth:

> "He could tell
> The inch where Richmond stood, where Richard fell;
> Besides what of his knowledge he could say,
> He had authenticke notice from the Play."
>
> *Ed. Gilchrist*, p. 193.

P. 59. *And garters which are* lost, *if she can shew them.*] As I understand this it means that if a gallant once saw the garters he would never rest till he obtained possession of them, and they would thus be *lost* to the family. Garters thus begged from the ladies were used by the gallants as *hangers* for their swords and poniards. See *Every Man out of his Humour*, vol. ii. p. 81. "O, I have been graced by them beyond all aim of affection: this is her garter my dagger hangs in;" and again p. 194. We read also in *Cynthia's Revels*, vol. ii. p. 266, of a gallant whose devotion to a lady is such that he

> "Salutes her pumps,
> Adores her hems, her skirts, her knots, her curls,
> *Will spend his patrimony for a garter,*
> Or the least feather in her bounteous fan."

P. 61. I leave *you, sir, the master of my chamber.*] Jonson wrote "*I'll leave* you," and so it ought to be printed.

P. 63. *These sister-swelling breasts.*] The latter part of Gifford's note is quite justifiable if Jonson's stage-directions are printed, but hardly so without them. "He growes more familiar in his courtship—playes with her paps, kisseth her hands, &c." The street must have been very contracted at the top, for the same directions say, "This scene is acted at two windows, as out of two contiguous buildings."

P. 65. *For you, you, sir, look to hear from me.*] This second *you* has been interpolated without the slightest authority, to the manifest injury of sense and rhythm.

P. 67. *That was your bedfellow.*] Or, as we should now say, *chamberfellow*, or *chum*. See vol. viii. p. 353, *An Epistle to master John Selden.*

P. 69. *There's Dickey Robinson.*] Gifford's brave words about the "blasphemous cant of those ferocious times," are a little thrown away as far as *Dickey Robinson* is concerned, for we find his name among the dedicators of the first Beaumont and Fletcher folio, two years after Basing house was captured; and the Register of St. Anne's, Blackfriars, tells us that he was quietly buried there on the 23rd March, 1647 (8). "Robinson the player," who was "slain

by the hands of Major Harrison, that godly and gallant gentleman," is supposd by Mr. Collier to be a William Robinson, who
was one of Queen Anne's players in 1619. See Collier's *Memoirs
of the Actors*, p. 272.

P. 71. *A* forest moves not.] I suppose Trains means, "It is
in vain to tell him of venison and pheasant, the right to the bucks
in a whole forest will not move him."

P. 71. *Tell him we'll* hedge in *that.*] The same phrase occurs
again in the last line but one of page 73. It appears to mean
"formally include," and to have no connection at all with the
pecuniary arrangement known as "hedging" in the present day.

P. 76. *In garrison, a wench of a* storer.] The word in the original
is *stoter*, which I have no doubt is the name of some small coin
current in the camps when Jonson was familiar with them.

P. 82. *At Christmas, and* St. George-tide.] Jonson wrote, *St.
George's-tide.*

P. 82. *And* take in Pimlico, *and kill the bush*
        At every tavern.] Pimlico was near Hogsden, and con-
sequently included in the ground over which the Finsbury sham
fights extended. To *take in* was to *capture*. At vol. viii. p. 410,
we read :
        "What a strong fort old *Pimlico* had been !
        How it held out ! how, last, 'twas taken in !"

As the major Sturgeons of those days "took in" tavern after
tavern, we can imagine them "killing the bushes." Three lines
lower down "*Bristol* stone" should be "*Bristo* stone."

P. 83. *There, they are just a hundred pieces.*] I prefer Jonson's
own version :
        "There th' are just : a hundred pieces !"

P. 84. *And cozen in your* bullions.] Mr. Dyce in his *Beaumont
and Fletcher*, vol. vii. p. 291, has a note in which I entirely concur.
"To me it appears that in their attempt to explain *bullions*, when
applied to dress, Gifford and Nares have been misled by connect-
ing the word with bullion (uncoined gold or silver). *Bullions*, I
apprehend, mean some sort of hose or breeches, which were
bolled or *bulled*, i. e. swelled, puffed out [in Jonson's *Sad Shepherd*, vol. vi. p. 240, we find, 'And hang the bulléd nosegays 'bove
their heads']: hence the epithet applied to them in the *Beggars
Bush, blistered.*"

P. 85. *Is* too-too-*unsupportable.*] See vol. iii. p. 54, and my
note on Mr. Halliwell's elucidation of "too-too." It occurs once
or twice again, and will each time be noticed.

P. 86. *I know her, sir, and her gentleman*-usher.] It is a great pity to drop Jonson's word *huisher*. Gifford's practice is quite incomprehensible, as he allowed it to stand only a few pages back:

> " For footmen for you, fine-paced *huishers*, pages
> To serve you on the knee." (p. 66.)

P. 87.   *A project for the* fact, *and venting*
> *Of a new kind of* fucus.] *Fact* must here mean *manufacture*, in which sense I have not met with it elsewhere. *Fucus*, as has been before mentioned, is paint for the face.

P. 88. Fitz. *I was so earnest after the main business,*
> *To have this ring gone.*
> Meer. *True, and* it is *time.*] Jonson printed, *True and it's time*, forcing the emphasis on *time*. The editors, whom Gifford in his careless way copied, found by their fingers there was a syllable wanting, and expanded *it's* into *it is*. I could point out scores of instances in which Jonson made his line a syllable short in order to compel the right emphasis.

P. 89.   *Answering*
> *With the French time,* and *flexure of your body.*] Here is more improving. Jonson wrote "*in* flexure of your body," which has somewhat more of meaning in it.

P. 97. *I am no kin to him, we but call cousins :*
> *And if* he *were, sir, I have no relation*
> *Unto his crimes.*] It is almost needless to say that Jonson printed *we* instead of *he* in the second line.

P. 98. *If we once see it under the seals, wench, then,*
> *Have with them for the great* caroch, *six horses,*
> *And the two coachmen, with my* Ambler bare.] "Have with them" is an idea borrowed from the gaming table, being the opposite of "have at them." For *caroch*, see *ante*, p. 35. To have the *coachman* bare (see *ante*, p. 55) was considered a main point, but *Ambler* was the *huisher*. For the " project of the toothpicks," mentioned just below, see Gifford's note, p. 130.

P. 99. Chewing *some grains of mastick.*] Jonson used the old form " chawing."

P. 102. *To all the fall'n, yet well disposed* mad-ams.] Here Wittipol's joke, such as it is, suffers considerably from inattention to what Jonson wrote :

> " To all the falne, yet well disposed, *mad-dames.*"

P. 103. *Your ladyship's fucus has no ingredient but I durst eat.*] This is exactly what, in a recent trial, Madame Rachel's mother, deposed as to the fucus which was "brought on swift dromedaries from the desert of Sahara."

P. 104. *Makes a lady of sixty look* as *sixteen.*] Jonson wrote, "look *at* sixteen," which, besides being the true word, is more in accord with the " keeps the skin *in decimo sexto*" of the next page.

P. 111. *Ay, for his valley is beneath the* waist.] See my note on p. 24, *ante.*. Here I think the spelling *waste* should be preserved, as making the play of words better by carrying on the idea of barrenness and cruelty of weather in the two preceding lines.

P. 119.   Ever. *You have made election*
            Of a most worthy gentleman!
            Man. *Would one of worth*
            Had spoke it! but now *whence it comes, it is*
            Rather a shame unto me, than a praise.] The words *but now* are inserted without the slightest authority, and without the slightest notice that they are not in Jonson's text. Had Gifford exercised his usual discrimination, he would have seen that the defect lay in the line above, which had appropriated two words not its own, and that the right reading was :

    " *Ever.* You have made election
    Of a most worthy gentleman !
    Man. Would one
    Of worth had spoke it ! Whence it comes it is
    Rather a shame unto me than a praise."

P. 120. *I think I* sous'd *him.*] Gifford candidly owns that this reading does not satisfy him, and Mr. Dyce has pointed out that the old reading of *sou't*, as given by Jonson himself, is perfectly correct. It is "nothing more than a variety in the spelling of *shu'd*. To *shu* is to scare away a bird." Dyce's *Webster*, p. 350.

P. 120. *To be made duke of Shoreditch.*] This was the mock title bestowed on the most successful marksman in the annual trials of skill among the archers of London. In the *Poor Man's Petition* of 1603, one item is that the king should not make the "good lord of Lincolne Duke of Shoreditch."

P. 123. *Spare your* parenthesis.] To understand this the preceding four lines should be printed as Jonson printed them :

    " Finding by conference with me that I liv'd
    Too chaste for my complexion (and indeed
    Too honest for my place, Sir) did advise me
    If I did love myselfe (as that I do
    I must confesse).
        Mer. Spare your *Parenthesis.*"

Why the marks of parenthesis should be eliminated here, when the context required them, and retained both above and below, it is not easy to explain.

P. 124. The art mentioned in the concluding lines of this page figures again in the *Staple of News, post,* p. 226.

P. 126. *Three-penny gleek.*] Sir John Suckling thought this a very dull game. On November 18th, 1629, he wrote to his friend D'Avenant, " Lying four nights on shipboard is almost as bad as sitting up to lose money at three-penny gleek."

P. 126. *As plain as* fizzling.] " To fizzle," says Mr. Halliwell, "is to do anything without noise."

P. 127. *Little Darrel's tricks.*] This worthy is mentioned again in the *Epigram on the Court Pucelle,* vol. viii. p. 422 :

" Take heed,
This age will lend no faith to Darrel's deed."

P. 129. *The laudable use of forks.*] See the *Fox,* vol. iii. p. 261, and Gifford's note. The most curious part of Coryat's account is his description of the use of this novel instrument. " The Italian and also most strangers that are commorant in Italy, doe alwaies at their meales use a little *forke* when they cut their meate. For while with their knife, which they hold in one hand, they cut the meate out of the dish, they fasten their *forke,* which they hold in their other hand, upon the same dish ; so that whatsoever he be that, sitting in the company of any others at meale, should unadvisedly touch the dish of meate with his fingers, from which all at the table doe cut, he will give occasion of offence unto the company, as having transgressed the laws of good manners, insomuch that for his error, he shall be at the least brow-beaten, if not reprehended in wordes." *Crudities,* 1611, 4to. p. 90.

P. 131. *For a matter of fifty,* in *a false alarm.*] Jonson wrote, "*on* a false alarm."

P. 135. Shackles. *Here you are lodged, sir ; you must send your garnish.*] This word *garnish* has been made familiar to all time by the writings of John Howard. " A cruel custom," says he, " obtains in most of our gaols, which is that of the prisoners demanding of a new comer *garnish,* footing, or (as it is called in some London gaols) chummage. *Pay or strip* are the fatal words. I say fatal, for they are so to some, who, having no money, are obliged to give up part of their scanty apparel ; and if they have no bedding or straw to sleep on, contract diseases which I have known to prove mortal." The next time a poet made the " divell " take a walk in

London, he represents him as receiving hints for "improving the prisons in hell." Pug might have done the same in this matter of "garnish."

P. 135. *Cast care at thy posterns, and* firk *in thy fetters.*] Steevens says, and Nares endorses his opinion, that the word *firk* was so licentiously used, that it is not easy to fix its meaning. In this instance it means that Pug should *hitch* himself in his fetters, as T. P. Cooke used to do in his trousers. ·So R. Brome, in the *Antipodes :*

> "As tumblers doe : when betwixt every feat
> They gather wind by firking up their breeches."

P. 138. *Thou hast been* cheated on, *with a false beard.*] Here Mr. Dyce notes in his copy : "There ought to be no point after *on*, for *cheated on* means simply *cheated*. The same mode of expression continued till Mrs. Centlivre's time. In the *Wonder*, Don Felix says to Violante, ' 'Sdeath, could not you have imposed upon me for this one night ? could neither my faithful love, nor the hazard I have run to see you, make me worthy to be cheated on ? ' "

Mr. Dyce might at the same time have noticed "hang out" being used twice for "hang" in this very place :

"That body back here was *hang'd out* this morning." (p. 135.)

"It is Gill Cutpurse was *hang'd out* this morning." (p. 139.)

P. 138. Provincial *of the cheaters, or* bawd-ledger.] Jonson here borrows terms both from Church and State. A *Provincial*, more particularly among the Jesuits, was the spiritual head of a province, and a *Lieger*, or *Ledger*, was a minister resident at a foreign court, as distinguished from an ambassador extraordinary. I suppose that what we now call consuls and vice-consuls would all have been called liegers in those days. See *post*, p. 176.

P. 141. *Wherever he put his head, with a* wannion.] Nares says : "Used only in the phrase *with a wanion*, but totally unexplained, though exceedingly common in use. It seems to be equivalent to *with a vengeance*, or *with a plague*." Latimer uses it when speaking ironically of some brother bishop : "Was not this a good prelate ? He should have been at home preaching in his dioces, with a *wannion*." It occurs again in the *Staple of News, post*, p. 247.

P. 146. *You cannot see* St. Pulchre's steeple *yet*.] St. Sepulchre's churchyard was the customary burial-place for the corpses of criminals taken from Newgate to be executed at Tyburn. The parishioners, however, occasionally raised objections, and many were buried close to the gallows. The word *steeple* was not used in the restricted sense to which we now confine it. The *tower* of St. Sepulchre's, in Jonson's time, must have been very much like what we now see it as most carefully and tastefully restored.

NOTES TO THE STAPLE OF NEWS.

P. 150, Note.

HE only play, &c.] This was one of the three plays printed under Jonson's own eye in 1631. See his letter to the earl of Newcastle, vol. i. p. cxxxviii.

P. 150. The motto from the *Ars Poetica* of Horace was thus translated by Jonson himself, vol. ix. p. 105 :

"Poets would either profit or delight;
 Or mixing sweet and fit, teach life the right."

P. 151. *The* Staple of News.] In the masque of *News from the New World discovered in the Moon*, vol. vii. p. 336, and presented at Court in 1620, five years before this play was produced, Jonson had said, " I have hope to erect a Staple for News ere long, whither all shall be brought, and thence again vented under the name of Staple-news."

P. 151. *Where? On the stage, ladies!*] It does not necessarily follow from this that ladies were ordinarily provided with seats upon the stage as gentlemen were.

P. 155. *Rolling himself up and down like a tun in the midst of them, and* purges, *never did vessel of wort or wine work so.*] Jonson's word is *spurges*, not purges. It means to *froth* or to *foam*, and the change is injurious in every way. Jonson has the word again, vol. vii. p. 117 :

" The spurging of a dead-man's eyes,"

where the spelling is not interfered with.

P. 158. Nut-crackers, *that only come for sight.*] This nuisance of nut-cracking is not felt in our leading London theatres, but it is only necessary to cross into Surrey to find it in full swing, in spite of prohibitory placards stuck up in every direction.

P. 161. *Gramercy, Leatherleg; get me the spurrier,*
     And thou hast fitted me.] I apprehend that *an'* should be the reading instead of *and*.

P. 161, Note. *Sir 'tis a* perspicil, *the best under heaven.*] Gifford may well be amused with Whalley's quotation, but his mistake was only in withholding what followed :

> " Sir, 'tis a *perspicil*, the best under heaven :
> With this I'll read a leaf of that small Iliad
> That in a walnut-shell was desk'd, as plainly,
> Twelve long miles off, as you see Pauls from Highgate."

P. 162. *Enough, enough, dear watch,*
> *Thy pulse hath beat enough.*] Nares cites this as an early mention of a repeating watch.

P. 165. Emissaries? *stay, there's a fine new word.*] Jonson appears to have been the introducer of this word. He has it again in the *Underwoods*, vol. viii. p. 301 :

> " You shall neither *eat* nor sleep,
> No, nor forth your window peep,
> With your emissary eye."

Bishop Hall had favoured *emissitious*, direct from the Latin.

P. 166. *I feel a* grudging *of bounty.*] *Grudging* here means *inclination.* The verb is used in the same sense by Shakspeare, " Perish they that *grudge* one thought against your Majesty." *First Henry VI.*, A. iv. S. 1.

P. 166. *Right Spanish perfume, the lady Estifania's,*
> *They cost twelve pound a pair.*] I suppose these perfumed pockets are the *sweet bags* of the following extract from Howe's *Continuation of Stow :* " Edward Vere, Earle of Oxford, came from Italy, and brought with him gloves, sweet baggs, a perfumed leather jerkin, and other sweet things." The favourite scent for gloves long continued to be called " the earl of Oxford's perfume."

P. 167. *That clothes do much upon the wit, as weather*
> *Does on the brain; and thence* [*sir*] *comes your proverb.*] Gifford interpolated the word *sir* I think unnecessarily, as in all probability the accent was thrown on the second syllable in *provérb.*

P. 168. *Is this same hat of the* block-passant,] i. e. of the fashionable shape. So D'Avenant has :

> "This hat looks like
> An old morion. 'Thas been my pillow 'bove
> Eighteen years—just off Methusalem's block."
> > *The Siege,* vol. iv. p. 396.

P. 168. *Rogue! rascal! slave! give tradesmen their true names,*
       And they appear to him *presently.*] To *him!* To *whom?*
Jonson knew his own meaning, and printed *them*, not *him :*—that
is, they appeared to the *names* of " rogue, rascal, slave," as the case
might be.

P. 169. *Thou should'st have been brought in too, shoemaker,*
       If the time *had been longer.*] Meaning if the *tune* had
admitted of it.

P. 170. *I do not like* these *paper-squibs, good master.*] Here the
those of Jonson is altered to *these;* and, by way of compensation,
in the same speech, the line below, which Jonson wrote :

       " To beat *these* pioneers off that carry a mine,"

has *these* changed to *those*.

P. 170. *Secure your* casamates.] "Casamatta," says Jonson's
friend Florio, is " a casamat, a canonrie or slaughter-house, so
called of enginers, which is a place built low under the wall or
bulwarke not arriving unto the height of the ditch [? counter-scarp],
and serves to annoy or hinder the enemie when he entreth the
ditch to skale the wall." This is what we should now call a
fausse-braye, but the " casa mate " which Jonson intended is no
doubt the "canonrie " described by Florio.

P. 170. *Stage direction,* They make legs to him.] It is rather
exceeding the license of an editor to interpolate without authority
directions worded like these.

P. 171. *Poor rascals! I* do *it out of charity.*] Jonson printed,
"I *do do* it out of charity."

P. 171.   *I was bred in the mines*
       Under sir Bevis Bullion.] At this place Mr. Dyce
wrote in his copy, " Here Gifford has no note. The name sir
Bevis Bullion contains an evident allusion to sir Bevis Bulmer,—a
well known personage of those days, who, I believe, was Superin-
tendent of the Royal Mines, or at least had some situation connected with them. Prince, in the *Proemium* to the *Worthies of
Devon,* mentions that that ' famous artist,' sir Bevis Bulmer, Kt.,
by his excellent skill in minerals, extracted a great quantity of silver
from the Combe-Martin mines, a portion of which he caused to be
made into two cups in 1593, and presented them inscribed with
verses,—the one to William Bourchier, earl of Bath, the other
(weighing 137 ounces) to sir Richard Martin, Lord Mayor of
London, ' to continue to the said city for ever.' "
Very shortly after his accession to the throne of England James
sent him beyond the Tweed to develop the mineral wealth of his

native land. On April 14th, 1608, the King made him a free gift of £500, and on the 24th he received a discharge for £2,419 16s. 10d. granted him to be employed about the mines in Scotland."

P. 172. *Set forth the table, the* carpet *and the chair.*] See the *Silent Woman*, vol. iii. p. 441.

P. 172. *O ! you are a* butter-*woman.*] Jonson writes it Butter-woman, with a capital *B.* Mr. Dyce, in a note at p. 73, vol. x. of his *Beaumont and Fletcher*, says, " Butter is mentioned in an early poem by Cowley, as one whose pamphlets of news were not greatly credited :

> " May be, though all his writings grow as soon
>   As Butter's out of estimation."
> *A Poetical Revenge.*

And in the above note as it originally stood on the fly leaf of this volume of Jonson, he added, " Butter is mentioned in Saltonstall's *Whimsies*, 1631."

P. 177. *We not forbid that any news be made,*
    But that it be printed.] These and the ten next lines are taken almost verbatim from the masque of *News from the New World.* See vol. vii. p. 337.

P. 179. *His father died on this day* seven-night.] Jonson, as a rule, gave the most minute attention to spelling. This word is printed *seventh-night.*

P. 180. *What are your present clerk's* habilities ?] This is a word of Spenser's. Sir Philip Sidney uses the still more unpleasant *hable.* On the 24th March, 1586, he wrote to his father-in-law Walsingham, " If the queen pai not her souldiours, she must loos her garrisons ; there is no doubt thereof. But no man living shall be *hable* to say the fault is in me." And it occurs again in the same letter.

P. 182. *I know it* [*I*]; *a right kind-natured man.*] This is another instance in which I think the line loses force by the interpolation of the tenth syllable.

P. 183.   *Her name is,*
        Or rather her three names are (for such she is)
        Aurelia Clara Pecunia, a great princess.] The " great princess" with the " three names" was, of course, an allusion to the Infanta. See *post*, p. 217, and Gifford's note. She is always called the Infanta *Maria* simply, and even Don Pascual de Gayangos has been unable to supply the two other names. When the match with Charles fell through, she married the king of

5   G G

Hungary, and became the ancestress of other Marias renowned in history.

P. 184. *I have had a certain itch*
    In my right eye.] Here Mr. Dyce notes, " Jonson as usual was thinking of the classics—*Theocritus. Idyl* iii. 37."

P. 185. *With* a *beggar to boot.*] This is no improvement on " With *the* beggar to boot" which Jonson wrote ; nor, five lines lower down, is *"could* have endured him" so good as Jonson's *"would* have endured him," as any one may satisfy himself by comparing the readings in each case.

P. 185. *And no man say* black is his eye.] In *Love's Cure,* Beaumont and Fletcher (vol. ix. p. 143) have the same expression, used by a justice to a damsel at whose evil courses he had been conniving :
    " I can say black's your eye, though it be grey,"
which seems to connect it with a vulgar saying of the present day, which may be occasionally heard, "No man can say black is the white of your eye."

P. 186. *He is an* errant *learned man that made it.*] At least a dozen times before this have I had to sigh over Gifford's change of Jonson's "errant," into his own or Whalley's *"arrant."* The word has been fortunate enough at last to escape.

P. 188. *Expect,* intend *it.*] Here Mr. Dyce wrote in his copy *" Intend it :* i. e. View it attentively, give all heed to it." See my note on vol. ii. p. 17.

P. 189. *My aged knees to* buckle.] This word in the sense of bending or doubling up is still used for the folds which will so often come in straining paper on a drawing board—in casting iron plates, &c. It is in this sense of involuntary and unwished-for bending that Shakspeare employs it.

P. 189. *A sordid rascal, one that never made*
    Good meal in his sleep, but sells the acates are sent him.] Archdeacon Nares, who would himself have made such an admirable editor of any of our old poets, suggests that the second line should be altered by transferring the word *but,* making it read :
    "Good meal but in his sleep, sells the acates are sent him."

P. 194. *That air of hope has blasted many an* aiery
    Of castrils *like yourself.*] A *castril,* generally written *kestril,* was a base degenerate hawk. See the *Silent Woman,* vol. iii. p. 431. Aierie is spelt in this way here, and at p. 200, partly to help a joke, and partly, perhaps, out of a mistaken idea

of the etymology of the word. It means a nestfull, and has nothing to do with airiness of situation. It should be spelt *eyry*, which is simply a form of *eggery*.

P. 196. *And you play Crop in the Fleet.*] This must have been a slang phrase for standing in the Pillory.

P. 197. *Out of the* custard-politic *for you*, the mayor's.] See vol. iii. p. 164, and *ante*, p. 13. Poets of comparatively a recent date continue to associate mayors and custards. Mat. Prior, for instance, says (*Alma*, cant. i.) :

> "Thus, if you dine with my Lord May'r,
> Roast beef, and ven'son is your fare ;
> Thence you proceed to Swan and Bustard,
> And persevere in Tart and Custard."

The following quotation of a letter from Bishop Warburton to Hurd (April, 1766) is too apposite to be omitted. "I certainly made them merrier than ordinary at the Mansion House, where we were magnificently treated. The Lord Mayor told me the Common Council were much obliged to me, for that this was 'the first time that he ever heard them prayed for.' I said, 'I considered them as a body that much needed the prayers of the Church.' But if he told me in what he abounded I told him in what I thought he was defective—that I was greatly disappointed to see no custard at table. He said that they had been so ridiculed for their custard that none had ventured to make its appearance for some years. I told him I supposed that Religion and Custard went out of fashion together."

P. 198.   *What* plover's *that*
            They have brought to pull ?] Plover is used here precisely as Dotterel was in the preceding play, and as Pigeon is among the Pennyboys of the present day. "Green" too, in the next speech, has exactly its modern signification.

P. 198. *You snuff the air now*, has *the scent displeased you ?*] Can anybody say that this is an improvement on what Jonson wrote ?

"You snuff the air now, *as* the scent displeased you."

P. 199. *Why, he's of years, though he have* little beard.] Jonson has many allusions to himself in this part of Madrigal. His own beard was thin and straggling at the sides, while the chin had no hair at all, and Dekker, among other jeers on the subject, makes captain Tucca "damn him for a thin-bearded hermaphrodite." And further on in this play (p. 265) he is called "my *egg-chin'd* laureate." See also vol. ix. p. 409.

P. 200. *Some* dosser *of fish.*] A pannier—what in Scotland is called a *creel*. Samuel Johnson does not recognize this form, but admits *dorsel*, and *dorser* with the same signification. Cotgrave has " *Hotte*, a dosser, or basket to carry on the backe, wide at the top and narrow at the bottome."

P. 200. *He may in time, he is his agent now.*] A word is omitted in this line. Jonson wrote :

"He may *be* in time, he is his agent now."

P. 202. *Thank your* dog-leech *craft.*] In the days of bear-baiting and bull-baiting, the poor dogs had a sorry time of it, and their " leeches " on the bank drove a roaring trade. In the opening scene of the *Alchemist* (vol. iv. p. 18) " dog-leach" is one of the worst terms of abuse which Face can find for Subtle.

P. 206. Spar *up all your doors.*] Cotgrave has " *Barre*, a barre, or sparre, for a door." " *Barrer*, to barre, or sparre ; to boult." It is still the word on board ship for such spare timber as is not large enough for masts.

P. 207. *What ? a clapper-*dudgeon !] The progress of this word to its present meaning is very curious, and I have never seen it clearly explained. 1. It appears to have stood for some peculiar quality for working possessed by the root of the box tree. 2. It then came to stand for the root of the box itself. 3. Then being the wood best adapted for daggers, when, coupled with *haft* or *handle*, it came to mean *wooden*. 4. Being the basest material used for handles, it was applied in the sense of *cheap* or *common* to things in general. 5. While, simultaneously, being the material most in use for dagger handles, it came to mean the *feeling* indicated by pointing to the haft of that weapon.

P. 212. *Stage direction,* "*Kisses them again.*"] I prefer Jonson's own marginal note, " He doubles the complement to them all."

P. 213. *But* mas Broker *here.*] This prefix of *Mas.* to Broker has now occurred several times in this play, and without any notice from Gifford, who at vol. iii. p. 199, has declared that it was a contraction of *Messer*, not of *Master*, as it obviously is here. See my note on that place. Brokers at that time were very unlikely to be called *Messer*. Henry Chettle in *Kind-heartes Dreame* (1592) says : " There is an occupation of no long standing about London, called *Broking* or *Brogging*, whether ye will, in which there is pretty Jugling especially to blind Law and bolster Usury." *N. Shak. Soc.* p. 74.

P. 214. *Old Lickfinger's the cook, here in* Ram-alley.] *Ram Alley* seems to be now represented by Mitre Court. Its cook-shops are mentioned by Massinger in *A New Way to Pay Old Debts* (vol. iii. p. 530) :

> "The knave thinks still he's at the cook's shop in Ram Alley,
>   Where the clerks divide, and the elder is to choose ;
>   And feeds so slovenly."

By this I suppose is meant that the clerks made up the messes for themselves, and selected by seniority, which would be well ascertained at the Temple gate. See *ante*, p. 200.

P. 214. *The blessed* Pokahontas.] This lady arrived in 1616. On the 22nd of June Chamberlaine writes to Carleton, "Sir Thomas Dale has brought from Virginia Pocahuntas, the daughter of Powatan the king, who is married to Rolfe, an Englishman. The country promises well, but no present profit is expected." And on the following 18th of January he tells the same correspondent : "The Virginian woman, Pocahuntas, has been with the king : she is returning home sore against her will." Finally, on March 29th he reports : "The Virginian woman died at Gravesend on her return." Two lines further on, for "hath been in *womb of tavern*," the folio reads, "hath been in womb of *a* tavern." In this note Gifford quotes Stow as to an event which took place in 1631, when the old chronicler was dead in 1605.

P. 215.   *Simon the king*
           Will bid us welcome.] Mr. Dyce thought there ought to have been a note here about the old song, "Sir Simon the King," but see *post*, vol. ix. p. 73—*Verses placed over the door at the entrance into the Apollo.*

P. 219, *Note. To the Reader.*] There is no reason why this notice, on which Jonson placed such importance, should have been detached from the text, and degraded in smaller type to a note.

P. 221. *With all the* migniardise, *and quaint caresses.*] This is pure French. Cotgrave has : "*Mignardise :* quaintnesse, neatnesse, daintinesse, wantonnesse ; smooth or fair speech ; kind usage." Jonson had before used the adjective *migniard.* See the *Devil is an Ass*, p. 24.

P. 221. *I move upon my axle like a* turnpike.] It is curious to think how the meaning of this word has changed in the course of time, and how it will soon vanish altogether. We should now, I suppose, say *turn-style*, but in Jonson's days that would certainly have involved the idea of climbing.

P. 224. *Why* have not you this, *Tom ?*] It is in vain to specu-
late why this has been changed from the "haven't you this" of the
original; or, ten lines lower down, why "'Tis but writing" is
altered to "It is but writing."

P. 225. *Betwixt the* costs *of a ship.*] Jonson wrote and printed
coasts, which was quite an ordinary form of the time. This blunder
did not originate with Gifford, but is complacently adopted by him
—and the judicious Nares too has been misled by it.

P. 225. *The eel boats here, that lie before Queen-hythe.*] Close to
Queen-hythe was Brooke's Wharf, and during Lent the Dutch eel-
boats lay here very thick. "At this time of the year the pudding-
house at Brooke's Wharf is watched by the Hollanders eeles-ships,
lest the inhabitants, contrary to the law, should spill the blood of
innocents, which would be greatly to the hindrance of these *butter-
boxes.*" *Westward for Smelts,* 1603 or 1623. *Percy Soc.* p. 5.

P. 225. *But what if* Spinola *have a new project.*] Spinola and
Gundomar, between them, had, in 1620, completely succeeded in
mystifying James as to the move upon the Palatinate. *Spedding's
Bacon,* vol. vii. p. 112.

P. 227, *Note. A marginal note describes this* first customer *as a
dopper.*] I have four copies of the folio, the only version, and in
no one of them is there mention of a *dopper* in this place. The
marginal note is simply: "1. *Cust. A she-baptist.*" But in the
text, where Gifford prints "1. Cust.," Jonson wrote DOP. See vol.
vii. p. 342, *News from the New World discovered in the Moon,* where
the doppers were found to be very numerous.

P. 230, *Note. The massacre of Amboyna took place in* 1622.] In
point of fact, the massacre of Amboyna took place on the 17th
of February, 1624, and the news of it did not reach England till
the commencement of 1625.

P. 232. *A precept for the wearing of long hair.*] Jonson liked
this joke. He told Drummond, "One who wore side hair, being
asked of one other, who was bald, why he suffered his hair to grow
so long, answered, It was to sie if his haire would grow to seed,
that he might sow of it on bald pates." See vol. ix. p. 404.

P. 233. *The poor English play was writ of him.*] Jonson, as if
to call more attention to this passage, has a marginal note: "Gundomar's use of the Game at Chesse, or Play so called." In the note
Gifford speaks of an engraved frontispiece, where Gundomar is engaged *in propriâ personâ* in no very friendly conversation with
Loyola, but Mr. Dyce has given a facsimile of a frontispiece where
Loyola does not appear at all, but Gundomar is represented hand-

ing a letter to the *Fatte Bishop* Antonio. The letter is from *His Holinesse.* The bishop takes it, but says *keepe yr distance*, on which the White Knight exclaims, *Check mate by Discovery.* Gifford should have called Gondomar the *Black Knight*, not the *Black House.* "Yonder Black Knight, the Fistula of Europe." The pecuniary profits must, for the time, have been enormous. On August 14th, 1624, sir F. Nethersoll wrote to Carleton (*Cal. Jac.* I. p. 327) that it was so "popular that the players gained £100 a night."

P. 236. *The very* brooch *of the bench.*] See the *Poetaster*, vol. ii. p. 383: "Honour's a good brooch to wear in a man's hat."

P. 236. *He says nothing, but twirls it thus.*] This was of course brought in for the sake of his favourite hit at Daniel's *Dumb rhetoric, and silent eloquence.* Gifford is certainly right in saying that "there was no great kindness between Daniel and our poet." In 1618 Jonson told Drummond that "Daniel was at jealousies with him," adding, however, that "he was a good honest man, had no children, but no poet." See *Conversations*, vol. ix.

P. 238. *Now, at the* coronation.] Gifford is certainly wrong about the bringing out of this play. The coronation did not take place till the 2nd of February, 1626, and "*now* at the coronation" would have been inappropriate so long previously as the preceding April. There are many traces of Jonson's having been offended at not being employed in preparing speeches for this occasion. His description (*ante*, p. 236) of Alderman Security, has every mark of being personal, and what he says (*post*, p. 246) of "a true receipt to make an alderman," is also evidence of what was rankling in his mind. See also the *New Inn, post*, p. 375.

P. 241. *Send in an Arion, in a brave broth.*] This passage is taken from the Masque of *Neptune's Triumph*, vol. viii. p. 29, which I believe was never acted except in rehearsal, and which Jonson therefore very properly regarded as available material for future use:

"I conceive you.
I would have had your isle brought floating in, now,
In a brave broth, and of a sprightly green,
Just to the colour of the sea ; and then
Some twenty syrens, singing in the kettle,
With an Arion mounted on the back
Of a grown conger, but in such a posture
As all the world should take him for a dolphin."

P. 244. *They must have* velvet haunches.] These important appendages figure in *Bartholomew Fair*, vol. iv. p. 497.

P. 244. *Of silver dishes, or gold chamber-pots.*] Golden chamber utensils were among the articles of luxury thundered against by him of the golden mouth in the ancient Constantinople.

P. 245. *I'll have no venture in your* shop, *the office,*
    Your bark *of six.*] The word *shop* in the first line is an unwarrantable and ridiculous alteration of Jonson's *ship*. The word *barque* in the next line ought to have stopped them from meddling.

P. 245. *A shrunk old* dryfat.] A *dry-fat* was a packing-case, or loosely put together cask. In Sylvester's *Du Bartas* we read of :

    "A dry-fat sheathed in latten plates without ;"

and in Dekker's *Works*, vol. iii. p. 338 : "In ! in ! if danger pursue you, in a dry-fat I'll pack you hence."

P. 246. *In Silver-street, the region of money.*] When Silver Street was mentioned before in the *Silent Woman*, it is as being famous for false hair ; if indeed the allusion be not rather aimed at the hue of Mrs. Otter's natural locks.

P. 246. *What fine* slips *grew in Gardener's-lane.*] Jonson's minute knowledge of Westminster localities has never been sufficiently appreciated by London historians. "Why I had it from my maid Joan Hearsay, and she had it from a *limb of the school*, she says, *a little limb not nine year old*," which we may suppose to have been Jonson's age when the great Camden first took him by the hand. "The mill" which he mentions has its memory still preserved in *Mill* bank. The stream which turned it ran where Great College Street now stands. Gardener's Lane, too, may yet be discovered. "Slips" were false coins, and so came to mean base-born children, as well as base productions of other sorts. Wenceslaus Hollar died in Gardener's Lane.

P. 247. *They make all their scholars play-boys.*] Jonson of course alludes to the annual performances of the Latin plays, which have long constituted so marked a feature in the curriculum of the famous old school. Camden was dead before the production of the *Staple of News*, but it is evident there was some one among the masters of 1625 who was a poet, or at least had acquaintance with a poet, and was cherished by Jonson accordingly.

P. 247. *Zeal-of-the-Land Busy and my gossip Rabbi Troubletruth.*] It is pleasant to see these old friends of *Bartholomew Fair* make their appearance again even in this passing way. None but men of real genius can venture on these allusions to the creatures of their own invention.

P. 249. *When we do speak at* volley.] Gifford most likely was not aware that *volley* is a technical term in the games of *tennis* and *racquets*. *To volley a ball* is to strike it before it touches the ground, instead of waiting for the rebound, which gives time for a steadier aim.

P. 250. *A* coat card *of the last order.*] It is not easy to say how this word came to be corrupted into the now familiar *court*-card. In 1681 the usage had become doubtful. See *Nares, sub voce.*

P. 251. *The perfect and true strain of poetry.*] The whole of the text, from this line down to "And 'tis divine," at l. 5, p. 253, is taken from the Masque of *Neptune's Triumph*, vol. viii. p. 24, *et seq.* There are several variations, a good deal appearing as prose in the Masque which is given as poetry in the Play, and so on. One line which reads something like nonsense in the play (p. 252),

"Some he *dry-dishes*, some motes round with broths,"
comes out clearly in the Masque—

"Some he *dry-ditches*, some motes round with broths."
The "brethren of the Rosy-cross," who are "airy" in the *Staple of News*, are "bare-breeched" in *Neptune's Triumph*.

P. 254. *What says my* poet-sucker?] Jonson had used this contemptuous word before. See *Bartholomew Fair*, vol. iv. p. 357. Nares says it is "formed by analogy from rabbit-sucker, which means a sucking rabbit."

P. 255. *It is his rose, he can make nothing else.*] This was a favourite joke of Jonson's. See *Conversations*, vol. ix. p. 404, and the prologue to the *Sad Shepherd*, vol. vi. p. 235.

P. 256. Pick. *Al-manach, though they call him Almanac; and Note* 9.] There is no authority whatever for giving this speech to Picklock. On *studying* the folio I am persuaded that the line belongs to the preceding speech of *Pecunia*. Gifford is rabid about the imaginary blunders of the folio, which is here the only authority.

P. 260.   *He had the use*
Of our bodies.] Coleridge proposed to print this :
                    "He had the use of
Our bodies;"

and goes on to say, "Now, however, I doubt the legitimacy of my transposition of the *of* from the beginning of this latter line to the end of the one preceding; for though it facilitates the metre and reading of the latter line, and is frequent in Massinger, the disjunction of the preposition from its case seems to have been disallowed by Jonson. Perhaps the better reading is :

'O' your bodies,' &c.,

the two syllables being slurred into one, or rather snatched or sucked up into the emphasized *your*. In all points of view, therefore, Ben's judgment is just; for in this way the line cannot be read as metre, without that strong and quick emphasis on *your* which the sense requires; and had not the sense required an emphasis on *your*, the *tmesis* of the sign of its cases *of*, *to*, &c., would destroy almost all boundary between the dramatic verse and prose in comedy: a lesson not to be rash in conjectural amendments. S. T. C. 1818."

P. 263.   *He must be a good scholar*
          Can *my descent*.] As Gifford tells us afterwards (vol. vi. p. 15,) "This is not the potential of some verb, but the present of the Saxon term for *know*, or comprehend."

P. 264. *I love all men of virtue*, from my *princess*.] In Coleridge's copy of this play the two words *from* and *my* had been run into one word, *frommy*, which led the great poet, philosopher, and critic to pen the following note on the "*frommy princess!*"—" Frommy, *fromme*—pious, dutiful, &c."

P. 265. *My* egg-chin'd *laureat*.] One of Jonson's many allusions to his beardless chin. See note on p. 198.

P. 270. *Set a beggar on horseback, he'll never* lin *till he be a gallop*.] To *linne* is to *stop*. Swift uses the word in his *Journal to Stella*, and says " *lins* is *leaves off*."

P. 271. *Some trick to beg him* for *his estate*.] The folio reads, " beg him *from* his estate," which I have no doubt is correct.

P. 271. *Run him out of the country like an Irish rat*.] Jonson works this fancy before in the *Poetaster*, vol. ii. p. 518.

P. 272. *A* mournival *of protests*.] John Cleavland uses this phrase in one of his ablest poems (ed. 1659, p. 39):

        " Like to Don Quixote's Rosary of slaves,
          Strung on a chain ; a Murnival of knaves
          Packt in a trick, like Gypsies when they ride."

P. 274.   *And is return'd,*
          As we do hear, grand captain of the jeerers.] Mr. Dyce here notes in his copy, "Q? is the word used here in the same sense in which we speak of a candidate being *returned* to Parliament?"

P. 275. *Like a Low-Country vorloffe*.] The note (8) which Gifford appends to this passage is an amusing specimen of his reckless arrogance. There may, however, have been less untruth in it in

1816, when The Duke's Despatches were for the most part unknown, and sir William Napier had not yet taught the world how history ought to be written.

P. 277. *Yet must maintain the thing, as* my own *right.*] Jonson wrote "*mine own* right," and he knew the force of the words he was using.

P. 278. *I will not change a* syllable *with thee more.*] Jonson, as usual with him, wrote *syllab*, for which Horne Tooke commends him, as does Gifford likewise in another place.

P. 281. Quoited over the bar.] This is even a more racy expression for *disbarring*, or *outbarring* than the "thrown over the bar," at p. 275.

P. 283. *With throwing* bed-staves *at her.*] See my note on *Every Man in his Humour*, vol. i. p. 36.

P. 284. Scene II. *A Room in Pennyboy senior's house.*] Coleridge notes here : " I dare not, will not, think that honest Ben had Lear in his mind in this mock mad scene."

P. 285. *Did you smell she was going ?*] This device of one person carrying on both sides of a conversation, may have suggested the immortal *Curtain Lectures* of Douglas Jerrold.

P. 286. *Who ? did Block bescumber*
      Statute's white suit ?] Mr. Dyce here wrote in his copy : "Todd quotes this passage but totally mistakes the meaning—he says '*bescumber* from *cumber*, to load with something useless or impertinent !' For example now, 'which working strongly with the conceit of the patient would make them bescomber to the height of a mighty purgation.'" *MS.*

P. 287.   *And from your jawbone,*
      Don Assinigo ?*] This Portuguese word, which means a young ass, occurs in *Troilus and Cressida*, and in Beaumont and Fletcher's *Scornful Lady*. It is right to mention this lest it should be thought an introduction of Jonson's, and taught by him to his servant, Richard Brome. See his *Mad Couple* (vol. i. p. 13). He introduces it in the *Expostulation*, vol. viii. p. 110, and carries on the suggested image :

    " Are you so ambitious 'bove your peers,
      You'd be an Assinigo by your ears ?"

P. 287. *No, nor* blushet *Wax.*] Nares thinks that this word *blushet* (one who blushes) is peculiar to Jonson. He uses it again, vol. vi. p. 467, as a substantive.

P. 289.   *To deride*
       The wretched, or with buffoon *license jest.*] Here Jonson,
as usual, prints *buffon*, which is necessary for the rhythm, and ought
on every account to be preserved.   .

P. 291. *My learned counsel tells me here, my* cook.] Here of
course a little joke is intended on the name of that great lawyer,
but narrow-minded pedant, the lord chief justice Coke.

NOTES TO THE NEW INN.

Page 296.

HE title page.] In the concluding lines, "Now at
last set at liberty to the Readers, his Majesty's servants
and Subjects to be judg'd *of.*" The word of is un-
meaningly added by the editors. Every word in this
title was most carefully studied, and the little volume
watched through the press, with more even than Jonson's usual
vigilance. The motto, as customary with him, has a word or two
altered to suit his particular purpose. The true reading of
Horace is:

"Verum age, et his, qui *se* lectori credere *malunt,*
Quam spectatoris fastidia ferre superbi."
                                        Ep. 2, i. 214.

Pope renders it very feebly:

"Think of those authors, sir, who would rely
More on a Reader's sense, than Gazer's eye."

P. 300. *Till by* reducing *her lord.*]   "*Domum reducere,* to bringe
saife home againe." *Cooper,* 1587.   To maintain his strange theory
that Jonson had fewer Latin words than other writers of the time,
Shakspeare, for instance, Gifford has slurred over this, and
hundreds of other equally palpable instances.

P. 300. Cock-brain'd *resolution,*] i. e. Wood-cock brained, i. e.
without any brains at all.   With sportsmen still the woodcock is
"cock" *par excellence.*

P. 300. *Make themselves merry with the accidents* on the by.] So
in *Catiline,* vol. iv. p. 248:

"And Fulvia come in the rear, or *on the by.*"

P. 301. *A* standard *of her own best apparel.*] A *standard* was a complete suit, or perhaps more properly a complete *wardrobe.* See *post,* p. 332.

P. 301. *Describing the effects of love so* vively.] Jonson has the word again in the *Magnetic Lady,* vol. vi. p. 47, where he speaks of seeing a "thing vively presented on the stage." And Wilson in his *History of James I.* has "the *vive* image of my own inward thankfulness."

P. 303. *Alias the lord* Frampul.] For further illustration of this word *frampul,* see note on *A Tale of a Tub,* vol. vi. p. 155. There are various modes of spelling it. In that place Ben Jonson writes *frampull,* while with Shakspeare it is *frampold,* and with Beaumont and Fletcher *frampel* and *frampal.*

P. 308. *Two turtles,* makes.] Coleridge here notes that *makes* for *mates* "is frequent in old books, and even now used in some counties for *mates* or *pairs.*" It is as old as the Chester Plays (*Shak. Soc.* i. 25):

> "Rise up, Adam, and awake ;
> Heare have I formed thee a *make.*"

P. 309. *A poor quotidian* rack *of mutton.*] *Rack of mutton* is what we now call *neck of mutton.* The learned say that it is derived from the Saxon *hracca,* the back of the head. In May's *Accomplished Cook* there is an instruction to "put in the *crag* end of the *rack of mutton* to make the broth good." The *crag* of course is the neck, still commonly called in Scotland the *craig.*

P. 310. *Balderdash, or* bonny-clabber.] Jonson had previously introduced this liquor in the *Irish Masque* (see vol. vii. p. 226) where Donnell pronounces it to be better to dance upon than usquebaugh.

P. 311. *Either owls or* rere-mice.] "Rere-mice" were *bats.* So *post,* p. 361 :

> "Once a bat, and ever a bat ! a rere-mouse,
> And bird of twilight."

Another name is *flitter-mouse,* which Nares says is a mere translation, *rheran* in Saxon being to *flutter.*

P. 313. *Titles were not* vented *at the drum,*
       Or common out-cry.] This is rather hard upon Jonson's old friend and patron king James, the inventor of this degrading plan for raising money, or at least of something very like it. See the *Calendars* of the State Papers of his reign.

P. 314.   *For a leap*
        Of the vaulting horse, to ply *the vaulting-house.*] Some
intermediate editor had substituted *play* for *ply*, which was restored
by Whalley.   Coleridge proposes to keep *play*, and goes on, "I
suggest *horse* for *house*.   The meaning would then be obvious and
pertinent.   The punlet or pun maggot, or pun-intentional, 'horse
and house' is below Jonson.   The *jeu d'esprit* just below :

                          ' Read a lecture
        Upon Aquinas at St. Thomas à Waterings,'
has a learned smack in it to season its insipidity."

   P. 315. *Cards of ten, to* face it
        Out *in the game.*]   On this Nares remarks that "it is
a common phrase which we may suppose to have been derived
from some game (probably primero) wherein the standing boldly
upon a ten was often successful."   It was most probably some
game in which, as in the present *Vingt-Un*, the *coat cards* all counted
the same as the ten.   Skelton introduces the expression in the
Bowge of Court (Dyce, vol. i. p. 42) :

        "First pycke a quarrel, and fall out with him, then
        And so *outface* him, with *card of ten*."

   P. 316. *A seat to sit* at ease *here*, in mine inn.]   This pleasant
expression, which the genius of Shakspeare has placed among our
household words, is always considered to refer to a tavern or
hostelry, as it probably does in the present instance ; but it had its
origin before the word *inn* came to mean anything more than my
lodging for the time being.

   P. 318. *Old master Gross, surnamed* Ἀγέλαστος.]   With regard
to Gifford's "observation once for all," Southey notes, "In the
text that occasions this note, the line might be read by quantity if
the true reading of the preceding word should be 'surnaméd.'"
Common Place Book, Fourth Series, p. 325.

   P. 319. *To the last* bodge *of oats, and* bottle *of hay.*]   For the
word *bodge*, Halliwell refers to the Songs of the *London 'Prentices*,
p. 76, and says it was "a kind of measure, probably half a peck."
A *bottle* of hay was a truss, and is still familiar to us in the proverb
about "looking for a needle in a bottle of hay," which most people,
however, believe to refer to the ordinary glass vessel which has
monopolized the name.

   P. 321. *Chalk, and renew the rondels.*]   This direction puzzles
me.   "Rondels" are the rounds or rungs of a ladder, and I should
guess that the *board* or *slate* on which the score was chalked, was
divided in a similar manner to keep the entries distinct.   In the

Tale of a Tub, vol. vi. p. 144, where the word *rondels* occurs again it is plainly in the sense of dancing, and here possibly it may have something to do with merry-making, although a floor of rushes would hardly have taken chalk kindly.

P. 325. *No knights o' the Sun, nor Amadis de Gauls.*] This passage attracted the attention of Southey, who remarks on Jonson's "contempt of Romances, with which he oddly couples Pantagruel:" Southey says that the same feeling of contempt again displays itself in the *Execration on Vulcan*, vol. viii. p. 400 :

> "Had I compiled from Amadis de Gaul,
>   The Esplandians, Arthurs, Palmerins, and all
>   The learned library of Don Quixóte."

P. 325. *Then shower'd his bounties on me, like the Hours, &c.*] When Coleridge arrives here he remarks, "Like many other similar passages in Jonson this is εἶδος χαλεπὸν—a sight which it is difficult to make one's self see—a picture my fancy cannot copy detached from the words."

P. 326. *Exeunt.*] At this point I find a MS. remark of Mr. Dyce's, which I most cordially echo: "I hardly know where to find a more admirable First Act of a Comedy than this—*Si sic*—— !"

P. 330. *So is your* sovereignty.] Gifford speaks very authoritatively in the matter of this word *sovereignty*, but Mr. Dyce maintains that he is altogether in the wrong. The present instance certainly is on his side, but general feeling is all against him in the quotation from *Hamlet*, and I suppose no one truly believes that to "deprive *your sovereignty* of reason" does not mean something higher than "deprive *your royal highness* of reason."

P. 332.   *A poor*, silly *fool*,
    But an impertinent *and sedulous one.*] Here *silly* means simple and unsophisticated ; and *impertinent* is, I suppose, a stronger form of *pertinent* in its best sense of immovably constant.

P. 333. *Drive in again, with the* coach-leaves *put down.*] We should now say *coach blinds*. The old name is strongly indicative of the clumsy nature of the ancient contrivance.

P. 334. *Who, my Fly?*] Here Mr. Dyce has a manuscript note, "It pleases mine host to say so in this place ; but in the last scene he gives us another account of Fly."

P. 335. *Enter* colonel Tipto *and* Fly.] Coleridge here breaks in with, "Though it was hard upon old Ben, yet Feltham, it must be confessed, was in the right in considering the Fly, Tipto, Bat,

Burst, &c., of this play, mere dotages. Such a scene as this was enough to damn a new play; and Nick Stuff is worse still—most abominable stuff indeed!" The lines of Feltham, referred to by Coleridge, will be found at p. 418.

P. 337. *Cuerpo! what's that?*] To be *in cuerpo* was to be stripped like a prize fighter of our time. Sir Thomas Urquhart describes the Admirable Crichton (I quote at second hand from sir John Hawkins): "Now, drawing to a closure he rents it first in *cuerpo*, and vapouring it with gingling spurs, and his armes *a kembol* like a *Don Diego*, he strouts it, and by the loftiness of his gait plaies the Capitan Spavento."

This is one of the passages which was transferred almost bodily to Beaumont and Fletcher's *Love's Pilgrimage*, A. i. S. 1. In the purloined version it commences:

"Dost thou think
Her good face e'er will know a man in cuerpo?
In single body thus? in hose and doublet,
The horse-boy's garb? base blank and half-blank cuerpo?"
Dyce's *Beaumont and Fletcher*, vol. xi. p. 226.

It is worth while also to compare the versions a few lines lower down:

"He would not speak with an ambassador's cook,
See a cold bake-meat from a foreign part,
In cuerpo: had a dog but stay'd without,
Or beast of quality, as an English cow,
But to present itself, he would put on
His Savoy chain about his neck, the ruff
And cuffs of Holland, then the Naples hat,
With the Rome hat-band, and the Florentine agate,
The Milan sword, the cloak of Genoa, set
With Flemish buttons; all his given pieces,
To entertain 'em in; and compliment
With a tame cony, as with the King that sent it."
Dyce's *Beaumont and Fletcher*, vol. xi. p. 227.

P. 338. *Know all, to the* gold weights.] In the then state of the currency every piece of gold offered at a mercer's counter was weighed before it was accepted, and the scales were for ever at work. See, for instance, Brome's *Mad Couple well Match'd*:

"*Lady.* Give me my purse . . . . your gold weights, Mrs. Sale-ware.
Mrs. Sale-ware. Here Madam, all in readinesse.
Lady. You take no gold but what is weight, I presume.
Mrs. Sale-ware. 'Tis but light paines to weigh it, Madam."
Brome's *Works*, vol. i. p. 20.

P. 338. *Without his* paramentos, *cloke and sword.*] Florio has, " *Paramento*, any kind of dighting, preparation, trimming, garnishing, or furniture."

P. 339. *So had* Caranza *his.*] In vol. i. p. 35, Bobadil speaks of " a most proper and sufficient dependance, warranted by the great Caranza." See notes on that passage.

P. 341. *They* lightly *go together.*] Here Mr. Dyce noted in his copy, " *Lightly*, i. e. commonly, usually."—MS. So in *Richard III.*, "Short summers *lightly* have a forward spring." A. iii. S. 1.

P. 342. *It is not now, as when plain Prudence lived.*] Mr. Dyce remarks in his copy that this is a " parody of a line in the much ridiculed *Spanish Tragedy*, by Kyd."

P. 346. *Do not* detract.] I cannot conceive why Gifford altered this from Jonson's " Do not *detrect*," which he intended for quite a different word, the Latin *detrecto*, to avoid.

P. 350. *That joy is too, too narrow.*] I always call attention to Jonson's use of the word " too-too." See *ante*, vol. iii. p. 54, and note.

P. 350. *Soft*, debonaire, *and amiable Prue.*] When king James *revised* lord Bacon's *Life of Henry the Seventh*, his " amendments " were very few, but among them was the substitution of *mild* for *debonnaire*. See Spedding's *Bacon*, vol. vii. p. 325.

P. 350. *Try but one* hour *first, and as you like*
    The loose *of that, draw home and prove the other.*] Here, as almost always with Jonson, *hour* is a dissyllable. *Loose* is the word which Gifford so strangely misunderstood in *Every Man out of his Humour*, vol. ii. p. 118.

P. 352.   *I did tell him of* Serly
    Was a great family come out of Ireland.] This chief of the M'Connells is only too well known to the readers of Mr. Froude. " Surley boy, otherwise spelt Sarley boy, or Sarle boigh ; meaning Sarley or Charley the yellow-haired." His family was ruthlessly massacred by the English at Rathlin in 1575 by order of Essex. See Froude's *History*, vol. x. pp. 527-9 (small edition).

P. 355. *A plague of all jades, &c.*] Here commences the second great transfer from the *New Inn* to *Love's Pilgrimage*. It closes at l. 19, p. 360. Weber's remark, that " Such an insertion could easily have been performed by the players " without the aid of a dramatist, is combated by Mr. Dyce, as the dialogue is a good deal and not unskilfully altered; nor was Weber, he adds, aware that in the earlier part of the play there are several minor "insertions" from the same source. See Dyce's *Beaumont and Fletcher*, vol. xi. p. 218.

P. 357. *As* gross *as hemp*.] Shirley (?) altered *gross* to *big*, because, perhaps, the former word, in this sense, was growing obsolete.

P. 360. Prolate *it right*.] This word is in Samuel Johnson, whose example from Howell admirably illustrates its use in this place. "The pressures of war have somewhat cowed their spirits, as may be gathered from the accent of their words, which they *prolate* in a whining credulous tone, as if still complaining and crest fallen."

P. 361. *His* tuft-taffata *night gear*.] A sort of silk, which Nares thinks had grown unfashionable in Beaumont and Fletcher's days; and Jonson's mention of it here, and *ante*, p. 332, confirms this idea rather than otherwise. In this place it is used for *night gear*, and in the previous one a charewoman was to be disguised,

> "With a tuft-taffata cloke, an old French hood,
> And other pieces, *heterogene enough*."

P. 363. *Take a* dejeune *of muskadel and eggs*.] Muskadel was the rich and high-flavoured wine made from the grape of that name. Jonson's meaning will be best understood by an extract from his *Conversations with Drummond*, vol. ix. p. 406: "A waiting woman having cockered with muskadel and eggs her mistresse page, for a shee meeting in the dark, his mistress invaded: of whom she would of such boldness have a reason. 'Faith, Lady' (said hee) 'I have no reason, save that such was the good pleasure of muskadel and eggs.'"

P. 364. "*Lo*, louting, *where he comes into the court*."] *Louting* was bowing obsequiously low. So bishop Latimer: "They came lowting and with low courtesy, as though they would creep into his bosom."

P. 368. *So knowledge first begets benevolence,*
Benevolence breeds friendship, friendship love.] Coleridge here remarks: "Jonson has elsewhere proceeded thus far; but the part most difficult and delicate, yet, perhaps, not the least capable of being both morally and poetically treated, is the union itself, and what, even in this life, it can be."

P. 368. *It is a mere degenerous appetite.*] The word sounds as if altogether obsolete, but it is in Samuel Johnson, and he quotes Dryden and king Charles among his authorities.

P. 369. *And all he speaks it is* projection.] This is indeed carrying out the idea of Lovell's tongue being tipt with the philosopher's stone.

P. 373. *And the old catch too, of* Whoop-Barnaby.] In the *Gipsies Metamorphosed*, vol. vii. p. 388, a wench laments that she has lost her *Practice of Piety*, and the "ballad of Whoop Barnaby." It seems also to have been a dance tune, for in the next generation Charles Cotton has a couplet in that piece of perverted ingenuity, his *Virgil Travestie :*

> "Bounce, cries the port hole ; out they fly,
> And make the world dance Barnaby."

P. 375. *Your shop citizens : they are rude animals.*] Here, as in the *Staple of News, ante*, p. 238, Jonson takes pleasure in girding at the citizens, by whom he conceived himself to have been injuriously treated.

P. 377.   *His mere cuello,*
Or ruff about his neck, is a bill of exchange.] This is best illustrated by an extract of a letter written about this time from Madrid by Howell. "His *Gravity* is much lessened since the late proclamation came out against *Ruffs*, and the King shewed himself the first example, they were come to that height of excess herein that twenty shillings were used to be paid for the starching of a Ruff! And some, tho' perhaps he had never a shirt to his back, yet he would have a toting huge swelling Ruff about his neck." p. 161.

P. 378. *Bird of the vespers,* vespertilio *Burst.*] Florio has " *Vespertillo*, a night-bat or reremouse."

P. 382. *She did but say the suit on.*] It may be convenient to mention that to *say on* is to *try on*. At p. 384, in the last line but six, the word *censure* means *judgment*.

P. 386. *The* Testament of Love *(and note* 4.)] I believe it has been established, beyond all question, that the *Testament of Love* has no claim to be the work of Geoffrey Chaucer.

P. 389. *The things true valour's exercised about.*] This description deserves to be well studied, as Jonson prided himself upon it greatly, and evidently had himself in his eye during the whole time he was penning it. He calls attention to it most particularly in the *Magnetic Lady*, vol. vi. pp. 65, 66 :

> " Only one virtue they call fortitude,
> Worthy the name of valour.
>
> * * * * * *
>
> O, you have read the play there, the *New Inn,*
> Of Jonson's, that decries all other valour,
> But what is for the public."

See also an important note of Gifford's, vol. viii. p. 349, where he justly says that the observations of Lovel on *true valour* will not be "easily paralleled for justness of thought, vigour of sentiment, and beauty of expression, in this or any other language."

P. 391. *How most ridiculous quarrels are all these, (and Gifford's criticism on Whalley's note).*] Here Southey has some remarks, distinguished as usual by good sense and good feeling. "Though the discourse is very ill laid, considering some of the company, the objection certainly does not hold good with regard to the Chambermaid, who is what Ben Jonson remembered female domestics to be, on the same footing as pages in the family. The one in this play is the friend and companion of her mistress, and thought a fit wife for a nobleman at the end of the drama." *Common Place Book*, Fourth Series, p. 325.

P. 391. *I am kept out a masque, sometime thrust out.*] This thrusting out, which so rankled in Jonson's mind, had taken place a quarter of a century before the writing of this play. See his *Conversations with Drummond*, vol. ix. p. 378, and my note on this very curious transaction. The masque on the occasion was written by Daniel.

P. 399. *And his branch'd cassock, a side sweeping gown.*] Southey in his *Common Place Book* quotes a passage from *Euphues*, in which one of the characters " pinches Philautus on the *parson's side,*" and the Rev. Mr. Warter, the editor, thinks he explains it by quoting the above line from Ben Jonson ! Whereas Lyly, of course, intended it as a euphuism, or euphemism, for that side of the body which, according to the libellers, a parson's life tends abnormally to develop. Gifford quotes a satire of Lyndsay's against the *sidetails* of the ladies' gowns in Edinburgh. What then does Calderwood, the Kirk historian, mean when he describes Queen Mary at Carbury Hill, as coming " with Grange to the Lords in a short petticoate, little *syder* than her knees " ? (vol. ii. p. 364.)

P. 400. *Hang him, poor snip.*] Is not this an early instance of the use of *snip* for a *tailor* ?

P. 400. *I had rather die in a ditch with mistress Shore,*
Without a smock, as the pitiful matter has it.] The title of
the old ballad, as given by Bishop Percy (*Reliques*, vol. ii. p. 285)
is "The woefull lamentation of Jane Shore, a goldsmith's wife in
London, sometime King Edward IV. his concubine."

> "Thus weary of my life, at lengthe
> I yielded up my vital strength
> Within a ditch of loathsome scent,
> Where carrion dogs did much frequent :
> The which now since my dying daye,
> Is Shore-ditch called, as writers say,"

—and as scores of people now alive are quite content to believe !
In the next page occurs the word *volary*, in the sense of *aviary* or
fowlery.

P. 402. *All-to-be married.*] *All-to-be* simply means *very much,*
entirely. It occurs again twice in the next play (vol. vi. p. 29
and p. 92.) One of the latest instances of its use is in a letter from
Swift to Pope, mentioning that lord Peterborough "all-to-be-
Gullivers me with very strong insinuations."

P. 402. *Room for* green rushes.] Browne presents a pleasing
picture in his *Britannia's Pastorals*, i. 2 :

> "Others in wicker baskets
> Bring from the marish rushes to o'erspread
> The green whereon to church the lovers tread."

P. 403.   *A sallad after supper,*
Of your own lettice here.] In case some unfortunate
reader may miss the little joke, it is perhaps as well to mention
that the young lady's name was Lætitia.

P. 405. *She'll prove a* counterfeit *mirth, and a* clipp'd *lady.*]
See my remarks on Gifford's note, vol. vi. p. 70. I believe that
"crack'd within the ring" and "clipped," as applied to woman,
had both their origin in the double meaning of the word "piece."
See vol. ii. p. 226.

P. 405. *Thou son of crumbs and* orts.] *Ort*, says Nares, is a
"scrap or trifling fragment of anything. It is of obscure derivation." Shakespeare has :

> "Let him have time a beggar's *orts* to crave."

P. 406. *The match is a good match (note).*] Mr. Dyce complains
that the passage from the *Widow* is "cited very incorrectly ;" but
solely by omissions (in this instance) to bring out as briefly as
possible the similarity of the stories.

P. 415. *Ode to Himself.*] Southey, who was always on the look out for new forms of versification, was struck by the peculiar metre of this Ode, " a ten-lined stanza, but sufficiently varied by the different length of the lines, though the rhymes are in couplets." May I be excused for mentioning that a friend who was smitten with paralysis at the early age of thirty-seven, has often been heard to describe the comfort which he derived from the fifth stanza of this noble Ode, which he happened to read a few days after his misfortune.

END OF VOL. V.

CHISWICK PRESS:—PRINTED BY WHITTINGHAM AND WILKINS,
TOOKS COURT, CHANCERY LANE.

www.ingramcontent.com/pod-product-compliance
Lightning Source LLC
Chambersburg PA
CBHW052344110726
47901CB00005B/1349